Ruthlessly his lips came down on hers, the touch of his warm, hard mouth engulfing her in a maelstrom of intoxicating, bewildering sensations. Ah, but it was sweet to have him kiss her...to have that taunting mouth moving so urgently on hers, to feel the thunderous beat of his heart against her breast. Compulsively, she pressed her slender body closer to his, seeking more than this half-savage, half-gentle assault upon her senses. Unknowingly, her arms crept up around his neck, her head tilted backward as she shamelessly, innocently offered herself to him...

The Tiger Lily

Shirlee Busbee

 CORGI    AVON

THE TIGER LILY

A CORGI/AVON BOOK 0 552 12714 0

First publication in Great Britain

Published by arrangement with Avon Books, 1790 Broadway, New York 10019

PRINTING HISTORY
Corgi/Avon edition published 1985

Corgi Books are published by Transworld Publishers Ltd.,
Century House, 61-63 Uxbridge Road, Ealing, London W5 5SA.,
in Australia by Transworld Publishers (Aust.) Pty. Ltd.,
26 Harley Crescent, Condell Park, NSW 2200, and in New
Zealand by Transworld Publishers (N.Z.) Ltd., Cnr. Moselle
and Waipareira Avenues, Henderson, Auckland.

Made and printed in Great Britain by
Hunt Barnard Printing Ltd., Aylesbury, Bucks.

For some "Lilies" of my own:

MRS. LILLIE HAYNES, Howard's sweet grandmother, a charming and wonderful lady.

LILLIE PATTERSON, a sister-in-law, who is absolutely tops and willing, at the drop of a hat, to feed the dogs and water the plants for me. Thanks, sweetie!

And a special sort of "Lily," STELLA SULARSKI, another sister-in-law, who has always been so good to me and is so dear to me. We miss you, Steller-feller!

And, as always, Howard.

The Tiger Lily

PROLOGUE

FIRST LOVE, FIRST CONFLICT

Natchez, Mississippi Territory
Spring, 1789

This bud of love, by summer's ripening
   breath,
May prove a beauteous flower when
   next we met.

William Shakespeare
Romeo and Juliet

CHAPTER ONE

"Will I be as beautiful as you, Tía Sofia, on my wedding day?" Sabrina asked wistfully, her big amber-gold eyes fixed admiringly on her aunt.

Sabrina asked the question as she stood next to a handsome satinwood dressing table in her aunt's elegant bedchamber. Her aunt, Sofia Aguilar, was seated on a velvet-covered stool and at the moment was critically viewing the image reflected in the dressing table's gilt-edged mirror.

At Sabrina's question, however, Sofia, looking absurdly young for a widow of thirty about to embark on a second marriage, stopped her nervous fidgeting. Momentarily ignoring the lovely cream-colored mantilla that covered her shining black hair, she shot her young relative an affectionate glance. With a twinkle in the dark Spanish eyes, she exclaimed with a smile, "Of course you will, pigeon!" Adding teasingly, "Aren't you *my* niece?"

Her niece promptly giggled. But then the small face was instantly serious as she demanded, "But I mean *truly.*"

Something in Sabrina's voice made Sofia turn around to stare at her niece. And while Sabrina waited anxiously, Sofia's gaze traveled consideringly over her.

It was difficult to tell, Sofia thought slowly, precisely what someone seven years old would look like when she was fully grown, but from the delicate planes of Sabrina's lively features, she rather suspected that in time her niece would be quite a beauty—though not a beauty in the usual Spanish mode. Her hair was too shocking a color, a glorious, flaming red-gold mane that defied all attempts to tame it; even now, after it had been freshly brushed and firmly plaited, tiny, unruly curls seemed to spring out defiantly and cluster around Sabrina's little face. Surprisingly

3

dark eyebrows and lashes intensified the impact of those incredibly colored amber-gold eyes, eyes that could go dark with deep emotion or burn an astonishingly bright gold when she was angry. A straight nose with a slight upward tilt at the tip, an as yet too large mouth, and a delightfully determined chin completed the features of what, Sofia was certain, would be in ten years' time a thoroughly fascinating face. As for the rest of Sabrina, her aunt smiled. At the moment her young niece resembled in both body and temperament nothing so much as a week-old thoroughbred colt—mischievous, spirited, stubborn, and possessed of a skinny body with long, unbelievably slender legs. But in time . . .

Smiling gently into Sabrina's anxious face, Sofia said softly, "Truly, *chica!* On your wedding day you will be a lovely bride—a *very* lovely bride!"

Inordinately pleased—for usually she cared nothing for her appearance—Sabrina threw her arms impetuously around her aunt's neck. "Oh, Tía Sofia, I am so happy that Madre and Padre allowed me to come to Natchez with them for your wedding! You are the very best *tía* anyone could ever wish for!" Her eyes suddenly brimming with laughter, she said dulcetly, "And you are as beautiful as I am, *sí?*"

Sofia laughed, and shaking her head, she answered, "You, pigeon, are incorrigible! And I think it is time that you changed your clothes—or do you intend to wear *that* to my wedding?"

That was a finely embroidered white linen nightshift which reached to Sabrina's slender ankles. With a smothered gasp of half-laughter, half-dismay, Sabrina disappeared out of her aunt's bedchamber like a small, fiery whirlwind.

Sofia's fond glance followed her. How fortunate, she thought with amusement, that while her own first marriage had been childless, Elena, her only sister, had presented her with such a delightful niece. And fortunate, too, Sofia admitted freely, that despite the distance which separated Natchez from Nacogdoches, where Elena lived with her only child and husband, she was able to see them all so frequently.

4

Alejandro del Torres, Elena's husband and Sabrina's father, was a wealthy man with varied business interests up and down the Mississippi River, and at least once every two years he came to New Orleans to oversee his expanding business affairs and to discuss progress with his local man of business. It was only natural that his family would accompany him, and it was even more natural that at some point during their stay in New Orleans they would travel up the river to Natchez to visit with Elena's only relative, Sofia.

Elena del Torres was the elder of the two sisters, and when Jaime Aguilar y Farias, Sofia's first husband, had died suddenly three years ago from one of the fevers so prevalent along the Mississippi River, she had descended upon a numb and stunned Sofia and whisked her away with much motherly clucking and concern to Nacogdoches, in the eastern part of Spanish Texas. The months spent at the lovely Rancho del Torres had been a healing time for Sofia, and gradually the heartache of her husband's untimely death had eased.

Sofia gave herself a shake—now was not the time to dwell upon the past! In just a few hours she would be marrying Hugh Dangermond, and this was no time to be remembering how sad she had been at the death of her first husband. Today was a new beginning, and it *would* be a happy day.

And yet, she wondered. The seven years she and Jamie had had together had been tranquil, contented years, while Hugh's first marriage had been anything but tranquil! For a moment, Sofia's eyes flashed angrily. How could Gillian, Hugh's dead wife, have been so deliberately scandalous—so scandalous with her lovers and extravagant expenses that all of Natchez had been atwitter with it? Even more disgraceful, Sofia thought, had been Gillian's complete indifference to her eldest son, Brett. It had long been the talk of Natchez that she clearly wanted nothing to do with Brett and lavished all the love of which she was capable on the second child, Martin. Martin, who so closely resembled her with his sapphire blue eyes and golden curly hair, while Brett was so obviously a Dangermond. . . .

Impatient with herself for again letting her thoughts stray, Sofia rose gracefully from the dressing stool and walked around the handsome room, trying to force herself to think of the happiness she and Hugh would share—and the love and affection she was more than willing to bestow upon his two sons . . . if they would let her.

She supposed that Hugh's sons were the real reason for her doubts. Hugh loved her. She was thankful that despite his disastrous marriage and the truly magnificent scandal Gillian's final escapade had caused, he had not become a misogynist, whereas Brett . . .

Sofia sighed. Brett had been ten years old seven years ago when his mother had run away with a traveling preacher, taking the then eight-year-old Martin with her. That Gillian had chosen a poor man upon whom to bestow her fickle affection was in itself surprising, but a man of the cloth! Natchez had been stunned! But only a year later when Hugh had finally found her in New Orleans, she had been openly living with a gambler well-known in the Natchez area. A gambler who had forced a duel upon Hugh, a duel that had left him nearly dead and permanently crippled.

Sofia was unhappily aware that Brett had been the one to suffer most. Clearly rejected by his mother, he had clung pathetically to his father, and Hugh's near-death had been the final agonizing blow. In a sense, Sofia thought miserably, that duel had also crippled Brett—it was very obvious that he had decided that women were not to be trusted, that they only maimed and betrayed. Which is going to make it very hard for me, Sofia mused regretfully, thinking of the aloof manner in which her seventeen-year-old stepson-to-be treated her.

Brett didn't trust her, *that* she knew. And it wasn't just her, it was *all* women, she reminded herself with a frown. Then suddenly her face lightened. All females that is, except Sabrina! Sabrina was clearly enchanted with the idea of having a tall, handsome stepcousin, and she had adoringly followed Brett about during the past two weeks since her arrival from Nacogdoches.

That Brett allowed it said much for the way Sabrina could charm *any*one, her aunt thought with a smile. Perhaps little Sabrina would be the one to teach him that women really weren't such terrible creatures.

As if her thoughts had conjured them up, she happened to glance out of one of the long windows that overlooked an expanse of green lawn and spotted Sabrina, now suitably attired in a gown of jonquil muslin, standing next to Brett. The two were underneath one of the many majestic oaks that dotted the landscape, and from the unusually gentle curve of Brett's finely shaped mouth, it was apparent Sabrina was weaving her innocent magic around him.

He is such a handsome youth, Sofia thought fondly, her gaze skimming the chiseled features that were just now beginning to lose the perfect beauty of childhood. His hair was dark, like Hugh's, and like Hugh's, his eyebrows were strongly defined. His dark green eyes, the color of jade, were deep-set, and their expression was frequently hidden by the sweep of long, thick, curling lashes, lashes, Sofia thought with a smile, she would have given a fortune to possess. Brett was tall; almost eighteen, he stood two inches above six feet. Although his shoulders and chest had not yet caught up with his height, it was obvious he would be a powerfully built man. If only, Sofia mused with exasperation, he would drop that icy barrier he keeps around him!

As she watched the two below her, Brett openly smiling now and gently tweaking one of Sabrina's neat braids, a third person joined them, and Sofia's sweet mouth twisted with dislike. Martin.

She had tried determinedly to like fifteen-year-old Martin, but it seemed impossible. Martin was spoiled, selfish, and a born troublemaker. The boy took enormous pleasure in reminding Brett that their mother had loved *him* enough to take him with her, and for that alone Sofia would have derived much joy from using a horsewhip on him! Particularly when she remembered the way Brett's face would close up and the way Martin's blue eyes would gleam with malice.

To be fair, and Sofia always tried to be, she supposed it was difficult for Martin to adjust to living with his father and brother after the years he had spent with his mother. And it was true, Sofia had told herself repeatedly during the past several months, that he was probably still grieving from his mother's unexpected death last year in a carriage accident in New York, where they had been living at the time. Gillian's death had meant Martin's return to Natchez and a family he hadn't seen in six years. It was bound to be difficult for him, but did he have to take such delight in being so very obnoxious? He was sullen and insolently disobedient to Hugh while committing acts of petty malice against Brett.

The sight of Elena in the doorway disrupted Sofia's unpleasant thoughts. Elena was very like Sofia, a little plumper, it was true, but she possessed the same wide, dark eyes and black hair, and although there was now a strand or two of silver mixed in Elena's dark hair, she had at forty the liveliness of a woman half her age. Elegantly dressed in a gown of soft green silk with a frivolous flounce that nearly swept the floor, a warm twinkle in the laughing dark eyes, she asked excitedly, "Are you ready? I know you dismissed your maid *ages* ago, and Sabrina has been filling my ears with how beautiful you look, so that I could not stay away any longer."

Sofia sent her an affectionate smile, and then pirouetting gracefully, the full skirts of her pale yellow, almost cream-colored, silk gown billowing out lightly from her slender, fine-boned body, she demanded, "Well? What do you think?"

Elena gave a gasp of pleasure. "Oh, Sofia, how *lovely* you look!" And taking in the delicate lace mantilla on her sister's head, she added warmly, "And I am so happy that you are wearing the mantilla that I wore at my wedding."

"Now if it will only insure that Hugh and I are as happy as you and Alejandro!" Sofia said teasingly.

Elena gave her a saucy wink and murmured, "It will, my dear, it will!" Then, glancing at the ormolu clock on the dressing table, she added, "It is almost time for us to leave for the church. . . . Are you excited or nervous?"

Sofia smiled ruefully. "Perhaps a little of both and . . . even a bit apprehensive."

"Oh, but you shouldn't be, *chica!*" Elena protested gaily. "Such a handsome man is your Hugh! And Brett is all that a stepmother could ask for, so polite and well-mannered."

"I notice," Sofia said dryly, "you didn't mention Martin."

Elena wrinkled her pretty nose. "Well, one must take the sour with the sweet!"

Sofia laughed, and from that moment on there was no more time for reflections of any kind—they would be leaving for the church in minutes.

It was a beautiful wedding, Sabrina thought blissfully as, ensconced between her parents, she watched Sofia marry Hugh Dangermond. Everything was exciting: her father had looked extremely handsome in his black satin jacket and white cravat as he had escorted Sofia down the flower-decked aisle, a shaft of errant sunlight turning his red hair to flame; her mother's new gown was lovely, as lovely as Tía Sofia's wedding dress; and the altar was breathtaking, with armloads of bright spring flowers— daffodils, lilacs, and roses. Señor Dangermond was most handsome, too, Sabrina admitted generously, the silver-headed cane he always walked with increasing his aristocratic bearing, his dark, lean face filling with a soft, warm light when Tía Sofia laid her hand in his and the black-robed priest murmured the words that would make them man and wife. Of course, Señor Dangermond was not as handsome as his son Señor Brett was, she decided judiciously. *No one* was as handsome as Señor Brett . . . not even his good friend Morgan Slade, although Señor Slade was very nice looking, too.

Shyly her glance strayed across the aisle to where Señor Brett sat with Señor Martin. He looked so handsome, she thought with a sigh, in his bottle-green jacket and buff breeches. But then, noticing that his features, usually so sunny and merry with her, were oddly rigid as he listened to the ceremony that married his father to Tía Sofia, Sabrina frowned. Wasn't he happy that Tía Sofia would now be his mother? The expression on his face made Sabrina vaguely uneasy.

The huge eyes puzzled, a troubled look on her little face, she continued to watch Brett's features. Didn't Señor Brett *like* Tía Sofia?

Brett *didn't* like Sofia. It wasn't that he held anything against her personally—for a woman, he would be the first to admit, she seemed perfectly pleasant—it was just the simple fact that she *was* a woman. A woman had hurt his father badly once, had almost been the cause of his father's death, and Brett would have preferred that the Dangermond men continue to live out their lives without the problems and interferences a woman could cause. Not that women didn't have their places—he and his boon companion, Morgan Slade, had discovered that exciting fact a few months ago from a complaisant, easygoing whore in Natchez "under the hill."

Despite having learned that women were at least capable of giving physical pleasure, Brett still would have stopped his father from committing what he was certain was folly. There was nothing spiteful in his motives; they sprang from love of his father and his wish to save Hugh the pain of further betrayal. But he was also dimly aware that Hugh, oddly enough, *wanted* this marriage to Sofia Aguilar, and not wishing to cause his father distress, Brett grimly held his tongue. But he didn't have to like it, he told himself unhappily. Or *her*.

While Brett didn't like Sofia, he didn't *dis*like her either. He merely refused to let her slip under his guard as she had his father's, having decided long ago, as he had sat terrified by his father's bedside, watching Hugh's desperate battle to live after the duel Gillian had precipitated, that *no* woman was to be trusted. In time that feeling might have lessened, but there was a constant reminder— every time he saw Hugh's silver-headed cane and watched his father's slow, careful steps, he was reminded. That cane had become a symbol, a constant painful, bitter reminder of the trouble a woman could create.

Certainly *he* was never going to be so foolish as to marry, nor would he ever let any woman mean anything to *him*. Women were made to be used, he decided cynically, and use them he would! But then, as if to remind him that his actions did not always follow the cold dictates of his brain, his gaze moved irresistibly across the aisle to meet Sabrina's troubled look.

Suddenly his brooding expression faded and the young hard face softened. Of course, Sabrina wasn't to be included with *women*—she was only a child. An adorable minx, he decided fondly, and wishing to dispel his own unhappy thoughts as well as erase the troubled look from the amber-gold eyes, Brett grinned and winked audaciously at her across the aisle.

Instantly Sabrina's worries fled, and she flashed him a sunny little smile, content now that Brett no longer seemed unhappy. She would never want Señor Brett to be unhappy.

CHAPTER TWO

Immediately following the wedding ceremony, everyone retired to the Dangermond estate, Riverview, so named for its commanding view of the roiling, turbulent Mississippi River below the bluff upon which it sat. It was a beautiful home built nearly sixty years earlier in 1730 by a reformed English freebooter.

At that time, Riverview had been little more than a charming cottage, the city of Natchez only a huddle of wooden buildings in the middle of a vast, unexplored wilderness. The wilderness was still mostly unexplored, but like Natchez, Riverview had grown until, in this spring of 1789, it was an elegant, imposing house that the very new Sofia Dangermond would now call home.

Since she and the del Torres family had been living at Riverview these last few days before the wedding, it already had a feeling of home for her. Her personal belongings were scattered throughout the house as if she had always lived there. Knowing that Elena and Alejandro would be staying at Riverview to keep an eye on Brett and Martin while she and Hugh took a brief wedding journey to New Orleans lifted every care from her mind. Her face radiant, the love she shared with Hugh obvious, Sofia moved happily among those who had come to wish them well.

A feast had been laid out for the many guests. There were punches in silver bowls, wines, and lemonade; flaky pastries filled with ham, shrimp, and chicken were piled high on ornate silver trays; but best of all to Sabrina's way of thinking were the cream cakes and syllabubs. Seeing where her eyes strayed so often, Brett laughed at such open greed.

Sabrina was the only child present—and she was included only because she was staying at Riverview with her parents. Being an only child, she was used to the exclusive company of adults and was quite happy to remain at her mother's side watching the ladies and gentlemen in their fine clothing. But Brett, moved by an emotion he didn't recognize, made it his duty to entertain her. His mouth curved in rueful amusement at his own actions; he held her small hand in his and manfully ignored Morgan's cocked eyebrow and Martin's unkind snicker as he escorted her about and saw that her plate was heaped with the delicacies that would appeal to the stomach of a seven-year-old.

Naturally Brett was teased unmercifully for his odd behavior. After the guests had departed, he and Morgan had appropriated a few bottles of Hugh's best wines and had stolen away to a grassy spot at the bluff's edge. Sprawled comfortably beneath a spreading oak tree, they had settled down to enjoy themselves and the wine. Which they did until, a few minutes later, Brett heard some suspicious rustling in a nearby bush.

Resignedly he grumbled, "You might as well come out, Martin. I know you're there."

Brett grimaced and Morgan rolled his eyes heavenward as Martin showed himself and began to threaten. "I saw you take the bottles from the cellar! If Father hadn't left for his honeymoon, I'd tell on you!"

When Brett remained unmoved and merely looked at him contemptuously, Martin whined, "I won't tell, though, if you let me have some. I'm almost as old as you, and I don't see why I can't do the things that you do . . . or why you never let me come with you but you let that brat, Sabrina, follow you about!"

Brett fixed him with a cool look and said icily, "Leave your tongue off Sabrina! As for telling—Father gave me permission to use the wine cellar as I wished when I turned sixteen."

His blackmail having failed, Martin scowled and started to turn away, but Brett, feeling guilty because he really didn't like his brother, called out, "Stay and join us, if you like." Martin liked, and he threw himself down on the grass near the other two.

There was a companionable silence for a while until Morgan said dulcetly to Brett, "You were quite the gallant this afternoon with your new cousin." His blue eyes opening very wide, he asked innocently, "Do I sense a romance? Has the family betrothed you to the young lady? Seven does seem a bit, er, *soon,* but I suspect you know your own mind. I wonder though, suppose she grows up to have spots and no bosom!"

Brett shot him a speaking look. "Cut line! She's only a child!" Somewhat defensively he added, "I . . . I felt sorry for her."

Morgan snorted, and Brett flushed. But unwilling to let his friend get off so easily, Morgan, a teasing slant to his full mouth, complained mournfully, "But you feel *sorry* for her all the time! I cannot think of any time during the past fortnight that Sabrina has been far from your side." Mockery dancing in his eyes, Morgan breathed in shocked accents, "Never tell me you've changed your mind about women? My God, can it be that you think to snaffle her young and train her to be the perfect bride?"

Brett's flush increased, and he appeared much younger than a few weeks away from eighteen. Martin, who had been listening avidly to the exchange, smiled maliciously at his older brother's discomfort. Deciding to contribute to the discomfort, Martin said slyly, "Oh, no, it isn't that, let me assure you! It's simply that he enjoys having a little slave running behind him. He can do no wrong in her eyes, and he finds playing god to an adoring audience a novel situation."

"That's not true!" Brett returned hotly, willing to let Morgan roast him but unable to bear Martin's making disparaging remarks about Sabrina. Growing more uncomfortable and defensive, he suddenly realized just how much time he had spent with the girl. Under his breath he muttered, "She's only a child. I was only being polite—anyone would have done the same thing."

Morgan smiled. "Of course . . . if you say so."

Throwing his companion a look of utter loathing, Brett said savagely, "Haven't you anything else to talk about? I wonder if *you* aren't nourishing a passion for her the way you go on!"

14

Morgan laughed, and the subject lapsed. They finished off the wine, and once they had escaped from Martin's company, Morgan and Brett found themselves irresistibly drawn to Silver Street. They were young and their blood was running hot, and it really wasn't surprising that Brett spent the remainder of the night discovering again the pleasure a woman could give a man.

Peculiarly, Sabrina was very much on his mind when he woke the next morning with a pounding head and an odd distaste for his actions the previous evening. Morgan's teasing, innocent though it had been, had flicked Brett on the raw. Grimly he made a vow that he would have nothing more to do with his young stepcousin.

That resolve lasted for all of two days. The hurt, confused expression on Sabrina's face when he curtly told her she couldn't come catfishing with him, the quivering lip when she learned that he didn't want her company on his morning rides any longer, and the pained shadows he detected in the usually bright eyes when he sharply reprimanded her for hanging over his shoulder in the evening while he played piquet with Morgan couldn't be borne any longer.

Rising the morning of the third day since the wedding, he deliberately sought out Sabrina. He found her sitting listlessly under one of the magnolia trees. When Brett saw the forlorn droop of her bottom lip and guessed the reason, his heart twisted painfully.

To make her smile again was certainly worth a little teasing from his friend, wasn't it? It definitely was, he decided firmly. Approaching her, a warm smile curving his finely shaped mouth, he said coaxingly, "I spotted a quail sitting on her nest yesterday. Shall I show it to you?"

A sparkle instantly leaped into her eyes, and Sabrina turned to stare at him. "Oh, *yes!*" she breathed before she had time to think. But then, just a little wary after her inexplicable fall from grace, she added coolly, "That is, if you don't mind."

The quail's nest was some distance from the house. They walked quietly through a tangled forest of blackberry and honeysuckle vines, wild plum trees intermingling with the pine, sycamore, oak, and chestnut trees, and eventually

15

they came to it. Putting his finger to his lips and dropping to his haunches, Brett pointed.

It took Sabrina several seconds to discern the quail's gray, brownish-black feathers among the mottled leaves that were scattered across the forest floor, but when she finally saw it, she sucked in her breath with clear delight. "Oh, Señor Brett!" she whispered. "How wonderful! She is very pretty, *sí?*"

Brett nodded, and together they stealthily crept away. The find of the quail's nest re-established their rapport, and it became part of the daily ritual to quietly inspect it. Each day Sabrina faithfully placed a handful of stale bread a short distance from the nest, the quail's bright little eyes watching her every movement.

"She knows us!" Sabrina said sincerely one morning. "She *must*, Señor Brett! She never moves off her nest or flies away when we come. Do you think she would let me pet her?"

Brett smiled gently down into her upturned face, his hand lightly caressing her bright hair. "Afraid not, sweetheart. She's a wild creature, and as soon as her eggs hatch, she'll be off with her chicks."

Sabrina's face fell. "Oh, I do hope we can see the babies."

"We will, don't worry," Brett promised, his dark green eyes full of affection.

It was only as they turned away that they discovered Martin had followed them. Coming out from behind an oak tree, he glanced over at the nest and sneered, "A quail's nest! Is that what you've been sneaking off to see each day?"

Earnestly Sabrina said, "Oh, but Señor Martin, she is not just any quail—she knows Señor Brett and me!"

Martin looked indifferent, but Brett stared at him hard for several seconds and then said softly, "You *will* leave the nest undisturbed, won't you?"

Martin reluctantly met his brother's green gaze. "Of course—why would I bother an old quail's nest?"

It was the end of the conversation, but for several days, Brett kept an eye out for Martin to make mischief. Brett

16

gradually relaxed, however, for it seemed that Martin had decided a quail's nest was beneath his talents.

Then came a morning when the little bird wasn't on her nest. Brett thought nothing of it, assuming that the bird was out hunting, and with a light comment he turned away, heading back for the house, certain Sabrina was following him.

Sabrina had been full of anticipation this particular morning, confident that today would be the day that the eggs hatched, and consequently she didn't immediately follow Brett but crept closer to the little nest. Seeing the broken shells, she clapped her hands with excitement and glanced eagerly around, positive *her* quail wouldn't have left without displaying the chicks. She had just opened her mouth to call joyfully to Brett when she spied the sinister shape coiled a few feet away from the nest. A copperhead snake. A copperhead with an obscene bulge in the middle of its sinuous length that cruelly revealed the fate of the quail and her eggs.

Horror choked Sabrina, and remembering the way the little quail had seemed to watch for her each day, she was filled with fury. A cry of half-anguish, half-rage came from her, and blindly she reached for a fallen oak branch and attacked the snake.

Brett heard her cry and spun on his heels, swiftly returning to the nest. He found Sabrina, weeping and furious, wielding the oak branch with fatal efficiency.

The snake was dead long before Brett could pry the oak branch from Sabrina's clenched fingers. She was still sobbing angrily, tears streaking down her cheeks, her eyes a pure gold glitter between the spiky dark lashes when she finally released her hold on the branch and flung herself into Brett's comforting arms.

"It *ate* her!" she cried with furious revulsion.

"I know, sweetheart, I know. But these things happen in the wild," Brett said helplessly. Lifting her from the ground, he gently enfolded her slender body next to his, murmuring soft, consoling sounds.

Sabrina's arms were tightly clasped around his neck, her face buried under his chin, but suddenly she flung

17

back her head angrily and said vehemently, "But it shouldn't have happened! Not to *my* quail!"

Brett looked down at her, intending to say something to ease her hurt, but the words stuck in his throat as he stared at the little face just below his. Her eyes were bright with tears and anger; her cheeks were flushed pink. The wide, generous mouth was inches from his own, and Brett was overwhelmed by a surge of tenderness.

Suddenly assailed by an emotion he had no business feeling for a seven-year-old girl, he instantly thrust her away from him and setting her urgently on the ground, put several feet between them. Drawing a ragged breath, he forced himself to concentrate on what she had said, and unsteadily he got out, "No, no, it shouldn't have happened, poppet, but it did. You have to realize that nature isn't always kind. Life can be cruel." Bitterly, ruthlessly ignoring the emotions that clawed through him, he said, "Life *is* cruel—you can't always have things the way you want them."

After that, it was as if the death of the quail had been the death also of their re-established rapport. Brett assiduously avoided Sabrina. What he had felt for her was damnably wrong, and he convinced himself that the incident was further proof of how dangerous women could be—even very young ones.

Sabrina suffered again at suddenly being anathema to her idol. She was bewildered, hurt, and angry at the same time to be now treated as if she had committed some unforgivable, terrible offense. As the days passed, and the time grew nearer for the del Torres family to depart for Nacogdoches, Sabrina took refuge in disliking her once beloved Señor Brett. He was a beast!

There was one other incident in connection with the quail. Two days after the discovery of the snake, as Brett was dismounting from his morning ride, he happened to overhear one of the grooms scolding Martin. That Martin was *very* aware of Brett's presence was obvious from the nervous glances he kept shooting his way. But Jem, the English groom, was completely oblivious of Brett as he grumbled, "Did you get rid of that snake? I don't mind you trapping animals and such, but I'll be damned if I'll have

18

you keeping snakes near the stables—and a bloody copperhead at that! Why you keep it and don't feed it is beyond me! If you haven't let it loose or killed it by now, do so today!"

A dangerous gleam in the dark green eyes, Brett said silkily, "Oh, I wouldn't scold him anymore, Jem. . . . I'm certain he let the snake go, didn't you, Martin? About two days ago?"

Martin swallowed uncomfortably and hastily backed away from his older brother. It did him little good. Brett stalked furiously after him, and later that day and for several days thereafter, Martin's blackened eye and puffed, swollen face weren't a pretty sight.

Sofia and Hugh returned from their brief honeymoon in New Orleans the day before Brett's eighteenth birthday. That marriage agreed with them was apparent from the shy smile on Sofia's lips and the warmth that leaped into Hugh's eyes whenever she entered a room.

After the initial greetings had been exchanged, Sofia noticed the estrangement between Brett and Sabrina. The next morning she asked Elena, "What in the world has happened between your daughter and my new stepson? Did she do something to enrage him?"

Elena shrugged her shoulders helplessly. "I don't know, but I would like to box his ears! It was not kind of him to be so pleasant to her and then avoid her like she had the pox. Men! Never will I understand them!"

Brett's birthday present from his father arrived that afternoon, and the entire family gathered at the whitewashed stables to admire it. It was a magnificent two-year-old golden chestnut stallion, a powerful, spirited animal that Brett was to tame and train himself.

Staring at the half-wild animal as he snorted and cavorted in the paddock, for a few minutes Sabrina forgot the gulf that had grown between her and Brett. The stallion was a thoroughbred, his Arab blood evident in the small, arrogant head and the long, incredibly slender legs, and Sabrina was enchanted.

Her antagonism forgotten, she watched enthralled as the sunlight turned the stallion's glossy coat to a fiery red when he reared up, lashing out with his hooves. It was a beautiful sight, and Sabrina sighed, "Oh, Señor Brett! He is so beautiful!"

Dazed by the gift, Brett, too, for the moment, was able to put aside his grim resolve. Grinning down at her, he murmured mockingly, "Handsome, Sabrina, handsome. Males of the species are not beautiful."

Sabrina grinned back at him, her spirits suddenly lifting skyward. Wrinkling her tipped-up little nose, she retorted firmly, "He is more than handsome. He *is* beautiful! Oh, see how the sun shines on his coat—he looks like a flame. A *beautiful* flame!" Earnestly she added, "That is what you should name him, Flame, for he is truly a horse of flame."

"What do you intend to name him?" Sabrina's father, Alejandro, asked.

Staring at the stallion, seeing the sleek, fiery coat and hearing Sabrina's words ringing in his ears, Brett said slowly, "Why not Flame? It certainly fits, and"—slanting a teasing glance down at Sabrina—"as Sabrina says, he is a *beautiful* flame."

Her eyes huge, her own red-gold hair flame-colored in the sunlight, she demanded, "You will truly call him that? You will use the name I chose?"

Unable to help himself, Brett flicked a caressing finger down her cheek. "Naturally. What gentleman could refuse such a lovely lady?"

There was a murmur of laughter, and then, ever inclined to press her luck, Sabrina asked eagerly, "And you will let me ride him, *sí?*"

"No!" came from the assembled adults, Brett's answer perhaps most fierce, a horrifying picture of what the untamed Flame could do to Sabrina's small body flashing through his mind.

Surprised at the collective answer, Sabrina looked crushed, and Brett was moved to explain, "He is totally untrained, Sabrina, almost a wild horse. No one has ever ridden him, and even the grooms say he is difficult to handle. He is too powerful and dangerous for you to consider riding. I forbid it."

All of her charity toward him vanished, and there was a

mutinous cast to her chin when she glanced away from him. "I could, you know," she muttered stubbornly.

Suddenly remembering that he wanted to keep her at a distance, Brett deliberately spoke coldly. "No, you couldn't. You're too young, just a child."

Nothing he could have said could have wounded her more deeply. Throwing him a look of positive dislike, she tossed her red head and angrily flounced away. She would show him . . . and then maybe he would like her again?

Sabrina's opportunity came sooner than expected, the very next morning in fact. Arising early, she discovered to her surprise that she was up before anyone else. After she had been put to bed the previous evening, there had been several toasts to Brett's good health, and with one thing and another, it had been extremely late when everyone had retired. Consequently, dressed and eager for the day, Sabrina found herself the only one of the family up. There were servants moving about, but they were busy with their tasks, and no one thought to demand that she stay indoors.

Hopping down the curving staircase of the house, Sabrina glanced wistfully in the direction of the stables, the brown roof of one of the buildings barely discernible through the trees. She was drawn irresistibly by the lure of Brett's stallion and soon found herself leaning against the paddock fence watching with open pleasure as Flame haughtily trotted over in her direction.

Cautiously they inspected one another, the big, untamed flame-red stallion and the little girl with the flame-colored hair. Eager to make friends, Sabrina hastily yanked up some clover growing near one of the posts of the paddock and lovingly held it out to the stallion. When Flame condescendingly nibbled the offering, Sabrina thought her heart would burst with excitement. Gingerly reaching up to touch his soft nose, she sighed blissfully when he blew softly and made no move to jerk away from her caress.

Wanting something more worthy of him than clover, she dashed into the stables and quickly found the bin of oat and grain that were regularly fed to the Dangermond thoroughbreds. She dumped several handfuls into a nearby bucket and then offered them up to her new friend.

She still hadn't really thought about riding the stallion, but as time passed and he seemed to accept her presence, she grew bolder and climbed to the top rail of the white paddock fence. Flame seemed unperturbed by this action, and Sabrina was delighted, even going so far as to gently pet his strong, straight back while he searched the ground for the last few kernels of corn that had fallen there.

It was too tempting to resist. Flame was standing right next to the fence, barely a handspan away from where Sabrina sat on the top rail, and before she had time to think, she leaned over and slipped onto the stallion's back.

Despite the late night, Brett had awakened not too long after Sabrina had skipped out of the house. And like Sabrina, he was drawn to the stables, wanting to reassure himself that Flame hadn't been only a wonderful dream. He arrived just in time to see Sabrina slide onto the stallion.

Flame was startled by the unaccustomed weight on his back, and he arched his neck uneasily, snorting loudly and dancing nervously. Having practically been born astride a horse, at his first movements, Sabrina instinctively clamped her legs to his sides and tightened her hold on his mane.

Brett froze. Aware of what could happen if the stallion decided to turn ugly, he forced himself to walk slowly toward the paddock, his heart beating with thick, painful strokes, his gaze locked on Sabrina's little figure. She looked so small, so defenseless, so incapable of controlling the stallion, that Brett felt a trickle of fright slide down his spine. Dear God, he pray fervently, dear God, don't let her be harmed.

The stallion was growing agitated about the creature on his back, and restlessly he pawed the ground, tossing his head and making little, uneasy sidesteps. Unaware of Brett's cautious approach, Sabrina was filled with excitement and pleasure at her accomplishment and wished passionately that Señor Brett could see her now.

Moving with agonizing slowness, Brett finally reached the fence. Not wishing to alarm the horse or the child, he said with far more calmness than he felt, "Good morning, Sabrina. I see you have managed to ride Flame after all."

Her face filling with delight, Sabrina jerked in his direction and cried joyfully, "Oh, Señor Brett! I was hoping you could see me! I *told* you I could ride him!"

But in that instant, Flame, with a whicker of anger, reared up suddenly on his hind legs. Caught off guard, Sabrina almost lost her hold, but instinctively she clung desperately to the rising stallion.

At Flame's first move, Brett had leaped to the fence and was instantly poised on the top rail. Horse and rider were only inches from him, and as Flame's feet hit the ground and the stallion gave a powerful buck, Brett's muscled arm lunged across the space that divided them and roughly plucked Sabrina from Flame's back.

Breathing heavily, beads of perspiration dotting his forehead, Sabrina clasped to his chest in a death hold, Brett slid thankfully onto the ground on the opposite side of the fence. Flame, relieved of his unwelcome burden, tossed his arrogant head and with a whistle of fury raced swiftly away.

Sabrina was not at all pleased with her rescue. Twisting around to glare at Brett, she said angrily, "I could have stayed on—I have ridden many, many horses. I am *not* an infant!"

Relief that she was safe had barely penetrated his brain when her words hit him, and instantly he was blindly, furiously angry. "Why, you little hell-born babe! I just saved your bloody life!" And then, as his anger fed on itself, the jade-green eyes nearly black with fury, he snarled, "And I forbade you to ride him! How *dare* you disobey me!"

All her hurt and confusion of the past days rising up to sting her, Sabrina glowered back at him, screwing her features up into an awful face and sticking her tongue out at him.

It was the final straw. Enraged as much because she could arouse emotions within him that he didn't understand as by her actions, Brett promptly turned her over his knee and gave her a hiding she was never to forget. His chest heaving, his mouth thinned, moments later he stood

23

her in front of him and snapped, "Let that be a lesson to you, brat—don't *ever* cross me again!"

Furiously Sabrina blinked back the tears that threatened to fall. The full lower lip quivering pitifully, the amber-gold eyes a startling incandescent gold, she spat, "I hate you, Señor Brett! *I hate you!* I never want to see you again!"

"Well, that suits me just fine!" he hurled back. Watching her stalk proudly away, he knew an urge to call her back, an urge to mend the breach between them, but fiercely he killed that urge. What a fool he was! It was a good thing that he had discovered her real nature before it was too late—an embryonic Jezebel, practicing her wiles already on the unwary male; headstrong, stubborn, and not to be trusted an inch!

PART ONE

BITTERSWEET AWAKENING

Nacogdoches, Spanish Texas
Summer, 1799

> For aught that I could ever read,
> Could ever hear by tale or history,
> The course of true love never did run
> smooth.

William Shakespeare
A Midsummer Night's Dream

CHAPTER THREE

လ August 1, 1799, Sabrina del Torres's seventeenth birthday, dawned bright and clear. It was one of those marvelous, lazy summer days that she so loved. Waking just as the sun was topping the tall, pungent pine trees that grew near the sprawling, gracious adobe house where she had lived all her life, she slid naked from her soft featherbed and ran gracefully to the double doors that opened to the rear of the room. Throwing them aside, she stepped out onto the small balcony that overlooked the back of the hacienda.

She had no fear of being observed—her rooms were upstairs at the very end of a long wing that had been added onto the main dwelling when her father had married, and it assured privacy. All that met her wandering gaze was the endless lush green forest.

Flinging her arms wide in pagan abandon, like a priestess of fire, she faced the glowing sun, her face and slender body bathed in its golden light. The sun lit the fire in the red-gold hair that tumbled to her waist, gilded the striking features that were upturned eagerly for its warm touch, and wandered like a lover's hand over the tall, slim body. The sunlight seemed to linger on the full, coral-tipped breasts, the flat, almost concave stomach, the fiery curls at the junction of her thighs, and the long, shapely legs as she stood there before it, her arms outstretched as if to embrace a lover.

The sun transformed her into a slender flame, all crimson and gold; sighing with unashamed ecstasy she slowly pivoted, reveling in its warmth. Her arms slowly falling to her sides, a smile of pure happiness on her young face, she walked to the black iron railing that encircled the balcony.

Leaning her elbows on the top of the railing, her chin

cupped in her hands, contentedly she stared out at the expanse of forest that met her eyes, the scent of honeysuckle drifting to her. In the distance, she could just make out the glitter of blue from the small lake where she frequently swam on days like this one.

But there would be no swimming today, she thought with a smile. Today was her birthday, and today there would be other delights in store for her. As her father's only child, and the heiress to a considerable fortune, her birthday was an important day in the lives of everyone connected with the Rancho del Torres. And not just the lives of those directly connected to the ranch—families with marriageable sons, neighbors and friends who had known her since birth would all be converging on the ranch to share in the joyous celebration of her seventeenth birthday. A fiesta had been planned for weeks, and for days the cooks in the kitchen had been baking and preparing foodstuffs. The grand salon had been thrown open and aired, scrubbed, and polished until every chandelier, every tile in the mosaic floor, every stick of furniture shone like a newly minted doubloon.

As she thought of the grand salon, Sabrina's face suddenly clouded. Today would be the first time it had been used since before her mother's death nearly ten years ago.

A shaft of remembered pain sliced through her like a knife as she thought of her mother's tragic death in Natchez in the summer of 1789. Such a sad and melancholy ending to what had been, for the most part, a wonderful trip to see Tía Sofia marry Hugh Dangermond.

Her soft, voluptuous mouth thinned as she recalled unexpectedly and for the first time in years her painful, disillusioned parting from Brett Dangermond. What a beast he had been, she reminded herself fiercely. Sabrina, while generally a sweet, generous girl, *never* forgot an insult or an injustice, and to her way of thinking, Brett's treatment of her after the death of the quail had been both . . . *especially* the morning she had ridden the stallion. She had suffered dreadfully from his inexplicable rejection, but it had been nothing like the pain and suffering she had endured when, two days before they were to leave for home, for Nacogdoches, Elena had been killed when her horse bolted

28

during a morning ride and she was hit in the head by the limb of a huge oak tree.

Everyone had been stunned. No one could believe that dear, laughing Elena was dead. Sofia had seemed to age ten years, Alejandro had been like a man possessed, and Sabrina had looked like a small, pale ghost, blindly refusing Brett's or anyone's offer of comfort, unwilling to accept that her beloved mother would never smile at her again, never hold her again.

They had buried Elena in the Dangermond plot in Natchez—it had been impossible to consider returning her body to Nacogdoches—and somehow that had hurt Sabrina even more deeply. Alejandro and Sabrina had not lingered in Natchez after the funeral. Natchez was now a place of unhappy memories for them both, and in the intervening years, while Alejandro had occasionally visited with the Dangermonds, Sabrina had never returned. Tía Sofia wrote regularly to her, and Sabrina eagerly replied, yet she wanted nothing to do with Natchez or its sad, painful memories.

She and her father had grown extremely close after Elena's death. They were complete with each other, neither needing nor wanting the intrusion of another person in the warm circle of love they had created for themselves. Elena was never forgotten, and a stranger listening to them converse would have thought that Elena had merely gone on a journey just yesterday and would return at any moment. Her name cropped up often between the two of them, Sabrina sometimes coaxing her father to order a new pair of pantaloons or an embroidered waistcoat by saying softly, "Madre would not like to see you appearing so shabbily dressed, Padre—not when you are going to visit with the commandant in town!" And if Sabrina's way was a trifle devious, Alejandro was just as guilty of using Elena in bending Sabrina to his will. When all other arguments had failed to sway her from a course he disapproved of, he would arrange his handsome features into a mask of sorrow and murmur unscrupulously, ""I do not think your *madre* would like you to do this, *chica.*" And Sabrina would instantly fall in with his wishes.

Despite Elena's untimely death, Sabrina's childhood

was a happy one. She spent an inordinate time with her father as he went about the ranch supervising and doing the daily tasks. Her life was less restricted and confined than it would have been if her mother had lived, but her father's unorthodox regime and the maturity forced upon her by Elena's tragic death had not been harmful. Though she was petted and pampered, in some ways Alejandro treated her as though she were a son.

And while there were some, notably Tía Francisca, Alejandro's eldest sister, who thought it outrageous that Sabrina could not sew a straight seam, had never fathomed the mysteries of the kitchen or instituted any of Francisca's multitude of orders for the running of a *proper* household, most found Alejandro's daughter a high-spirited, enchanting young creature. But if Sabrina might be found lacking in some of the necessary requirements for a young lady of her station, she most definitely made up for them with the uncommon and questionable skills she had learned from her father and the vaqueros on the ranch. She could ride like a Comanche, could shoot far better than most men, was unusually proficient with a knife, and could boast, if she wished, of a vocabulary that would make a drunken guttersnipe blush. Sabrina was unique; she was also, not surprisingly, the pride and darling of the Rancho del Torres, her warmhearted, unselfish nature making her all the more endearing. Which of course explained why her birthday was such a special event in the Nacogdoches area.

Conscious that soon Bonita, her maid, would be appearing with her breakfast tray, Sabrina ceased her profitless musing and went back into the room. She spared one last long look at the bright sky and murmured softly, "Wish me well, Madre . . . I will think of you often today."

Splashing some cold water into a china bowl, she swiftly completed her morning ablutions and then, picking up her silver-backed brush, quickly brought some semblance of order to her night-tousled curls. Crossing to her bed, she lifted up the white linen nightdress that had been laid out the previous evening and with a wry grimace, put it on. Too many mornings the sight of her naked body had unleashed a torrent of displeasure from Bonita—it was not

proper, it was *sinful* to sleep naked. Bonita's plump face
would set in determined lines. Every night with stiff, angry movements she would lay out a fresh, clean nightgown, and, of late, every morning Sabrina resignedly put
it on—it was easier than offending Bonita.

Sabrina had just settled herself back in bed, several lace-
edged pillows plumped up behind her, when Bonita, a
warm smile on her swarthy face, waddled into the room
carrying a large silver tray that held Sabrina's usual
breakfast: hot chocolate and a sweet cake called *pan dulce.*
Different from most days, however, was the huge bouquet
of yellow roses and the small cloth-covered box that lay in
the center of a plate.

Seeing the roses, Sabrina gave an exclamation of pleasure, and Bonita's lined face softened. "Happy birthday,
little one," she said, the affection she felt obvious in the
wise brown eyes and the crooning tones of her voice.

Bonita had been Elena's nurse, and when her mistress
had married the dashing Alejandro del Torres, she had accompanied her from Natchez and had settled down in the
wilderness of Spanish Texas to devote herself to the house-
ful of babies she was certain would be arriving in due
course. But there had been only one baby, Sabrina, and
consequently Bonita had lavished all her love and not a
few scoldings on Sabrina, much like a cat with one precious kitten.

Watching as Sabrina took a deep, delighted sniff of the
fragrant roses, Bonita was conscious of a feeling of bittersweet satisfaction. How proud Dona Elena would have
been of her daughter on this day! Then, eyeing suspiciously the uncreased state of the demure nightgown that
covered Sabrina's body, she thought how shocked Elena
would have been that her daughter could have acquired
such wanton habits.

Bonita was old and fat, her once-dark hair liberally
streaked with gray, and whatever shape she had possessed
had long ago disappeared. She had a merry face, though,
and a deep, rich chuckle that made one smile involuntar-
ily. She ruled the del Torres household with an iron hand;
that is, all the household with the exception of Señorita Sabrina and Don Alejandro. Don Alejandro had only to pinch

her cheek and smile whimsically at her and she instantly melted. As for Sabrina, well, try as she might, Bonita could never resist the appeal of those amber-gold eyes. She had been heard to mutter on more than one occasion that Señorita Sabrina could have charmed the devil or slain him with just one glance.

As Sabrina opened the cloth-covered box, those incredible eyes darkened with deep emotion, and staring at the beautifully wrought gold hoop earrings that lay on the white satin, Sabrina breathed reverently, "Oh, Bonita, you are too good to me—you spoil me."

"Sí, this is true," Bonita returned with her rich chuckle, and reaching over to tweak a strand of the curly hair, she added, "But there are days when you deserve it, and today is one of them."

Oblivious to the nearly spilt chocolate pot and the wobbling vase of roses, Sabrina twisted in bed and flung her arms around Bonita's neck. "Oh, Bonita, I love you so much! And I will always treasure these lovely earrings. I will wear them tonight for the fiesta."

The remainder of the day proved to be as enjoyable as its beginning. There was a constant stream of well-wishers arriving and congratulations from everyone she met, and from her father and relatives and the servants of the ranch there was an almost overwhelming variety of gifts to help celebrate her birthday: a gold hair comb from the women in the kitchen; a fine leather bridle embossed with silver from the stablemen, a beautiful white lace mantilla from Tía Francisca and her family, a breathtaking silver-inlaid saddle from the suddenly shy vaqueros, and from her father a curious combination—a delicate blade of wonderful Toledo steel and a necklace of glittering emeralds.

That evening as she dressed for the fiesta in her honor, she managed to wear as many gifts as possible. Bonita had piled the red-gold curls high on Sabrina's head and secured them with the gold comb; Bonita's gift of the earrings hung from her small ears, and around her neck were the emeralds given to her by her father. She wore a simple gown of white silk, a profusion of lace flowing around its deep decolletage and around the hem of the wide, full, swinging skirt, Tía Francisca's gift of the white mantilla draped fashionably about her bared shoulders and arms. The effect was striking, the brightness of that flame-colored hair, the honeyed tones of her soft skin against the emeralds, and the white silk of the gown making more than one young caballero that night think of a goddess of fire—a goddess in whose embrace it would be heaven to burn.

Unaware of the thoughts she aroused in the young males and not a few older ones, Sabrina took a child's unaffected delight in the evening. She danced every dance, her gay laughter and heartstopping smile heard and seen continually, and Alejandro, watching her proudly from a short distance away, was aware of a curious mixture of pleasure and pain. If only Elena could see her, he thought, could be with us . . .

For just a moment he allowed the uneased agony of Elena's death to sweep over him, and almost compulsively he fingered the unique turquoise and silver bracelet he always wore—a bracelet that Elena had given to him to seal their betrothal. But then, conscious that even from a distance, in spite of the whirl of gaiety around her, Sabrina would uncannily sense his unhappy thoughts, he quelled the pain that welled up inside him. Tonight was a joyous one—and Elena would be the last person to want him sad, he reminded himself with a forced smile.

"They make a lovely couple, do they not?" Francisca de la Vega said abruptly from his side, her eyes on Sabrina and the young man with whom she was presently dancing.

Wryly Alejandro returned, "I agree. But don't you think we are a bit prejudiced? After all, Sabrina is my daughter and Carlos is your son."

Francisca gave a satisfied smile. "That is true, but they are a handsome couple nonetheless—and it would be a wonderful alliance. The del Torres *rancho* and the de la Vega *rancho* under one ownership would make them the largest and richest landowners this side of the Sabine River."

Alejandro remained silent. Though his sister might prefer one to think her motives were totally altruistic, he knew the de la Vega finances were not flourishing. Luis de la Vega, her husband, had casually intimated as much to

33

him not a month ago, and Carlos only last week had laughingly stated that while they had land and cattle aplenty, he would probably have to marry an heiress if he wished to see any amount of gold in the near future. Every landowner occasionally suffered from lack of ready money, Alejandro admitted wryly to himself, even he did periodically, and he assumed that this was the current situation with his sister's family—next month, next year, things would right themselves and all would be well. Carelessly he dismissed as unworthy the notion that there was any desperate need for a marriage between Sabrina and Carlos. Francisca had *always* wanted the marriage, and he guessed that at the moment it probably looked even more attractive than usual to her. But to Carlos? Thoughtfully he gazed at his nephew as that handsome, smiling young man spun Sabrina lightly around the grand salon.

Alejandro had no real reservations about Carlos de la Vega—certainly his lineage was impeccable, and at twenty-six he was mature enough and hopefully wise enough to control Sabrina. But even knowing the scheme was dear to his sister's heart, Alejandro had for the past two years resisted her attempts to formalize a match. There was much to be said for a marriage between Sabrina and Carlos, he would freely concede, and yet . . .

Consideringly he scrutinized Carlos as that young man laughed across at Sabrina. Carlos was a handsome devil, typically Spanish in his features—thick black hair; black eyes; a thin, aristocratic nose; and a mouth that was at once sensual and cruel. Like so many Spaniards, he was not a tall man, and yet there was such command and arrogance in his bearing that one immediately forgot his lack of height. His was a slim, graceful physique, and whether on the back of a horse or on a ballroom floor, he always gave the impression of complete control. Tonight, attired in black velvet calzoneras, the Spanish equivalent of a pantaloon, the borders trimmed with filigree buttons and tinsel lace; a matching *chaqueta* that ended just above the gold silk sash that tightly encircled his firm masculine waist; and a white silk shirt that intensified his dark good looks, Carlos was, Alejandro had to admit, an eminently eligible young man whose suit would make most of the

34

unmarried women there that night swoon with delight. Somehow, though, he didn't think Carlos would make Sabrina swoon. And that, he admitted ruefully, is the crux of my problem.

Born into a proud Spanish family where arranged marriages were commonplace—even when, as in the case of Alejandro's father, Don Enrique, a younger son had chosen to seek his fortunes in the new world—Alejandro had resisted such a fate. He had gone, as his father before him, to Spain to choose a bride, but unlike his father, Alejandro had found no dark-eyed *señorita* who aroused anything more than tepid interest within his heart. He had returned home to the family ranch in Mexico, much to Don Enrique's disgust, unmarried. It was only some five years later, when he was busily wresting the present Rancho del Torres from the wilderness of East Texas and had by chance visited Natchez, that he had met Elena Sevilla . . . met and fallen passionately in love with her. They were married three months later, and even now, ten years after her death, Elena lived in his heart. His marriage to her had been idyllic, filled with laughter, love, and passion. I want *that* for Sabrina, he thought fiercely. I want her to love with every fiber of her being, I demand that the man she marries will love her beyond death, and I want *him* to be her very reason for breathing. Nothing else will satisfy me . . . or Sabrina.

And yet, tonight as never before, he was aware of the fact that when he died, Sabrina would be alone in the world without the much-needed protection of a man. Oh, to be sure, his sisters, Francisca at his side, and the younger one, Ysabel, in Mexico City, would see that no real harm befell her; Sofia, too, could be counted on to care for Sabrina. But the thought of either of his sisters or their husbands having control of his vibrant, headstrong daughter distressed him. Sofia and Hugh Dangermond now . . .

Alejandro's sixty-two years sat lightly on him, his carriage and bearing as straight and proud as it had been thirty years ago. He was tall for a Spaniard, standing nearly six feet in height. He had passed this trait on to his daughter—in her stocking feet she was only three inches shorter than her father. His vivid red hair was untouched by silver; the amber-gold eyes were still magnificent, the passing years unable to dull their brilliance. But while he enjoyed the best of health, he was conscious that someday, perhaps not too far away, Sabrina would be alone. To have her safely married was the only way he could think of to protect her, and yet he felt instinctively that Carlos de la Vega was not the man to capture her heart—or the man to love her as she would need to be loved. But how to explain that to Francisca?

Francisca de la Vega was precisely ten months older than her brother, a fact she constantly threw up in his face. She was also a creature endowed with few emotions, a rigid woman to whom family and duty came before anything else. She had been disbelieving when Alejandro had refused to marry for anything less than love, and if he were to have explained his reservations about a match between her son and his daughter, she would have been outraged and incredulous. *She* had not loved their longtime neighbor in Mexico, Luis de la Vega, when Don Enrique had arranged her marriage to him, but what did that matter? Luis, though a younger son, had been wealthy enough, and he had been blue-blooded enough to satisfy Don Enrique. It had been her *duty* to marry as her father demanded, and she had done it without argument. It had also been her duty to follow her husband when, much to her fury, he had decided to follow his brother-in-law's lead and remove his family from Mexico and settle in the Nacogdoches area. Francisca absolutely *hated* living in this barely civilized outpost of Spanish dominion, and through the years she had complained bitterly about its lack of the elegance of life. Elegance she would have enjoyed had they remained in Mexico. But it had been her *duty* to stay with her husband and run his household and bear his four children, including Carlos, the youngest, the only son and heir. Why couldn't Sabrina do the same?

If Francisca and Alejandro were far apart philosophically, they were also greatly dissimilar physically. Francisca was the epitome of a highborn Spanish matron. Swathed in bright silks and glittering, heavy gold jewelry, she was a little plump and not very tall, with lustrous dark hair not as yet showing any sign of silver, and possessed a pair of lovely, liquid brown eyes. She, too, carried her age well, her aristocratic features still showing signs of the beauty she had been. Unfortunately, neither she nor her sister, Ysabel, shared their brother's lively sense of humor or zest for living, nor would either of them have understood his reasons for not agreeing to a match that was so advantageous.

Which brings me back to where I started, Alejandro sighed with frustration.

As he remained silent, making no reply to her statement, Francisca grew impatient and demanded sharply, "Have you nothing to say?" And when Alejandro merely shrugged his shoulders, she added heatedly, "Why will you not admit that their marriage would be a splendid thing? I do not understand you, *mi hermano!* Surely you can have no objections?"

Reluctantly Alejandro confessed, "No, I would have no objection . . . if it were what Sabrina wanted."

Francisca looked offended at the notion that Sabrina could have any say in their plans for her future, but deciding not to be sidetracked by such nonsense, she pressed on. "I didn't agree with you when you suggested we postpone any serious settlements when Sabrina was younger, but as there was no real urgency to the matter being decided then, I held my tongue. Now, however . . ."

His eyebrow rising sardonically, Alejandro murmured, "Do you *ever* hold your tongue?" But before she could reply, he asked innocently, "You mentioned urgency. Is there some urgency now? And as I recall, you made quite a few objections when I wouldn't discuss a marriage between them before Sabrina went to spend those six months with Ysabel when she was fifteen. Could it have been that you were frightened she might have found a young caballero in Mexico City who would have suited her better than your son? Like perhaps Ysabel's oldest son, Domingo?"

Francisca's opulent bosom swelled with indignation. "There is," she spat furiously, "no one *better* than Carlos!"

Suddenly enjoying himself, Alejandro said meekly, "Ah, forgive me, what you say is perfectly true. But tell me, why are you so insistent that we decide anything now? Nothing has changed." His tongue in cheek, he added, "Unless Ysabel has written to say that Domingo is coming to visit?"

Francisca's dark eyes flashed, and her full mouth tightened. Controlling her temper with an effort, she ignored his provocative statements and said levelly, "Sabrina is now seventeen years old. There is no reason why an engagement cannot be agreed upon."

Annoyed with her persistence, Alejandro finally muttered, "Francisca, cease your machinations! Tonight is Sabrina's seventeenth birthday, and I have no intention of making any decisons." He said inflexibly, "You were eighteen before our father betrothed you to Luis, so why should Sabrina have less time? She is young yet, and I will not have you or anyone else stampeding her into a marriage she may not want."

Her jaw clenching, Francisca inquired acidly, "Are you saying she may not want to marry Carlos?"

Alejandro sighed. "I don't know what her thoughts are. Rest assured that if Sabrina wishes to marry Carlos, I will put no obstacles in their way."

"How generous of you!" she said scathingly. "But do not be surprised if, by the time you condescend to talk of a marriage, Carlos has already decided he no longer wishes to marry your daughter."

"So be it."

Making no attempt to hide her displeasure, Francisca stalked off, and Alejandro breathed more freely. But the conversation they had exchanged did not go away from his mind, and much later that night, when all the guests were gone and he and Sabrina were settled comfortably in a small, cozy, slightly shabby sitting room at the end of the main wing of the house, he casually said, "I noticed that you danced quite a few dances with Carlos. Do I sense a romance?"

Sabrina, in a very *un*ladylike position, barefooted, her long legs dangling over the side of a huge, high-backed chair of Cordova leather, stared at her father with astonishment. "A *romance?*" she demanded incredulously. "With *Carlos?*"

Alejandro smiled, thinking of Francisca's reaction if she had heard Sabrina's answer. Pushing the thought of Francisca's chagrin and anger from his mind, he said idly, "Hmmm, Carlos. Do you like him?"

Puzzled, Sabrina answered readily enough, "Of course I like my cousin—we've grown up together."

"But have you considered marrying him?"

A look of complete bewilderment on her lovely face, Sabrina glanced at the crystal snifter of brandy that sat just inches from her father's hand. Alejandro laughed out loud at that glance, instantly feeling happier. Lightly he said, "No, I have not overindulged myself, pigeon. It is just that your Tía Francisca would like to see you married to Carlos, and I wondered how you might react."

Sabrina wrinkled her slightly tilted nose with displeasure. "Tía Francisca interests herself in matters that are not her concern. I do not wish to marry yet, and," her features suddenly dreamy, she added, "when I do, I want to love as you and Madre did—nothing less will do."

Relieved and pleased at the same time, Alejandro raised his brandy snifter and said solemnly, "Nothing less than love for us."

Despite the reassurance of his own beliefs about Sabrina, after she had gone to bed that night, Alejandro found himself thinking seriously of her future—and possible marriage. There was, he knew, no man of any age in the area who had caught her fancy. Or, he admitted ruefully, one that she would not lead around like a bull with a brass ring through its nose! But yet, even as that thought crossed his mind, he remembered a young man with a dark, lean face and hard jade-green eyes . . . his nephew-in-law, Brett Dangermond.

Now there, he conceded almost smugly, was a man. A man strong enough and devil enough to handle *any* woman—even Sabrina.

If Sabrina had not seen Brett Dangermond since she was seven years old, the same was not true of Alejandro. He had seen Brett several times during the ensuing years, in Natchez and New Orleans, and though the meetings had been far apart and fleeting, each time he had met Brett, he had been more impressed. But until this evening, he had never considered that unsuspecting rakehell in the light of a possible son-in-law.

A smile of pure devilment on his face, Alejandro rummaged around in the carved pine desk he was sitting behind and found some paper and his quill and inkpot. For several seconds he stared off into space, suddenly realizing that he had to have some reason for so unexpectedly inviting Brett to visit with them. He racked his brains for some plausible excuse, and then, remembering vaguely something about Brett winning a plantation in lower Louisiana on the throw of the dice, he began to write.

That had been two years ago, and Alejandro seemed to recall that when he and Brett had met by accident in New Orleans, Brett had made some mocking comment about perhaps turning his hand to being a planter like his father. The plantation Brett had just acquired had been devastated by the indigo crop failure back in 1792, but Brett, Alejandro remembered clearly now, had mentioned he'd like to try experimenting with sugar cane. As Alejandro recalled, Brett had known a surprising amount about the cultivation of this fairly new crop in Louisiana, and his smile widened. Of course. Sugar cane was the answer! He would write Brett, indicating that he was considering planting several hundred acres in sugar cane and would like Brett's advice. It was weak, but it was not *un*reasonable. Swiftly, before he had time to change his mind, he began to write. When he had finished, he sat back and grinned.

Thinking of Brett Dangermond had reminded him of how fond Sofia and Sabrina were of each other, and he was aware that he had suddenly solved several problems that Francisca's conversation tonight had raised: if something happened to him, under the current situation, Sofia Dangermond would be the only person he would want to have care for Sabrina, but in the meantime—his grin widened—in the meantime, who knew what would happen once Brett received his letter?

CHAPTER FOUR

When Alejandro's gracious invitation to visit the Rancho del Torres to discuss planting sugar cane finally arrived in Brett Dangermond's hands, it was a wet, stormy day in late November. Brett had returned to Riverview, where he was temporarily staying at his bachelor quarters situated some distance from the main house, after a day spent in the company of his friend Morgan Slade.

Cursing the damp weather, in the narrow entry hall of the small house that had been built for his exclusive use five years earlier, he tossed aside his dripping greatcoat. Walking through a doorway to his right, he entered a large pleasant room and strode rapidly across an elegant red Turkey rug to stand before the welcoming fire that blazed on the bricked hearth.

The room where he stood served as both a salon and a dining room. There were comfortable green leather chairs scattered indiscriminately about it, a heavy oak table and sideboard were situated at one end of the room, several Louis XV chairs covered in brown velvet were nearby, and soft gold drapes hung at the rain-splattered windows. From the haphazard mixture of furniture and the hunting prints on the walls, it was obviously a room that had never known a woman's touch—which suited Brett just fine.

Having warmed his hands, he turned to face the room, and it was then that he noticed the travel-stained letter reposing on a small inlaid marquetry table near his favorite chair. Curious and frowning slightly, he reached for it. Fingering the ripped edge of the packet that contained the letter, he glanced through the doorway where his butler-cum-valet, for want of a better designation, was grumpily hanging up the discarded greatcoat. Resignation lacing

41

his deep voice, Brett asked, "When did this arrive? And who delivered it?"

"Arrived about two hours ago, guvnor. A peddler delivered it, said he got it from a Spanish soldier in New Orleans," Ollie Fram replied laconically, the cockney accent still obvious even after nine years in Brett's service.

Brett looked over the top of the letter at his servant. Dryly he commented, "And of course you just couldn't help opening and reading it."

A pained expression on his ugly monkey face, Ollie Fram replied indignantly, "It might 'ave been important, guvnor—I might 'ave 'ad to send for you."

Brett snorted and settling himself comfortably in the chair nearest the fire, quickly read the letter.

A thoughtful cast to his features, Brett stared moodily into the fire for several seconds. It was only when Ollie placed a mug of mulled wine at his elbow that he stirred. Glancing at the small, dark youth who was so completely the opposite of what a proper butler, or valet for that matter, should look like, he asked, "Well? Shall we accept Don Alejandro's invitation?"

"Don't see why not. You've been getting more and more restless since we came 'ome from England in October. Seems to me it's time we were moving on again. Besides, we ain't never been west of the Sabine River," Ollie answered promptly.

If it seemed odd for a gentleman to seek his servant's opinion about anything other than his cravats and boots, it was an even odder occurrence that Ollie Fram was Brett's servant at all. By rights, as Brett had told him often enough, Ollie should have been hanged on Tyburn Hill years ago—and if the pocket that young scamp had tried to pick that day at Bartholomew Fair had been anybody else's but nineteen-year-old Brett Dangermond's, that might have been Ollie's fate. But while the fates had been unkind to Ollie most of his life, leaving him an orphan in the notorious slums of London at age six, they did not desert him completely: until he was ten, he had managed by methods best not described to survive in the cesspool of Whitefriars. Certainly the fates had smiled upon him the day he had attempted to pocket Brett's watch.

Feeling his gold watch sliding ever so slowly from his waistcoat pocket as he wandered carelessly through Bartholomew Fair, Brett had violently rounded on the culprit. Finding himself face to face with a small, incredibly ugly boy dressed in rags, whose mouth spat the most shocking filth imaginable, Brett had been nonplussed. To have the boy brought before a magistrate would practically have been the child's death warrant, and so, moved by a compassion he couldn't explain (insanity, he said in later months), he had brought the ungrateful ragamuffin into his household in London. It had been difficult for everyone, for Ollie had not been at all thankful for his escape from possible death if it meant bathing and learning some manners as well as to read and speak the King's English. But over the years the rough edges had been shaved off, and not surprisingly, Ollie had come to the belated conclusion that Brett was nothing less than a god.

Brett was never quite certain how it came about, but Ollie gradually took the places of his butler and valet. He filled their departed shoes admirably, if peculiarly, and Brett was satisfied. Ollie was always a bit of a shock at first meeting, his small, wiry stature making him appear at nineteen much younger than he was—until one noticed the cynical wisdom in his brown eyes. And then, unfortunately, there was his occasional lapse from grace, when a particularly exquisite stickpin or watch sported by one of Brett's acquaintances would inexplicably find its way into Ollie's clever hands. Despite his obvious failings, Ollie was quick and intelligent, and to someone as ripe and ready for mischief and danger as Brett was, he was the perfect servant. No questions from Ollie about some of the strange goings on in which Brett had taken part; no arguments from *him* when Brett was leaping blindly into some harum-scarum escapade. Instead, Ollie was likely to join in the madness. Of course, Brett had been very young in those days. He had come alone to England to claim a handsome fortune left to him by a great-aunt, and the results had been entirely predictable. He had been let loose on Europe with too much money, too much time on his hands, and few restraints, so it was only natural that his high spirits would lead him along dangerous paths, paths that soon earned him the nickname "Devil" Dangermond.

There was a rapping at the outer door just then, and Ollie disappeared to answer it. He reappeared a second later, saying laconically, "Guvnor, your father would like you to go up to the house. A General Wilkinson is staying the night, and your father would like you to join them for a brandy after dinner."

Brett grimaced, realizing that his father's invitation was actually a plea to save him from having to endure an entire evening alone with the unctuous Wilkinson. Reluctantly he said, "Very well, send word that I shall be up later."

He found his father and the General by the fire in a small, cozy room at the rear of the house when he finally arrived. After greeting both men politely, he poured himself a brandy and said lightly, "A filthy evening to be visiting, General, isn't it?"

Wilkinson gave a hearty laugh. He was only a few years over forty, but his once-attractive features were bland and heavyset. "Indeed it is!" he replied jovially. "But I was in the area and decided that I would beg a roof over my head from your father rather than spend it in some drafty inn." He smiled slyly. "Besides, your father keeps the best brandy in Natchez."

Hugh Dangermond smiled and murmured, "That may be the case now, but there was a time when it was not true. When Manuel Gayoso was our governor under the Spanish, *he* had the best brandy."

Hugh's fifty odd years lay sedately across his handsome face and body. There was a liberal sprinkling of silver in the black hair, a fine network of laugh lines spreading out near his eyes, and just the slightest padding of weight around his waist to show that time had left its mark on him.

The comment about Gayoso brought a frown to Wilkinson's ruddy face. His hands folded complacently over a noticeably rotund stomach, and he said casually, "Such a shame about him. It seems impossible to think it was only this past summer that he died in New Orleans." The General shook his fair head. "I was there the night he died you know." He gave a long sigh. "Couldn't believe it when they told me the next morning that he was dead. Such a shock! One of my dearest friends, dead in an instant!"

Brett said nothing. His opinion of the General had never been high, and there was something about Wilkinson's manner that bothered him. He sensed hypocrisy in the words about Gayoso's death . . . and he wondered how friendly the General had really been with the late Manuel Gayoso de Lemos.

Wilkinson's friendship with the Spanish was well-known, and there were many, Brett and Hugh among them, who viewed it with suspicion, privately thinking that for a high ranking officer in the United States Army, Wilkinson was a little *too* friendly with the Spanish. There had always been rumors about Wilkinson and the Spanish, but no one had ever proved anything. Unsavory rumors seemed to follow General James Wilkinson; rumors of bribes and crooked dealings trailed behind him like dark shadows.

As the three men talked politely for several minutes, Brett calculated how soon he could leave without deserting his father or offending the General. But then Wilkinson said something that caught his interest.

Placing his glass of brandy on a marble-topped table near his chair, Wilkinson murmured, "I had hoped to see my young friend Philip Nolan before now, but it seems that he has not yet returned from Spanish Texas. I will wait here in Natchez a few days longer, but then I must be off." He smiled affably. "Official duties, you know."

Philip Nolan was Wilkinson's unofficial protégé; he had been Wilkinson's agent before striking off on his own, disappearing for years at a time in the vast, untracked wilderness of the Spanish lands west of the Sabine River. Why would Wilkinson want to see Nolan as soon as he returned from his latest trip in those lands? Brett wondered to himself. Speculatively he eyed the General. What were those two planning? Certainly something that would line their pockets—Wilkinson was always notoriously short of ready money.

Hugh provided a clue, saying innocently, "Strange how Gayoso turned against Nolan before he died. I remember

45

when they were the best of friends. I believe Gayoso actually issued a warrant for Nolan's arrest. . . . We hear rumors up here about the Spanish in New Orleans. It's as if they believe Nolan has discovered some marvelous treasure out there in that wilderness.'' Hugh shook his head disgustedly. ''The Spanish never seem to realize that there is *no* Cíbola, no seven cities of gold. They probably think poor Nolan has found some hidden Aztec treasure.''

The effect of Hugh's words on Wilkinson was electrifying. His entire body stiffened; a look of fury and fear flashed through his blue eyes, though he quickly hid it. Hugh had turned aside to pour himself another brandy, but Brett clearly saw Wilkinson's reaction. Incredulous, Brett stared at the pudgy features. Did the General believe such nonsense? Was that why he wanted to see Nolan? To find out first hand if Nolan had indeed found a treasure? And yet, paradoxically, there was also an air of smug satisfaction about the man, as if he already possessed some enlightening information, as if he knew something that others didn't. . . .

Suddenly intensely curious, Brett began to question the General, but Wilkinson, as if realizing that he had betrayed himself, replied with bland answers, deftly turning the conversation away from Nolan and the Spanish. Reluctantly Brett allowed him to do so. But sometime, he thought slowly to himself as he rode the short distance to his house later that evening, it might prove interesting to do some quiet investigating—to discover how Gayoso had really died and why Wilkinson was so eager to see Nolan. . . .

Unusually restless that evening, Brett roamed about the snug little house like some caged predator. He tried sleeping, but finding sleep elusive he finally donned a black silk robe and wandered downstairs to the salon. Poking irritably at the smoldering fire, he was eventually rewarded by the flicker of flames. Staring at the dancing flames, he found himself remembering a child with hair the color of fire, and his fine mouth tightened.

When he had read Alejandro's letter, he had been aware of a reluctance to renew his acquaintance with the del Torres family, but he was also unbearably curious about the changes that were certain to have occurred in his step-cousin. I wonder what she looks like now, he mused, if she's grown into those incredible eyes and that impudent mouth. . . .

Certainly he had changed in the ten years since they had last met. Yet in the man of nearly twenty-eight there was still a definite resemblance to the youth he had been. Barefooted he stood four inches over six feet with a lean, steel-honed body that possessed the grace and leashed power of a hunting lion. As Sofia had predicted, his shoulders had broadened, his arms swelling with hard muscle now that hadn't been there ten years ago. A wide chest matched his shoulders, his waist and hips were lean and narrow, and his long, elegantly muscular legs showed to perfection in the tight pantaloons and breeches that were currently fashionable.

Perhaps the greatest change lay in his facial features; ten years of dangerous, devil-may-care living were clearly stamped on the harsh, dark face. His hair was just as black, the black eyebrows were just as forbidding, the jade-green eyes . . . The green eyes had acquired a deeply cynical, almost insolent gleam, and the full, mobile mouth frequently had a reckless slant to it, a derisive, faintly contemptuous twist that strangely enough intensified his charm. There was no doubt that Brett Dangermond had grown into an extremely handsome young man despite his unconscious arrogance and air of weary disdain.

He possessed everything—aristocratic breeding, fortune, and a devastating charm and manner that, when he wished, could annihilate any obstacle that lay in his path. And yet there was a constant driving urge within him to seek to allay the boredom and emptiness that were his ever-present companions.

Before he was twenty-five, with Ollie as his eager guide, he had toured the seamy underside of London's danger-ridden slums, had drunk blue ruin until he was nearly blind, had gambled and whored his way to Spain, to France, to England, to America, and back again. There had been duels and madcap pranks along the way—he had fought bulls in Madrid, killed a man in a duel over a woman in Paris; on a drunken wager he had played the highwayman along Hampstead Heath—returning the ill-gotten gains undetected to the rightful owners had been the part of the wager Brett found the most exciting; he had smuggled aristocrats meant for the guillotine out of a France gone mad; and for a year he had thrown his lot in with an American privateer plying the waters off the coast of Mexico. But the escapade, if it can be called such, that had given him the most danger and satisfaction had been the three months he had spent infiltrating a gang of smugglers in the New Orleans area almost three years ago.

It had been no prank, no drunken wager, that had driven him into their notorious ranks, but rather a thirst for vengeance—above all else, Brett was fiercely, savagely loyal to his friends. During the year he and Ollie had sailed with the privateer, Samuel Brown, Brett had grown to like and respect the gruff old captain. Sam Brown had been an honorable man in his rough fashion, and returning from one of his lightning visits at Riverview, Brett had been both grieved and furious to hear of his death at the hands of a renegade band of smugglers. Deliberately Brett had coolly inveigled his way into their network and just as coolly had brought about their ruin. With the help of the Spanish magistrate in New Orleans, he had effectively destroyed the gang from within, watching impassively as the death sentence for Sam Brown's murder was meted out to the guilty party.

It had been shortly after that incident that he had won the decayed indigo plantation in Louisiana and had considered the possibility of a more sedate life. For about a year he had thrown himself into the challenge of bringing back from the brink of disaster the land he had won, and like everything he turned his hand to, he had succeeded. But he had also grown bored with it. He had put a manager in charge of the acreage and had again let his fancy wander where it would, his curiosity aroused by the continuing war between France and England. However, he had discovered to his dismay that danger simply for the sake of danger no longer held the appeal it once had, and driven by a boredom he couldn't dispel, he had returned to Natchez in the fall of 1799 to consider his future.

Danger for danger's sake might have lost its allure for

him, but one thing that had not changed was his deep, abiding contempt and distrust for women. And, unfortunately, in the intervening years there had been certain incidents that had only hardened his beliefs. With all the arrogance of a handsome, much-sought-after youth of twenty-one, he had thought himself immune to Cupid's arrows, but such had not been the case. Returning to England from a turbulent, revolution-torn France in the spring of 1792, he had met Miss Diana Pardee at Almack's one evening. He and two friends, on a dare, had entered those sacred portals to add a bottle or two of fine French wine to the innocuous punch that was always served. They had succeeded in their plot and had settled back to watch the results when Brett had been caught by a pair of wide blue eyes set in the most beautiful face he had ever seen. Curly dark hair framed those wondrous features, and like a man in a daze, instantly forgetting his fierce vow never to be trapped by a woman, he had found himself fervently courting the beautiful Miss Pardee. He had fallen rapturously, blindly in love, and deaf to the warnings of his friends that it was well known that nothing less than a duke would do for Miss Pardee, he had continued for weeks to ply his ardent suit. He had been captivated by her—and it had been clear that she returned those passionate feelings. She had encouraged his advances at every opportunity.

It had come as a particularly painful and distasteful surprise when her betrothal to the Duke of Alward was announced . . . especially since two days previously she had met Brett clandestinely in Hyde Park and had responded enthusiastically to the sweetly urgent kisses he had rained over her upturned face.

Stunned, disbelieving, humiliated, Brett had descended upon the Pardee town house on Half-Moon Street. Lord Pardee, Diana's father, had looked him up and down with pity, and deciding cynically that his daughter could best rout this romantic young firebrand, he had allowed Brett to speak privately with Miss Pardee. It was a shattering blow to hear from his love's lips that she had never had any intention of accepting his suit—he was handsome, much handsomer and younger than the Duke, and she had thought to enjoy herself before she settled down to boring domesticity with a man old enough to be her grandfather. Besides, she couldn't marry an untitled nobody, no matter *how* rich and eligible he was. And of course, everybody knew the Duke of Alward was much, *much* richer than Mr. Dangermond.

Pride had come to his rescue, and cloaking his anguished hurt, his bitter disillusionment, Brett had regarded her contemptuously across the long, handsomely furnished room where they stood. His heart feeling as if it were ripping in two, his face hard and cold, he had taken his leave of Miss Pardee. How blind he had been, he viciously berated himself, living in a fool's paradise, believing even for an instant that there was *one* woman who was different! And how unwise of him to forget the lesson first taught to him by his own mother: a woman meant only pain and betrayal.

If the lesson had needed any strengthening, regrettably, that had been provided in the summer of 1797, when, returning to Natchez for one of his infrequent visits at Riverview, he had accompanied Morgan Slade on that young man's tragic pursuit of his runaway wife. Morgan's faithless wife had taken their child with her as she fled with her lover, and Brett had been with Morgan when they had discovered their bodies on the Natchez Trace. Brett didn't think he would ever forget the expression of stark anguish on his friend's face when Morgan had looked upon his son's little body. Brett had vowed then and there that he would *never* allow any woman to be in a position to hurt him that way, that a woman would never slip under the cold steel guard he would keep around his heart.

And yet, over the years, as he grew older, there were times when he questioned his own beliefs, times when he saw the love and joy that his father shared with Sofia that caused him to wonder. . . . Perhaps, he had mused one night not too long ago, perhaps once in a *great* while there occurred a rare and precious jewel among females—a warm, beautiful woman who was loving and loyal, whose heart was true and steadfast. He didn't really believe it, but Hugh's happy marriage gave him pause every time he came home to visit.

The marriage was definitely a resounding success, the huge house now ringing with the laughter of children, a feeling of warmth and love immediately recognizable the moment one stepped into the elegant marble-floored hallway. Even Brett, steeped in his own bitter cynicism, recognized it, and that might have been why he had grudgingly begun to think that just *maybe* Sofia was as adoring and caring as she appeared to be. Reluctantly he had to admit that his father was ecstatic with his wife and young, growing family, Hugh's face more relaxed and smiling than Brett could ever remember it.

Sofia, to her delight, after a first childless marriage, had proved to be remarkably fertile. A boy, Gordon, had been born in 1790, in 1794 there had been a girl, Roxanne, and another girl, Elisa, had appeared barely a year later, in 1795.

Of Martin one seldom spoke—he had continued his disagreeable ways, making himself thoroughly disliked during his short life. When he had died unexpectedly of yellow fever at the tender age of nineteen, there were those in Natchez who had whispered that it was a profound blessing for the family.

Though Brett had never had a warm relationship with Martin, he viewed his younger siblings with a tolerant affection, and they in turn were comically slavish in their love of the tall, handsome giant who appeared and disappeared with such puzzling irregularity. Brett had once laughingly accused them of cupboard love, since no matter where he had been, or under what circumstances, there always seemed to be an intriguing and dazzling gift for each of them.

Whether it was the children's innocent charm or his father's blatant happiness Brett didn't know, but he had become increasingly aware of an emptiness within himself—an emptiness that danger and excitement no longer seemed to fill. Staring blindly at the dancing fire, he wondered uncomfortably if he didn't envy his father's joy, if deep in his heart, he didn't long for that same happiness. Which made him decidedly uneasy and suspicious about the reasons behind his sudden certainty that he was going to accept Alejandro's unexpected invitation.

Was he going to Nacogdoches because he wanted to help Alejandro and wished to renew his acquaintance with a distant member of the family . . . or was he going because he had never quite forgotten the emotions a child of seven had aroused in him?

Furious with himself for considering for even a moment such a possibility, he almost dashed off a curt refusal of the invitation. But he didn't. Instead, cursing himself for a fool and muttering under his breath something about "mawkish, maudlin, midnight thoughts" he stalked out of the salon and sought his bed.

Ollie found Brett somewhat surly and bad-tempered during the weeks that followed, and even though this unusual state of affairs lasted clear into the new year, he paid it no mind—it would pass. Morgan Slade, arriving the following Wednesday for an evening of drink and cards, wasn't quite so amiable about it.

Watching his friend as Brett scowled at the cards he held in his hand, Morgan asked bluntly, "Is something biting you? You've been like a sore-headed bear all evening."

Brett grimaced. Throwing down the cards on the oak table, he admitted, "Nothing I'm certain of. I think it must be this bloody weather. God, how I hate rain!"

Morgan grinned in commiseration. It was true that the past several days had been unpleasant, but knowing it was unlike Brett to let something as mundane as the weather disturb him, he probed lightly. "Is just the weather making you such disagreeable company?"

Rising to his feet, Brett approached the sideboard and poured them both a snifter of brandy. He handed one to Morgan and reseated himself. Staring at the amber-colored liquor in his snifter, Brett said somberly, "Hell, I don't know what's wrong with me! I think I've been here in Natchez too long. It's time I was moving on again, but I find that no place in particular has any lure for me."

"But I thought you were going to visit that relative of yours in Spanish Texas," Morgan said with surprise, his vivid blue eyes puzzled.

"Oh, I probably will," Brett admitted moodily. "It's just that . . . oh, damn and blast! I don't know what's the matter with me—I just can't seem to arouse any enthusiasm for anything these days. Not even the thought of seeing new territory pricks my interest."

Thoughtfully Morgan said, "Have you seen Philip Nolan since his marriage last month to Fannie Lintot?"

Surprised and showing it, Brett answered, "No. Why?"

"Well," Morgan began slowly, "if going to visit your uncle in Nacogdoches doesn't appeal to you, why don't you consider going with Nolan later on this year when he goes to capture more wild horses west of the Sabine River?"

"He just got married this past December and he's *already* thinking of leaving his bride? That doesn't speak well for the state of matrimony!" Brett said sardonically. Then he could have cursed himself for the spasm of pain that crossed Morgan's face. "Forgive me!" Brett burst out contritely. "I didn't mean to—"

Morgan gave him a twisted smile. "It doesn't matter," he interrupted easily. "Time does heal the pain, my friend." His features suddenly hard, he added, "Time also teaches one that women are never what they seem."

Women and their deceitfulness was one subject upon which Brett and Morgan never disagreed, and for the next hour, each reinforced the other's bitter assessment of the opposite sex. Having exhausted the sins of women they had known, Brett brought the conversation back to Philip Nolan.

"Do you think he is really going to go horse hunting so soon after his marriage?" he asked casually.

"I doubt he means to leave within the next few months, but he did say something to me last Tuesday that made me think he might be going west this fall some time. With Nolan, you never know what he is going to do. Although, like you, I find it peculiar that with a new bride and after his last brush with the Spanish . . ." At Brett's expression of interest, Morgan explained, "He almost didn't make it back to Natchez; the Dons apparently wanted his hide rather badly. And of course he asked for it, telling them he had papers to hunt horses in one place and then being detected in another part of Texas where he had no business. You know how suspicious the Spaniards are, they're so certain we're going to steal their land from them."

"And we aren't?" Brett interjected sardonically.

Morgan shrugged his shoulders. "As long as they let us use the Mississippi and the Port of New Orleans unhampered, I doubt there will be any trouble on that score!"

Brett grunted and then inquired, "You seem to know a great deal about Nolan's plans. Are you going to go with him?"

"I might," Morgan admitted slowly. "Like you, since I returned home from New Orleans last fall, I've found myself growing more and more restless. There is nothing to hold me to Natchez—I very well might just throw my lot in with Nolan if he does leave."

"It sounds interesting, but I doubt I can control my boredom until, and *if,* Nolan goes horse-hunting again," Brett said dryly. "I suspect that before spring arrives, I'll have shaken the dust of Natchez from my feet and wandered God knows where."

"Well, if you do go to Nacogdoches, it doesn't entirely preclude the trip with Nolan. He had friends in that area, and I believe he frequently stops there, so it's possible you might meet up with us."

Brett nodded his dark head in agreement. "That may well be. We'll just have to see how things develop. But in the meantime, I believe I won the last hand. . . ."

They played cards for hours, but despite his late night and the consumption of a prodigious amount of brandy and wine, Brett woke the next morning feeling more satisfied than he had in days. He supposed it was because at last he had settled in his own mind the question of the trip to Nacogdoches. He was definitely going, even if the true reasons behind his decision were obscure. He told himself he was bored, he'd never been to Nacogdoches; he liked Alejandro and he'd once held Sabrina in affection, so why not go visit them? That he was oddly eager to see his young stepcousin he stubbornly pushed to the back of his mind. Besides, he reminded himself forcibly, at seventeen she was still a child.

Having settled that point to his satisfaction, in the following days Brett found himself impatient to begin the journey to Nacogdoches and the Rancho del Torres. Sofia was delighted with his decision, and for one awful moment he was afraid she might decide to accompany him. Sofia took an amused, knowing look at his carefully controlled features and burst into laughter. "No, I don't intend to come with you. Of course, if Sabrina would like to return with you and visit with us awhile, would you mind acting as her escort?"

"It would be my pleasure," he muttered politely.

Bad weather conspired to delay his departure, but it also gave him time for reflection, and for the first time in his life he seriously considered his future. Certainly, he admitted wryly, he could not continue as he was—gaming and whoring, living with his past reckless abandon. Ideally he should settle down at Riverview and prepare himself for the day the plantation would be his. But with a twisted smile he finally conceded within himself that he would never live comfortably at home for very long—within six months the small tight-knit community of "Upper Natchez" would stifle him and the smooth running of Riverview would leave him with too much time on his hands.

Having admitted that much, he suddenly realized that he *never* would be happy living at Riverview, and his jaw tightening, he came to a decision. He gave it careful consideration, and then, his mind made up, he sought out his father.

Brett found Hugh going over the account books, and Hugh looked up with delight when Brett walked into the study the next evening. Laying aside his quill, he smiled warmly and said, "This is a pleasure! I wanted an excuse to escape these dull books!"

The two men talked desultorily for some minutes, Brett sprawling lazily in a crimson channel-backed chair near his father's walnut desk. They had served themselves snifters of brandy from the crystal decanter that always sat on the marble-topped table near Hugh's desk, and eventually Brett said quietly, "I had a specific reason for calling upon you tonight."

"Oh?"

Bluntly Brett said, "Before I leave on this trip to Nacogdoches, I would like you to have the papers drawn that dispose of my interest in Riverview. Gordon should have it.

It is *his* home now, and God knows I've fortune enough without it."

Hugh was stunned. Blankly he murmured, "Gordon will not be penniless, you know. Sofia had money of her own, and I have also added to it." His voice deepening with emotion, he added, "You are my eldest son, my heir. Riverview has always gone to the eldest son."

A curiously gentle expression on his hard features, Brett said softly, "Father, just because I was born first is no reason to leave Riverview's fate in my hands." His lips twisted into a derisive smile. "On the turn of a card I have lost and won a fortune equal to Riverview. Would you want it in the hands of a wastrel and a gambler? Doesn't everything you have worked for deserve a better caretaker? I want Gordon to have it."

Brett's startling announcement had shaken Hugh, reminding him miserably that Brett's memories of Riverview could never be happy ones, that while now the house rang with laughter and joy, it had not always been so. His son might claim he was renouncing the plantation because he was satisfied with his fortune, but Hugh suspected that there was a deeper reason.

They never spoke of the early unhappy years at Riverview, years in which they both had lived in the hell created by Gillian, but Hugh was sadly aware that those years had much to do with Brett's rejection of the estate. His comments about being a wastrel and a gambler Hugh dismissed without further thought—he had no doubts that his son would do the very best by Riverview should it come into his possession. But would Riverview, with all its bitter memories, be best for Brett? Inwardly Hugh sighed and candidly admitted to himself that there was much to be said for Gordon's being the next owner of Riverview. But it had always been understood that Brett was the heir, and Hugh was reluctant to change that fact. Out loud he asked, "What about your own heirs? Someday you may marry, and when you have children you may feel differently about it."

Brett looked cynical. "Father, marriage is the *last* thing you can expect from me!"

Staring at the scornful young face, Hugh was reminded

vividly of himself during the painful, ugly years following Gillian's defection. Then he had been full of hatred and contempt for women, believing there wasn't a woman alive who didn't practice deceit as easily as she breathed.

How bitter I was then, Hugh thought with surprise, as bitter and cynical as Brett is now. As bitter and cynical as I would be now except for Sofia. . . .

With a wrench he brought his mind back to the question of Riverview. His expression troubled, Hugh asked heavily, "Are you positive about this?"

A slightly quizzical smile on his lips, Brett inquired wryly, "Have you ever known me to change my mind? I believe you once said that my stubbornness was either my greatest vice or my greatest virtue—you hadn't at the time decided which."

An unwilling smile tugged at the corners of Hugh's mouth. "I still haven't," he replied dryly. The smile faded, and sending Brett a searching look, he asked again, "You're certain? There is nothing of Riverview that you want for yourself?"

Thoughtfully Brett admitted, "I wouldn't mind having the house I'm living in now and some acreage to go with it." An impish grin flashing across his dark face, he added dulcetly, "For my decrepit old age."

A week later, Brett was once again sitting in his father's study. Giving his son an unsmiling look as Brett sat across the desk from him, Hugh said testily, "I've done as you wished. When you sign these documents you sign away all claim to Riverview—it will all go to Gordon."

Brett reached for the quill, but his father's hand stopped him.

"I don't like this!" Hugh burst out explosively. "Riverview should be yours! What if you lose that blasted fortune you have now? Then where would you be?"

"I would be precisely where I deserved to be!" Brett answered swiftly. Conscious of his father's distress, he said seriously, "Father, have you forgotten the plantation in Louisiana? The money and houses in New Orleans? The lands in England? The funds in the bank in London? Good God! I have no need of more!"

Hugh gave a sigh, lifting his hand from Brett's. "I suppose you're right." A brief smile flitted across his face. "I deeded you that house and a hundred acres—for your decrepit old age, of course."

The weather had begun to clear, and it appeared that the worst of the winter storms were over. Two days after the meeting with Hugh, weighted down with messages and gifts, Brett and Ollie rode eagerly away from Natchez, heading for the Sabine River and Nacogdoches.

It wasn't an easy trip. They were starting out early in the year, and all the rivers and streams were swollen and rampaging. The trail they followed—and often there was no trail—was first through gloomy, swampy wastelands inhabited only by alligators and other wildlife. Eventually the countryside improved in appearance despite being trackless and virtually uninhabited. There was thick vegetation that nourished teeming game—bear, panther, and deer—and Brett enjoyed the hunting; Ollie did not. Huddled next to a smoking camp fire and being bitten to death by the hordes of mosquitoes that were just hatching as the weather warmed, he was heard to grumble, "And to think I thought this would be exciting!"

Brett merely grinned, aware that while Ollie was ever ready for adventure, he had never been introduced to the vast and varied wilderness that comprised the largely unexplored American continent. He was perfectly suited to life in the dens of iniquity to be found in the major cities of Europe, but nothing in his young life so far had quite prepared him for living so close to nature.

And while the same could probably have been said of Brett, he discovered that he was enthralled by the varied countryside. The wild, untamed land appealed to him; the savage joy of the hunt sung in his veins; the green solitude of swamps and forest insidiously wrapped itself around him, making him more relaxed and carefree than he had been in years.

Eagerly Brett embraced the hardships of the trail: the unyielding ground for a bed at night, the smoky camp fires, the need to secure their own fresh meat, and the inherent dangers that were ever present along their journey —predatory animals . . . and men.

The Sabine River area was gaining a reputation as a haunt for desperate hunted men, and twice they had been accosted by strangers whose demeanor and manner had made Brett reach carelessly for the pistols he kept tucked in the wide leather belt at his waist. And twice those same strangers had taken a long look at Brett's shoulders, the cool green eyes, and the pistols held so expertly in his lean hands and had ridden on.

Ironically, by the time their last night on the trail arrived, Brett very closely resembled those hard-featured desperadoes they had outfaced. His raven hair was long, brushing the collar of his shirt; a half-grown black beard partially disguised his features; and the rough clothing he wore was definitely not that of a man of wealth. Attired in an open-necked red calico shirt, a wide brown leather belt, buckskin breeches, and boots, he bore little similarity to the elegant rakehell who had graced some of the wealthiest homes in Europe. And with his bearded face and a practical wide-brimmed brown hat pulled low across his forehead, it wasn't surprising that when Sabrina saw him, she thought she had fallen into the hands of a desperado.

CHAPTER FIVE

Sabrina, unaware of Alejandro's invitation to Brett Dangermond, had found the months following her seventeenth birthday fiesta uneventful. No, that wasn't quite true, she admitted with a frown one sunny morning in early April. There were subtle differences within herself, and she was conscious of a flicker of dissatisfaction with the easy regularity of her days.

There was nothing or anyone she could blame for her disquietude—her father was the same loving man he had always been, her home and the servants were unchanged, and she was still the darling of the Nacogdoches district. But there was something missing . . . some unnamed yearning growing inside of her made her restless and moody, uncertain and expectant at the same time. She wasn't *un*happy, nor was she precisely disenchanted with her usual pursuits, it was just that . . .

Balefully she scowled at an unoffending display of vivid pink morning glories that caught her eyes. She was sprawled comfortably in a patch of spring clover that grew under the shady branches of a beech tree, her slim body clothed in what was positively indecent attire for a young lady: a loose-fitting white linen shirt and a pair of disreputable-looking russet calzoneras. A wide-brimmed sombrero lay on the ground near her booted and spurred feet, and just a short distance away, the palomino mare that had been her sixteenth birthday gift from her father lazily cropped the lush green grass.

This was a favorite spot of Sabrina's. It was less than a mile from the hacienda, and she often came here to sit and allow the peacefulness and beauty of the sheltering beeches, pines, flowering dogwood, and myrtles to sweep over her. She had spent many a pleasant afternoon lying here daydreaming. Unfortunately, of late, her daydreams had been vague, shadowy affairs that increased rather than diminished the growing turmoil within her.

Still glaring at the morning glories that were attempting to twine themselves around the base of a towering pine tree, she plucked a stem of clover and idly chewed it. Maybe it is Carlos, she thought reluctantly. Or maybe it is Father.

Her soft mouth curved ruefully. No, it wasn't anything her father had done, but she wished he had never brought up the subject of marriage to Carlos.

Sabrina had never thought too deeply about the man she would one day marry, but marriage was something she had always accepted as inevitable. Until the night of her seventeenth birthday. Or rather, until the weeks following it.

Meeting the sons of the neighboring ranchers, dancing with them at other fiestas, dining at their homes with her father, she discovered with surprise that there wasn't one she would want to marry. Not even dear Carlos, she conceded wryly.

Since the conversation with her father she had begun to look at the men of her acquaintance with new eyes, particularly her cousin Carlos. And while she still found him delightful to dance with, to laugh with, and to ride with, she was becoming increasingly aware that she definitely did *not* want to marry him—or any man she had met so far.

As if to give lie to that thought, a dark young face with jade-green eyes danced before her, and with an exclamation of disgust, she tossed the mangled clover stem away and rolled over onto her stomach. Brett Dangermond was certainly the *last* man she'd ever think of marrying! And right behind him came Carlos, she decided grimly.

If she had begun to look at Carlos with new eyes, she had also begun to be aware of the fact that their relationship had undergone a delicate change during the months following her birthday. He seemed to call more frequently at the Rancho del Torres than he had in the past . . . or was it just because she was now more conscious of him? And hadn't his hand seemed to linger longer on hers than necessary? And wasn't there a look in his dark eyes, a hungry, assessing look that hadn't been present before? She couldn't tell for certain; she only knew that the way his eyes seemed always to follow her had begun to disturb her slightly and that she didn't take quite as much enjoyment from Carlos's presence as she once had.

Suddenly annoyed and angry with her train of thoughts, she sprang lithely to her feet and reached for her sombrero. Hurriedly twisting her red-gold hair up on top of her head, she secured the fiery mass with an ivory comb she always carried with her for just that reason, and jamming on the wide-brimmed sombrero, she whistled for the palomino mare, Sirocco. Well trained by Sabrina, Sirocco instantly trotted over to her mistress, whickering softly. Sabrina smiled, her foul mood vanishing, and gently she caressed the silken muzzle that pushed against her breasts.

"What a fool I am, Sirocco," she said absently, "to be brooding on such a lovely morning." The mare tossed her golden head as if in agreement, and Sabrina laughed.

Looking more like a slim youth than an heiress, she swung up lightly into the ornate silver saddle the vaqueros had given her for her seventeenth birthday. Grasping the silver inlaid bridle given at the same time, she leaned over and crooned mischievously into Sirocco's twitching ear, "Shall we see if you live up to your name? Will you run for me like the fiery wind you are named after?" And ever so gently she touched the gleaming golden hide with her spurs.

Spiritedly Sirocco reared up on her hind legs, and then very like her name, she plunged from the green glade where they had been and raced like the wind across the wide, marshy meadow that stretched in front of them. This was familiar ground to them both, and recklessly Sabrina urged the mare on to an even faster pace, reveling in the feeling of the mare's powerful strides and the humid air rushing coolly across her face. A joyous sparkle in the amber-gold eyes, a smile on the full mouth, Sabrina felt the last remnant of her earlier dissatisfaction evaporate, and with a soft laugh she loosed her hands on the reins, giving Sirocco free rein, willing to lose herself in the sheer pleasure of this wild, mad dash.

To Brett and Ollie, just entering the meadow to the left

of where Sirocco had burst from the forest, the situation looked anything but pleasurable. The first clue they had that they were not alone in this seeming uninhabited wilderness was when, like a creature gone mad, the golden mare with her slim, boyish rider suddenly exploded into their view and began to race crazily across the meadow. Never once dreaming that anyone would deliberately ride with such a disregard for life and limb, assuming that the horse had escaped the control of her inexperienced rider, Brett tossed the reins of the pack horse he'd been leading to Ollie. With a muttered curse under his breath about the stupidity of young males, he dug his spurs into his stallion's side and shot away after the disappearing horse and rider.

Sirocco was fleet and light-footed, and at four years of age she was just coming into her full strength, but Firestorm, Brett's stallion—a son of Flame's—was at his peak, and with his longer legs and more powerful strides, Firestorm swiftly closed the distance between them. Still unaware that he was not rescuing a young boy, as Firestorm raced alongside Sirocco, Brett leaned over in his saddle and made a desperate attempt to catch the silver bridle that dangled so uselessly against Sirocco's extended, lathered neck.

Sabrina hadn't been conscious of anything but her own enjoyment of this wild ride, but the instant the lean brown hand made a grab for Sirocco's bridle, she was alerted that she was no longer alone. Catching only a glimpse of a hard, dark, bearded face beneath the wide brim of a hat, she took immediate evasive action, jerking the reins and causing Sirocco to swerve sharply in another direction. She heard the other rider curse furiously, and glancing over at him, she saw that his own horse had already changed direction and was once again coming up fast alongside Sirocco.

Her heart beating painfully in her breast, certain she was about to be attacked by one of the many brigands who had been drifting into this area, Sabrina tightened her mouth, and during the following minutes she did her damnedest to escape. But it was all to no avail—the other horse was too powerful, the other rider too determined, and in an open field there was no place to do more than let

Sirocco have her head and pray the mare could outmaneuver the big chestnut horse.

It still hadn't occurred to Brett that the boy he was attempting to rescue didn't want to be rescued. The erratic movements of the mare he put down to inexcusable handling, and by the time he was again in position to attempt to stop the runaway horse, his temper, never the coolest in the best of situations, was boiling. And this time he made no move to snatch at the reins. Instead, with the suddenness of a striking snake, he reached out and roughly plucked Sabrina from Sirocco's back. With more force than necessary, he flung her facedown across the saddle in front of him.

Sabrina was not at all grateful for her supposed rescue, and being handled like a sack of meal, the breath momentarily knocked out of her, did nothing for her frame of mind. Furious that this lawless creature would dare to attack the daughter of Don Alejandro del Torres on his own land, she didn't even wait for the galloping horse to slow down before she began to fight.

The Toledo steel blade her father had given her for her birthday was neatly sheathed in the top of her boot, and if she could only reach it . . . Quickly recovering her breath, she twisted and squirmed, trying uselessly to escape from the iron hand that pressed down so forcefully in the middle of her back as her captor gradually reined in his horse. Determined to get away, she continued her wiggling, hoping that if she couldn't use her knife, she could shift her weight to the side her feet dangled from and then slide down the side of the slowing horse and possibly make it to the protection of the nearing forest.

Brett didn't exactly realize what his unwelcome burden was up to, but he was aware that if the confounded boy didn't stay still, the young whelp stood an excellent chance of falling to the ground and being trampled under Firestorm's hooves. Grasping the waist of the calzoneras, he ungently shifted Sabrina so that her head was now lower than her thrashing feet. Harshly Brett commanded, "Be still, you young cretin, until I stop the horse!"

The blood rushing to her head, as much from his words as her position, Sabrina furiously began to struggle even harder. The sombrero, which had miraculously remained on her head until now, went flying, the ivory comb with it, and the red-gold hair came tumbling down around her flushed face.

Busy with stopping the powerful stallion with only one hand on the reins, Brett saw neither the sombrero nor the ivory comb disappear. He also wasn't paying as much attention to his captive as he should have been, and just as the stallion finally came to a stop, with a burst of incredible agility, using her hands for leverage against the side of the horse, Sabrina was able to flip herself over and practically in the same movement twist herself into a sitting position in front of her captor.

Like lightning her hand snaked to the top of her boot, and in a second her fingers closed around the blade. Before Brett even had time to assimilate that the "boy" wasn't a boy at all but a furious fire-maned young hellcat, the knife swung in a determined arc, deeply slashing him across the shoulder and down the upper portion of his muscled arm.

Taking no notice of the almost blinding flash of pain, Brett reacted instinctively, and moving with a deadly swiftness, he captured the slender arm that wielded the knife so efficiently. Cruelly twisting the arm behind Sabrina's back, he glared down into the angry features so near his own. Astonishment held him speechless as his stunned gaze took in the disheveled mass of flaming curls rioting around the most enchanting face he had ever seen— thickly lashed amber-gold eyes fairly spitting defiance and fury were set under haughty dark brows, a delicate straight nose with a delightful tilt at the tip was thrust arrogantly into the air, and below it was a generously curved mouth that fairly challenged any man to taste its sweetness.

It was that glorious hair and those unforgettable eyes that brought recognition to him almost instantaneously, and on a note of incredulity, he breathed, *"Sabrina?"*

At the sound of her name, Sabrina froze, and suddenly oblivious to the brutal hold on her arm, she stared up into the dark bearded face so near her own. It wasn't precisely reassuring. Heavy black eyebrows curved sardonically over deep-set, cynical, jade-green eyes ringed by remarkably long, thick, black lashes—the impact of those eyes was mesmerizing. With an effort she tore her gaze away from his and swiftly took in the arrogant nose, the slightly flaring nostrils, and the full, mobile mouth with its mocking slant. The half-grown beard hid most of his face, but with her heart unexpectedly racing in her breast, her gaze once more fastened on the hard green eyes—green eyes that she had never quite forgotten. "Señor Brett?" she got out huskily, unable to believe that it was really he.

The chiseled mouth curved into a wry smile, and slowly he loosened his cruel grip on her arm. "Yes, I'm afraid it is, sweetheart," he said dryly. The pain from the knife wound making itself felt, he winced as he dropped his right arm and muttered, "I could have wished for a less violent welcome, but considering how we last parted, I suppose I shouldn't be surprised at being met with naked steel!"

Guiltily Sabrina's eyes went to his injured arm, her stomach lurching as she took in the bloodstained calico shirt. "I . . . I . . . I'm s . . . s . . . sorry," she stammered unhappily. "I wouldn't have struck if I'd known it was you! I thought you were an outlaw."

He laughed mirthlessly, his gaze on her soft mouth. "Perhaps I am, spitfire, perhaps I am."

Suddenly aware of the way they were sitting, her full breasts crushed up against his hard chest, her hip pressed intimately into his groin, she moved slightly away from him. Almost primly she said, "Well, you certainly gave a good imitation of one, the way you attacked me just now."

"Attacked?" he questioned sharply. "I was under the impression that I was saving you from a runaway!"

Sabrina stared at him open-mouthed. "Sirocco? You thought she was running away with me? Is that why you grabbed at the bridle?"

"Of course it was!" Brett returned testily, her astonishment making it abundantly clear that he had mistaken the situation, which didn't soothe his temper any. His injured arm was aching like the very devil, adding to his discomfort, and he was much too conscious for his liking of the slender body so close to his own. Brusquely he said, "If I erred, I apologize. However," he went on harshly, "if that sample I just saw was any indication of your usual riding

66

habits, I won't be at all astounded to hear shortly that you've broken your bloody neck!"

Not unnaturally Sabrina bristled at his comments, but before she could make a spirited rejoinder, Brett said sarcastically, "And if this is a sample of the hospitality your father wrote me about, I'd just as soon forgo it, if you don't mind."

"My father?" she repeated stupidly. "My father wrote to you?"

Brett smiled at her unkindly, and as if speaking to an imbecile, he said, "Why else would I be here? Surely you don't think I just *happened* to be here, do you?"

Shooting him a glance of dislike, she replied heatedly, "I haven't had time to think of anything yet!"

Infuriatingly Brett murmured, "I have found over the years that thinking isn't something that women do very often . . . or well."

Smothering an urge to slap his mocking mouth, Sabrina contented herself with returning sweetly, "Perhaps not, but then neither do they attempt acts of such foolish bravado, as you just did!"

Surprisingly, an appreciative grin curved Brett's full mouth. "Very good, infant, very good!"

"I am not an infant!" Sabrina gritted out, for some unknown reason wanting that fact to be made very clear to Brett Dangermond.

One black eyebrow quirked upward, and insolently his green eyes traveled over her slender body. No, she definitely was *not* an infant any longer, he admitted slowly to himself—he'd been *very* aware of that disturbing fact from the moment he'd realized who she was. But if the change ten years had wrought *had* escaped his initial notice, the soft white linen shirt that clung lovingly to the firm breasts and the delicate shape of the long legs revealed by the tight-fitting calzoneras would have made it evident to anyone but a blind man. And Brett was not blind. Quite the contrary, as his eyes lingered on the rise and fall of her bosom before his gaze was drawn irresistibly to the innocently provocative mouth.

His eyes locked on her lips, he murmured teasingly, "I

67

stand corrected, sweet cuz—you are definitely *not* an infant."

His words should have given her satisfaction, but instead they caused her throat to go suddenly dry and a curious breathlessness to assail her. Swallowing nervously—and Sabrina was never nervous—she muttered, "I'm not your cousin either."

"You might add," Brett drawled with a derisive gleam in his eyes, "not very welcoming in the bargain! And while ordinarily I do not go around reminding my hostesses of their duties, in this case I shall make an exception and suggest that unless you wish for me to bleed to death, you set about showing me the way to your home."

Sabrina flushed, and she looked once again at his injured arm, seeing that there was a great deal more blood soaking into the calico shirt than there had been only moments before. Instantly filled with concern for him, she abandoned her belligerent tone, and her eyes shining with contrition, she murmured unhappily, "Forgive me, Señor Brett. I . . . I . . . haven't meant to be *un*welcoming, and I will show you to the hacienda immediately—it isn't far, and Bonita, my maid, will see to your arm."

She started to scramble down from the horse, but despite the needles of pain that were pricking along the open wound, Brett's left hand tightened compulsively on her shoulder, halting her movements. She glanced at him questioningly, and slanting her a crooked grin, he said audaciously, "Couldn't you give me a more explicit sign of welcome? A kiss between cousins meeting for the first time in ten years wouldn't come amiss."

Her heart hammering painfully in her breast, her tongue frozen to the roof of her mouth, she could only stare at him mutely, the amber-gold eyes huge in her face. For a second Brett regarded her, and then with something between a curse and an imprecation, he bent his head and his hard mouth claimed hers.

Besides the paternal salutations of her father, Sabrina had never experienced a man's kiss, and nothing in her life so far had prepared her for the jolt of sweet fire that swept through her veins as Brett's lips pressed ardently against hers. She was giddily conscious of the warmth emanating from the male body so close to hers, of the faint, pleasing odor of horses, wood smoke, and tobacco that clung to him, but most of all she was unutterably moved by the hungry longing that his touch evoked deep within her.

It was a strangely chaste kiss that they shared, but it made her aware of her body as she had never been before, made her bewilderingly aware of a pleasurable tingle in the pit of her stomach, of the tightening of her nipples, and of an insane urge to press herself closer, to cling unashamedly to him. It also, oddly enough, alarmed her, a part of her shrinking away, guessing instinctively that there was danger in feeling the way she did. Danger and a beckoning, tantalizing promise of ecstasy.

For Brett the reaction to her nearness, the soft, innocent yielding of her mouth, was far more powerful, far more violent. The second his lips touched hers, his body exploded with such a fierce surge of almost uncontrollable desire that he trembled. He had known desire before, had carelessly slaked desire before, but it had never been like this, this wild, intoxicating yearning to pleasure, to give, to share and yet possess so completely, so powerfully, that she would remember and bear the stamp of his possession forever. Stunned and shaken by the depth of his reaction to a simple kiss, he was even more appalled at how much he wanted to deepen this embrace, how very much he wanted to part her lips and explore the inner sweetness. Her mouth was achingly soft against his, and for one wild second, he almost lost his head completely and kissed Sabrina as his body prompted him to, but Ollie's voice, sharp with indignation, brought him instantly and unpleasantly back to reality.

"Well, if that don't beat the Dutch!" Ollie exclaimed hotly. "First the bloody bitch pulls a knife on you, and then you kiss her!"

With a sigh, Brett reluctantly lifted his mouth from Sabrina's. Recovering himself quickly, a rueful grin tugging at the corners of his mouth, he murmured to Sabrina, "I think I can safely say that you have welcomed me properly, sweet cuz."

Dazed by his kiss, Sabrina gazed at him blankly for a second, the world slowly coming back into focus. Belatedly she became aware of Ollie, who had ridden up pulling the two heavily laden pack horses behind him. Staring at the small, monkey-faced young man who was regarding her balefully, she asked bewilderedly, "Who is he?"

"Well you may ask," Brett said easily. "This is Ollie Fram, my, er, man." Glancing at Ollie he added, "This is my cousin, Sabrina del Torres. We will be staying at her father's house."

Assessingly, Ollie and Sabrina eyed one another. To Ollie there were only two classes of females—good women and bad women, and Sabrina looked like a bad one to Ollie. The fact that she had just stabbed his employer didn't precisely endear her to him either. As for Sabrina, Ollie's misleading youthful appearance, as well as his travel-stained clothing and sparse beard, wasn't exactly what one expected in the servant of a well-bred, wealthy young man like Brett Dangermond. But then, risking a glance at Brett's own bearded face and rough clothing, she decided that they probably suited each other. Cautiously she acknowledged Ollie with a slight inclination of her head. Ollie merely sniffed disapprovingly.

Rattled by the morning's events, she wasn't quite as calm and collected as she would have liked to be, and slipping lightly off Brett's horse, she said stiltedly, "If you'll follow me, I'll lead you to the hacienda."

It took only a second to whistle up Sirocco, and within minutes, the trio was riding down the dusty red road that led to Sabrina's home. Forest pressed thickly against the road—more a path than a road—pines, black willow, redbud, and sweet gum intermixed with coral honeysuckle, wild azaleas, and cinnamon ferns.

Sabrina's home, Brett discovered a moment later when the forest stopped and they rode out into the open, was a pleasant example of rustic graciousness. The outbuildings in the distance were of adobe and rough-hewn lumber; the corrals and paddocks of split rails were unpainted, but the weather had worn the unprotected wood to a rich, warm, sienna brown that was extremely pleasing to the eye. The hacienda, the *casa grande,* was nestled among the encroaching forest and constructed with tiled roofs and arched walkways and windows in the Moorish fashion. It was impressive in its size and reminded Brett vividly of Spain.

Made of adobe and exposed square beams, the main portion of the house was single-storied, built long and low to the ground. The eaves of the roof had been extended, and they formed wide, welcoming corridors of shade that served as outside hallways. Jutting out at right angles to the rear of the main building was a two-storied wing; a black filigreed iron railing enclosed the narrow balcony that overlooked the front of the hacienda. A courtyard shadowed by graceful, sprawling redbud trees and orange and lemon trees led to wide double doors. As Brett gingerly dismounted, favoring his wounded arm, those doors flew open and Alejandro, a warm smile on his face, came rushing across the courtyard, saying, "How good to see you! I have been looking for you these past weeks and had just about given up hope that you would accept my invitation." His smile faded though as his eyes took in the bloodstained shirt and Sabrina's disheveled appearance. Concern on his face, he inquired, "What has happened? Were you attacked by bandits?"

Brett grimaced. "No. Let's just say that Sabrina and I had a . . . misunderstanding."

Well aware of his daughter's volatile temper and propensity for rash action, Alejandro frowned darkly, and he threw Sabrina a look full of disapproval. "What have you been doing this time, *chica?*" he asked half-angrily, half-resignedly.

Sabrina's soft mouth tightened, and she was slightly indignant that she should have to explain herself to her father. But before she could formulate something less than the heated reply that trembled on her lips, Brett broke in with, "It wasn't her fault. She thought I was an outlaw intent upon, er, ravishing her, and I thought she was a boy on a runaway—my actions were somewhat abrupt and to the point. Before either of us realized our mistakes, I'm afraid she defended her honor rather effectively." A twisted grin on his mouth, he nodded in the direction of his bleeding arm and added lightly, "Don't worry about this bit of nonsense. I assure you I have suffered far worse in the past."

71

"I see," said Alejandro slowly. He sensed that there was more to the tale, but not one to force confidences, he turned away, and clapping his hands, he called loudly, "Bonita! Josefa! Clemente! Elias! Come quickly! We have visitors!"

The next moment the courtyard was swarming with servants and filled with the murmuring of voices as Brett was welcomed and his wound exclaimed over. With much clucking he was led away by Bonita and Josefa, Ollie following jealously behind. Clemente and Elias swiftly and competently saw that the baggage was unloaded and taken to the rooms that would be Señor Dangermond's during his stay. Another call from Alejandro brought more men running from the stables to take charge of the horses.

The courtyard deserted now except for Sabrina and her father, Alejandro sent her a thoughtful look as she stood there, her hair tumbling down to her waist, the boyish garb somehow intensifying her femininity. Just the faintest note of censure in his voice, Alejandro said slowly, "I think the time has come for you to put aside this unsuitable apparel. You are a young woman now, not a wild savage." A slight smile softening his words, he continued lightly, "Your *madre* would not be happy if she could see you now, *chica.* She would think I had done badly in raising you." He quirked an eyebrow at her, as if encouraging an answer, but there was a stubborn tilt to her chin that he knew too well, and a second later he turned away and entered the house in search of his guest.

Feeling strangely bereft and oddly resentful at the same time, Sabrina glared at the empty courtyard. Inside she was a mixture of emotions: ashamed and angry at her father's words, not precisely happy with Brett Dangermond's arrival, and yet not unhappy, more confused and a little insulted at the way he had treated her. One thing was certain though—Brett Dangermond had come back into her life with the suddenness and violence of a lightning bolt, and she was very much afraid that her world was never going to be the same again.

CHAPTER SIX

꿩 It was several hours later before Brett and Sabrina saw one another again, and the intervening time had been used to good effect by both of them. Brett's wound had been tended to by Bonita, and while she muttered that it would have to be sewn and that it was going to leave a scar, there was no real worry about it.

Bathed, shaved, and clothed in a white cotton shirt and black breeches and boots, his wounded arm resting in a sling of scarlet silk, Brett bore little resemblance to the brigand Sabrina had first thought him. Only those deepset, cynical jade-green eyes betrayed that while he wore the trappings of a gentleman, underneath his aristocratic bearing might very well lurk a brigand.

It was true that the sudden meeting with Sabrina had thrown him momentarily off guard and that for one dangerous moment, as he had tasted the sweetness of her lips, his defenses had suffered a serious breach. But that insanity had lasted only for as long as it had taken him to realize the folly of what he was feeling, and he had cursed himself roundly for being such a fool. By the time they had arrived at the hacienda, he had convinced himself that the incident meant nothing.

Sabrina's emotions were harder to define and were certainly far more confusing. She had never known desire until he had kissed her, never before been overly curious about what went on between a man and a woman. But Brett's warm lips on hers had awakened a host of sensations that she wasn't positive she wanted to feel, suspecting that they could plunge her into treacherous waters.

After her father had left her in the front courtyard, she had wandered upstairs to her room. As she had walked past the open doorway of Brett's room she had had no inclination to linger in that vicinity. Sabrina knew she should have inquired after his wound, but she was too angry and distressed by the entire series of events to do so. She was also vaguely conscious of an uneasiness at knowing he would be situated just down the hall from her own room.

Not that she expected Brett to creep down the hall and ravish her, she thought with a contemptuous snort as she pushed aside the voluminous yards of filmy mosquito netting that ringed her bed. Flopping down on the bright yellow and green silk quilt that lay atop the mattress, she propped her chin up on her hands and stared blankly into space. Unable to help herself, once again she relived the moment she had recognized the dark-faced devil who had held her captive. She should, she realized bleakly, have been relieved. But she hadn't been then and she wasn't now. Instead she was filled with an odd mixture of resentment, bewilderment, excitement, and anger.

I don't want him here! she finally decided. He was too disturbing, too disruptive, and she just knew he was going to interfere with the even tenor of her days—completely ignoring the fact that only hours before she had been bewailing those same even-tenored days. Already his presence was making itself uncomfortably felt, she mused rebelliously—never before had her father offered the slightest objection to her usual riding attire . . . or her boyish activities. Yet today, within moments of Brett Dangermond's arrival, he had done both, criticizing her clothes and reminding her to act like a young lady. He also, she thought moodily, had neglected to mention anything about a possible visit from Brett Dangermond.

Frowning, she considered that thought and its implications. There had never been any secrets between her and her father. While he didn't tell her everything that he did, it seemed odd that he would withhold information about a simple invitation issued to, if not a blood relative, at least a close connection to the family. Unless there was more behind Brett's visit than just a family visit? But what? And why had Brett Dangermond decided to accept that invitation?

74

Her brow puckered in concentration. Throughout the years that had passed since Sofia's wedding to Hugh Dangermond, quite a lot of information had come Sabrina's way about Brett, and now, as much because of her father's inexplicable, almost secret invitation as a need to understand why Brett himself should suddenly appear in the wilds of Spanish Texas, she dredged it up from memory. Brett had left home at an early age, that she knew. She also knew from Sofia's frequent letters that Hugh worried about his eldest son a great deal and even upon occasion threatened to disown him. There had been a few scattered references to gambling and duels and the wish on Hugh's part that Brett would settle down and take an interest in Riverview, but there was nothing that Sabrina could recall that would explain why he was now at the Rancho del Torres. It made no sense, she decided heavily—from Sofia's letters it was obvious he was far more at home in the sophisticated, vice-ridden capitals of Europe than in Nacogdoches. Small Nacogdoches was scarcely more than a wilderness outpost and had little to offer a man of Brett's background. So why was he here? she wondered uneasily. Had Hugh finally disowned him and thrown him penniless upon the world? Did he think to recoup his fallen fortunes from her father? Or had he been forced to flee the civilized world because of some heinous crime?

With a chill she remembered her first impression of him, of the leashed, dangerous power, of the hard face and harder, cold eyes. He had looked a renegade, a brigand on the run . . . was he? Or was she simply letting her imagination run full rein? A small, rueful smile curved her mouth. She rather suspected it was the latter, but still the unpleasant thoughts lingered in her mind for some time.

As for Brett's kiss, *that* she resolutely refused to think about. Not wanting to remember the sweet ache that had coiled in her stomach or the wild urge she'd had to cling helplessly to his solid, warm body, she blotted the incident from her mind. Besides, she vowed tightly to herself, it would *never* happen again!

Sabrina would have liked to have stayed where she was, locked away from the rest of the household and its activities, protected from Brett Dangermond's unsettling pres-

75

ence, but she knew it would appear childish to remain sequestered in her room. And, for some reason not wanting Brett Dangermond to think of her as a child, and aware that her father would be rightfully displeased if she were blatantly rude to their guest, she eventually set about changing her clothes and mentally preparing herself to face her disturbing cousin-in-law once again.

By taking her time, by deliberately loitering over her usually brief toilet, she managed to postpone the meeting until twilight, near the time for the light evening meal she and her father preferred. She also, for motives not entirely clear to herself, took special care with her appearance.

Lingering over a bath and luxuriating in the silky foam from a bar of violet-scented Pear's soap, she found herself falling into a ridiculous daydream in which, by methods unknown, Brett Dangermond ended up her adoring slave and she of course coolly spurned his advances. It was a *very* satisfying daydream, and for several moments she sat staring absently off into space, until with an angry jerk she realized what she was doing. Heavens! She certainly didn't want *him* to look at her as Carlos did . . . did she? Confused and a little annoyed with herself, she hurriedly finished her bath.

Wrapped in a huge white towel, for the first time in her life she took an inordinate amount of interest in the contents of her wardrobe. She had always loved beautiful clothes, despite her preference for calzoneras when riding, and being the only child of a wealthy, indulgent father, she had all the gowns and fripperies a girl could wish for. But somehow, as she stared with displeasure at the rainbow array of exquisite clothes that met her eye, nothing quite appealed to her this evening. Then, suddenly angry with herself, gallingly aware of why she was being so selective, she thinned her lips and reached in and yanked out the first garment that came to hand.

It was a lucky yank. The gown of soft apricot silk was one of her newest and prettiest. Expertly made, the bodice fitted snugly along Sabrina's rib cage to her slender waist, and the yards and yards of silk that comprised the skirt fell in graceful folds to just below her ankles. Bell-shaped sleeves ended a few inches above her elbows and were lavishly trimmed with blond lace, as was the low, square-cut neckline. Observing herself in the long cheval glass, she wondered if perhaps the gown wasn't just a little too low-cut—it seemed to her that an unseemly amount of her bosom was exposed. But then, remembering that she had worn the gown previously and hadn't been self-conscious about the amount of smooth golden flesh it revealed, she tossed her curly head and defiantly sat down at her dressing table.

With nimble fingers she began to arrange the tangled flame-colored hair. Several minutes later, she stared back at her handiwork with a certain amount of gratification. Unlike so many of her contemporaries, Sabrina seldom needed or wanted the services of a maid, although upon special occasions Bonita would insist upon being allowed to dress her hair. As Bonita had taught her, she had piled the unruly locks high on her head and had secured the fiery mass with a gold and pearl comb; a few tendrils had been coaxed to curl enchantingly near her ears and temples. Fastening the huge gold hoop earrings that Bonita had given her, Sabrina decided with grim satisfaction that Señor Brett would *not* mistake her for a boy when next they met.

Feeling as if she were going into battle, Sabrina draped a black lace mantilla about her shoulders and her chin held high, sailed out of the safety of her bedroom. Walking down the broad curving staircase that led to the ground floor, she told herself that she had taken such care with her appearance to please her father, and yet, as she approached the small salon where she assumed she would find her father and probably Brett, it was Brett's reaction that she wondered most about. A polite smile on her mouth, she took a deep, fortifying breath and marched into the room.

It was anticlimactic to find the salon empty, and for a moment she glanced about her in puzzlement. But then, noting the double doors that were flung wide and hearing her father's voice coming from that direction, she realized that he must have decided to sit outside on the rear patio.

This proved to be the case, and as the evening was a fine one with a slight breeze blowing to discourage the mosquitoes and other insects, it wasn't surprising that Alejandro had chosen to enjoy the cool tranquillity of the open air. The patio was a favorite place of Sabrina's, she and her father often partaking of their breakfast here, and, on pleasant evenings such as this one, their last meal of the day.

The hacienda itself was L-shaped, and consequently the patio was sheltered on two sides, several sets of double doors opening onto it from the house. To create a greater degree of seclusion, a reverse L-shaped wooden lattice had been constructed to completely enclose the patio. Virginia creeper, honeysuckle, and bougainvillea had long ago entirely covered the lattices, and now they were two tall, green, fragrant walls broken only by the delicate iron-worked gates. A large stone fountain graced one corner of the patio, water spouting from the mouth of a statue of a rearing stallion that rose up from its center. Near the center of the patio a majestic pine tree gave welcome shade during the heat of the day; gaily painted pottery urns containing hibiscus and jasmine were placed on either side of the archways created by the wide, extended eaves of the house. Next to the pine tree was a filigreed iron table, with several chairs scattered nearby.

Alejandro was seated in one of the chairs, a crystal glass near his elbow. As she walked out from the concealing shadows of the eaves, Sabrina caught the faint scent of tobacco that drifted on the night air. Seeing Alejandro seated there alone, she decided she must have been mistaken about hearing his voice a moment ago. Pleased and yet oddly disappointed at Brett's absence, she approached him.

The patio was in a pleasant gloom, and if it hadn't been for the few lanterns that had been lit in two of the archways, there wouldn't have been light enough to see anything beyond dark shapes. But in that faint light, Sabrina's gown glowed like soft gold and her hair shone like fire as she reached her father's side.

Stepping in front of Alejandro, she threw him a saucy look, and then pirouetting provocatively, she said teasingly, "Is this ladylike enough for you, Padre? Or shall I find a gown that is even more daring?"

Alejandro laughed easily, relieved that Sabrina had

taken his words to heart. His eyes warm with pride and love, he replied, *"Bella, bella,* my little pigeon! You are indeed the picture of a lovely young lady. But perhaps I am a bit prejudiced in your favor, *si?* We need, I think, another opinion." And looking beyond her, over her shoulder, he asked, "Tell me the truth, *amigo,* is she not a daughter to be proud of?"

The smile dying on her lips, Sabrina turned slowly around, silently furious with herself for having made the mistake of not scanning the patio area before showing herself. She had been so certain that Alejandro was alone that she had looked no farther than his chair, and it came as an unpleasant surprise to find that Brett Dangermond was lounging indolently against one of the adobe columns that supported the extended eaves, watching her.

She might not have been quite so furious and disconcerted if she could have known that the sight of her as she twirled in front of Alejandro had left Brett feeling as if he had just received a fist in the solar plexus. There was a crazy leap in his pulse, and his heart contracted painfully in his chest as he stared intently at the lovely vision.

The infant was definitely an infant no longer—she was a beautiful, desirable woman, he admitted grudgingly. Too desirable, his brain warned; she is a woman, a silken, corrupt trap. A sardonic expression on his face, Brett conceded the wisdom of the warning, grimly ordering himself to treat her as the child, the "infant" he had once had a fondness for. He didn't dare view her as a woman. She *was* a child, and children could be teased, indulged, and petted. Women could not. Women were dangerous.

Assessingly his gaze ran over her slender body again, and despite his vows, despite his icy determination not to be moved by her, he could feel the heat of desire coiling up through his loins. Virulently he cursed under his breath, enraged at his body's betrayal. He was going to have a damned dangerous time of it, what with one part of him insisting that she was a child while another part responded violently to the young, vibrant woman that she was.

Becoming uncomfortably conscious of his prolonged stare, Sabrina lifted her chin angrily. She was clearly seen in the light of the lanterns, but Brett had chosen a shadowy archway in which to lounge, and she could see only the gleam of his white shirt, the scarlet sling appearing almost black in the gloom. His features were completely hidden in the darkness, only the red tip of his cigarillo revealing the location of his head.

A tight smile on her soft mouth, with far more forwardness than she knew she possessed, she walked coolly up to him and then swept him a deep, disdainful curtsy. A challenging glitter in her eyes, she asked dulcetly, "Well, *señor*? What is your verdict?"

This close, his features were plainly discernible, although the expression in his eyes was hidden from her. As she stared at him, seeing for the first time the lean, hard face without its disguising beard, she was aware of a curious flutter in the region of her stomach. He was undeniably handsome, but not in the most accepted sense—Carlos, she admitted reluctantly to herself, was actually the more handsome of the two, but there was something about Brett's face. . . .

His mouth was absolutely beautiful, full and perfectly chiseled, the lower lip possessing a frankly sensuous curve; his nose was an arrogant blade in the dark face, the nostrils too wide and flaring for classical beauty. The heavy black brows had a naturally insolent slant; the jade-green eyes were deep-set and shadowed by ridiculously feminine lashes. His jaw was too square and determined for perfection, and yet taken all together, his features comprised an intensely masculine face, such an arresting, powerful face that its imperfections were instantly forgotten.

As Sabrina stared, that beautiful mouth curved into a mocking smile, and taking the cigarillo from between his teeth, he murmured mockingly, "Perhaps we should have your verdict of me first. . . . You've certainly studied me long enough."

Sabrina flushed, her temper rising. "I apologize," she said stiffly. Then she added smartly, "You seemed to be hiding here in the shadows, and I couldn't help wondering if your features were so frightful that you dared not reveal them."

"Sabrina!" Alejandro expostulated, but Brett only smiled, not a very nice smile.

Lazily pushing himself away from the adobe column, he stood in the pool of light that shone on Sabrina, and, the green eyes hooded, he demanded softly, "Well? Now that you can see me clearly—are my features so very frightful?"

He made an extremely romantic figure as he stood there in the golden, flickering lantern light, the scarlet sling vivid against his white shirt, the black breeches hugging his long, muscular legs, the black boots gleaming. A lock of thick blue-black hair had fallen across his forehead, increasing his rakish air, and as the dancing light played across his hard face, Sabrina muttered unwillingly, "No, as I'm certain you know very well!"

It was as if the two of them were alone on the patio, Alejandro's presence momentarily forgotten. Intently Alejandro watched them, not displeased by the almost tangible tension between them, or the sarcastic exchange of words. They strike fire from each other, he thought with pleasure. A fire that could consume them both and burn forever.

Brett grinned at Sabrina's reply, his strong white teeth a brief flash in the darkness of his face. "Such graciousness, infant! You'll unman me!"

Unsettled, confused by the contradictory emotions he aroused within her, she abandoned any attempt at politeness. He was laughing at her, teasing her, mocking her, and Sabrina's volatile temper rose further. Under her breath, she hissed, "I'd like to unman you—with a razor-sharp blade!"

Brett's infuriating laughter rang out across the patio, and an imp of mischief dancing in the depths of his eyes, he murmured silkily, "It's been tried, infant, believe me." The mischief suddenly vanished from his eyes, and he added harshly, "It's been tried by women far more proficient than you at castrating a man!"

Staring at that unexpectedly dangerous face, Sabrina shivered, angry and wary at the same time. We're like two mortal enemies, she thought wildly, compelled to fight the moment we see each other, for reasons neither of us even knows. Why? Why do I feel the need to quarrel with him, she wondered painfully, and at the same time long for . . . ? Even she wasn't certain what she longed for, and bewilderedly her eyes searched his face, seeking an answer.

His eyes were on hers, his gaze as intent as hers, and catching a glimpse of the expression buried in those jade-green eyes, she was instantly very glad that she was a woman—and that her father was seated nearby.

Alejandro had not heard their last exchange, but he was aware that something had passed between them, something that wasn't making either of them exactly happy, and knowing how quick-tempered his daughter could be, he called out hastily, "Come now, you two, you must share this conversation with me."

With an effort, Brett tore his eyes away from Sabrina's, and shrugging his broad shoulders, he said easily, "I was merely agreeing with your earlier statement—Sabrina is indeed lovely. You have good reason to be proud of your daughter . . . even if she has a tongue that can wound fatally."

Alejandro smiled wryly and nodded his head. "Sí, this is true. Often I have wished that she had been born dumb."

The tense moment disappeared and with an unladylike snort, Sabrina started to turn away, but Brett reached out and captured her arm. Adding to her confusion and conflicting emotions, he took her hand, and bending low over it, he pressed his warm mouth into the palm. His lips seemed to sear where they touched, and her heart began to behave most erratically.

An unbelievably attractive smile on his mouth, he said huskily, "Shall we cry peace, infant? I promise to behave myself—as best I am able—if you will promise to curb that wicked little tongue of yours."

Suffused with an inexplicable, intoxicating burst of happiness, all her earlier reservations gone, she gave him a radiant smile. An enchanting dimple appeared in one cheek, and she agreed almost shyly, "Sí, Señor Brett, I would like it above all things."

Brett blinked at the blinding smile, feeling suddenly as if he had drunk too much wine. Reluctantly releasing her hand, he placed it on his forearm, and with teasing gallantry, he escorted her the short distance to where Alejandro sat. His eyes brimming with laughter, Brett tweaked one of the fiery tendrils that curled near her ear and murmured, "Now that your daughter and I have made our peace, I have a strong feeling that I shall indeed enjoy my stay with you."

The harmony between them was fragile, but it *was* harmony, and as she prepared for bed that night, Sabrina was aware of a pleasurable tingle of anticipation for the morrow. Dinner had been delightful, Brett amusing them with some of his less outrageous escapades in Europe. They had exchanged family gossip, of which, not unnaturally, Brett had little to contribute, but he was able to answer their questions about Sofia, Hugh, and the children easily enough.

But while Sabrina had enjoyed dinner and the cessation of the unexpected and confusing hostility between her and Brett, she hadn't quite been able to control a slight feeling of disappointment and perhaps just the tiniest bit of resentment when, after dinner, Alejandro had banished her as if she were still a child. He and Brett had retired to the small salon to enjoy a glass of fine Madeira that Brett had brought as a gift and to smoke their cigarillos. As Sabrina usually joined her father in this ritual, partaking of a glass of sherry or something else equally innocuous, her reaction wasn't surprising. The after-dinner relaxation, the casual mulling over the events of the day, the planning of what would be done the next, was one of Sabrina's favorite times with her father, and she was dismayed at being denied it. When Tía Francisca came to dinner or they were entertaining other guests, she perfectly understood the reasons why she couldn't join the gentlemen, but Brett? When Carlos came to dinner, she wasn't excluded, she thought mutinously. What made Brett so different? Forlornly she wondered if, for the duration of his stay, she was to be banished each night, to spend the hours before retiring in lonely solitude while Brett usurped her place in the salon with Alejandro. She didn't think she was going to like that—or put up with it for very long!

Unhappily conscious of the fact that she was whipping herself into a rage against Brett, and for a petty reason at that, Sabrina determinedly focused her thoughts on more agreeable things. Like how Brett's presence had pleased her father, and how he had made her laugh at dinner. And then there was tomorrow, too, when they would show their visitor the ranch.

Suddenly feeling more charitable toward the situation, Sabrina snuggled down into her soft featherbed mattress. It was pleasant, she decided sleepily as she lay there, to see Señor Brett again, and unwilling to delve any deeper into her emotions, she left it at that. She would not think of his kiss, or the way her heart jumped when he smiled at her, or the way her blood skipped in her veins when he looked at her a certain way. . . . No. She would keep the peace between them.

CHAPTER SEVEN

The next day was a fine one, warm and sunny without the debilitating humidity that would become more apparent as the days grew longer and hotter. Sabrina joined her father and Brett as they lingered over breakfast, discussing the possibility of growing sugar on the Rancho del Torres.

Surprised at the topic and the discovery that it was the reason behind Brett's visit, Sabrina listened intently as the two men talked, but she found her thoughts wandering down an unpleasant path. Why hadn't Alejandro mentioned the idea of growing sugar to her before now?

During the past few years, there hadn't been any major decision made concerning the ranch that Alejandro hadn't asked her opinion on first, and she was perplexed that he hadn't done so this time. She was not angry, not even piqued, but confused. She had always understood that one of the reasons Alejandro had solicited her views about the running of the ranch while she was still a child and had encouraged her less than womanly pursuits was that he had been training her for the day when she might have to run the ranch alone. She had grown used to being consulted about the disbursement of their fortune—the cattle they would sell, the horses they would buy, the crops they would grow—and yet now it was clear that without a word to her, Alejandro was embarking upon an ambitious scheme that would commit a large amount of their land, time, and money.

She glanced at her father, a slight frown marring her forehead. Why? Why had he been so . . . so *secretive* about the sugar project and Brett's impending arrival? It didn't make sense. Unless it was Brett's influence upon her father. . . .

Her frown deepened and she shot Brett an assessing look. This morning there was no sign of the previous day's bandit. His face was freshly shaved, his clothes were clean and unrumpled, but she couldn't quite shake the memory of that bearded, dangerous male who had confronted her yesterday. She had sensed an air of lawlessness about him. But now, completely oblivious of her, he was involved with explaining the cultivation of sugar to Alejandro, his handsome face relaxed, the green eyes lacking that disturbing cynical gleam.

Why was he here? she wondered again. Nacogdoches had nothing to offer him. Perhaps he *had* lost his fortune and was here to swindle her father? Knowing her thoughts were unworthy, she writhed with embarrassment that she had even considered such ideas.

Ashamed and just a little angry with herself, she set about being as charming and welcoming to their guest as possible. After a prolonged breakfast, the three of them wandered about the grounds near the hacienda, Sabrina on her very best behavior, and then later in the day, after siesta, they all walked down to the stables.

The del Torreses were noted breeders of both horses and bulls, and as the three of them ambled from one corral and stable to the next, there was much to hold Brett's interest. Unlike most ranches, Rancho del Torres had many facets; the fortune that Sabrina's grandfather had brought from Spain with him had allowed the family far more license to follow their own inclinations than was normal. Their wealth had grown since the first day Enrique del Torres had stepped forth in the New World. There were warehouses and wharves in New Orleans, a cotton plantation in upper Louisiana, silver mines and land in Mexico. With almost unlimited wealth behind them, they lived a life very different from that of most of the settlers who came to the Americas—the majority of the Spanish settlers were only able to eke out a meager living in the untracked wilderness, but the del Torres family lived in baronial splendor. They were able to indulge their fancies, so it wasn't surprising that the del Torres ranch was meticulously maintained, or that their stables contained some of the finest imported Spanish brood mares and stallions to be found west of the Mississippi River. Most of the breeding stock for the bulls, too, had come originally from Spain to Mexico in Enrique's time, and looking with an experienced eye at the size, the breadth of shoulder, the powerful haunches, and the wicked horns on some of the huge black beasts, Brett decided that not even in Spain had he seen such magnificent animals.

Idly he asked, "Do you sell them just for breeding, or do any of them end up in the bull rings in Mexico City?"

Alejandro's face creased in a wide smile. "Would you believe, *amigo*, that last year I was able to sell several to a marquess in Madrid? It was, I think, the height of my ambition—del Torres bulls bred, born, and raised here in the province of Texas returning triumphant to the land of their ancestors. Ah, yes, but I was pleased. But to answer your question—most of them are used by breeders here in Texas to improve their own herds, although some are used locally in the bull ring."

Brett looked surprised. "Bull ring? Bullfights, here?" he asked, one eyebrow rising skeptically.

"*Sí*, here," Alejandro replied. A twinkle in his eyes, he added, "A Spaniard is a Spaniard no matter where he is, and where he is, you can be assured that there are bullfights. It is a passion with us! Shall I arrange one for you while you are our guest?"

Brett nodded his head, his gaze on some of the powerful beasts as they trotted and snorted in a huge corral nearly half a mile away from the horse stables. "I'd like that," he replied simply.

Like the del Torres fortune, the ranch was huge and far flung. It comprised nearly fifty thousand acres of almost tropical lushness, and it would have been impossible to view it in one day. The majority of the lands were still in virgin wilderness, and it was only near the hacienda and outbuildings that the civilizing hand of man was revealed. Most of the cattle and horses roamed freely throughout the seemingly endless acres of the ranch, numerous vaqueros keeping watch over them. Only the finest, the prize animals that were used to maintain the excellent standard of the del Torres herds, were kept in the corrals and paddocks that sprawled out some distance from the hacienda.

After days in the saddle, Brett found it a pleasure to stretch his long legs, the leisurely walk through the stables and barns just what he wanted. His arm was still in the sling, but he would have discarded it this morning if Bonita hadn't been so outraged at the notion. It still ached some, and as the hours passed and the ache became more pronounced, he decided wryly that she had been right—it *was* much too soon to lay the sling aside.

Sabrina noticed the faint look of pain about his mouth, and aware that it was probably caused by his wound—the wound *she* had given him—she asked with compunction, "Is your arm bothering you? Have we walked too far for you? Would you like us to return to the hacienda so that you can rest?"

If Brett had been on the point of flagging, nothing could have stiffened his spine more effectively than her contrite words. Pity, he thought sourly, he could do without, and to be viewed as an object of pity by the little devil who had given him the wound was at once amusing and annoying. He chose to be amused though, and, a crooked smile curving his mouth, he said, "Infant, I may be years older than you, but I am not in my dotage! My arm does ache a little, but it's nothing that you should bother your pretty little head over. Besides, you should be pleased—you meant to cut deep."

Sabrina's lips tightened. *Well!* See if she ever offered him sympathy again! He could die for all she cared!

The day turned out to be one of mixed enjoyment for her. She found the conversation stimulating, and as she was nearly as knowledgeable about the ranch as Alejandro was, she frequently took part in the discussions. Brett's infuriating attitude though, did nothing for her temper. Being mocked, teased, and treated as if she were a child, a *brainless* child, considerably lessened her enjoyment of the day. *No one* had ever treated her as he did. Even her father, in his most paternal moments, listened, if not always intently, at least interestedly, to what she had to say. Brett merely smiled indulgently as she spoke and then turned away to converse with her father about the very thing she had just explained!

But if she found Brett's attitude infuriating, she was

also almost unbearably conscious of his tall form next to hers as they walked about the stables, of the way he smiled, of his deep, husky laugh and the attractive crinkles that formed near his eyes when he grinned. She was irritated with herself for being so very aware of him, and a dozen times during the day, she scolded herself, telling herself repeatedly that she was not seven years old! She was not to be charmed into a childish adoration as had happened in Natchez. Remember how *that* particular incident ended, she reminded herself sternly, the humiliating spanking Brett had given her suddenly vivid in her mind.

The following days sped quickly by as Brett and Ollie settled down in the gracious del Torres hacienda. Alejandro was an exemplary host, and his home was both luxurious and delightful. There was not even the barrier of language to make his guests feel uncomfortable—Alejandro and Sabrina spoke excellent English, and Brett and Ollie had picked up the occasional Spanish phrase in their travels.

By the time the visitors had been at the ranch five days, Brett's wound had healed sufficiently for Bonita to decree that the sling was no longer needed. With a mocking gleam in his eyes and suspect meekness, Brett laid it aside.

Sabrina had grown so used to that scarlet sling that the morning he joined them for breakfast on the patio without it, she was startled.

"Your sling?" she inquired.

Brett grinned. Seating himself across from her, he helped himself to a warm tortilla, slathering it with butter and blackberry jam. Lightly he said, "Your guardian angel has decided that I don't need it any longer—thank God! I was afraid she was never going to let me be rid of it."

Alejandro, who was seated next to Sabrina, laughed. "You must make allowances for Bonita—she is a thwarted mother and cannot help but cluck over us all."

His mouth full of tortilla and jam, Brett rolled his eyes expressively and nodded his dark head energetically.

Instantly defensive, Sabrina said stiffly, "You should be grateful for her care—she is well known for her success with the ill."

Swallowing his mouthful, Brett retorted mockingly, "I am not, as you can see for yourself, ill. As I told you at the time, I've survived worse wounds."

Sabrina snorted and buried her nose in a cup of hot chocolate, wishing perversely that he didn't look so disgustingly vital as he sat across the table from her. Five days of his company had done nothing to resolve the turmoil within her. One moment she was drawn irresistibly to him, and the next she was certain that she had never met a more arrogant, condescending swine in her life!

Alejandro obviously had no such problems, and more and more Sabrina found herself pushed into the position of mere onlooker. It was with Brett that Alejandro discussed the day's events, Sabrina supposedly amusing herself with womanly tasks. It was Alejandro and Brett who rode out to inspect the possible sites for the sugar cane—Sabrina spent the day indoors writing out the invitations to the fiesta they were to give on Saturday to introduce Brett to their friends and relatives. Brett seemed to dominate all of Alejandro's waking hours, and while Sabrina could make excuses for her sudden rejection—they were men, they hadn't seen each other in a long time, Brett was their guest—she still couldn't help but feel forlorn and a little resentful. She could deal with Brett's intrusion into their lives; it was her exclusion she had trouble coming to grips with.

Alejandro was orchestrating his attempt at matchmaking badly. Not wishing to reveal his fond desire, or to appear to throw Brett and Sabrina into each other's arms, he did the exact opposite. Unconsciously he kept them apart, inadvertently banishing Sabrina from her common routine and his company.

Alejandro was also taking much pleasure in the company of a man he would have been proud to call his son. He adored his daughter and he would no more have hurt her than he would have cut off his right arm, but he wouldn't have been human, or Spanish, if there hadn't been times when he dreamed of a son. As Sabrina had grown older, he had put aside such dreams, delighted with her quick intelligence and her boyish skills. But in Brett's *very* masculine company, Alejandro lost his head a little and the dreams

90

came back. His current absorption in that young man was understandable, if excessive. Sabrina's growing resentment and bewilderment were also understandable, and Alejandro would have been utterly horrified if he had realized what he was accomplishing.

This morning began as a repeat of other mornings, Brett and Alejandro busily discussing the day's plans while Sabrina sat in silence. Gritting her teeth, she tried to stem her rising temper. It soon became apparent that she was again to be left to her own devices, presumably feminine ones, when the two men rode out to view various sites for the sugar mill.

Determined not to allow the situation to continue, when there was a brief halt in the conversation, Sabrina said firmly, "I'll come with you. If we are to go into the sugar business, I think I should begin to learn about it, too."

Alejandro looked at her, taking in the mulish slant of her chin. Dimly realizing how much she had been excluded of late, he smiled guiltily and said weakly, "But of course, *chica*. Your company is most welcome, and you are right— you should know what is planned." To her outrage, he glanced across to Brett, and almost as if seeking approval, he asked, "It is a good idea, don't you agree?"

Brett shrugged. "If you think she should come along, I have no objections." Rising to his feet, he added, "I'll walk down to the stables and see that her horse is saddled and brought along with ours. Shall we meet in front in half an hour?" Not expecting a reply, he glanced at Sabrina and asked lazily, "A half hour *will* be sufficient for you to make ready? Women are notorious for always being tardy."

Sabrina smiled tightly. *"Some women."*

Brett inclined his head mockingly. "As you say."

Her eyes smoldering, she watched as he sauntered out the back gate and disappeared. Not trusting herself to speak, she hastily took a gulp of her chocolate, and setting the cup back down in its saucer with a clatter, she said flatly, "I'll go change. I wouldn't want to keep the arrogant beast waiting!"

When she returned, barely fifteen minutes later, she was defiantly attired in the rust-colored calzoneras, and her glorious hair was subdued in a long, thick braid, just a few unruly tendrils curling near her temples and neck. There was a set expression on her usually merry face as she stalked toward the patio.

To her pleasure she found Carlos sitting at the table with her father. Her features softening, she said warmly, "*Buenos días,* Carlos! What brings you here this early in the day?"

Carlos smiled, his black eyes roaming appreciatively over her slender body. "I would like to say that it was your own lovely self," he began teasingly, then, his face and voice becoming somber, he said, "but unfortunately that is not true. As I've just told your father, the bandits have struck again, and this time, they've murdered their victims."

"No!" Sabrina cried, shocked. "When did this happen? Who was murdered?"

Alejandro answered her. His face troubled, he said heavily, "Last night they attacked the Rios *rancho* and killed Señor and Senõra Rios."

Sabrina's fist clenched, and she burst out angrily, "Curse these devils! Something must be done to stop them!"

Alejandro nodded his head, but it was Carlos who spoke. "*Sí!* It is time that we took action against them!" he stated grimly. "My father is inviting everyone to our hacienda tonight to discuss the problem."

They continued to speak of the outrage for a few minutes more, then Carlos rose to his feet. Regretfully he said, "I cannot stay longer. There are others who must be notified of tonight's meeting." Glancing at Sabrina he asked, "Walk with me to my horse?"

Eager to escape a possible reprimand from Alejandro for her clothing, she instantly agreed. Carlos had tied his horse behind the foliage-covered lattice, and upon reaching the animal, he commented lightly, "Your servant arrived yesterday with the invitation for the fiesta to welcome Señor Dangermond. We are looking forward to meeting this *americano.*"

Sabrina made a polite reply, but Carlos knew her well, and there was a note in her voice that made him look at her keenly.

"Who is he?" he asked. "I didn't realize that your Tía Sofia had an adult son. Madre was most surprised when she read your invitation—his visit had not been mentioned previously."

Sabrina shrugged. "He is Tía Sofia's stepson. And I suppose the topic of his visit never came up before." Not for the world would she reveal how surprised *she* had been at Brett's arrival!

His curiosity evident, Carlos prodded, "Will he be staying with you long?"

Again Sabrina shrugged. "I don't know."

His gaze sharpening, with deceptive idleness Carlos questioned, "Is he handsome? Will the ladies adore him?"

"I don't know," Sabrina repeated unhelpfully.

Dissatisfied, Carlos frowned. "What *do* you know about him?" he finally demanded with exasperation.

Neither one of them was aware of the tall man who was approaching, or that upon seeing them he stopped abruptly. Before he could make his presence known, Sabrina spoke.

She had instinctively recognized the reason behind Carlos's probing, and while not normally a vain young woman, the knowledge that he was jealous of Brett gave her pleasure. The past five days had been disruptive ones for her, and Carlos's obvious jealousy acted as a balm upon her lacerated emotions. Smiling with uncharacteristic coquettishness, she said teasingly, "I know that you are far more handsome than he is." She wasn't lying either; Carlos was handsomer, with his perfect features and genial manners. But there was something about Brett. . . .

Pleased by her words, Carlos relaxed slightly, his eyes on her soft mouth. "And?" he questioned huskily.

Sabrina did not usually encourage Carlos's attempts to flirt with her, but Brett's arrival had awakened feelings within her that she didn't yet know how to control—didn't even exactly understand—and she eyed her cousin speculatively. He *was* handsome, his olive skin smooth and unblemished, his eyes flashing pools of ebony, and she knew that he held her in great affection—that at the slightest sign from her, he would boldly cross the distance she had always kept between them. Would Carlos kiss her as Brett had? she suddenly wondered. And more importantly, would his kiss unleash all the wild, turbulent feelings she had experienced when Brett had kissed her? Surprising both of them, she blurted out, "Would you kiss me?"

Carlos recovered himself instantly, and his eyes filled with an ardent light, he murmured, "With pleasure, *querida!* With pleasure!"

His mouth was warm and tender on hers, his arms strong and possessive as he passionately crushed her against his hard chest. He even smelled faintly of tobacco and horses as Brett had, but for Sabrina there was no breathless ecstasy in his touch. She felt nothing more than a mild enjoyment in his embrace, and gently, when he would have deepened the kiss, she stepped back from him, her eyes shadowed.

Carlos was breathing rapidly, and there was a faint flush on his cheeks. *"Querida,* you must know how I feel about you!" he began, but Sabrina put her fingers up to his mouth, silencing him.

Ashamed at the way she had used him, appalled at how little his kiss had affected her, she whispered regretfully, "Hush, *mi amigo.* I should not have asked such a thing of you. It was unkind."

He started to protest heatedly, but irritably aware that this was not the time or place, he muttered thickly, "We shall talk of this later."

Sabrina smiled at him repentantly, shaking her head slowly. "No. You must forget my foolishness—what just happened changes nothing between us. It cannot."

He looked at her steadily for a long moment and then lithely swung up onto his horse. Sending her an unsmiling glance, he said harshly, "For the moment I will bow to your wishes. But it will not always be so. Remember that!"

Unhappily she watched him gallop away. Carlos was her friend, and she had taken advantage of that friendship, she thought wretchedly. If only Brett had never kissed her, this wouldn't have happened! It was all *his* fault! she decided irrationally.

She spun on her heel, intending to return to the courtyard, when she caught sight of the object of her thoughts leaning negligently against the mottled trunk of a large sycamore tree. She froze and glared at him, wondering how long he had been there.

The expression in his eyes was hard to define as he walked up to her, but his voice was filled with mockery. "Lover's spat?" he inquired interestedly.

"That is none of your affair!" she snapped. "And if you were any sort of gentleman, you would have made your presence known." Her breasts heaving beneath the thin cotton shirt, she demanded angrily, "How long were you there?"

"Long enough," Brett returned dryly. "Who is he, infant? Someone your father doesn't approve of? Is that why you were sneaking out here to meet?"

All the resentment that had been simmering just under the surface erupted. "How dare you!" she hissed. "That was my cousin Carlos, and we weren't *sneaking* anywhere! He'd been to see my father, and I was merely saying good-bye!" Her eyes glittering like golden stars, she said hotly, "As for my father's approval—there has long been talk of a marriage between us." Just why she told Brett that information she wasn't certain, nor was she certain why she didn't tell him that Carlos would never be more than a dearly beloved friend to her. But she had, and slyly, insistently, her mind questioned her reasons. Had she told him because *women* married, not infants? Might the knowledge that she was old enough to talk of marriage make him see her as a woman? And if Carlos could be moved to jealousy, could Brett? She knew that last idea was ridiculous—didn't he treat her with barely concealed tolerance? Contemptuously she thrust away the other thoughts.

Brett's face was unreadable as he stared down at her, his thumbs hooked carelessly in the broad leather belt around his lean waist. "Marriage? Aren't you a trifle young?" he drawled.

Her fingers curving into claws at her sides, she said tightly, "I will be eighteen in less than four months."

"Such a great age," he teased, a gentle smile hovering on his lips. Lightly he flicked a tanned finger down her smooth cheek. "Don't rush into anything, infant—even eighteen isn't *that* old. You'd still be a babe."

A challenging sparkle in her amber-gold eyes, she said

breathlessly, "Carlos didn't think I was a babe . . . neither did you when you kissed me."

A muscle twitched in his lean jaw, and his smile vanished. "No, I didn't," he admitted reluctantly. His eyes narrowed suddenly as an ugly thought occurred to him, and, his voice grim, he demanded, "Is that what you were doing? Comparing us? Seeing which one of us treated you less like a child?"

Sabrina's eyes were huge as she stared up at his dark face, a guilty flush staining her cheeks as she realized that she had indeed been comparing them. Not deliberately perhaps, but she *had* wanted to know if Carlos could affect her the same way that Brett did. Attempting to brazen out the situation, she gave what she fervently hoped was a sophisticated shrug and returned carelessly, "And if I was?"

Since he had kissed her in the meadow, Brett had purposely kept his distance from Sabrina. Intentionally he had made himself as derisive as possible, doing everything he could to destroy the almost overwhelming desire within him that demanded he do the exact opposite. Without volition, he had found himself responding violently to her warmth and charm, and daily he battled not to succumb to the increasing surge of attraction he felt for her. At night in his rooms, he dreamed of her, her bewitching smile beckoning him toward untold delights, her slender body driving him half mad with longing. But waking each dawn, he would furiously deny the images and yearnings of the night. The painful lesson that all women were false was too deeply ingrained for him to forget it, and viciously he had sworn that he would *not* be drawn into the treacherous enchantment that she represented.

The sight of Sabrina in the arms of another man, however, had stunned him, sending a savage flood of conflicting emotions through his body. He was at once grimly satisfied that she was proving to be as vainly flirtatious as he knew women to be, but there was also an odd sense of betrayal, of crushing disappointment and some other powerful emotion . . . jealousy? Stung by his thoughts, he had jerked away from pursuing them further.

He was already angered by his reactions, and Sabrina's flippant words were too provocative to ignore. A glitter in his jade-green eyes, he reached for her, yanking her brutally against him. His mouth inches from hers, he snarled softly, "If it's comparisons you're making, add *this* to your samples!"

Ruthlessly his lips came down on hers, and the touch of that warm, hard mouth engulfed Sabrina in a maelstrom of intoxicating, bewildering sensations. Ah, but it was sweet to have him kiss her again, to be once more in his arms, to have that taunting mouth moving so urgently on hers, to feel the thunderous beat of his heart against her breast. She was hazily aware that she had wanted this to happen. She pressed her slender body closer to his, seeking more than this half-savage, half-gentle assault upon her senses. Unknowingly she slid her arms up around his neck, her head tilted backward as she shamelessly, innocently offered herself to him.

At her sudden surrender, Brett's anger vanished, and he forgot everything but the bewitching soft body in his arms. All the hungry desires that he had kept so tightly leashed sprang free, and his arms tightened around her, crushing her fiercely against him. His mouth moved with increasing demand across hers, but it soon wasn't enough, and huskily he commanded, "Open you mouth to me. I want the taste of you on my tongue."

The words sent a quiver of excitement through Sabrina, and when his lips touched hers, she obediently opened her mouth. His tongue plunged hotly between her parted lips, filling her mouth as he slowly, sensuously explored the inner warmth.

Stiffening with shocked, pleasurable astonishment, Sabrina wondered giddily what he was doing to her. Her knees felt weak, her head was swimming, and there was an increasingly painful yearning in her loins that the touch of his probing tongue in her mouth only intensified. Her nipples were unbearably sensitive, and she moaned softly, wanting incredibly for him to touch her there, to feel his hard, knowing hands on her breasts.

Brett had been weeks without a woman, and his body was one long ache of desire. His manhood was hard and throbbing between their bodies, his blood was thundering in his brain, and Sabrina's artless response to his lovemaking nearly smashed his control. Nearly made him forget who she was, who he was, and why it was both ungallant and dangerous to be kissing her this way. He might treat women callously and with contempt, but he had made an ironclad vow ages ago never to chose his ladybirds from among the female relatives of his friends. Nor was it his custom to share his bed with young girls like Sabrina; his preference ran to older, experienced women who knew what they could expect from him: skilled lovemaking and generous settlement—no emotions.

Realizing sickly how close he was to throwing scruples to the winds, with a smothered curse, he thrust Sabrina from him. His breath labored, he said sardonically, "I think that was sample enough, don't you?"

It took Sabrina a moment to slide back into reality, to leave behind the sensuous world she had glimpsed in his embrace. She stared up at him blankly, her mouth slightly swollen from his kiss, her eyes still drowsy with desire, but then the import of his words sunk in.

For a second she glared up at him, and then before he could guess her intentions, she drew back her arm and slapped his dark face as hard as she could. "You black-guard!" she spat wrathfully.

Gingerly he reached up to touch the cheek she had just slapped, and mockery creeping into his eyes, he said mildly, "For an infant, you certainly pack a wallop!"

Sabrina gritted her teeth and said thickly, "Don't call me 'infant'! I am not an *infant!*"

He suddenly grinned and murmured, "I'll have to admit—you certainly don't kiss like an infant!"

Choking back a gasp of fury, Sabrina spun on her heel and stormed through the iron gate into the courtyard. Fortunately it was empty, and as she marched angrily toward her room, she wondered blackly how she was going to endure Brett's infuriating presence for an indefinite amount of time. She was either going to explode with rage—or murder him!

CHAPTER EIGHT

If Alejandro noticed, as they inspected the various sites for a sugar mill, that his daughter treated their guest with icy disdain, he made no comment. Nor had he commented on the suspicious scarlet mark on Brett's cheek. But he speculated.

Sabrina speculated about nothing. She was so furious, so ashamed and alarmed by her reactions to Brett, that she refused to even think of what had happened between them.

Still ruffled by the morning's events, she declined to accompany the men when they rode over to the de la Vega ranch that evening. Besides, she told herself sourly, she didn't want to sit through a grueling inquisition by Tia Francisca and all the other curious ladies.

Sabrina might have escaped Francisca de la Vega's merciless interrogation, but Brett did not. Alejandro had gently warned him about his sister, but even Brett hadn't been prepared for such blunt questions.

They had arrived at the de le Vega ranch a few minutes early, and Francisca had used that time to good effect. Barely allowing the introductions to be made, she had instantly launched her questions. When had he arrived? How long was he staying? Why was he here? What were his prospects? Was he unmarried? Why wasn't he married? Was he on the lookout for a bride?

Even if Brett hadn't heard from Sabrina about the possibility of a marriage between her and Carlos, Francisca's barely disguised hostility and rude questions would have indicated where the land lay. That and Carlos's even less thinly veiled dislike.

There had been almost a tangible air of tension between the two men when they had been introduced. Brett had sized up Carlos immediately—arrogant, selfish, and cruel

99

. . . and displeased that a possible rival was on the scene. Carlos was also quick to take his opponent's measure—a rich, ruthless gringo, and one who was far too blatantly masculine not to have an effect upon Sabrina. The *americano* was also too confident and had too easy a relationship with Alejandro for Carlos's liking.

Almost by unspoken assent, the two men moved away from the others and toward the courtyard. Carlos instantly opened the hostilities. His black eyes cold and unfriendly, he murmured softly, "How strange that you should appear so suddenly in our midst. Alejandro has said nothing of your impending arrival. We were surprised even to learn of your existence—my uncle seldom speaks of his dead wife's family, but I am certain that he has never mentioned you before. Nor has Sabrina. I wonder why?" The words in themselves were innocuous, but Carlos's tone of voice implied that there was something unsavory and sinister about the entire thing.

Brett quirked an eyebrow, well aware that he was being baited. "Oh?" he said mildly. "Perhaps the reason my name has not been the topic of conversation is simply that Alejandro does not gossip. As for Sabrina"—Brett shrugged his broad shoulders, a mocking light leaping to his eyes—"women do not tell all their secrets . . . especially to other men."

As Brett watched interestedly, Carlos flushed angrily, his hand clenching into a fist. "It is not *gossip,*" he ground out, "when one merely acknowledges the existence of a relative—no matter how distant the connection!"

It was very apparent that as far as Carlos was concerned, the connection wasn't distant enough. Señor Dangermond annoyed him, and there was also something elusive about those jade-green eyes and that reckless mouth that bothered him—where had he seen this man before? As he stared at Brett, he had the most curious sensation that he had met him before. But where? And when?

Brett had the same sensation—I've met this Spaniard before. Somewhere our paths have crossed, but where? And when? New Orleans was the most logical place. There, or Spain?

As Brett made no reply to his earlier comment, Carlos,

realizing the uselessness of open warfare, forced a smile and said smoothly, "You must forgive my seeming rudeness, but Sabrina is my *novia*, and I am not unnaturally concerned that a virtual stranger has taken residence in her home."

"Your fiancée?" Brett questioned sharply, aware of a sudden inexplicable knot forming in his gut. A slight frown darkening his brow, he added, "I was under the impression that nothing formal had been decided upon—Alejandro did not tell me that Sabrina had been formally betrothed." Nor had Sabrina, he reminded himself dryly.

Carlos sent him a superior smile. Malice gleaming in the black eyes, he said mendaciously, "Between Sabrina and myself it has long been settled, the announcement is a mere formality. Our parents know and wholeheartedly approve of the match. In fact, they are eager for it—almost as eager as Sabrina and I."

"I see," Brett said slowly. He distrusted Carlos's words, and yet . . . This morning he'd seen Sabrina in this man's embrace, and Sabrina herself had alluded to the possibility of a marriage between them, so why did he resist the idea? Because Sabrina hadn't kissed *him* like a young woman engaged to another man? He smiled cynically. Now that was a foolish notion. She wouldn't be the first to act so—hadn't the lovely Diana done the same thing, and with him?

Alejandro called to Brett just then, and there was no chance for further conversation with Carlos. Which was just as well, Brett thought wryly. The more I know of him, the more I find myself holding him in extreme aversion! Almost with relief he joined Alejandro and was introduced to some gentlemen who had just arrived. Shortly they all adjourned to the library, leaving Francisca to reign over the ladies who had accompanied their husbands and sons.

The de la Vega library was a long, narrow room. Slightly worn but comfortable leather chairs were scattered about; a huge pine *trastero* served as a liquor cabinet, and at one end of the room was a rather untidy oak desk. Colorful rag rugs lay on the wooden planked floor, and for the first time Brett became aware of an impression that had been

101

forming in the back of his mind since he had first seen the de la Vega hacienda.

The de la Vegas were obviously prosperous, but their wealth did not compare with that of the del Torreses. Their hacienda was smaller, the outbuildings were not as extensive and the furnishings were noticeably less luxurious. He suddenly wondered if money wasn't behind Carlos's engagement to Sabrina. Not that Sabrina herself wasn't reason enough for Carlos wanting marriage, but was it *just* love that motivated Carlos? Brett's mouth curved sardonically. What did it matter to him? Marriage for wealth and position was common among people of his class, but he found the idea of Sabrina being married for such a reason oddly distasteful. *She* certainly had little to gain from the match! Carlos would be the one to reap the benefits—a lovely wife *and* a fortune!

Luis de la Vega called the informal meeting to order, and for the next several hours, Brett listened alertly to what was being said. A few times he frowned and almost joined the discussion, but aware that he was a newcomer and a stranger, he saved his questions and comments until he and Alejandro were riding home.

They were quietly traveling along the winding trail that led to the hacienda when Brett asked suddenly, "How long has this trouble with the bandits been going on?"

Alejandro grimaced. "We have always had trouble with bandits—we are too far away from civilization for rogues and robbers not to flourish. But this latest series of attacks began, I think, about four or five months ago." His features brooding, he added, "They are very clever these bandits. They seem to know exactly when to strike—and precisely whom to rob. The Rios attack is a good example of their work—Señor Rios had just returned home from New Orleans after selling a fine herd of wild horses there, and that very night his hacienda was attacked and he and his wife were killed. Carlos had been by to visit them only that afternoon, and he said that poor Rios had been so pleased and relieved to have made it home safely with his gold." Shaking his head, Alejandro muttered, "Such a tragedy. Such good people, and now they are dead, their home looted and burned to the ground."

"Is this the first time something like that has happened?"

"*Sí.* Before it was only robberies—no one had been hurt. But now . . . Now it worries me that they grow so brazen."

"What about your hacienda—will Sabrina be safe?" Brett asked curtly.

Alejandro smiled, suddenly feeling more confident about his attempt at matchmaking than he had since Brett's arrival. "My hacienda is safe. For weeks now I have armed my vaqueros and warned them particularly to be wary of strangers. As for my daughter"—he nodded his head slowly—"she will be safe, but only if she will stop her willful rides alone."

Brett's face hardened. "While I'm here you can be damned certain she won't be doing anything like that!"

Alejandro smiled again, a very pleased smile.

Brett wasn't smiling, however, his thoughts on the bandits. Abruptly he inquired, "You said they seem to know whom to rob. What did you mean?"

"Only that they make no mistakes; their victims are always affluent people, and they are robbed, like poor Rios, only when they have great sums of money on them."

Frowning blackly, the suspicion that had been forming all evening in his brain becoming a certainty, Brett asked tersely, "Any strangers in the area lately?"

"No. At least no more than usual. We are a frontier settlement, *amigo,* and as such, we see a constant flow of strangers. But none of them has seemed any more suspicious than any other, and more importantly, except for a few with families who have staked out their farms, none has remained."

"Then your bandits have to be someone you know and trust. There is no other answer," Brett said flatly.

Alejandro appeared startled. "But you must be wrong! I know of no one who would do such a thing! We are a small community—you saw yourself how outraged my fellow citizens were tonight. *Everyone* wants these murderers caught and punished!"

Brett's brows rose skeptically. "I doubt that. And I would be willing to wager that your bandits, when found, will turn out to have been at that meeting tonight—

probably wanting to know precisely what is being planned to stop them."

Alejandro would not countenance such an idea, and for the remainder of the ride home, he very earnestly tried to argue Brett around to his way of thinking, all to no avail. As they dismounted in front of the hacienda, Alejandro said half-angrily, half-teasingly, "You cling to your stubborn ideas like an honorable woman does her virtue!"

Brett smiled. "You should write and tell my father so—he would agree with you."

Alejandro snorted, and a few minutes later they parted, Alejandro to seek his bed, Brett to light a cigarillo and wander out into the empty courtyard. He was strangely restless this evening, and though the hour was fairly late, almost midnight, he found himself unwilling to retire to his bed. His *lonely* bed, he thought with a twist to his mouth—women did have their uses, and a warm, willing woman would have done much to relieve the tension that was slowly building within him. The trouble was, he admitted grimly, the only woman he wanted was a half-child, half-seductress with flame-colored hair!

Angry with himself and displeased by the admission that he did indeed want Sabrina, he coolly switched his thoughts to the evening he'd just spent at the de la Vega hacienda. More particularly, to Carlos de la Vega. Where the hell had he seen him before? A cynical expression flitted across his face as he realized that half his interest in the arrogant Spaniard stemmed from this morning's incident with Sabrina. That and the irritating fact that Carlos claimed to be engaged to her. Was there really an understanding between them? he wondered disagreeably.

Furious that once again he was focusing on Sabrina, he took another drag on the cigarillo. For a little while he was able to consider other things—the bandits, his enjoyment of the Nacogdoches area, and Alejandro's surprising proposition to grow sugar—but soon he found himself thinking again of Sabrina, remembering how she had felt in his arms, the way her mouth had tasted when he had kissed her. With a disgusted motion he ground out the cigarillo under his boot heel.

Turning away sharply, he started to enter the hacienda

when he noticed a light in one of the rooms downstairs. The entire house was in darkness except for that one light. Knowing that Alejandro had already retired and curious about why someone was up at this time of night, he walked in that direction.

Silently he stepped under the extended eaves, and quietly he pulled open one of the double doors that faced the courtyard. Hearing no sound from within the lamp-lit room, he glanced in.

At first examination the room appeared to be deserted, Brett's gaze traveling slowly over the contents: the wall of leather-bound books directly across from him, the velvet-covered chairs, the small marquetry tables, and the fine Brussels carpet on the floor. It was a wealthy family's library, and remembering the simple furnishings of the de la Vega library, he was again struck by the differences in wealth. A long, elegant couch of dark green velvet faced the wall of books, the high back of it being all that Brett saw, and the light that had first caught his attention came from a tall, ornate candelabrum that sat upon a small table at one end of the couch.

Assuming a careless servant had left the candles burning, he walked across the room intending to snuff out the flickering yellow flames. Reaching the couch, he happened to glance down, and his breath caught sharply in his throat as he spied the figure sprawled on the velvet cushions.

Sabrina lay sound asleep on her side, her head resting on one outflung arm, the red-gold hair tumbling across her face and spilling like living fire onto the green velvet couch. She was wearing a simple gown of soft yellow silk, and it had rucked up around her knees, her bare feet and slim legs gleaming palely against the rich green velvet. The book she had been reading lay open on the floor nearby.

For a long moment Brett stared down, mesmerized by her sleep-softened features. She was so lovely, he mused painfully, his eyes moving almost tenderly over her thick, dark lashes, the slightly tilted nose, and the generous mouth. And she looked so damned *young!* he thought with vexation. Had he *ever* been that young? Ever been so innocent and vulnerable? For a moment his mouth tightened as he remembered the pain of his mother's rejection. Surprised by the bitterness and hurt that memory aroused, he was aware that at one time, long, *long* ago, he had been as innocent and vulnerable as Sabrina was now. She appeared untouched by the world's cold indifference, he reflected bleakly, and looked in need of protection against those who would corrupt that innocence. Ruefully he added, so *very* much in need of protection against cynical bastards like myself! Again his gaze slid slowly over her slim body, lingering on the rise and fall of her full bosom and the length of the long, slender legs.

Unwillingly he felt desire stir, and, aware of the potential danger of the situation, he bent down and lightly shook Sabrina. Beyond a muffled rejection of his touch, she continued to sleep, and Brett smiled faintly. God! He'd forgotten how deeply the young slept. The smile still curving his mouth, he knelt down beside the couch and softly touched the bright hair where it grew near her temple. "Wake up, sleeping beauty," he murmured huskily.

Oblivious to both his touch and his voice, Sabrina slept on, and, unable to resist the temptation of that sweet mouth, he leaned over and very gently kissed her. For just a moment he let the hungry desire that was clamoring for release sweep through his body as slowly he kissed her soft, warm mouth. But then, with a regretful sigh, he lifted his mouth from hers and sank back on his heels, a twisted smile on his lips.

That smile was the first thing Sabrina saw as she slowly drifted awake. That and the mockery that was dancing in those dark green eyes. She thought she had been dreaming that he had kissed her, but as she gradually awakened and saw his smile, she realized instantly that she had *not* been dreaming.

Oddly enough she wasn't angry. Sabrina might not forget an insult, but she did not hold grudges, nor did she stay truly angry for very long. And she'd had a long, lonesome evening in which to mull over everything. Brett *was* infuriating, but she had to admit uncomfortably that she had, at least partially, invited both his embrace and his enraging comments. Further thought on the subject of Brett Dangermond had left her feeling only confused and frustrated, and she had come to the reluctant conclusion that she was going to have to come to grips with his disturbing effect upon her.

It wasn't a pleasant admission for her, but she had finally conceded that it was *her* reaction to him that was the problem and not necessarily *his* actions. Having gotten that far in her musings, she had made a grim little vow not to allow herself to be provoked anymore by him, and more importantly not to let her volatile emotions get the better of her. She would treat him with courtesy and politeness and make a determined attempt to rekindle some of the rapport they had once shared—which didn't mean, she had thought with a snort, that she would fawn over him with childlike adoration! She would be *adult* about it—*not* an infant!

Pleased with her deductions, she had happily settled down to read and await the return of the gentlemen. Perhaps worn out by the constant conflicts within herself, she was fast asleep not too many minutes later, her dreams, unfortunately, at complete variance with her resolutions.

Sheltered and innocent as she was, though, her dreams were not very explicit beyond the point of Brett's sweeping her into his arms and kissing her, but they were quite satisfying, and to awake and find the object of those fantasies smiling at her, his lips only inches from her, was quite, *quite* gratifying.

Still only half-awake, Sabrina smiled at Brett sleepily, completely unaware of how seductive that smile was. She made no move to change her position on the sofa beyond bringing the outflung arm down next to her body and nestling her cheek against her hands. Drowsy amber-gold eyes met his as she said softly, "*Buenas noches,* Señor Brett. Did you enjoy your meeting?"

His smile a bit wry, he replied lightly, "Did you expect me to? Especially my meeting with your so very curious Aunt Francisca?"

Sabrina giggled. "Did she ask an inordinate number of questions?"

Nodding his dark head, he rose lithely to his feet and sat down on the sofa next to her, resting one arm along the high back. The mocking light in the green eyes becoming

107

more pronounced, he answered, "She certainly did! At this moment, I don't believe there is one aspect of my life that she isn't aware of. You should have warned me!"

There was a sudden easy relationship between them, as if all the earlier days of stormy emotion had never existed. For these few precious moments, Brett seemed to have banished the taunting, galling manner in which he usually treated her, and was, unwisely, allowing himself the pleasure of responding unguardedly to her natural charm. Sabrina, too, for once at ease with herself, was acting more normally; she was relaxed and unruffled, content merely to enjoy his fascinating company.

The circumstances themselves deepened the growing intimacy—it was very late, the house was still and quiet, they were the only two people awake, and the flickering candlelight cast a soft, golden glow over them, intensifying Sabrina's fiery beauty, illuminating Brett's dark, sardonic features. Even their positions increased the cocoon of warm intimacy that was slowly, inexorably surrounding them. Brett's hard hip was nearly touching Sabrina's stomach as she lay on her side on the dark green velvet cushions, his upper body looming almost protectively above her.

They continued to talk for some minutes longer, neither willing to break the spell that seemed to have fallen over them. Brett knew he was playing with fire, knew that it was sheer insanity to prolong the dangerous interlude, and yet he could not escape her web of enchantment. He could not take his eyes off her, watching with an odd, hungry intentness the way her smile lit her entire face, the way the amber-gold eyes would shyly meet his and then flicker away. The faint scent of orange blossoms came from her body, and he was suddenly assailed by an insane desire to seek out the source of that beguiling perfume.

Sabrina was not immune to the situation either, and she had far less control of her emotions than Brett did. She was absolutely mesmerized by him in this charming, teasing mood, and her gaze roved eagerly over his features—the thick black hair, the deepest jade-green eyes with their extravagantly long lashes, and the full, mobile mouth. The dancing candlelight shadowed the hollows beneath his high cheekbones, and Sabrina stared fascinated at the way the wavering light played across his handsome nose and the hard jawline. But it was his mouth that riveted her attention, and, unable to help herself, she found herself remembering the texture and pressure of those warm, knowing lips against hers. Uncomfortable with the direction her thoughts were taking, and far too aware of his disturbing nearness, she shifted her position slightly, turning onto her back and moving a little farther away from him.

It was an uncalculated move, but it only increased Brett's awareness of how very desirable she was. The soft material of her gown tightened across the firm young bosom, bringing his eyes to the smooth golden flesh that rose so temptingly above the lowcut neckline. The yellow gown was an old-fashioned peasant design, that bared her shoulders and laced up the front with delicate ribbons of green silk, and his fingers trembled at the idea of undoing those green ribbons and exposing the satin-smooth flesh beneath. He swallowed with difficulty, the longing to jerk her into his arms and make violent love to her almost overpowering him. Tearing his gaze away from her, he stared grimly at the candelabrum and said with an effort, "I think we should say good night now. Your father has already retired, and I was on my way to do the same when I saw your light."

Regretfully Sabrina agreed. "You're right, of course," she said quietly, and then, unable to help herself, she added breathlessly, "I'm happy that we had these moments alone to talk. . . ." Impetuously she reached up and touched his hard chest with her hand. "It . . . it makes things easier between us, no?"

Her touch was his undoing. Their eyes suddenly met, and Sabrina's heart began to hammer at the glitter of raw desire in those dark green eyes. Compulsively Brett's fingers closed around hers, and bending his head, he pressed his warm lips against the palm of her hand and muttered in a tormented voice, "Sweet mother of God! What are you doing to me?"

In the grip of awakening awareness of her own sensuality, Sabrina stared dumbly up at him, desperately wanting him to kiss her again, her lips parting in unconscious invitation. With a groan, Brett dropped her hand and capturing her slender shoulders, dragged her roughly up against him, his mouth crushed demandingly against hers. Mindlessly she returned his kiss, trembling with pleasure when his tongue entered her mouth and began to hungrily probe the inner warmth. She didn't understand everything that was happening to her; she only knew that Brett alone aroused an urgent need within her, that she craved his kisses, his touch, that she wanted to be in his arms and have him kiss her in this almost savage manner. Her arms closed around his waist, and ardently she embraced him wanting more, wanting . . .

Desire, warm and sweet like honey, spread languidly through her body as Brett continued to kiss her, his hands sensuously kneading her shoulders, his chest hard against her tingling breasts. Driven by instinct, hesitantly her tongue flicked his, and with a bewildering mixture of delight and fright, she felt the shudder that went through his body. Blindly she followed his lead, kissing him more deeply, her exploring tongue taking the same liberties that his had. He tasted of tobacco and brandy, but to Sabrina it was as intoxicating as the headiest wine ever served, and she was helpless against the powerful tide of passion that suddenly rocked her.

The couch was soft beneath them, but never disrupting their kiss, Brett slid slowly to the floor, pulling her unresisting body with him. They landed with Sabrina on top, but gently he rolled her over until they were lying side by side, his tall, muscled length straining against hers. He continued to kiss her, long, drugging kisses that left Sabrina weak and dazed. But kissing didn't satisfy the blazing hunger that raged through him, and swiftly he unlaced the green ribbons of her bodice. Before Sabrina realized what he had done, she was stunned to feel his warm, seeking fingers on her naked breast. It was incredibly erotic as lightly, teasingly, his long fingers stroked and caressed her small nipple, and she moaned low in her throat with pleasure.

At her small sound he reluctantly stopped kissing her. His voice thick with desire, he got out, "Did I hurt you? I

110

didn't mean to, but . . . oh, Jesus, Sabrina, you're driving me insane! I must have you! I must!''

Somberly they stared at one another, and seeing the wondering passion in her lovely eyes, he muttered something under his breath and urgently sought out her mouth. Sabrina was lost, she was drowning in his lovemaking, her young untaught body aflame with needs she had never envisioned, aware of nothing but the magic of his touch.

For the first time in his life, Brett was totally ruled by his emotions, Sabrina affecting him in a way no other woman ever had—perhaps ever would. He knew he should halt this wild madness, but he simply could not. He wanted her too badly, she was too tempting, too warm and responsive in his arms, for him to gain control of the fierce desire that was dictating his actions. Compulsively his hand once again closed over her breast, his thumb moving rhythmically over the pulsating nipple. Pushing her onto her back, he slid his mouth sensuously down her throat, across her chest, to the breast he had bared. Tantalizingly, savoringly, his tongue curled around the nipple, his teeth lightly grazing it.

The hot ache of desire that had been coiling within Sabrina's stomach tightened unbearably at the touch of the knowing mouth on her nipple, and convulsively her fingers clenched in the dark hair of his head, pulling him even closer to her. Shockingly the thought occurred to her that she wished they were entirely naked, that her hands could roam at will over his hard body, that she could put her lips to his breast and do the wonderful things to him that he was doing to her.

As if guessing her thoughts, Brett lifted his head, and with infinite slowness he undid the remainder of the lacings, shoving the bodice of the gown down around her waist. His gaze seemed bewitched by the smooth golden flesh that he had exposed, the firm breasts jutting proudly under his look, the coral nipples full and erect.

Shyly Sabrina watched the expressions that chased across his face, the wanting and the passion that were so clearly revealed, and she shivered with both joy and fear. He wanted her as a man wanted a *woman!* And, oh, dear God, it might be wrong, her soul might be damned for all

111

eternity, but she desperately wanted him to complete her initiation into womanhood. No matter what happened in the future, she would have this to remember—the sweetness of his touch, the passion of his mouth, and the ecstasy of his possession.

And yet, when at last his hand slid up her thigh, his fingers seeking that most intimate part of her, she stiffened. What exactly went on between a man and woman making love was a mystery to her, and despite her arousal, despite wanting him to be the one to teach her, she was totally unprepared for what possession really meant. His fingers caressing her inner thigh suddenly frightened her, and when he touched the soft red-gold curls between her legs, her heart beat with a suffocating tempo.

He was kissing her passionately, but Sabrina was oblivious of it, all her concentration on that searching hand. What was he doing to her? Her fingers painfully clutched his broad shoulders, her throat tight with apprehension as gently his exploring fingers parted the springy curls and softly stroked the tender flesh.

A flood of heat and desire swept through her body at the probing intimacy he was wreaking on her, but it warred with a growing feeling of alarm. Moaning with a curious blend of fright and pleasure, she began to struggle against his invading fingers, her hands pushing him away, her body rejecting his advances.

Tearing her mouth from his, she said breathlessly, "Please, *señor,* please stop! I . . . I don't want you to . . . Oh, *please* stop!"

Through a red haze of passion, Brett heard her words, heard the faint undertone of panic, and with an agonizing effort he painfully brought himself back to reality. For a long moment he stared blindly down at her, forcing his breathing back to normal, forcing his brain to think coherently. Almost with surprise he noted their positions on the carpet, the rumpled disarray his searching hands had created with her yellow gown, and suddenly aware of the enormity of what had nearly happened, he was engulfed by a wave of revulsion and disgust. His eyes closing with repugnance at his actions, writhing with embarrassment and fury at how easily he would have betrayed his own ironclad rules and Alejandro's trust, he flung himself away from Sabrina. Lying on his back, one arm thrown across his eyes, he muttered, "Dear God in heaven! What possessed me?"

Sabrina made some inarticulate sound, appalled and as shocked as he was by what had transpired. Her face flaming with shame, she was fumbling with her gown, trying miserably to cover her naked breasts.

Brett heard her, and putting his arm down, he glanced over in that direction. Passion gone now, filled with anger and disgust at himself, he sat up and with less than gentle movements quickly and efficiently made short work of the green ribbon lacing. In a matter of seconds, Sabrina was correctly clothed, the only sign of their passionate interlude her still swollen mouth and some suspicious creases in the yellow silk gown.

She could barely bring herself to look at him she was so embarrassed, and when she finally did, her heart sank. His face was cold and implacable, the dark green eyes shuttered and unfriendly, and the full, sensuous mouth had a grim slant to it.

She wanted to say something to break the increasingly hostile silence that grew between them, but the words stuck in her throat, and Brett's expression didn't help. Once they were standing, she risked another glance at him, wondering with a dull ache in her heart at how swiftly the teasing, mocking, passionate lover had disappeared, leaving only this hard-faced stranger.

Never a particularly kind man, distrustful of women and unused to denying himself anything he wanted, Brett was at odds within himself. The unpleasant thought occurred to him that this entire episode might have been cleverly planned, and yet he didn't want to believe such a thing of either Sabrina or Alejandro. He wasn't a conceited man, but he would have had to be both blind and deaf not to know that he was considered a more than eligible party, and Sabrina wouldn't be the first gently reared young lady to use her body as a way to snare a husband. What made him angriest, though, was the galling knowledge that he had almost fallen into the trap, if indeed it had been a trap. The jade-green eyes hard and icy, he looked across at her

113

and said evenly, "I will not apologize for what just happened—or nearly happened. However, I will admit that my conduct was both insane and inexcusable." His voice bitter, he added, "You can rest assured that I will not forget myself again—no matter what the provocation!"

Stiffly he bowed and without another word stalked from the room, leaving Sabrina to stare after him in stunned dismay.

CHAPTER NINE

✑ It was nearly dawn before Sabrina finally fell asleep. Embarrassment and shame had given way to confusion and bewilderment at first, but then even that had faded, and she was left with only humiliated anger. She couldn't lay all the blame for what had happened at Brett's feet either—she had certainly not *dis*couraged his very improper advances! No, she remembered with shame, she had blatantly courted them.

Her thoughts tormented her. One moment she was appalled at herself, and the next she was assailed by a feeling of sharp disappointment that she hadn't experienced fully what being a woman meant. Even now, several hours later, just the thought of the way he had caressed her caused her body to ache for the touch of his hands and mouth. With a muffled sob, she turned her head angrily into the pillow, wondering miserably why he alone affected her as he did. No one had ever aroused within her the fierce, terrifying emotions that he did, not even Carlos, and with a jolt she suddenly realized why.

Her tears drying, she uttered softly, disbelievingly, "I'm in love with him! *That's* why I've been such a goose since he arrived. *I love him!*" The knowledge should have brought her joy, but it didn't. She might have stupidly fallen in love with him, but it was glaringly apparent that she was caught in a situation that could only bring her pain—had already brought her pain. She turned her face once again into the pillow, realizing now so many things—why his indifference had hurt, why she had been so eager for his touch . . . and why Carlos or any other man had never touched her heart or emotions.

Restless and unhappy she rose from her bed, unwilling to spend more time in the fruitless search for sleep. In-

115

stinctively, like a wounded animal, she sought a place in which to soothe her pain, and a few minutes later, dressed in a white cotton shirt and calzoneras, she slipped quietly from the house.

Intent upon reaching the one place that spelled solace for her, she hurried through the darkened pine-wood forest, oblivious to the night sounds and the movements of the wild creatures. There was the barest glimmer of the dawn light to guide her, but Sabrina was as familiar with these woods as she was the hacienda, and shortly she reached her destination—a tiny clearing at the edge of the small lake that could be glimpsed from her balcony.

It had been a favorite spot of her parents also when Elena had been alive, and the place held happy memories for Sabrina. The family had come here often, and Alejandro had even overseen the construction of a small, graceful gazebo for their further enjoyment. Sabrina could remember long, hot summer afternoons spent here, laughing meals held alfresco, her mother smiling and merry, her father's face full of the love he felt for them both.

Alejandro never came here anymore, but he had maintained the gazebo, knowing that Sabrina took comfort from the place. Inside was a small round iron table, and built against the lower walls were wide wooden benches. The benches were covered with comfortable cushions of vivid orange, and large, soft pillows of bright yellow and green were scattered about. With a sigh, Sabrina sank down onto one of the cushions, unknowingly wrapping her arms tightly around a yellow pillow.

The bottom half of the octagonal gazebo and the roof were of solid whitewashed wood, but the upper half of the charming building was made of a delicate latticework. The doorway was a tall, wide archway cut into one of the walls, the other seven being broken by long, narrow open arches in the latticed walls. Honeysuckle and trumpet vines completely covered two sides of the gazebo, the sweet scent of the honeysuckle filling the air as Sabrina stared blindly out of one of the arches.

She sat there for a long time, her mind blank, letting the peacefulness and tranquillity of the place seep into her body. The lake lapped gently at the shore, a hunting owl hooted in the distance, and there was the faint rustle of a light breeze.

Sitting there in the chill of the April dawn, staring numbly at the silver glitter of the lake as the rising sun struck it, she admitted bitterly that she had always loved Brett Dangermond. She had loved him as a child in Natchez, and unconsciously she had carried that memory of him with her always. Flinging the pillow away from her, she clenched her fist in angry denial. How ridiculous! she berated herself savagely. Children didn't fall in love! But they did, a part of her persisted sadly. They did . . . *you* did!

Her lovely face pensive, her fist slowly unclenched in defeat, and with a low moan she threw herself facedown on the orange cushion. She might have learned that she loved him, but it changed nothing; he was not in love with her . . . . or ever likely to be, she thought wistfully, remembering the cold look in his eyes tonight just before he had stalked from the library. Various phrases of Tía Sofia's letters came back to haunt her. . . . "I worry continually about Brett—he is so cold and distant with women. I sometimes feel that he actually hates us all." . . . "We had hoped that he would make a match of it with a suitable young lady when he visited Spain last year, but nothing came of it. When Hugh asked him about it, Brett just got that contemptuous look I so dislike on his face and said something awful about a wife being needed only for an heir and that Hugh had plenty of those! I could have boxed his ears!" In another letter she wrote, "Brett has all the young ladies in the area atwitter—he is so handsome and manly that I am not surprised, but he cares nothing for any of them. He sneers about love and has made it plain that women have only two uses (*most* improper of me to mention *that* to you, but I'm certain I'll be forgiven). He stated flatly on his last visit home that he doesn't need the one and the other can be easily obtained without love or marriage! How Gillian's rejection has eaten into his heart! And then there was that terrible affair with some English girl. I doubt very much that he will ever experience love or even consider marriage—pity the woman, Sabrina, who makes the fatal mistake of loving *him!* He would be a devil! People call him 'Devil' Dangermond sometimes, and I wouldn't be at all surprised to learn that a woman coined that name!"

Sabrina's face twisted. Half of what Tía Sofia had written had gone over her head at the time she had read those letters, but not any longer. Now she knew what Tía Sofia had been referring to. How *could* her foolish heart love so unwisely? Sabrina wondered helplessly. Her plight was hopeless, and knowing what she did about him, how could she even dare to think that he might suddenly fall in love with *her?* He'd had the choice of every beautiful, eligible young woman in Europe and America, so why should he single out an unsophisticated young lady like herself for his attentions? Especially one who greeted him with a knife!

Sitting up ramrod straight, Sabrina faced her problem squarely. It was both unwise and idiotic to love Brett Dangermond. She must somehow protect her unruly heart and teach it not to love him. She didn't want to love him, and she was quite positive that he would never love her. So. A lifetime of unrequited love holding absolutely no appeal at all, she reluctantly and painfully concluded that her safest and most sensible course was to armor herself against his dangerous, insidious charm. She wouldn't love him! *She would not!*

Finally having gained some measure of peace, she drifted off into uneasy sleep just as the sun rose fully above the tree tops. Brett was not so fortunate.

When he strode swiftly into his rooms after leaving Sabrina so precipitously in the library, Ollie, who had been waiting up for him as usual, took one look at the black scowl on Brett's face and bit back the impertinent greeting that had been on his lips. Instead he walked over to the tray of liquors that sat upon a heavy mahogany chest and splashed an overly generous measure of brandy into a glass. Handing it to Brett, who stood rigidly staring out the opened balcony doors at the courtyard below, and treading where no proper servant would have dared, Ollie asked brazenly, "Something wrong, guvnor?"

Brett swallowed the brandy in one long gulp, and passing the glass back to Ollie, he muttered, "Shut up, Ollie, and give me another one."

Silently Ollie did as he was told. When he turned around with the refilled glass, he found Brett lounging carelessly in a large chair of red Cordova leather. His long legs stretched out in front of him, his dark head resting on the back of the chair, Brett appeared to be absorbed in studying the open-beamed ceiling, but when Ollie approached, he looked at him and demanded grimly, "As long as you've known me, have I ever seduced an honorable young girl?"

His lips pursing thoughtfully, Ollie finally said, "Can't say that you ever 'ave, guvnor. There's been many a rum doxy you've set up as your mistress for a brief spell, but I can't recall that there was ever one that wasn't already in the trade, so to speak. Now then, there 'ave," he added fairly, "been one or two leg-shackled gentry morts among your ladybirds, but never one that you could call *honorable.*"

Brett tossed down the second glass of brandy as quickly as the first, and slamming the empty glass on the table, he snarled, "Then why in the hell am I on the point of doing it now, for God's sake? My very kind and honorable host's own daughter at that!"

"Never say your fancy's lit upon that red-haired termagant!" Ollie gasped incredulously, his first unfavorable impression of Sabrina having faded little during their stay.

Brett sent him a look that made Ollie wish he had not been *quite* so forthright in his speech, and in a tone of voice that did nothing to calm him, Brett asked silkily, "And if it has?"

Ollie swallowed. In the many years that he had served his master there had been several sharp exchanges; Brett allowed him unthinkable license, and Ollie was not at all inclined to keep a civil tongue between his teeth. But for the first time in their odd association, Ollie was aware that he was treading on dangerous ground. Warily he eyed Brett's set features. Obviously there was more to this queer situation than Brett was telling him—women *never* cut the guvnor up rough, but that she-viper, Sabrina, apparently had. Concluding that a conciliatory reply was his

119

wisest course at the moment, at least until he could get to the bottom of this, Ollie answered cautiously, "If that's the way the wind sits, guvnor, it's no bread and butter of mine." Piously he averred, "It's certainly not for your most 'umble servant to tell you 'ow to go on."

His black mood lifting slightly, Brett snorted with laughter. "And you are running a rig, jackanapes! I know you well enough—you are merely waiting for a more opportune time to give me the sharp side of your tongue."

Ollie grinned, relaxing. "Now guvnor, 'ave I ever been anything but a dutiful servant to you?"

Brett grinned back at him. "I won't answer that question. My plate is quite full enough as it is!" His grin faded, and moodily he stared down at his booted feet. "I think I must be just blue-deviled, Ollie—leave me alone and go to bed. Forget what I asked earlier."

Ollie hesitated. "Guvnor, if there's anything I could do . . ."

"Nothing," Brett said flatly. But forcing his thoughts away from his tangled emotions, he asked abruptly, "Do you remember a young Spaniard by the name of Carlos de la Vega? We might have crossed paths with him a few years ago."

Ollie shrugged his narrow shoulders. "Can't say as I do. Describe him for me."

Brett did, and when he finished Ollie frowned. "Seems to me, guvnor, there was a fellow in New Orleans who looked like that. Don't know if it was the same one, though—them Spaniards all look alike to me. But remember when the old captain was killed and we joined the smugglers? Remember that 'igh and mighty Spaniard that cut up Frenchie's favorite girl?"

Brett suddenly sat up straight, Ollie's words reminding him vividly of the incident. Of course, that's where he'd seen de la Vega before! It had been a minor confrontation, just one of the many violent encounters he'd experienced, and he had completely forgotten about it until Ollie reminded him.

Frenchie had been the leader of the renegade band of smugglers that had killed Sam Brown, and it was while Brett was part of their band that the incident with Carlos had occurred. Frenchie had operated a saloon and bordello on Girod Street in the notorious area known in New Orleans as "the Swamp." It had been there that Frenchie conducted his business of disposing of the smuggled goods. The actual transactions took place privately in a back room, and afterward it was Frenchie's policy to send his best customers upstairs to sample on the house some of the latest wares procured from all over the world. Nubile young girls direct from Africa were the most common commodity Frenchie had available, but there were also unfortunate young women from India, the Orient, Europe, and even Greece.

It had been near the end of Brett's sojourn as a smuggler that Carlos had appeared on the scene, and he had been there in the back room playing his role as Frenchie's newest right-hand bully when Carlos had come to bargain for the latest cargo of smuggled goods. Brett couldn't remember what it was that Carlos had purchased, but he did remember clearly being the one to escort the swaggering Spaniard upstairs to where the girls were kept. And it had been the shriek of fear and pain coming from the room where Carlos had been shown that had caused Brett to burst through the door to discover the naked and bleeding body of the young Greek girl who'd been Carlos's choice. Fortunately she wasn't dead, only badly frightened and horribly slashed by the thin-bladed stiletto Carlos still held ready in his hand. Carlos had been fully dressed, and his narrow lips had drawn back in a sneer as he had said coolly, "She tried to steal my money. I am disappointed in Frenchie. He should have known better than to try that trick with *me!*"

It was possible Carlos had been telling the truth, but it didn't excuse what he had done to the Greek girl. Controlling his blazing temper with an effort, Brett had urgently hustled the affronted Carlos out of the room and out of the saloon. It was only when they stood outside the low-gabled cypress building that Brett had threatened him. Carlos had looked him up and down and then shrugged his shoulders and drawled, "I don't fight with ruffians, nor do I brawl over common whores."

The dark green eyes glittering with suppressed violence, conscious of the dangerous role he played, Brett had dared not reply in kind. Instead he had taken a deep breath and promised, "Perhaps someday I'll make you change your mind about that. You might just find a brawl with a ruffian better sport than knifing an unarmed girl."

Carlos's face had whitened, but he had not pushed his luck. He'd spun on his heel and disappeared quickly, leaving Brett wishing he could forget his masquerade for about five minutes. He had figured that was about all it would take him to teach that arrogant Spaniard a lesson. And now, he thought with a grim smile, I might just get to teach Carlos that lesson after all.

Looking across at Ollie, he said, "You're right. That was the fellow. And he's Alejandro's nephew."

Ollie whistled with dismay. "That could be right bad for us, guvnor. This de la Vega saw you when you were acting the part of a smuggler. It'll be a bit difficult to explain what you were doing there."

Brett made a face. "It won't be that bad. Remember, Alejandro already knows what I was doing there. He was in New Orleans when Frenchie and the rest were brought to trial, and I explained to him my part in their arrest. The problem will be Carlos. I got the distinct impression tonight that nothing would give Carlos greater pleasure than to see me discredited. Even if I were to explain myself to him, he wouldn't believe it, wouldn't want to believe it. He'll definitely try to cause trouble if he càn, but I think I can probably stand the nonsense. The most that will arise out of it should be nothing more than a few raised eyebrows and whispers. As long as Alejandro isn't affected by it, and I don't believe he will be, I really don't give a damn what Carlos says or does!"

Ollie looked skeptical. "You going to mention this to Señor Alejandro?"

Frowning, Brett regarded his manservant. "It's a bit delicate, my little friend. Carlos is his nephew, and I don't like tale bearers. I can't very well march into Alejandro's room and say, 'Oh, by the way, I had a bit of trouble with a nasty customer when I was posing as a smuggler, and imagine my surprise when it turns out that *my* nasty cus-

122

tomer is *your* nephew!' A little difficult, wouldn't you say?"

"I see your point," Ollie replied glumly. "What are you going to do?"

"Nothing. Carlos may not even remember the incident. And if you'll recall, I looked the part I was playing. Hopefully there is a great deal of difference between Brett the smuggler and Brett the nephew of Alejandro del Torres." A glimmer of laughter deep in his eyes, he murmured, "And if there isn't, it must be the fault of my rascally valet! Hmmm?"

Missing the lurking laughter, Ollie bristled. "Well, if that don't beat the Dutch! I work my fingers to the bone turning you out proper, and you doubt my craft!"

Smiling, Brett dismissed him. "Go to bed, Ollie, and don't worry your head over tonight. We'll come about, you'll see."

Once he was alone in his rooms, Brett wished he were as confident as he sounded. This evening's interlude with Sabrina had left him badly rattled. And the ugly suspicion that he might have been the one seduced couldn't be dismissed. In the black, suspicious mood he was in at the moment, he wouldn't have been at all startled to have Alejandro suddenly come barging through his door, demanding that he do the honorable thing by his daughter. But he found it almost impossible to believe such a thing of Alejandro, and as the time passed and the house remained silent, he dismissed that notion. That Sabrina had planned tonight's confrontation all by herself wasn't quite as easy to dismiss. Even her youth did not stand in her defense— women were trouble right from the cradle as far as Brett was concerned.

Of course there was Carlos. . . . But he shrugged. Sabrina could simply have decided that Brett was a better catch—even Carlos had admitted that the engagement had not been formally announced. So had she planned what had nearly happened tonight? Or had it been as innocent as it appeared on the surface?

Unable to resolve that problem, he deliberately turned his mind away from it. But if he could push aside the question of Sabrina's innocence or guilt with reasonable ease, he could not ignore his own part in tonight's near disaster.

How could I have lost control of myself like that? he wondered bitterly. Not only had he transgressed his own code, he had nearly dishonored and abused the trust of a man he held in high regard. Disgust and fury at himself rising up in his throat, he got up and poured another glass of brandy. If she hadn't called a halt when she did . . . He closed his eyes in pain. God! He had wanted her! And he was bleakly aware that in another moment or two he wouldn't have been able to stop—no matter what she'd said or done. Just thinking of her warm body, of that soft mouth beneath his, made his body harden and burn with desire. Outraged that even now she could arouse him so powerfully, he cursed helplessly under his breath. Unwilling to admit to any reason other than simple lust and propinquity for his body's betrayal, he was eventually able to convince himself that all he really needed was a woman— *any* woman! Once he'd broken his celibate state, this ridiculous obsession with Sabrina would disappear completely.

Assured that he had discovered the reason for having nearly broken the rules of a lifetime, he relaxed slightly. He had nothing more to worry about, he told himself repeatedly. Sabrina's attraction had been merely that she *was* a desirable young woman and she had been close at hand. *Too* close at hand, he reminded himself tightly.

Those conclusions should have allowed him to seek his bed and sleep soundly, but such was not the case. He found himself instead increasingly restless, and like Sabrina he finally left his room and wandered downstairs.

Idly he walked through the darkened hacienda. Eventually he ended up in the library, and lighting the candelabrum at the end of the couch, his gaze went reluctantly to the floor where he and Sabrina had lain together. The image of her lying there came back to him, the flame-colored hair spread out like a cloak of fiery gold around her, the amber-gold eyes drowsy with desire, the lush ripeness of her mouth begging for his kiss. He swallowed dryly. He had to stop thinking about her!

Like a man chased by demons, he left the library instantly, fleeing unwanted memories. Reaching the stables just as the faintest glimmer of light broke on the eastern horizon, he declined the services of a sleepy stablehand and quickly saddled Firestorm himself.

How long he rode, or even where, he never remembered, but the movement of the horse beneath him seemed to soothe the devils that ate at him, and the instinctive need to pay attention to Firestorm's spirited attempts to increase their pace kept him from thinking too deeply.

When he finally did return to the hacienda, the sun was high in the sky and the place was bustling with the usual daily activity. Dismounting, he tossed the reins to the waiting stablehand and began to walk toward the house. Passing one of the paddocks, he absently noticed Sabrina's mare, Sirocco, joyfully frolicking with two other handsome horses. He stopped for a moment to watch the fluid, graceful movements of the sleek palomino, the sunlight turning Sirocco's gleaming hide to pure spun gold. A beautiful animal worthy of her owner, he decided.

Pleasantly exhausted now, he wanted nothing more than his bed, but crossing the front courtyard, he was stopped by Bonita, a faintly worried expression on her plump features.

"*Buenos días,* Señor Brett," she began politely. "Don Alejandro apologizes for having to leave this morning before seeing you, but a puma killed a calf last night, and he didn't want to delay the hunt for it until you could be found." A slightly scolding note in her voice, she said, "We were concerned that you were not in your room when word of the kill came, but once it was discovered that your horse was gone, your servant explained that you often go for an early morning ride." Her lips pursing sternly, she admonished, "You are as bad as Señorita Sabrina—both of you seem to forget that there are bandits in the area and it is foolish for you to disappear without letting someone know your whereabouts."

His suspiciously meek demeanor at odds with the twinkle of amusement deep in the dark green eyes, Brett murmured, "I am sorry, Bonita, if you were worried about me—I will try to be more considerate of your fears for my safety in the future."

Bonita sniffed, not at all placated by his words. But

letting the subject drop, she went on, "Don Alejandro does not think that the puma hunt will take too many hours, and he suggested that you might care to accompany him this afternoon, after siesta, when he plans to ride into Nacogdoches."

Brett nodded his dark head in agreement and would have gone on his way, but Bonita seemed to hesitate, and then she asked anxiously, "Señor, did you see Señorita Sabrina this morning? Or notice if her horse was in the stables when you were there?"

Brett stiffened, wondering immediately if this was another calculated move in whatever game Sabrina might be playing. "I haven't seen her since last night," he answered warily. "I did see Sirocco just a few minutes ago, though, in one of the paddocks. Why do you ask?"

Bonita wrung her hands, the expression of worry deepening. "She is not in her rooms! I was not alarmed at first, because, like you, señor, she comes and goes as she pleases, but it is almost mid-morning and still there is no sign of her. Never has she been gone this long without telling me! I had hoped that she had gone riding with you—but now you tell me that this is not so and that her horse is here." Her big, round brown eyes frightened, Bonita wailed, "Where can she be, señor? With the bandits around . . ."

Something decidedly unpleasant slithered down his spine, and because he had never experienced the feeling before, it took Brett a second to realize what it was—fear. Bonita's unspoken words raised horrifying specters in his mind—Sabrina helpless and at the mercy of the cruel, unscrupulous bandits; Sabrina suffering rape and worse at the hands of those same brutal murderers who had attacked and razed the Rios ranch . . . Savagely he reined in his racing imagination.

Concealing his own niggling fear, Brett said soothingly, "Now, Bonita, don't work yourself up into a frenzy. She's probably just gone for a walk and taken longer than she expected. Have you had any of the servants look for her?"

"Sí, señor!" Bonita answered quickly. "I had them search the grounds thoroughly when I could not find her. I myself was on my way to the stables when I met you."

"Well, dammit, she must be someplace!" Brett bit out,

torn between worry and irritation. "She can't just have disappeared on foot. Isn't there someplace you haven't looked, someplace she might have gone?"

Suddenly Bonita's face cleared. "Ah, *señor,* of course! What a silly old woman I am—she must have gone to the gazebo at the lake. It is a favorite place of hers, and she often goes there for an early-morning swim. How foolish of me not to have had someone look there. I shall see to it immediately!"

"Never mind. Just tell me where it is, and *I'll* do it," Brett growled. If Sabrina was there, he was going to wring her neck for alarming old Bonita. And if she wasn't . . .

His face hard and unfathomable, he listened to Bonita's directions, and in a mood of mingled suspicion and uneasiness, he set out swiftly for the gazebo. Finding Sabrina sound asleep inside the little building did not allay his mistrust of the situation. If anything it reinforced it—the scene was too reminiscent of last night for him not to be instantly on his guard. Last night had not gained her what she wanted, so she would try again. And yet, while his suspicions were fully alive, the feeling of relief that swept over him when he discovered her slim form stretched out on the orange cushions left him curiously shaken and weak. Unfortunately that feeling didn't last very long, and in a matter of seconds, relief was replaced by an odd fury. How could she frighten poor Bonita this way? he thought irrationally, completely ignoring the fact that he, too, had been frightened and that half his anger was simply because he *had* been, even for a moment, filled with fear for her.

Walking over to where she lay, he looked down at her, his mouth curling in a sneer. Violently he shook her, saying roughly, "Wake up, Sabrina, if you're really asleep! Bonita's had the entire household looking for you."

Groggily Sabrina stared up at him, momentarily disorientated. But then suddenly everything came flooding back and she jerked upright, the bright sunlight causing her to blink. Childlike, she rubbed her eyes with her fists and then yawned hugely. Still not quite fully awake, she glanced at Brett standing so rigidly nearby and muttered crankily, "What did you say? Something about Bonita?"

"Merely that this little stunt of yours has her frightened to death! She's been entertaining notions of your capture by the bandits!"

Sabrina appeared incredulous. "Bandits? Here? They are not so foolish as to try such a thing! The Rancho del Torres is safe. No one could harm me here!"

"Not only is this place not safe," Brett said nastily, "but you shouldn't be roaming about like some wild gypsy! What the hell is your father thinking of! Anyone could come across you here!"

Instantly enraged at the implied slur upon her father, Sabrina sat up even straighter and said frostily, "I beg your pardon!"

"You'll do more than beg, little girl, if you pull another escapade like this! Next time, if there is a next time, I'll tan your backside so hard you won't sit for a week!" Brett said brutally, and grabbing her arm, he jerked her to her feet. "Now let's get going. I haven't had any sleep, and I'm in no mood to argue with you."

"Let go of me!" Sabrina snapped, ineffectively trying to free her arm from his iron-hard grasp. "You're hurting me!"

"I thought you said no one could harm you here?" he shot back sarcastically, giving her a painful little shake.

Sabrina was dimly aware that he was deliberately being disagreeable, but it didn't stop her temper from flaring, and as he dragged her out of the gazebo, she quickly reached down into her boot and pulled out her knife. Before Brett realized what she was about, the blade had cut a neat slice across the top of his hand and Sabrina had danced free of his slackened grasp.

The jade-green eyes nearly black with fury, Brett first glanced at the thin line of blood on his hand and then at her. "You little hellcat!" he muttered thickly. "You're a damned sight too quick with that knife, and I think it's time that someone taught you some manners with it!"

He was very handsome as he stood there outside the gazebo, the lake shimmering in the distance behind him. A slight breeze ruffled the thick blue-black hair; his black silk shirt intensified the darkness of his hard, lean features, and the hip-hugging black breeches made her very aware of those long, powerful legs. Legs that had pressed intimately against hers only hours before, she thought with a catch in her breath. The air of suppressed violence that radiated from him frightened her, though, and nervously her hand tightened on the knife. She didn't want to fight him—all she wanted was for him to love her!

But Brett wasn't giving her any choice. With the quickness of a hunting cat he was on her, and instinctively Sabrina raised the knife in defense. Her defenses were useless; he had fought too many brawls in too many dark alleys to be stopped by a slim if determined girl. Unerringly his fingers closed around the hand with the knife, and with one sharp movement he brought her hand down painfully on his thigh, the shock of the impact against those steel muscles breaking her grip. The knife went flying, and with a sound of satisfaction, Brett saw it land near the edge of the lake.

Releasing Sabrina, he whirled and moved to pick it up, and looking back at her, a tight smile curving his mouth, he asked softly, "And now how are you going to defend yourself?"

"I'm not," Sabrina said calmly. Disconcertingly she began to walk slowly toward him.

Brett eyed her warily as she approached. When she was only inches from him, she stopped and extended her hand, palm down. Coolly she said, "You may take your own if you like. Perhaps it will make you feel better."

He stared at her for a long moment, wishing she weren't quite so lovely or that he weren't quite so conscious of her slim body and the isolation of this spot. He looked at her, looked at the knife, and then shrugged his shoulders. A twisted grin creasing his face, he handed her the knife. "Your win, I think," he said dryly.

CHAPTER TEN

There was silence between the two of them as they walked slowly back to the hacienda. Each one was very conscious of the other, but neither was willing to break the fragile peace that existed at the moment.

Upon reaching the hacienda, they were greeted by a scolding and vastly relieved Bonita, and any opportunity for private conversation was lost. Her round face wreathed in a smile, she said to Brett, "Oh, *señor*, thank you! I am so pleased that you found her!" And turning to Sabrina, she frowned and muttered, "And you, *chica*, should not be so free in your ways—there are bandits about, and you would make a tasty morsel for them!"

Like a hen whose lone chick has been returned, Bonita continued to fuss and hover, and with an amused grin, Brett bade both women good day and gratefully went in search of his bed. He slept until late afternoon, rising barely in time to shave and bathe before joining Alejandro for the proposed trip into Nacogdoches.

The mission Nuestra Señora de Guadalupe de Nacogdoches had been carved out in the early 1700s, but it had never been more than a not very successful outpost inhabited by only a few soldiers and even fewer gritty priests. At times it had been abandoned, and it wasn't until the late 1770s that a village had grown up around the old mission site. Presently, though, the village supported a thriving population of nearly six hundred residents. And as Brett rode down the narrow red-dirt streets lined with various framed buildings, he saw a wide variety of people—Indians, farmers, traders, soldiers, and robed priests.

The most imposing structure in the village of Nacogdoches was a large stone building that served as a storage area for merchandise. It had been built by Gil Antonia

Ybarbo, one of the leading settlers of the area, in 1779, and staring at the stone walls nearly a yard thick, Brett decided slowly that it would serve admirably as a warehouse for Alejandro's sugar crop—*if* there ever is a sugar crop, he reminded himself wryly.

It hadn't taken him long to realize that Alejandro's whim to suddenly grow sugar was just that—a whim. Granted the land was suitable for it, but a great deal of time and back-breaking effort was going to be involved before the crop could be planted. And more importantly, except for the residents of the Nacogdoches area, there was no commercial outlet for any surplus. Once harvested and milled, the sugar would have to be sent overland to Natchitoches, in the Louisiana Territory, and from there sailed by barge through a long, circuitous and uncertain route to New Orleans. It was both an unprofitable and an unpractical situation, but when Brett had pointed out this fact, Alejandro had shrugged and smiled charmingly. "We shall see, *amigo*, we shall see," Alejandro had murmured carelessly.

Brett had thought to argue further, but then he, too, had shrugged his shoulders—if Alejandro wished to waste time and money, why should he care? The problem was that he did care. And while Alejandro seemed in no hurry to begin the project, Brett threw himself into the scheme wholeheartedly. It might prove to be a foolish whim on Alejandro's part, but Brett was going to see that it did not fail because of poor planning. The preparing and clearing of the land, the planting, and the harvesting would be faultless. What Alejandro did with it after that would be no concern of his—he would have done his best.

The visit to town was more for social reasons than because of any desire on Alejandro's part to seek a warehouse for his crop, and as they rode slowly down the streets, they stopped often to converse with first this person then that. It was obvious that Alejandro was an important, well-respected member of the community, and it was only natural that Brett's presence at his side aroused a great deal of friendly curiosity. Proudly Alejandro made the introductions to the various people they met, and by the time they started homeward, Brett's head was reeling from trying to remember the many names and occupations of the individuals he had met.

They were at the edge of the village, just entering the pine woods, when they encountered someone Brett would have been pleased to avoid—Carlos de la Vega. The dislike between the two younger men had escaped Alejandro's notice, and seeing Carlos at the side of the road he reined in his horse with an exclamation of pleasure. Doffing his heavily embroidered sombrero, he acknowledged Carlos and the young woman who stood nearby.

"*Buenos días,* Señora Morales. Good day to you, too, Carlos," Alejandro said warmly before introducing Brett to Carlos's companion. "Señora Morales, allow me to present my nephew, Brett Dangermond, to you. He is newly arrived here from Natchez and will, I hope most sincerely, be making an extended visit with us at the Rancho del Torres. Brett, I would like you to meet Señora Constanza Morales y Duarte. Carlos you of course met last evening."

Constanza was a full-blooming Spanish rose, who could have been any age between twenty and thirty, although Brett suspected she was nearer thirty than twenty—there was something about the way her eyes lingered on his mouth and shoulders that bespoke amatory wisdom. A lovely, sensuous creature, Brett thought to himself, his gaze moving appreciatively over her beautiful face and ripe figure. Lustrous black hair veiled by a black lace mantilla framed her features, intensifying the creaminess of her magnolia skin, making her ebony eyes gleam. There was a slightly feline cast to her face, which Brett found intriguing, but there was nothing feline about her body— the lush, voluptuous curves were decorously but clearly revealed by her stylish gown of amber-bronze silk.

Brett suddenly became aware that Constanza, from beneath her lashes, was assessing him almost as thoroughly as he had her, and he grinned. When their eyes met, a look of complete understanding passed between them.

The introductions having been made, the four of them stood talking for some minutes, until Constanza, her fine, dark eyes revealing her unmistakable interest in Brett, suggested softly that the gentlemen might prefer some refreshments at her house. "It is only a short distance down

132

this street. Señor de la Vega and I were on our way there when we met you. Do say that you will!"

When Alejandro would have demurred, it was Brett who said casually, "An excellent idea, Señora Morales. It is very kind of you to offer your hospitality to a stranger like myself."

Oblivious to the other two men, Constanza smiled coyly and said dulcetly, "But you are no stranger, Señor Dangermond—not when Señor del Torres is your uncle."

Alejandro frowned slightly, not at all happy with the turn of events, especially not Constanza's undisguised eagerness to ingratiate herself with Brett—or Brett's apparent willingness to allow her to do so. It was Sabrina who was supposed to make him look as he did now—admiring and attracted—not this forward young widow of uncertain means!

Carlos, who had been noticeably silent, suddenly smiled sourly and murmured, "You will find that we Spaniards are a very hospitable people, Señor Dangermond—even to relatives who can claim no blood tie."

"Carlos!" Alejandro said reprovingly. "Where there is great affection and trust, there is no need for blood!"

Carlos flushed and muttered something under his breath. The subject was dropped, but an odd air of tension seemed to hang over the remainder of the visit.

Constanza's home turned out to be a modest but elegant frame house only a few yards from where they were standing. Leaving their horses tied to a shrub nearby, Brett and Alejandro followed the other two to a small, pleasant patio at the rear of the wooden building. A sharp clap of her slim hands brought an Indian servant to Constanza's side, and in minutes the three gentlemen were seated at a small table enjoying a glass of Madeira. Constanza contented herself with a tall glass of sangría, saying with a sigh, "I do hope that the Madeira is satisfactory. Since my husband's death three years ago, I seldom entertain any gentlemen, and it is surprising that there was anything in the house suitable for your palates." She glanced over at Brett and added, "I live here with my husband's maiden sister, but as she is very old and cares nothing for worldly things, she is little help to me in chosing what would be appropriate to have on hand for the occasional male caller. She is nearly deaf, so I suppose that might account for her reluctance to mingle with others." Her eyes moved on, and sending Carlos a pensive smile, she said fondly, "Señor de la Vega has been most kind to me during my widowhood. He and my husband were good friends, and I don't know what I would have done without his help after Emilio died. . . ."

The conversation went on from there, consisting of polite chatter, but by the time Alejandro and Brett departed, Brett knew all he needed to know about Constanza Morales y Duarte. She was a widow who wasn't averse to male companionship, and he was fairly certain that if she and Carlos weren't lovers now, they had been at some time in the not too distant past.

Constanza Morales was the type of woman Brett recognized instantly, the type of woman he usually chose for his mistress—a lovely, amoral creature, whose only difference from the common whore was an aristocratic birth and family. She had also made it clear that she wouldn't be reluctant to share a deeper intimacy with him. He was too well versed in the art of dalliance not to have understood immediately what was behind the seductive glances, the swiftness with which she had made her widowed state known, and the fact that her only companion was an elderly deaf sister-in-law! He smiled cynically. She had made so very certain that he knew she was available, even going so far as to murmur low when they said good-bye, "I am sorry to see you leave, Señor Dangermond. It is very lonely for me since Emilio died. Perhaps we will meet again . . . soon?"

His eyes meeting hers, he had said softly, "Of that you can be certain, *señora. Very* soon."

Alejandro hadn't been blind to what was going on, but as Constanza was considered a respectable young woman, he merely dismissed her actions as perhaps more forward and flirtatious than was strictly proper. If he could have overheard the conversation taking place between Constanza and Carlos just then, he would have drastically changed his mind and forbidden Sabrina even to acknowledge Constanza on the street, much less allow the woman access to his home.

"Are you going to take him as your lover?" Carlos asked interestedly as he and Constanza continued to sit on the patio after Brett and Alejandro had departed.

Constanza sent him a teasing glance. "Would you be jealous, *querido?*"

Carlos frowned and stared at the Madeira in his glass. "I don't know," he said at last. "But yes, yes, I think I would be jealous."

Surprise on her face, Constanza said perplexedly, "But you never were of the others. Why him?"

"The others were different!" Carlos snapped defensively. "They were not like Brett Dangermond. They meant nothing to you. But Dangermond . . . Dangermond is different."

"How? He is a man like the others. Perhaps more handsome, it is true, but you have nothing to fear from him—just as I have nothing to fear from the other women in your life, *sí?*"

"I do not fear Dangermond!" Carlos ground out angrily.

Well used to Carlos's outbursts of anger, Constanza looked almost amused as she said, "Very well then, you don't fear him. And you will not be jealous of him either, will you?" When Carlos did not reply but continued to look sullen, she leaned across the small pine table, and touching his strong hand with hers, she murmured, "Come on, *querido,* what is bothering you? Surely it is not that he will share my bed? We decided long ago, before I even married old Emilio, that we would put no bonds on each other. I have my men and you your women, and in between"—she smiled impishly—"we have each other. So why are you so disturbed by this man? Besides," she added slyly, "I thought the entire purpose of your visit today was to ask my help in seducing him. You did say you wanted me to make him so mad for me that he would have no eyes for Sabrina, didn't you? Am I not to provide a distraction for him and keep him away from Sabrina? Keep him enthralled so that you will have no rival for her hand? Is that not what we planned?"

Carlos relaxed suddenly and grinned across at her. "I should have married you, instead of allowing that old lecher, Emilio, to have you."

Constanza shook her dark head decisively. "No. No, *amigo*—we know each other too well. If I were your wife, I would be jealous of your other women and you would not want me to have my lovers. I like my life the way it is, Carlos. I would be lying if I didn't admit that I wish Emilio had left me with more money so that I could live in elegance in New Orleans or Mexico City, but on the whole I am satisfied with my life. I come and go as I please, I *very* discreetly take the occasional lover when it suits me, and when I am pressed for money or have need of a particularly expert lover, I have my good friend Carlos. What more could a woman ask for?"

"You are unnatural," Carlos said mildly, his eyes resting on her full mouth. "All women want marriage and children. It is what they are born to do—marry and provide their husbands with heirs."

Aware of his glance on her mouth, she slowly, provocatively moistened her lips with the tip of her tongue. "Bah! Because it is what you want with your Sabrina, you think I should want it, too! What I want at the moment is Brett Dangermond in my bed. Next week or next month it will be something else, but for now . . ." She smiled coquettishly at him, her hands lightly caressing his. "You shall have your Sabrina, and all the lands and riches that come with her, and because I have been accommodating in the matter of Brett Dangermond, you will share your new wealth with me, *sí?*"

When Carlos remained silent, his gaze still on her mouth, she touched his lips softly with one finger. Sensuously she outlined the shape of his mouth. "You will have everything you want, *amigo,*" she breathed huskily. "Everything . . . including me."

"Sí," he muttered thickly, rising to his feet. "Everything, including you."

Roughly he pulled her eager body into his arms, and he kissed her upturned mouth hungrily. He glanced around the deserted patio and demanded, "Where? Your room? Or the forest?"

"The forest," she replied against his throat, her hands touching him intimately.

His manhood nearly bursting from his tight calzoneras,

136

Carlos kissed her once more. Lifting his lips, he growled, "When you lay with the gringo, you will remember this afternoon." And then, dragging a very willing Constanza behind him, they disappeared into the thick, concealing forest.

Sabrina was in the forest, too, that afternoon, but unlike Carlos and Constanza she was alone. Or had thought she was . . .

Having declined to accompany Brett and her father into Nacogdoches, she had saddled Sirocco and gone for a ride, allowing the palomino mare to wander where she would. Sabrina had grown up in the forest surrounding the Rancho del Torres, and it had never held any fears for her. She was as familiar with it as she was the grounds of the hacienda, but today she was suddenly aware of how easily the tangled maze of trees and verdant undergrowth could conceal an enemy. Bonita's harping about bandits, as well as the horrifying news of the sacking of the Rios ranch had begun to prey on her mind, and perhaps that was why she gradually became conscious that she was no longer alone. Someone was stealthily following her. Not someone well versed in the forest either, she thought calmly, as a fallen branch cracked loudly behind her.

More curious than alarmed, she continued on her ride, imperceptibly changing her direction so that she was now heading back toward the hacienda. Passing under a tall pine tree, she slowed Sirocco long enough to allow herself time to swing up into a low, overhanging tree limb and then softly commanded the horse to move on. Obediently the mare did so, leaving Sabrina to wait for her follower.

She didn't have long to wait. Only minutes after Sirocco had ambled on, a horse and rider came cautiously into view. Sabrina recognized neither the animal nor the man upon its back, and with thoughts of the murdered Rios family in her mind, she reached down and slid her knife from the sheath in her boot. A feral gleam in the amber-gold eyes, the glorious golden-red hair a fiery halo about her head, she dropped down on the hapless rider below.

There was a startled croak from her victim as she landed behind him on the horse, her arm quickly and efficiently passing around the man's neck, the knife blade pressing menacingly into the rider's throat. In a voice that was surprisingly fierce, considering how fast her heart was beating, Sabrina demanded, "Your name or your life!"

Everything had gone according to her hastily improvised plan up until now, but she hadn't anticipated the violent reaction of her victim. A sinewy hand suddenly gripped the wrist that held the knife, even as the well aimed elbow of the man's other arm jabbed powerfully into her solar plexus. Winded from the unexpected blow, she momentarily slackened the arm that held the knife, and he took quick advantage, swiftly increasing his hold and forcing her hand down and away from his throat.

Realizing what was happening, Sabrina fought back, and they began to struggle violently to gain control of the knife. While they fought their grim, silent battle, the horse fidgeted nervously, finally rearing up and throwing both combatants to the ground. They hit hard, but rolling and twisting, they continued the fight until Sabrina, her breath coming in deep, painful gulps, finally gained the upper hand. Sitting on his chest, her knees digging into his arms, pinning them uselessly to the ground, she finally saw her opponent's face.

"Señor Ollie!" she burst out, the savage expression fading from her face. Unconsciously she sagged, sinking deeper onto his narrow chest, her knees now on either side of him, no longer trapping his arms. The knife, which she had been in the process of placing against his unprotected throat, once more lay limply in her hand. Her bewilderment obvious, she asked, "Why were you following me?"

His face a mixture of bafflement, embarrassment, and chagrin, Ollie ignored her question and burst out with a string of profanity of such hair-curling virulence, such boundless variety and innovation, that Sabrina blinked.

"I beg your pardon!" she said sharply, understanding not even one word in fifty of what he uttered. "Speak English!"

"I am speakin' bloody H'glish!" Ollie returned in an aggrieved tone.

Assessingly they eyed each other, and then, with a frustrated exclamation, Sabrina stood up. Impatiently she gestured for Ollie to rise.

Ollie did so, and dusting off the debris that clung to his clothes, he muttered disgustedly, "If this don't beat the Dutch! Bested by a dimber mort! And me a flash cove up to every rig and row that's ever been run!"

Torn between curiosity about his peculiar way of speech and an odd feeling of amusement, Sabrina suddenly found the situation preposterous. An attractive gurgle of laughter escaped her, and Ollie glanced at her with dislike.

"Laughin' at me!" he said, outraged. His brown eyes sparkling angrily, he shook an admonishing finger at Sabrina. "It ain't polite to crow over a man's misfortune! I would have thought even in a 'eathenish place like this, you'd 'ave been taught better. Seems I was wrong!"

Laughing now in earnest, Sabrina sought to soothe his ruffled sensibilities. "No, no, Señor Ollie. I was not laughing *at* you—it is this ridiculous situation." She sent him a blinding smile, inviting him to share her laughter, and Ollie stared at her open-mouthed, entranced.

She was a lovely thing, he thought to himself, his earlier distrust and animosity fading away. Aware suddenly of the enormity of what he had said and done, he hung his head and blushed like a girl. Now he was in for it! When the guvnor heard about *this* escapade, he'd be lucky if he wasn't dismissed on the spot. Miserably he said, "It's me, miss, that should be explaining things to you."

Sabrina's face softened. He was so very unhappy and uncomfortable that she could not find it in her heart to be very stern. "Very well then, if you will not join me in laughter, tell me why you were following me," she said softly.

Ollie swallowed painfully. He couldn't very well admit that the guvnor's uncustomary mood last night had anything to do with his actions. How could he say, "You had the guvnor fair blue-deviled, and as I always watches out for the guvnor, I wanted to know what kind of woman could do that to him?"

When Ollie remained silent, Sabrina asked quietly, "Was it because of the bandits? Did Señor Brett ask you to follow me?"

For a moment Ollie almost seized on the excuse, but figuring his lie would be found out, he shook his head. Improvising, he said, "I didn't mean to follow you. It was just that I was at the stables when you left, and as I 'aven't seen much of the countryside, I thought I'd just follow along behind you. That way I wouldn't get lost." Embellishing his tale, he looked suitably downtrodden and explained mournfully, "I shouldn't be saying this to you, miss, but the guvnor's no easy taskmaster. This is the first day I've 'ad any time to myself. I didn't mean any 'arm, miss." Putting his best pleading expression on his face, he begged pitifully, "You won't tell the guvnor, will you, miss?" He shuddered theatrically. "He'll fair beat me to death if he finds out about this, I can tell you!"

Completely hoodwinked by Ollie's manner and pathetic tale, Sabrina was firmly allied on his side. Why, Brett must be an ogre to his servants! she thought. *Poor* Señor Ollie, to be so frightened of his master. Her eyes kindling with the light of battle, she said grimly, "You have nothing to worry about. I shall say nothing. And Señor Ollie, if your master dares to lay a hand on you while you are at the Rancho del Torres, you let me know. We do not mistreat our servants *here!*" She glanced across at Ollie and smiled reassuringly. Then, looking at the sun, she said briskly, "We had best find our horses and head back to the hacienda if we wish to arrive there ahead of your master and my father."

Relieved and yet feeling the tiniest bit guilty about the easy way she had swallowed his story, Ollie agreed with alacrity. A cheeky grin on his face, he started to step out smartly when he heard a curious buzzing near his foot, and Sabrina commanded urgently, "Do not move! Stay like a stone, *señor,* if you value your life!"

Ollie froze, and looking down at his toes, he saw, curled not a foot away from him, the sinister shape of a serpent. But no serpent like he had ever seen before. This creature had a tail that vibrated so swiftly that the eye could not follow the movement, and the ugly triangular head was poised aggressively above the coiled, thick body. Ollie barely had time enough to realize that he might be in mortal danger when, out of the corner of his eye, he saw a

140

flash of steel. The next thing he knew, the snake was writhing furiously on the forest floor, its head staked to the ground by Sabrina's knife.

His face held a green tinge, and he stepped quickly away. "Bloody eyes! What in the 'ell is that?"

Placing her booted heel firmly behind the head, Sabrina coolly removed her knife and efficiently cut off the snake's head. Ignoring the twisting carcass, she dug a hole and gingerly deposited the head. "That, Señor Ollie, *was* a rattlesnake. They are venomous and quite, quite deadly," she said sincerely. "Our land is beautiful, but it is also dangerous. You must take care within our forests or we may bury you here."

Shaken, Ollie said piously, "God love you, miss! You saved my life! If ever Ollie Fram can do you a favor, I'll do it."

Opinions completely revised about one another, in increasing rapport, they caught their horses and rode back to the hacienda.

Later that day, as he was laying out Brett's apparel for the evening, Ollie glanced across at his master, who had just finished shaving, and said with studied carelessness, "Miss Sabrina saved my life today, guvnor."

Wiping his face with a white towel, Brett looked at him with a frown. "What do you mean, she saved your life?"

Looking very innocent, Ollie answered, "Well, guvnor, I was down at the stables, intending to take a little ride about, when I notices Miss Sabrina riding off all by herself. And I recalls the fuss that was made this morning about her maybe being captured by bandits, and I says to myself, 'Ollie, you best ride along with her. It's what the guvnor would want.' And so I did."

Brett's eyebrow rose skeptically. "And she allowed you to?"

Ollie nodded his head vigorously. "Indeed she did, guvnor! She was right 'appy to 'ave Ollie Fram nearby, I can tell you that!"

"Oh? And why was that?" Brett asked dryly.

For a moment Ollie appeared nonplussed, but then, warming to his tale, he said quickly, "Why, because of the bandits, guvnor! We rode quite some distance, and as you know, I'm no great 'orseman, so after a bit, I suggests that we walk and give me shanks a rest. Miss Sabrina, kind lady that she is, agreed, and guvnor, *that's* when she saved my life!" Ollie shot a look to see how Brett was taking his story so far, and if not reassured by the expression of amusement on Brett's face at least not worried by it, he said breathlessly, "Right by my feet was the most awful, deadly serpent in the world! A rattlesnake! And before I could even speak a word, quick as a wink, Miss Sabrina had nailed that creature of the devil right to the ground! Six inches of cold iron she put through its 'ead. Just like *that!*" And he snapped his fingers. His eyes gleaming with the deep admiration he felt, Ollie said blissfully, "Guvnor, she's a diamond of the first water! Why, she looked like a tiger when she killed that snake, them eyes of 'ers all glittery-gold like and that red hair like fire around her head, and yet she was the kindest, the sweetest lady I ever met. I take back everything I said about 'er last night—she's a *prime* article!"

Not as easily duped by Ollie as Sabrina was, Brett looked at his manservant for a long, unnerving moment. "I see," he finally said noncommittally, and Ollie breathed a sigh of relief.

There was a companionable silence between them as Brett dressed, Ollie obediently handing him first one piece of clothing and then another. Attired in black satin breeches, a crisp white linen shirt fitted snugly across his broad shoulders, Brett slowly fastened the buttons of a yellow waistcoat gaily embroidered with black. Casually he murmured, "You won't have to wait up for me this evening, Ollie. I will be riding into Nacogdoches later and have no idea when I shall return." He smiled cynically. "I suspect I shall be gone all night, if I have read a certain situation aright."

Ollie knew very well what that meant—the guvnor had found a new mistress. But for once, that fact disturbed him. Somewhere between the time Sabrina had killed the snake and now, Ollie had come to the happy conclusion that Miss Sabrina was the perfect mate for his master. And he wasn't best pleased that the guvnor was now chasing after some common light skirt when he should be paying proper suit to Miss Sabrina. "A Covent Garden Nun," he sniffed disdainfully, handing Brett an ivory-backed brush.

"Hardly a prostitute, Ollie," Brett chided as he brushed his thick black hair. "Although she probably has all the instincts of one." With a cynical grin, he laid down the brush and murmured, "But who knows! I might be wrong—she might even be perfectly respectable."

Brett wasn't wrong. Having made his excuses to Alejandro, he rode into Nacogdoches, arriving at his destination just as dusk was falling. Tying his horse discreetly at the rear of Constanza's small house, he quietly made his way across the patio and knocked softly on the wooden door.

It opened instantly, almost as if he had been expected. He obviously was, he thought sardonically, his gaze sliding lazily over Constanza's scantily clad body. She was wearing some sort of gauzy silk wrapper that revealed almost as much of her ripe body as it concealed, and his lips widened in a slow, appreciative grin.

Constanza smiled sleepily at him, touching his cheek lightly, her ebony eyes languorous and seductive. "So you did come to me, *querido*. I had hoped you would."

There was no need of conversation between them, Brett taking his cue from Constanza and pulling her into his arms, his hard mouth claiming hers in a devastating kiss that sent her mind reeling. It was only later, much later when he lay awake satiated and exhausted beside Constanza's naked body, that he was conscious of a queer sense of guilt and disgust. Infuriatingly, Sabrina's slender form rose up to mock him, to fill him with such a hungry desire that it was as if the hours just past of violent lovemaking with Constanza had never been. With a virulent curse, he turned to Constanza, jerking her against him, and proceeded to make wild, almost savage love to her. But it did little good. No matter how many times he lost himself in Constanza's warm, welcoming flesh, Sabrina's lovely face condemned him, made him writhe with an unquenchable longing to have her in his arms, to have her mouth against his, to have *her* body beneath his.

PART TWO

A HEART IN CONFLICT

For to be wise, and love,
Exceeds man's might; that dwells with
gods above.

William Shakespeare
Troilus and Cressida

CHAPTER ELEVEN

The evening of the fiesta welcoming Don Alejandro's American nephew was a fine one. The air was warm, the stars were glittering brightly in the black sky overhead, and on the slight breeze wafted the faint scents of honeysuckle and lilac.

The patio had been strung with lanterns, and the light flickered gaily across the courtyard, revealing the ladies in their loveliest gowns, the gentlemen in their finest clothes. A quartet of the best vaquero musicians softly serenaded the guests on guitars and marimbas, the lively music floating lightly into every corner of the courtyard.

Alejandro was well-pleased at the reception being accorded Brett. Everywhere Brett wandered through the throng, he was greeted warmly and with enthusiasm. The gentlemen liked his conversation and easy manner; the ladies were enamored of his dark good looks. But if Brett's popularity with his neighbors and friends delighted Alejandro, there were others present who viewed the matter far differently.

Her dark eyes full of dislike, Francisca complained to Sabrina, "I don't see why your father is making such a fuss over this gringo. Why, he is not even *really* related to us! I think it is disgraceful the way Alejandro fawns over his every word." And then, revealing the true source of annoyance, "Your father never listens to Carlos the way he does Señor Dangermond!"

Sabrina smiled wearily. Her aunt had done nothing but find fault since arriving with Carlos and Luis a half hour before. The affair was arranged too hastily, the refreshments were not sufficient, the night air was injurious to the health, and it was foolish to use the patio this time of year. But Sabrina knew that those complaints were

147

merely a guise to cover her aunt's real grievance—Alejandro's open admiration and affection for Brett Dangermond.

Unerringly Sabrina's eyes sought out Brett's tall frame as he stood talking to Señora Morales near the edge of the fountain. Her heart squeezed painfully when she saw the intimate way he was smiling down at the other woman, and she sighed softly.

She might have realized the folly of loving him, but her heart was proving to be dreadfully stubborn about the situation. Time is what I need, she thought despairingly. Time in which to outgrow this foolish fascination I have with him. But there was no time. Every day she saw him—across the table at breakfast, in the afternoon when they all met to go riding, and then again in the evening for the last meal of the day. There were few hours in which she was spared the sweet agony of his presence, and like a hunted doe, she had begun to spend more and more time alone in the deep forest. At least there she could think clearly and soothe her lacerated emotions, hoping and praying that the next time she saw him, she could remain unaffected by his magnetic presence.

Brett's manner toward her these past few days had helped Sabrina regain some semblance of normality. He was withdrawn and cool when they met; what conversation they exchanged was nothing more than the polite mouthing of words one would give a stranger. If she avoided him, it hadn't escaped her notice that he, too, was doing his share of making sure there were no intimate moments between them, and she was torn between relief and despair.

She had guessed that the evenings when he excused himself after dinner and rode into Nacogdoches, returning long after she and her father had retired for the night, had been to escape further chances of intimacy between them, but that there was a woman involved had not occurred to her. In her innocence she had assumed he went to one of the taverns and spent the time dicing and drinking. Carlos was to make very certain that she learned the error of her ways.

He had seen the look she had sent Brett and Constanza,

148

and with a slightly cruel smile on his mouth, he walked up to Sabrina where she stood next to his mother and said carelessly, "They make a handsome couple, don't you agree?" His eyelids dropped, and he added, "Almost as handsome as you and I."

Pasting a smile on her lips, Sabrina glanced at him, and ignoring his latter statement, she said with apparent obtuseness, "Who? There are so many handsome couples about this evening."

His eyes watching her expression closely, he murmured, "Sí, that's true, but I think Señor Dangermond and Señora Morales make an exceptionally handsome pair. She is so very beautiful, and though I personally think Dangermond too raw-boned and hard-faced, I will concede that when he is with Señora Morales one forgets those things."

Francisca sniffed scornfully. "Señora Morales may be beautiful, but she is nothing but a grasping hussy as far as I am concerned! I am certainly pleased that you came to your senses and recognized her for what she is. Poor Emilio was not so fortunate, and he was old enough to know better!"

Curious about Señora Morales on several counts, Sabrina turned to Carlos and teased gently, "Did you court the beautiful Señora Morales?" Her eyes full of mockery, she added dolefully, "And to think I believed you when you said you loved me."

Carlos shot his mother a look that boded ill for that lady, and, his voice sharp with annoyance, he muttered, "I do love you! My association with Constanza Morales, or Duarte as she was then, happened when you were a child." He smiled warmly across at Sabrina, his eyes lingering on the smooth golden skin that was enhanced by the deep azure blue of the silk gown she wore this evening. "I was waiting for you to grow up, querida, and you will not blame a man for a few peccadilloes, will you? Not when you have his heart as you have mine?"

It was very pleasant to bask in Carlos's admiration, his professed affection and obvious appreciation of her charms a soothing balm to her aching heart. Enjoying herself for the first time all evening, Sabrina giggled, as she usually did when Carlos spoke of love. "I think that you have a facile tongue!" she said laughingly, unwilling to take any of Carlos's lovemaking seriously.

The music changed tempo then, the strands of the fandango curling around them, and suddenly wanting to dance, to lose herself in the joy of swaying to the music, she grabbed Carlos's hand and said gaily, "Dance with me! Señora Morales and Señor Brett may be the handsomest couple here, but you and I will be the best dancers!"

Carlos eagerly joined her, and together they danced to the fandango, one moment flying around the courtyard, the next moving in slow, decorous rhythm to the music of the guitars and marimbas. Sabrina's lovely face was flushed with pleasure, the azure skirts whirling about her, the lantern light glinting on the gold hoop earrings that dangled near her cheeks as she moved gracefully in Carlos's loose embrace.

Among so many dark heads, her bright red-gold hair was like a beacon, and unwillingly Brett found himself watching her, unable to take his eyes off that lovely, laughing face as she twirled about in Carlos's arms. Her hair had been arranged in artless curls on top of her head, revealing the slim beauty of her neck, the exquisite slope of her slender shoulders, and Brett knew a sudden, fierce impulse to tear her out of Carlos's embrace, to jerk her next to his own hard body and bury his mouth in that tempting spot where her neck joined her shoulders. Furious with himself and unable to watch her in the arms of another man, he turned away, his eyes bleak and cold. Obviously Carlos had not been lying about his relationship with her, and that meant that when she had responded so sweetly, so ardently, to *his* kisses she had been betraying the man she had agreed to marry. His mouth thinned contemptuously. Little slut! Perhaps Constanza was the more honest of the two—she made no bones about the fact that she wanted him, that she enjoyed his lovemaking, and that she expected nothing from it but physical pleasure. She didn't pretend innocence, nor use her body to trap a man into marriage. He'd take an honest whore over the tricks and deceits practiced by a "good" woman any day!

A derisive smile on his handsome mouth, he looked

down at Constanza standing beside him and murmured, "Shall we dance?"

Smiling limpidly up at him, she agreed huskily, "But of course, *querido,* if that is what you want."

Pulling her next to him, he stepped out into the middle of the dancers and muttered, "What I want will have to wait until later."

Constanza fairly purred as she matched her steps to his, and they moved in perfect unison with the music. Glancing up at him, she commented lightly, "For a gringo you dance the fandango very well. Why is this?"

"My great-grandmother was Spanish for one thing, so there is Spanish blood in my family, and for another I spent several months in Spain some years ago." He grinned down at her, a mocking glint in the dark green eyes. "I learned many things of Spanish origin then. Shall I show you some of them . . . later?"

Her breathing quickened, and she lowered her eyes demurely. "I have never been fortunate enough to visit the land of my father, and I would be *most* interested in *anything* you could show me."

Brett laughed, his black mood lifting. His lips curving sensuously, he gazed at the ripe, full mouth inches from his. "It will be my pleasure," he promised softly.

The fandango ended, and Carlos led a breathless, smiling Sabrina over to a long refreshment table. Procuring for her a glass of sangría, he said, "Shall we sit over there?" and nodded toward some chairs that had been placed in a quiet, secluded area under the wide, extended eaves of the hacienda.

Sipping her sangría, Sabrina hesitated, not wanting to give Carlos an opportunity in which to press his attentions upon her. She liked her cousin, but she was not in love with him, and she didn't want him to love her. It was all very well to listen to his flirtatious nonsense under the approving eye of Tía Francisca, but it was quite another matter to hear it without the protection of another person.

But Carlos didn't give her any choice. Taking her silence as an affirmation, he firmly guided her to the chairs and saw that she was seated. Sitting down beside her, he said with deceptive idleness, "You seem very quiet this evening, *querida*. Is there a reason? Is something wrong?"

While dancing, Sabrina had been able to push aside her unhappy thoughts, but now they all came rushing back—especially since she had spied Brett leading a smiling Señora Morales from the dance floor. She had never been a jealous person, but watching the seductive sway of the older woman's black silk skirts, seeing the proprietorial way Constanza laid her white hand on Brett's arm, Sabrina viewed the pair through a decidedly green haze. With an effort she forced her gaze away from the other two and replied stiltedly, "Of course there is nothing wrong. I am just not in a talkative mood, that's all."

"I see," Carlos said slowly, seeing far more than Sabrina realized. Carlos's gaze went to Brett and Constanza, and he murmured, "I am glad there is nothing wrong. I would hate for the gringo to cause you any pain."

Sabrina gave a nervous laugh and said sharply, "Don't be ridiculous! *He* means nothing to me."

"Which is just as well," Carlos replied smoothly. "I would be very jealous, *querida*, and besides, it is apparent that he is deeply enamored of Señora Morales."

"Oh, I wouldn't say that!" Sabrina protested too quickly. "They only met tonight, and while he has been paying her a great deal of attention, I suspect it means nothing." Her jawline suddenly hard, she said grimly, "He is just a practiced flirt—he cares for no woman."

"They didn't just meet tonight," Carlos stated slyly. "They met last Wednesday when your father brought Señor Dangermond into town. I was there, and it was obvious even then that they were much taken with one another. Who knows—if Constanza had a fortune there might be a marriage in the wind."

Stiffly she muttered, "I think you make too much of a few chance encounters."

"Chance encounters, my dear?" Carlos questioned with a cynical lift of his thin eyebrow. "Hardly that! Especially not since I have seen his horse tied behind her house for the past few evenings. *Late* in the evening."

Sabrina swallowed with difficulty, wishing she could tell Carlos to shut his mouth. She didn't want to hear what he was saying, she wanted only to bury her head in the sand and pray that Señora Morales would simply disappear.

But instead she lifted her head proudly and looking Carlos straight in the eye, said bluntly, "I wonder if your interest in Señora Morales really has faded! You certainly seem to be *very* concerned about her affairs! Even to the point of spying on who comes to visit her!"

"I was not spying!" Carlos returned furiously. "It merely happens that I have had business in town that takes me past her home."

"The *rear* of her home? Late?" Sabrina asked sweetly.

Carlos flushed, but then, forcing a smile on his mouth, he reached for one of Sabrina's hands and said softly, "Come now, don't let us argue! Constanza and Dangermond mean nothing to us, so let us not talk of them anymore."

"I never was talking about them!" Sabrina said tartly. "*You* were the one who kept bringing them into the conversation."

Suppressing an urge to slap her, Carlos contented himself with merely shrugging his shoulders and saying mildly, "Perhaps this is so, but I no longer want to talk about them." An intimate note in his voice, he murmured, "I would far rather talk about us . . . and our marriage, *querida.*"

Sabrina snatched her hand away from him. "Carlos, I'm not in love with you, and I don't want to marry you," she said sincerely, the amber-gold eyes troubled as she looked at him. He was so dear, was such a good friend to her, but she could not allow him to entertain false hopes that one day she would change her mind. She touched his cheek lightly. "Find someone else," she said softly. "There are many lovely young girls here tonight who would make you a far better wife than I ever would, even if I consented to marry you. I would only make you unhappy."

"I don't want anyone else!" Carlos ground out exasperatedly. "A marriage between us has long been the wish of our parents, and you are just being contrary in refusing me!"

Trying to lighten the atmosphere, she smiled at him

teasingly and said, "See! I *would* make you unhappy—you're angry with me already."

Conscious he was pushing her too fast and too hard, Carlos smiled back at her and dropped her hand. "Very well, *querida*, for now I shall let you have your way." A humorous twist to his mouth, he added, "Just as I always do."

Relieved that Carlos had followed her lead so easily, Sabrina relaxed back in her chair and gratefully sipped on her sangría. The subject of Brett and Constanza may have been ended between them, but Brett's pursuit of the lovely widow was certainly uppermost in Sabrina's mind. Unwillingly her eyes went to where they were standing, and not even aware of what she was saying, she muttered, "If he does marry her, she has my pity—he would be a devil of a husband!"

Carlos stiffened in the seat beside her, his black eyes suddenly intent. "Devil," he said slowly, as if trying the word out on his tongue. *"Devil* Dangermond." Memory flooding back, he snapped his fingers, saying excitedly, "Of course! *That's* where I've seen him before! Devil Dangermond! The smuggler Frenchie's bully!"

Bewilderedly Sabrina looked at him. "What are you talking about?"

Carlos swiveled in his seat to face her, his narrow, handsome face alight with a curious satisfaction. "I kept thinking that I had met Dangermond somewhere before, but I couldn't remember where—until you said the word 'devil,' and then it all came back to me." Grasping both her hands tightly in his, he said urgently, "He is a bad man, Sabrina, a dangerous man! I wonder if your father realizes what sort of depraved creature he has opened his house to. A smuggler's bully and a murderous brute, that is what the fine Señor Dangermond really is!"

Her face shocked and disbelieving, Sabrina said faintly, "You must be mistaken! I know from my Tía Sofia's letters that he has a wild reputation, but never that he has done anything shameful or unlawful."

"And I tell you that he has!" Carlos returned passionately. "Remember when I went to New Orleans the last time?" At Sabrina's affirmative nod, he went on, "Just before my sister Catalina's wedding?" Sabrina nodded again. "Madre had asked that I purchase some particularly elegant material for Catalina's wedding gown, and that was when I met the smuggler Frenchie." His eyes grave, he said, "This Frenchie has a terrible reputation, Sabrina, including robbery and murder. They say he even betrays and murders his own kind, but he is so powerful that even if they fear for their lives, the ship captains still trade with him."

A self-righteous note entering his voice, he murmured, "Normally I would have had nothing to do with such a creature, but having exhausted the resources of New Orleans in search of material that would please Madre and Catalina, I was told to seek out Frenchie because he had just received an excellent supply of wonderful French silks." Carlos shrugged his shoulders. "What could I do? I could not return home empty-handed! And so I went in search of this notorious smuggler, and I found him in an ugly part of New Orleans. He did have the silks that I wanted, so I forced myself to deal with him." His voice lowering meaningfully, he announced, "And it was there, in that awful den, that I met Devil Dangermond! I had heard all sorts of wicked things about Frenchie's newest right-hand man, and so, when he showed me into Frenchie's back room, I was prepared for anything. All during my talk with Frenchie, he stood there glowering at me, almost as if he wished I would make some wrong move so that he would have an excuse to slit my throat then and there—not that his type needs an excuse," Carlos said darkly.

Still not wanting to believe Carlos's tale, Sabrina proposed hopefully, "Perhaps you were mistaken? I cannot believe it was the same man."

Carlos looked at her pityingly. "Señor Dangermond is not a man easily forgotten, nor is his name a common one. Are you going to have me believe that there are *two* Dangermonds of the same size and build, both with black hair and devil-green eyes?" Slowly Sabrina shook her head.

Triumph gleaming in his eyes, Carlos said bluntly, "Sabrina, he is a killer, a man beneath contempt! Why, he nearly killed a defenseless girl while I was there—I saw it with my own eyes!"

A gasp of shocked dismay came from Sabrina. "He struck a woman?" she demanded angrily.

"Worse," Carlos said smugly. "He cut her horribly with his knife!" Deferentially he muttered, "I had to stop him, even though the girl was not . . ." He looked embarrassed. "She was a woman of the streets, Sabrina. And they say he abused her disgracefully." Hastily he added, "I only learned that part later . . . after I had dragged him off her and thrown him out into the street."

Sabrina's hand was clenched into a fist. "Good for you, Carlos! It is too bad you did not mark him with his own knife—I wish you had!"

Modestly Carlos murmured, "It was nothing, my dear. And it was only the sheerest accident that I happened on the scene—I was on my way out of that place of depravity when I heard the most pitiful scream imaginable coming from the upper floor. Like any honorable gentleman, I immediately raced up the stairs to lend aid if I could. The screams were coming from a room to my right, and without thinking I broke the door down and there discovered, to my horror and revulsion, that black-hearted creature standing over the body of this poor young girl." His features revealing his pity and disgust, he continued, "Fortunately she was not dead, but he had marked her savagely with his knife, and when I faced him, he claimed she had tried to steal his money. It was all I could do to stop myself from taking that knife of his and marking him as he had that poor girl! Instead I had to content myself with showing him out of the building and threatening him with the law if he laid a hand on her again. And *that*, my dear, is the story of how I first met your Señor Dangermond."

Appalled and revolted by Carlos's tale, Sabrina glanced across at where Brett was talking to Constanza Morales. He didn't look like a depraved monster, but she had no reason to doubt her cousin and she had every reason to be suspicious of Brett Dangermond. What did she really know of him? Even Tía Sofia's letters seemed to condemn him, she thought, as she recalled Tía Sofia's worries about his wild life. He was seldom in Natchez, and so it was very possible that he had been in New Orleans, smuggling and abusing young women. Her heart rebelled against such thoughts, but her mind accepted them: she believed Carlos's tale.

Sickened and enraged at the way Brett had wormed his way into her father's affection, had traded shamelessly on that affection, she said breathlessly, "We must tell my father! He must be warned about him!"

Oddly enough, Carlos seemed to hesitate, but then, after a moment, he agreed. "Of course. It is what must be done! But I suggest that we wait until after the fiesta—there is no reason to cause an unfortunate scene now. Once your father knows the truth, he can send this villain away quietly, and no one except ourselves will ever know of this distasteful episode."

Slowly Sabrina nodded her head, knowing Carlos was right. After the fiesta would be soon enough for her father to learn the full extent of the depravity of a man he loved as dearly as he would have his own son. She quailed at the thought of her father's pain and disillusionment when they told him about Brett's sordid past, and for a second, she considered facing Brett alone and demanding that he leave. But she had to put that idea aside—her father had to know so that he would never again be deceived by that charming viper!

Looking at him filled her with rage, and it was all she could do not to stalk across the courtyard and denounce him. To think she'd been sorry that she had stabbed him! Her eyes glowed with that same fierce, feral gleam Ollie had seen. I wish I'd cut his throat! she thought vengefully.

That she was hiding behind anger and rage never occurred to her, any more than it had occurred to her to doubt Carlos's story. It was so wonderful after days of pining and feeling miserable to be able to *hate* the person who had captured her heart so underhandedly. To have a *reason* to treat him with disdain, to have all her earlier suspicions confirmed, was like a healing potion.

The remainder of the fiesta dragged for Sabrina, because her thoughts were so taken up with the coming confrontation. In a state of anxious anticipation, she waited impatiently for the moment in which she could unmask Brett Dangermond as the scoundrel he was. And yet, when that moment was finally upon her, she was struck by a sudden deep desire to say nothing. She didn't want to see her father's disillusionment . . . nor could she bear it if Brett tried to brazen out the situation and denied Carlos's story.

But Carlos would not let her retreat, and urging her forward, he was there at her side when she said to Alejandro, "Father, after the guests are gone, there is something important that Carlos and I must discuss with you."

His heart sinking, fearing that Carlos had convinced her to marry him, Alejandro said reluctantly, "Must it be tonight?"

Sabrina would have thankfully seized the postponement, but Carlos was taking no chances. His face determined, he said, "No, Tío, it *will* not wait! It is imperative that we speak tonight."

Sighing, Alejandro muttered, "Very well then. After the guests are gone, I will meet you in the library."

Sabrina nearly cried out in protest, not wanting the room where she had so nearly given herself to him to be the place where Brett's sordid and ugly past was laid out before her father. But Alejandro was already walking away.

When the actual moment came, it was nothing like Sabrina had expected. For one thing, her father seemed disappointed and displeased with *her,* and yet, when Carlos said quietly, "Sir, it is about your nephew, Brett Dangermond, that we must talk," Alejandro seemed to relax and appeared almost relieved.

"Oh?" he said mildly. "What has that young devil done now?"

"It is appropriate that you should call him a devil," Carlos said pompously. "For it is as *Devil* Dangermond that I first met him!"

Slightly mystified, Alejandro remarked, "You've met him before? *That's* what you wanted to tell me? And he was going by that ridiculous nickname of his?"

Carlos looked annoyed. "No, that is not what I wanted to tell you!" he snapped irritably. "When I was in New Orleans two years ago, I met him there, and"—his voice lowered portentously—*"he was aligned with, actually working for, the notorious smuggler Frenchie!"*

"Oh, *that!*" Alejandro said lightly. "I know all about it."

Her mouth open, Sabrina stared at her father. "You know about it?" she almost squeaked.

Alejandro nodded his head. "Of course. I was in New Orleans that summer, too, and I saw Brett then." Carelessly he added, "He told me all about it one evening when we had dinner together." There was a tap on the door just then, and after a nod from Alejandro, Sabrina went to open it. Her eyes went cold with dislike when she discovered Brett standing there. "What do *you* want?" she demanded ungraciously.

Brett quirked an eyebrow at her. "Bad mood, sweetheart?" he teased gently.

Hearing Brett's voice, Alejandro said, "Come in, Brett, come in. You should find this interesting."

Suddenly wary, remembering what had happened, or nearly happened, in this room, Brett entered. Seeing Carlos standing by the green velvet couch, he instantly guessed what was going on.

A smile on his face, Alejandro said with amusement, "We were just discussing your smuggling days."

"Oh, were you now?" Brett murmured easily, his eyes on Carlos's rigid face.

Sabrina came to stand next to Carlos, her face outraged and perplexed, and she asked her father, "Doesn't it *bother* you? I mean he was *smuggling!* And working with one of the most notorious smugglers in New Orleans!"

In a very good humor now that an announcement of their marriage wasn't forthcoming, Alejandro eyed Sabrina and Carlos fondly. "Oh, I don't let things like that bother me, my child. Besides, Brett has explained it all, and there was nothing shameful about it. Quite the contrary—it was very brave and noble of him."

"Noble!" Sabrina choked, staring at her father as if she had never seen him before. The fury she felt glittering in the amber-gold eyes, she shot Brett a look that should have felled him where he stood. *"That* is noble?" she spat scathingly. Turning back to her father, she demanded, "What about—"

Carlos gripped her hand painfully and spoke smoothly to his uncle. "Well, I see that our fears were totally unfounded. I am sorry that we took up your time, Tío. Will you excuse us? I will say good night to Sabrina and be on my way home."

Alejandro waved them affably from the room, and in an instant Carlos had whisked Sabrina away.

CHAPTER TWELVE

The door had barely shut behind them when Sabrina turned wrathfully on Carlos. "What did you do that for?" she snapped angrily. "Why didn't you let me tell him about the poor girl in New Orleans?"

Glancing over his shoulder at the closed door and then putting a finger to his mouth, he motioned for her to follow him.

Indecisively Sabrina glared at the door and then at Carlos's retreating figure. Her features set in stubborn lines, she turned reluctantly and walked in the direction Carlos had taken.

When they reached the front courtyard, Carlos stopped and looked at her. Heavily he said, "It is obvious that your father is completely within Dangermond's control." When Sabrina appeared unmoved by that statement, he added urgently, "Don't you see, I couldn't let you say anything about that girl—he wouldn't believe us. He might even think that we had made up the entire tale, that we were maliciously trying to discredit Dangermond in his eyes."

A mutinous expression on her face, Sabrina retorted hotly, "My father would never believe such a thing of me! But it's a risk I'm willing to take. He should know immediately just what sort of monster he has embraced!"

"I, too, want your father to know the truth!" Carlos said quickly. "But Sabrina, I don't think we can convince him right now of anything detrimental." His expression earnest, he complained bitterly, "You saw how lightly he took the news of Dangermond's involvement with the smugglers! Don't you see—Dangermond has won him over entirely! He will believe no wrong about him, no matter what we say!"

Some of the fury dying out of her face, an unhappy curve

to her mouth, Sabrina muttered bleakly, "What are we going to do? Let him increase his power over my father? Let him continue to deceive him?"

"No, no, of course not!" Carlos replied adamantly. "But we must bide our time, *querida*. And while doing that, we must do our best to protect your father from himself." Looking at her keenly, gauging the effect of his words, he said quietly, "You must watch this Dangermond and make certain he does nothing to cheat or trick your father. You must tell me everything that you learn, and together we will defeat this devil and save your father from his evil influence." Comfortingly he pressed her hand with his, his dark eyes full of compassion. "I will not let you fight this battle alone. Do not worry, my dear, now that we know Dangermond for the scoundrel he is, we will be able to circumvent whatever dastardly schemes he may plan. As for the incident with the unfortunate creature in New Orleans . . ." He hesitated and then said slowly, "I think we should say nothing more about it. It will be our secret, and when the time is right, we will face Dangermond with it in front of your father."

Miserably Sabrina agreed, seeing the wisdom of Carlos's words and yet uncomfortable with the situation. The thought of conniving against Alejandro with Carlos made her even more uncomfortable. Gloomily she said, "I never dreamed the day would come when I would find myself on opposite sides from my father." Uncertainly she bit her lip and then asked almost hopefully, "Don't you think we should try once more to convince my father of the truth?" Earnestly she added, "We don't know what that devil has told him—perhaps he lied about things, told my father only part of the truth. It may be my father doesn't really understand the full extent of Dangermond's actions. If we told him about the girl—"

"*No!*" Carlos retorted so sharply that Sabrina looked at him in surprise. He sent her a slight smile. "Not yet, *querida*. I know you are impatient, but you must trust me. When the time is right, I shall know it, and we will strike." His voice harsh, he went on, "Dangermond is clever—for all we know, he has already told your father some lying tale about the girl. He might even have claimed that *I* was the one who disfigured her and that *he* was the one who saved her!"

Her face filled with revulsion, Sabrina clenched her hand into a fist. "That contemptible swine!" she said heatedly. But then a puzzled expression flitted over her features. "He can't have done that, Carlos," she said slowly, thoughtfully. "If he had, my father would have said something to you about it . . . don't you agree?"

Carlos shrugged. "It's possible, but who knows what your father is thinking these days." Throwing her a grim look, he continued, "But I must warn you to be prepared for Dangermond to pull some sort of trick like that."

Her mouth tight, she replied gruffly, "I will be on my guard! Dangermond will not blind me as he has my father!"

Rather satisfied with the night's events, Carlos was able to take his leave of her a few minutes later with an almost light heart. There was even the faintest suggestion of a smile on his lips when he rode away from the del Torres hacienda.

Sabrina certainly wasn't smiling, nor was she satisfied with the evening's revelations. She was acutely miserable. The man she loved was a blackguard, and her father trusted him.

Alone in her bedroom, still wearing the lovely azure silk gown, she lay on her bed staring blankly at the ceiling overhead. If only Brett had never come to visit them. If only she had never seen him again, never fallen in love with him. She gave a bitter laugh. If only I loved Carlos, she thought suddenly, then none of this would matter so very much. It wouldn't hurt so deeply to hear that Brett Dangermond is a monster.

No, that wasn't true, she admitted honestly. Alejandro's unwavering admiration and affection for a man she knew to be an unscrupulous villain troubled her greatly. How *could* her father dismiss Brett's smuggling activities?

She knew that smuggling was a common practice in New Orleans; she was aware also that many people in that area considered it almost a respectable pastime. It was also true that many law-abiding citizens had regular business dealings with certain smugglers, but from what Carlos had said, it was apparent that this Frenchie was definitely not one of those. From Carlos's tale it was obvious that Frenchie was a true criminal, one of the lowest kind, a man capable of all sorts of wickedness—and Brett Dangermond, "Devil" Dangermond, had been his confidant.

It didn't seem possible that her father, so honest and fair, so very honorable, could easily forgive a man for doing the ugly things Brett must have done as Frenchie's trusted lieutenant—and yet it appeared he had. Heartsick and disillusioned, as much because of Alejandro's apparent culpability as the knowledge that the man she loved was nothing but a rogue, Sabrina felt her eyes fill with tears. Angrily she blinked them back. I will *not* cry, she vowed through gritted teeth.

She took a deep, shuddering breath, forcing herself not to dwell on her own unhappiness. At least, she thought bleakly, she was on her guard now. She would have to be the wise one in this situation. As Carlos had said, Alejandro was completely in Brett's power, and it was up to her to save him—somehow she must find a way to protect her father from Dangermond's wicked influence.

For a moment, thinking of Carlos and what he had said that evening, her unhappiness abated and she was suffused with a rush of warmth and affection. How eager Carlos had been to help, she reflected fondly. He had said that together they would defeat Dangermond, and together they would! she thought with growing confidence, her heartache easing just a little. She wasn't alone anymore—Carlos would help her!

She was too young and inexperienced to realize that she might be the one who needed protection. She and Carlos saw each other nearly every day, Carlos made sure of that; and any wavering or uncertainty on Sabrina's part was quickly and ruthlessly squashed. Repeatedly he counseled her to beware—Dangermond was an obvious fortune hunter. Her mind listened intently and absorbed his warnings and hints of even darker deeds, but her heart . . . her heart resisted, and she was torn by the fierce battle that raged within her.

164

At first it was simple to let anger rule her head, and during the weeks that followed the fiesta, she treated Brett with ill-concealed contempt. Protective of her father, suspicious of every move Brett made, she guarded Alejandro like a tigress with cubs. Every suggestion Brett made was met with a barrage of questions and mule-headed resistance on Sabrina's part. Particularly anything to do with the sugar cane project. Carlos had warned her repeatedly when they met at the gazebo that Brett was probably using the sugar cane scheme as a way to swindle a fortune out of Alejandro, and consequently she fought bitterly against it.

Her attitude toward Brett did not go unnoticed by the men in the household, that and the jealous way she dogged Alejandro's footsteps. Brett chose to be amused by her antics, finding it far safer to have her greeting him with hostility than with her nearly irresistible charm. He was annoyed, though, having guessed correctly that Carlos had a hand in her actions, but then he dismissed even that emotion—he was *not* going to let himself get involved with Sabrina del Torres!

For the most part Alejandro, too, was amused by Sabrina's attitude, and like Brett he was also annoyed and just a little worried. It wasn't like Sabrina to take someone in such sudden, inexplicable dislike, and it was hardly the frame of mind needed for her to fall in love with Brett. The meetings with Carlos at the gazebo had not been missed by Alejandro either, nor the fact that Carlos seemed to spend an inordinate amount of time at the del Torres hacienda these days. Too many afternoons he and Brett returned home to find Sabrina and Carlos laughing and talking on the patio as they drank tall glasses of sangría. The fear that Sabrina was falling in love with her cousin could not be dismissed, and coupled with her dislike of Brett, it dismayed Alejandro.

He was dismayed on several counts, not least of which was the fact that the de la Vega finances had not improved in the months since Sabrina's birthday. The full extent of their money problems had been made apparent to him when recently he had lent his brother-in-law a sizable sum to help the family during their time of trouble. The loan didn't worry him, but Carlos's attitude did.

Alejandro had always known that Carlos was spoiled —as the youngest child, he was his mother's pet and his father's pride. Often Alejandro had chided both Luis and Francisca for the way they pandered to and coddled Carlos, but it had never really bothered him. Of course, he had never seriously thought that Carlos would one day be his son-in-law either! It was not a pleasant reflection on Alejandro's part. One evening when Carlos joined them for dinner, he surreptitiously compared the two young men sharing his table. Seeing the lively humor that danced in Brett's jade-green eyes, as opposed to the hint of malice that occasionally flickered through the black eyes of Carlos, Alejandro shook his head disgustedly. How could Sabrina possibly choose Carlos over Brett? It was totally incomprehensible!

The weeks and months that followed the fiesta which introduced Brett to the neighbors and friends of the del Torreses were curious times. No one at the hacienda was deeply unhappy, and yet no one was particularly pleased with the atmosphere either. There was nothing that could be pinpointed as a problem, but there was a feeling of tenseness, of unease and concern, that seemed to permeate the air they breathed. Life was serene and untroubled on the surface, but underneath it was rife with a wide variety of violent and often conflicting emotions.

Brett began to spend more time working with the men who were busily clearing the forest, and Alejandro viewed his accomplishments and dedication with a mixture of admiration and frustration. The scheme of growing sugar had been only an excuse to invite Brett to visit, and to see that young man throw himself into the project so wholeheartedly made him feel just a trifle guilty. He was pleased with the work being done, but he would have preferred that Brett spend *some* of his time wooing Sabrina. The important thing was that Sabrina and Brett fall in love. With Brett slaving all the daylight hours in the widening areas of cleared land and Sabrina spending languid hours with Carlos, how could that come about? As the days passed, Alejandro's hopes for a marriage between his daughter and the man of his choice grew dimmer.

Had he been privy to Brett's dreams and Sabrina's thoughts, Alejandro wouldn't have been so downcast. Sabrina might have had frequent dealings with Carlos, but she was in no danger of losing her heart to him. He was her cousin and her friend, nothing more. And as far as she was concerned, he never would be anything else to her despite his efforts to change the relationship between them.

In the beginning, numb and unhappy, Sabrina had only listlessly countered Carlos's amorous advances. As April gave way to May, and May faded into June, she found herself growing more and more annoyed and ill at ease in his company. She didn't like the position she was finding herself thrust into more and more. Nor was she ever really comfortable with repeating to Carlos conversations that she had either had with Brett or overheard between Brett and her father. There was something so very *sneaky* about it.

Carlos's constant harping on what a fortune hunter Brett was, how they must watch and be ever alert for his nefarious schemes, also began to wear on her patience. And to her surprise she began to argue back with him. "Carlos," she had said firmly, one day in late June when they had met at the gazebo, "you're wrong about Brett using the sugar cane as a means to get money from my father. *He* isn't getting one peso! Instead, we are gaining a very competent overseer who has accomplished much during these past weeks—look at how many acres have been cleared! Look at how swiftly the sugar mill is progressing." An admiring gleam in the amber-gold eyes, she had murmured softly, "He may have had dealings with smugglers, but I think he must have put that part of his life behind him. I've seen nothing and heard of nothing that should alarm us."

An unbecoming flush staining his cheeks, Carlos had snapped, "Have you forgotten about the girl? The one he cut up and disfigured in New Orleans?"

Her eyes suddenly shadowed, Sabrina had turned away. "No, I haven't forgotten," she had said slowly. "But people do change. . . ."

His face had twisted with thwarted fury, and Carlos had raged, "I do not believe this! This man is a smuggler, a thug, and a bully, a defiler of young women, and you dare to make excuses for him! Bah! Run along, Sabrina! Run back to him and let him whisper lies in your ears! Let him work that specious charm of his on you until you are no more than a fawning bitch running at his heels like Constanza Morales!"

Nothing could have been better calculated to bring Sabrina once more under his influence. Seeing the angry flash of her amber-gold eyes and the determined slant to her finely molded jaw, Carlos had smiled.

But while Carlos could poison her mind against Brett and arouse her temper, there was one thing he could not do. He could not stop her from discussing events with her father. And there came an afternoon when Sabrina and Alejandro found themselves alone as they shared a tall glass of lemonade on the patio. They were seated at the iron table, relaxing in the cooling depths of the shadows of the tall pine tree that overhung the patio. It was the first time in ages that they had spent any time alone together, and each was savoring it. The conversation was desultory, and then somehow, out of nowhere, the subject of Brett's days in New Orleans came up. From there it was only moments before the truth of Brett's activities came out.

Alejandro stared at Sabrina's stunned face and murmured teasingly, "Chica, I cannot believe that you thought I would harbor a criminal in my house! When the smuggling was mentioned the night of the fiesta, I naturally assumed that you and Carlos knew the truth. It never occurred to me that all these weeks you've been under the impression that I have been in the clutches of a—what did you call him? A monster?"

Sabrina sent him an embarrassed smile and nodded her head. Defensively she muttered, "We had no way of knowing otherwise. Carlos's meeting with him was brief. How could he have known that Brett was only there to trap his friend's murderer?"

Alejandro's voice hardened slightly. "I am surprised at Carlos. Surely he must have realized that I would never have introduced such a man to my relatives and friends,

168

let alone allowed him free access to my house?" Shaking his head, Alejandro finished, "I do not understand Carlos these days. He must know that his father needs all the help he can get to save the *rancho,* and yet Carlos does not appear willing to raise a hand to help him." His face grew grim. "Instead he spends his time filling my daughter's head with nonsense!"

Sabrina hastened to reassure him, and the conversation went on to other topics. She had not mentioned the girl. Carlos's strictures on the need for complete secrecy were too deeply embedded in her brain. But with the news of Brett's real reasons for being in the smuggler's den, her faith in her father was restored, and if the treatment of the girl in New Orleans had tarnished her image of Brett, at least she felt easier about him.

The next day, she ran to meet Carlos with a happy glow in her cheeks, and almost merrily she blurted out the story to him. As could be expected, Carlos was not well pleased with the situation.

"And you believe this tale?" he sneered.

"Why shouldn't I?" she asked with obvious bewilderment.

"Because, you little fool," Carlos ground out, "it is apparent that Dangermond must have concocted this lying story to appease your father. Are you so stupid, so blind, that you, too, will be tricked?"

Perhaps if this confrontation had come the day after the shocking news of Brett's involvement with smugglers, Sabrina might have been swayed by Carlos's words. But as it was, she'd had time to deal with her hurt and disillusionment, and her own common sense had reasserted itself. Brett's actions these past months had not been those of a villain, and while she might concede it was all an act to lull them into a sense of security before he struck, she doubted it. And she certainly did not appreciate Carlos's inference that Alejandro was both stupid and blind! Her face cold, she said icily, "My father is neither stupid nor blind! Nor, may I add, am I! I think you are the one who is being blind, *amigo!* You have nourished a dislike against Brett, with what I will admit appeared good reason, but now it is you who will not recognize the truth! You *want*

169

him to be a smuggler, and because of that you will not listen to the real story."

Aware that he had crossed onto dangerous ground and unwilling to destroy the tenuous thread that existed between them, Carlos quickly capitulated. But it wasn't quite the same. Now that there was obviously no longer the need to spy on the men of her household, Sabrina found herself more and more disinclined to meet so often with Carlos.

If the rapport between Sabrina and Carlos had lessened, the current of awareness that flowed between Brett and Sabrina had not. Now that she knew the truth of his days with the smugglers, Sabrina caught herself once again responding foolishly to his potent masculinity. She hadn't forgotten what he had done to the girl in New Orleans, but she couldn't help but wonder if perhaps there wasn't some explanation for that, too.

Brett noticed the change in her attitude toward him almost immediately, and he speculated warily on what had caused it. Where before she had scowled when he entered her presence and had thrown him a look of scathing dislike, she now spoke pleasantly and even, upon occasion, smiled at him. Bemused by that sweet smile, he hadn't been able to resist her shy overtures of friendship. And when Alejandro had explained the misconception she had been laboring under, Brett had been astounded at how delighted he was that Sabrina had discovered the truth and was no longer treating him as if he were a leper.

His affair with Constanza had been extremely carnal in nature . . . and short-lived as well. By the time mid-July arrived, that casual liaison had ended amicably. And whatever satisfaction he may have gained from Constanza's ripe, willing body had been completely negated by the so very *un*satisfactory dreams of a certain flame-haired young witch that had haunted his sleep all too frequently. Grimly denying the unwanted attraction he felt for Sabrina, he had thrown himself into the physically exhausting work of taming the virgin wilderness. He was not often to be found at the hacienda; he rose at dawn and worked until twilight fell despite the increasingly hot and humid weather.

170

After Sabrina's conversation with Alejandro, the atmosphere at the hacienda lightened perceptibly. Brett began to stop work earlier and earlier in the afternoons. Arriving back at the hacienda, he would swim in the lake by the gazebo and then spend the remainder of the day with Sabrina and Alejandro. They whiled away long, enjoyable hours in the cool, shaded courtyard, sipping tall, icy refreshments prepared by the servants. With pleasure and relief, Alejandro noticed that Sabrina no longer met with Carlos so frequently. Alejandro almost began to hope that his fondest desire might actually come true—Sabrina had taken to wearing her prettiest gowns for their afternoons together, and Brett didn't appear exactly immune to her beauty.

Sabrina's eighteenth birthday was less than a week away. The hacienda was bustling with preparations for a grand fiesta. Staring thoughtfully at Brett and Sabrina one evening as they slowly wandered through the outer grounds of the hacienda, Alejandro could not help thinking that the night of the birthday fiesta would be an excellent time to announce their betrothal.

The swiftness with which this wonderful state of affairs had come about had been startling to both Brett and Sabrina. They seemed to have put aside their reservations and were enjoying a rapport that was similar to the one they had shared years ago—with one very vital difference—Sabrina was no longer a child. Watching her laughing face as they walked through the forest, he wondered how he had ever thought that Constanza's opulent charms would overshadow the powerful attraction that Sabrina held for him. That realization had caused him to end his relationship with Constanza weeks earlier. In the time that had followed, as he fell more and more under Sabrina's spell, that brief liaison faded from his mind. There was only room for Sabrina in his thoughts, and for the first time in his life, the iron guard around his heart began to slip.

Constanza was only a faint niggle in the back of Sabrina's mind; she was fairly certain that he was no longer seeing the other woman. When she glanced at Brett and saw the warm glint in his eyes as their gazes met, her heart leaped. Surely he wouldn't look at her like that if he was still seeing Constanza? A bubble of joy surged through her as she sent him a blinding smile of pure happiness.

Brett blinked at the sheer charm of that smile and said huskily, "Infant, you should warn us poor males before you flash that sweet smile—it can have a devastating effect on the unprepared!"

Sabrina dimpled and Brett was unable to stop himself from reaching out and gently caressing her mouth, his finger lingering on her bottom lip. Sabrina nipped him lightly and Brett smiled, a smile no other woman had ever seen. Softly he said, "I think you are bewitching me. I find that I am looking forward to these afternoons together far too much for my liking—if I am not careful, you will command all of my time."

"Would that be so very bad?" Sabrina asked breathlessly.

His smile faded and his gaze wandered over her upturned face. "No," he said slowly, "no, I don't think it would be at all."

Sabrina looked away. Shyly she murmured, "I have noticed that you spend more time at the hacienda . . . is there nothing in Nacodgoches that holds your interest these days?"

Gently Brett turned her face to his. His expression was tender as he said quietly, "Nacodgoches has nothing for me—it really never did, only I was too blind to see it. . . ."

But if the situation at the hacienda had grown better, the situation with Carlos was deteriorating rapidly. Though Sabrina refused to meet him as often as she had in the past, she did still see him frequently. But the encounters between them were uncomfortable and strained. She was unhappily aware that Carlos had not really changed his opinion of Brett, and there were even times, late at night, alone in her room, when she wondered if she wasn't allowing herself to be caught up by Brett's dark charm. Perhaps Carlos was right. . . . No! She didn't want to believe it! But if she who loved him had doubts, how could she possibly condemn Carlos for his suspicions?

On the Monday afternoon before her birthday fiesta on Friday, Sabrina made her way reluctantly toward the gazebo to meet Carlos. She had made up her mind to tell Carlos that there was no longer any need for these secretive assignations. Somehow, whenever she met with Carlos at the gazebo, she felt as if she were doing something unsavory.

The day was hot, and even though she had just donned a gown of cool lavender linen, by the time she reached the gazebo it was sticking uncomfortably to her back. Pushing back a strand of the red-gold hair that had a tendency to tumble across her forehead, she slowly entered the welcoming shade of the gazebo.

Carlos was already there, lounging carelessly against the bright yellow and green pillows.

At Sabrina's entrance, the petulant expression that had been on his face vanished and he stood up and smiled at her warmly. *"Querida,* you came! I had just begun to fear that today also you were going to disappoint me." Almost a note of censure in his voice, he added, "I miss you a great deal, and since you no longer meet with me as frequently as you once did, I find my days long and lonely."

Sabrina sent him a strained smile. Moving nervously around the gazebo, she said distractedly, "I would have thought that you would have been very busy of late. I know that Brett is."

Seeing the way Carlos's eyes narrowed and his mouth tightened, Sabrina could have bitten her tongue. Placatingly she muttered, "But, of course, he wouldn't be if it weren't for the sugar cane lands."

Carlos snorted. "Sugar cane! Do not speak to me about *that!* I still cannot understand your father's reasoning. If you want my opinion, it is a foolish waste of time and money! Brett Dangermond is the only one who is going to gain anything!"

Knowing it was useless to try to convince him otherwise, and aware of a small flicker of doubt within herself, she said coolly, "Perhaps. But I didn't come here to discuss either Señor Brett or my father."

Recognizing that he was doing his own cause little good, Carlos forced himself to act naturally. His black eyes soft, he patted the orange cushion next to him. "Come, *querida.* Come and sit by me, and let us talk. Of late it seems too often we quarrel."

Sabrina cast a longing glance at the doorway and then slowly walked over and sat down beside him. Wanting the unpleasantness over as soon as possible, she said abruptly, "Carlos, I don't really think we have much to talk of these days. I . . . I . . ." She hesitated and sent him a troubled look. "I don't want to come here to meet you anymore." Having got the most difficult words out, she smiled encouragingly at him and said in a rush, "We can still see each other as often as you like—you know that you are always welcome at the hacienda."

Carlos stiffened, and something ugly entered those black eyes. His voice slurred with anger, he snapped, "It is Dangermond, isn't it? He has turned you against me!" Warming to his theme, he raged, "I have seen it coming! The way your eyes light up when you say his name, the way you praise him, and now you will allow him to destroy what is between us!"

"That's not true!" she retorted hotly. "There never was anything between us! You delude yourself if you think there was."

"Oh, do I?" he said softly, in a tone of voice alarming to Sabrina. That and the way he turned to look at her, his mouth twisting into a smile that wasn't a smile at all. Slowly the black eyes roamed over her face, and then, to her surprise, he reached out and gently touched her cheek. His voice low, he muttered, "I think you delude yourself. Always there has been something between us, but you will not let it grow. You hide from it, but I tell you that it is there, and I cannot let you ignore it any longer." Almost crooning, a glazed look in his eyes, he went on, "You are meant to be mine, *querida*. And I will not let Dangermond poison your mind against me. Today I shall have to prove to you how completely you are mine." An arrested expression flickered across his face, and he murmured almost to himself, "Of course. Why didn't I think of it before?" His hands moved to capture her shoulders, and swiftly he dragged her up against his chest. His mouth inches from hers, he muttered, "Forgive me, *querida*, for what I am about to do, but there is no other way! You *must* be mine, my wife, and I can see only one way in which to bring that about!"

Sabrina didn't understand what he meant, but instinctively she began to fight, her hands pushing ineffectually against his chest. Carlos ignored her struggles, his mouth pressing down avidly on hers, his tongue forcing its way into her mouth.

Furious and frightened, Sabrina fought like the tigress she so often resembled, but while she and Carlos were of much the same height, he was much stronger, and her attempts to escape were fruitless. He was like a man possessed, his hands tearing at her gown and his own clothes. Sabrina's dress was torn from her shoulder, and with mingled rage and fear, she felt his sinewy hand fondling her naked breast. To her horror she realized that he had ripped away the upper portion of her gown and she was naked from the waist up.

Aware that she could not best him in a battle of strength, she stopped her wild thrashings, and freeing her mouth from his, attempted to reason with him. "Carlos, *querido*," she pleaded softly, "please, *please* . . . ." Her sentence wasn't finished as Carlos muffled her lips with his.

During their fight, Sabrina had been pinned down on the cushions by Carlos's heavier body. She hadn't been deeply frightened at first, but as the moments passed, and Carlos showed no inclination to stop his assault, fright grew within her. His hands seemed to be everywhere, his mouth plundering hers with increasingly passionate, probing kisses that affected her quite, *quite* differently from Brett's kisses. She could feel nausea rising up in her throat—that and hysteria. When his hand slid up her thighs, pushing the lavender gown up around her waist, Sabrina knew a quiver of pure panic. *He was going to rape her!*

She heard the sound of her delicate undergarments being torn away, and it galvanized her into further fight. Uselessly her fists beat against Carlos's back, and frantically she twisted and squirmed beneath him, trying desperately to throw off his crushing weight. Her mouth ached from his brutal kisses, and feeling him pressing his loins against hers, feeling his body slipping between her thighs, was terrifying. This was no delight; there was no joy, no pleasure, in what was happening to her. She was

175

full of fear and fury, and blindly she struck out at Carlos's face.

He muttered something guttural under his breath, his chest heaving with his exertions and the passion that consumed him, but her blow did not slow or deter him. If anything it seemed to goad him on, and he groaned deep in his throat, grinding their bodies together in an obscene parody of lovemaking. His hand fumbled with the fastenings of his calzoneras, and for one sickening, terrible moment, she felt his hardened flesh probing between her legs.

She stiffened in shocked rejection of his actions, her mind refusing to accept what was about to happen. *This can't be happening to me!* Carlos would never treat me this way! she thought with stunned disbelief. But he was, and his hand stroking the soft hair between her thighs, his fingers preparing the way for him, infused her struggles with a new, maddened strength. It seemed to have no effect on him, and with something akin to enraged despair, she sensed he was readying himself to join their bodies together as he braced his hips and pulled her closer to his engorged manhood. Then, suddenly, like a frigid blast from the Arctic, an icy voice inquired, "Am I interrupting something?"

CHAPTER THIRTEEN

The sound of Brett's voice was the sweetest sound in the world to Sabrina, and her body sagged with relief. Carlos jerked furiously away from her and with angry movements pulled the calzoneras back up around his waist. His face a vicious mask, he stared ferociously across the gazebo at Brett.

Sabrina struggled up into a sitting position, her trembling hands automatically trying to make some semblance of order of her ripped and torn clothing. Thank God Brett had come! Another second, another moment, and she would have been utterly ruined!

Shame and gratitude warred in the oddly timid glance she flashed to Brett, but at the expression of disgust and contempt revealed by the hard, set features of his lean face, she was flooded with mortification so intense that her entire body ached with it. Surely he didn't think . . . He couldn't think . . .

It appeared he did. The dark green eyes flickered disdainfully over her disheveled state, and in a taut, distasteful voice, he drawled, "You'll forgive my interruption, I hope. I didn't realize that the gazebo was . . . *occupied.* If you'll let me know what hours you use it for your assignations, I'll arrange my swim for a later time."

Sabrina's face flamed with both humiliation and fury. Smothering a gasp of outrage, she gathered her tattered clothing to her, and after throwing a look of utter loathing at the two men, she fled the gazebo.

There was an ugly, dangerous silence after she left. Casually Carlos straightened his clothes, a complacent smile on his lips. "You gringos," he said lightly. "Always so impetuous and impolite. Surely you knew the gazebo was occupied—and what we were doing. Sabrina is never quiet in her lovemaking, and you must have heard her begging for me to take her." Shaking his head, he added with apparent good humor, "Ah, well. It is too bad you arrived when you did. But in the future you will take more care not to disturb us, *sí?*"

Brett *had* heard Sabrina pleading, "Please, please." But he hadn't believed his own ears. He had come down to take his usual afternoon swim, and upon catching a glimpse of the writhing bodies through the lattice of the gazebo, had started to turn away, assuming a pair of servants were using the small building for a lovers' rendezvous. The sound of Sabrina's voice had stopped him dead in his tracks, and like a man of ice, a frozen zombie, he had walked up the stairs of the gazebo and looked in. The sight that had met his eyes was seared agonizingly in his brain. Sabrina's nearly naked body thrusting lustfully beneath Carlos's as they kissed hungrily, her arms flailing about wildly as passion consumed her.

Coldly he said, "You'll understand if I don't care to discuss the situation with you. What you and Sabrina do is your business! But I'd be damned careful not to let Alejandro be subject to a scene such as the one that I just interrupted. I don't think he could handle it as unemotionally."

Carlos shrugged. "It wouldn't matter. He would demand that Sabrina and I marry at once, which would suit us admirably."

"Which makes me wonder," Brett mused out loud, "why you're waiting? What do you hope to gain?"

Carlos shrugged again. Malice gleaming in the black eyes, he said softly, "I do not want to wait. I haven't since Sabrina first gave herself to me—but then *you* appeared!" With loathing he spat, "You with your great fortune! And now she delays, unwilling to commit herself fully to me, until she knows that there is no hope of a marriage with you."

His face unrevealing, the dark green eyes shuttered and empty, Brett turned away. Over his shoulder, he said curtly, "Rest assured, *amigo,* that you have nothing to fear from me! I wouldn't marry Sabrina del Torres if she were offered to me wrapped in diamonds and lying on a golden platter!"

178

A pleased smile on his mouth, Carlos watched Brett stride away. Things really hadn't worked out too badly, he thought smugly, as he caught up the reins of his tethered horse and prepared to ride away from the gazebo. The plan to dishonor Sabrina and force their marriage had been hasty and ill-conceived. This was *much* better. Dangermond was disgusted by her and certainly would not ever, *now,* consider her for a wife. It was true he was going to have to mend his fences with Sabrina, but with patience and charm, Carlos was positive, he could re-establish himself in her affections. It would be difficult, but he had all the happy years of their childhood to help him.

The passion that Sabrina had aroused gnawed at him, and cruelly he dug his spurs into the silken hide of the fine animal he rode. Constanza. He would go to Constanza.

A short while later, he pulled his lathered horse to a stop in the pine forest behind Constanza's small house and with rapid steps, crossed the empty courtyard at the rear of the house. He rapped emphatically on the wooden door, and when a servant opened it, he roughly brushed past her, demanding curtly, "Your mistress, where is she?"

"In the *sala, señor.*"

Swiftly he found his way to the salon, and he breathed a sigh of relief at seeing Constanza alone.

She looked up expectantly when he entered the room, but when she saw who it was, something died out of the fine, dark eyes. *"Buenos días,* Carlos," she said coolly. "What have I done to deserve your visit?" Almost petulantly, she added, "You have not been by to visit me for some time now."

Carlos smiled sarcastically. Cruelly he said, "Six weeks ago, you would not have been pleased to see me—then you had the gringo."

Slowly her eyes traveled over him, noting with a slumberous glow the slight swelling near the crotch of his calzoneras. Her mouth curving sensuously, she murmured, "But you did *not* have your Sabrina . . . or did you?"

With a low growl, he crossed the room and jerked her off the elegant silk-covered sofa. Ruthlessly his mouth plundered hers, Constanza's body melting against his, her lips

179

opening eagerly under the demand of his. *"Querido,"* she breathed deeply a moment later, "I have missed you."

"Especially these past weeks," he taunted, his hands busily exploring her ripe curves.

An odd smile on her mouth, she agreed huskily, *"Especially* these past weeks." Deliberately she reached down and freed his throbbing manhood from the calzoneras, her fingers sliding warmly around it.

Carlos groaned low in his throat and buried his mouth on hers. In the grip of blind, animal passion, he pushed her down to the floor. Savagely he shoved her skirts up, and grunting his pleasure he entered her.

They mated like animals, Constanza driven wild by the fierceness with which he took her, and the delicious fear of discovery made the act even more exciting. If a servant should enter . . . Carlos's teeth closed over the breast he had just freed, and Constanza thought of nothing else but the ecstasy of having a man once more.

Ten minutes later, she rang for a servant, and the heavyset Indian woman who entered the room would never have imagined that only minutes before her mistress and Señor de la Vega had been writhing on the floor in a paroxysm of passion. Stony-faced, Maria, the servant, listened as her mistress demanded refreshments for the guest.

Alone again, Carlos sprawled comfortably in a high-backed chair of brown leather. Constanza sat demurely across from him, her skirts discreetly arranged.

They said nothing until after Maria had returned with Madeira for Carlos and hot chocolate for Constanza. When the servant had departed, Constanza said, "The suit with Sabrina must be prospering if she sends you to me in such a condition."

Carlos made a disgruntled sound. "Yes and no. Today I would have forced her into a position in which it would have been imperative that we marry—but that cursed gringo interfered!" His hand closed into a fist, his face twisting. "I should kill him!"

"No!" Constanza blurted out before she could stop herself. To her mortification, she felt a blush rush into her cheeks at the knowing look Carlos sent her.

180

"Ah!" Carlos purred, his black eyes unkind. "This gringo means something to you."

Constanza bit her lip and for something to do, took a sip of the hot chocolate. "Not exactly," she said a second later. A queer look flashed across her face. Her voice full of bewilderment, almost as if she didn't understand her own emotions, she muttered, "He was very different from what I expected. And with his wealth and . . ." She shrugged her shoulders. "It was a foolish notion of mine, one he never encouraged or guessed. Besides, I'd make him a wretched wife."

"You actually considered marriage?" Carlos said, his face full of incredulity. Sneeringly he added, "He must have been wonderfully proficient. And magnificently well-endowed."

"He was indeed!" Constanza snapped, her dark eyes sparkling with anger. "He would split your sweet Sabrina in two—and leave her moaning for him to do it again!"

Carlos sucked in his breath with rage. Sitting up in the chair, he snarled, "He will never have Sabrina! I saw to *that* this afternoon!"

Both seemed to realize how very near they were to a falling out, and with an obvious effort, Carlos brought his temper under control. Throwing himself back against the chair, he said conciliatorily, "Come now, *querida,* don't let *us* fight! It is Sabrina and Brett who must be kept in dissension."

Constanza gave him a rueful smile. "You are right, *amigo.* I do not know what came over me." She shook her head and said teasingly, "Perhaps I needed you more than I knew." They smiled at each other.

Casually Constanza inquired, "What did you mean about seeing to *that* this afternoon?"

Carlos took a long swallow of his Madeira. Satisfaction written across his dark features, he said smugly, "He caught Sabrina and me in a *very* compromising situation—I let him think that we were lovers and that we made love often. He will not touch her now. He would not want what he thinks is my leavings."

An odd note in her voice, she asked, "Do you think there was any danger of him wanting her in the first place?"

"I don't know. I only know that these past few days, Sabrina has seemed to change. She speaks highly of him, and there is something that comes into her eyes that I do not like. A marriage between them would be intolerable!"

Her face whitened, and Constanza asked harshly, "Do you think that is likely?"

"Would it bother you?" Carlos inquired with deceptive idleness.

"A little," Constanza answered untruthfully.

Carlos smiled, recognizing the lie. Dropping his eyes to the glass in his hand, he murmured, "Then I suppose that if, by chance, the improbable happened and a marriage between them was imminent . . ." He glanced across at her. "You *would* do anything to stop it, wouldn't you?"

Her mouth tightened, the dark eyes blank and shuttered. "Yes," she replied grimly. "Yes, I would. *Anything!*"

It was a *very* satisfactory answer, Carlos thought to himself as he took another swallow of his Madeira.

Brett was also swallowing Madeira at that time, but he had no feeling of satisfaction as he did so. He was seated in a chair also, but the person across from him wasn't female—it was Alejandro, and Carlos would have been extremely *dis*pleased to discover that he, himself, was the topic of their conversation. The two men were seated on the patio, resting from the heat of the day.

Brett's thick black hair still showed damp traces of his swim in the lake, and his long legs were stretched out in front of him. He looked relaxed, the glass of Madeira held loosely in one lean, tanned hand, his head thrown back against the chair as if he were contemplating the rough bark of the tree overhead, and yet . . . There was a curious stillness about that lounging, elegant form that bothered Alejandro.

Covertly he eyed Brett's face, noting that the features had a fine-drawn appearance to them. His face was thinner than it had been when he had first arrived, and the weeks in the hot, blistering Texas sun had darkened it until he had the swarthiness of a Spaniard—or a gypsy, Alejandro thought with a smile.

The smile faded from his lips when Brett asked bluntly,

182

"Did you know that Sabrina is meeting Carlos alone at the gazebo?"

Taken aback, dismay obvious in his voice, Alejandro replied, "Still? I had hoped that those assignations had stopped."

"You *know* about them?" Brett demanded incredulously. "And have done nothing to stop it?"

Alejandro moved restlessly in his chair. "They are cousins, *amigo!* They have known each other since birth! Why, Carlos is like a brother to Sabrina. I could not forbid her to meet him. I have been perturbed about it for some time, but you do not have to fear that it will in any way besmirch Sabrina's reputation. Everyone knows how it is between them. They are like two young puppies—it is harmless." On a lighter note, he added ruefully, "I have not tried to stop it, because to do so would make my very headstrong daughter all the more determined to meet with her cousin."

"Harmless!" Brett spat with an ugly laugh, and then caught himself up swiftly. He had debated mentioning the meeting to Alejandro, but his conscience had demanded that he do so, if only to forewarn a man he admired and respected that dishonor could come from an unexpected source. But his conscience would not allow him to reveal what had *really* been happening. *That* would smack too much of tale-bearing. No. Not even with Alejandro's best interests at heart could he reveal what an angel-faced little slut his daughter was. "Forgive me!" he said immediately. "You know your daughter best." Floundering helplessly for some excuse for his outburst, he muttered, "I guess I was just surprised that a gently reared young girl of her station would meet alone with a man other than a brother or a father."

Eagerly Alejandro leaned forward to reassure him. "But don't you see, *amigo,* Carlos *is* a brother to her!"

The jade-green eyes were expressionless. "As you say," Brett agreed noncommittally, images of Sabrina's long golden legs as she thrashed beneath Carlos snaking torturously through his brain. Deliberately, he shattered the images that tormented him. *No* woman, no matter how lovely and desirable, was worth pain. Hadn't he learned that lesson at his mother's knee?

Alejandro was elated at Brett's concern. Surely there had been a note in his voice that had been, well, almost jealous? Alejandro prayed so, but he was disturbed to hear that the meetings with Carlos had not ceased. His handsome face troubled, he said slowly, "I do not fear that Sabrina will come to any harm with her cousin, but under the present circumstances, if it is your wish, I will see if I can persuade her not to act so indiscreetly."

Stiffening, catching an inflection that rang like a warning bell through his mind, Brett questioned grimly, "Under the present circumstances?"

Embarrassment crept across Alejandro's features. How vexatious of him to have said that! Searching for an excuse to cover up his dangerous lapse, he said hastily, "The bandits! You haven't forgotten about them?"

Brett relaxed slightly. What a fool he was—and arrogant, he admitted wryly. Until then his host had never given the smallest inkling that he had ever considered Brett in the light of a son-in-law. Brett smiled mirthlessly. To have read even a hint of matrimony into Alejandro's simple phrase had been lunacy. "The bandits," he said slowly. "I *had* forgotten them." Keenly he glanced back to Alejandro. "Have you heard some new word of them? I thought that since the Rios attack there has been nothing more heard of them."

"Yes, that's true," Alejandro agreed quickly. "But though they seem to have disappeared from the district, one can never be too safe. I must impress upon Sabrina the danger of going alone to the gazebo—even if it *is* only to visit with her cousin."

Brett remained silent, his eyes fixed intently on the shining toes of his black boots. He took a long swallow of his Madeira.

The silence spun out, a companionable quiet between the two men. But eventually Alejandro was moved to break it. Irritably pushing his glass back and forth across the table in front of him, he suddenly said, "I must confess that those meetings with Carlos do weigh heavily on my mind."

"Oh?" Brett inquired warily.

Alejandro looked at him and made a face. "I do not like to discuss other people's business affairs, but I know you will say nothing, and perhaps it will do me good to get it off my mind."

Brett nodded his dark head slowly. A lopsided grin curving his mouth, he murmured, "Sometimes the only manner in which I can see my way clear is to discuss a particular problem with my friend Morgan Slade."

Nodding his head, much like Brett, Alejandro murmured thoughtfully, "Yes, I can understand that." He took a sip of his Madeira and said reluctantly, "The de la Vega family is in great financial trouble. Just a short while ago, I lent Luis a *very* large sum of money. The money doesn't concern me—Luis will repay me when he can. What does concern me is Carlos! I cannot understand what that young fool is thinking! His family is as close to ruin as a family can be, and yet he spends his time at some low cantina in Nacogdoches, gaming and wenching."

At Brett's expression of surprise, Alejandro admitted uncomfortably, "Several of the vaqueros from our *rancho* have seen him in there. And they talk. When the family *had* the money, I could understand Carlos's wasteful habits, but now . . ." Alejandro shook his head sadly. "Now he continues just as he always did, and instead of helping his father, he lazes the days away visiting with Sabrina!"

A curiously bleak slant to his mouth, Brett said dryly, "Perhaps he comes to her for compassion. Or in the hope that she can find a way to solve his dilemma—you said that they are close."

"That's not the point! The point is that Carlos should be working like the devil to save his home, his inheritance. He acts as if it means nothing to him. Luis is showing the strain; even my sister, who would rather die than let me know she is disturbed, has begun to bear the marks of worry." Glumly Alejandro confessed, "She hated it when Luis asked me for the money. She has *such* pride, and worse, she never wanted to leave the de la Vega *rancho* in Mexico and make Nacogdoches her home." Alejandro sighed. "How she pleaded with Luis not to come with me when I wanted to settle here! Even my own father wasn't

185

precisely pleased about it, but at least he understood a young man's yearning for adventure. I tried to explain to Francisca at the time that Luis, being the youngest son, would never be more than merely a cipher next to his older brother, that here he could be his own man, forge his own fortune." He smiled whimsically. "But Nacogdoches cannot compare to the splendor and delights to be found in Mexico City, and though she hides it well, I know she still resents the fact that Luis listened to my stories of the beauty and grandeur of this country, of the opportunity for a man to gain a fortune, and decided to come with me when I left Mexico." He shook his head sadly. "She always feared that they would come to ruin, and now . . ."

"But how did it come about?" Brett asked curiously. "This land is so rich, so very fertile, that I cannot believe a man could fail so dismally. It is obvious that they prospered for some time."

Alejandro grimaced. "It is always a battle out here, *amigo*. Floods can drown your herds, Indians can steal them, and crops can fail. And then there are bandits and four-legged predators like bear and puma that can devastate an area. But in Luis's case, I think it has simply been mismanagement of his money. A rancher, like many plantation owners, lives from season to season, from one year of plenty to the next of famine, and Luis has not always been wise with his funds." Alejandro's patrician features hardened. "And I fear that his indulgences with Carlos have also eaten deeply into his actual monies—he cannot, or will not, deny his only son." Alejandro shook his head again. "I never suspected how unworthy Carlos is. I knew he was spoiled and perhaps a little wild, but I never dreamed he would be so indifferent in the face of true adversity. These past few months have left me very disappointed in Carlos."

A little smile of embarrassment tugged at the corners of his mouth. "And now," he said apologetically, "I have disappointed myself, by boring you with such a maudlin tale." He glanced at his glass. "It must be the Madeira that has made me such a poor host."

Brett hastened to assure him that he was indeed a fine host, and a few minutes later they were busy talking of

186

other, more interesting things. It was only when the shadows were lengthening into the duskiness of early evening that Alejandro looked up with surprise and murmured, "It just occurred to me that Sabrina should be here with us. I wonder what has delayed her."

Brett remained silent, not trusting himself to speak, his eyes fixed on his glass. But then there was no need for him to speak. Almost as if waiting for her father's words, Sabrina suddenly walked out from under the overhanging eaves of the house and joined them at the table.

It had taken a great deal of bravery for her to do so. Outwardly she looked quite composed—no sign of the angry, disheveled young woman who had raced away from the gazebo in shame was apparent in her appearance. The red-gold curls were demurely caught in a chignon at the base of her neck, and her gown was a delightful concoction of embroidered yellow muslin. The color enhanced her own golden-toned skin and deepened the intensity of the amber-gold eyes; a profusion of lace edging the modest neckline formed a charming frame for her lovely features, and around her neck was an emerald-green velvet ribbon; topaz earrings gleamed in her ears. But if outwardly Sabrina showed no signs of agitation, inwardly she was a quaking mass of jangled emotions. She was furious with Brett, and the hours between their parting and now had done nothing to soothe her ire. How dare he think her capable of welcoming Carlos's attack! And yet, a more rational part of her admitted that the scene *had* looked compromising. She didn't want to think about that, for her humiliation was too deep.

Her attitude toward Carlos was a mixture of disbelief, anger, bewilderment, and hurt. How could he have acted so despicably? She had been nearly in a state of shock when she had gained the safety of her bedroom, and for several moments she had just stood in the center of the room staring blindly at nothing. Fortunately, no one had seen her arrival back at the house, and she had shuddered just thinking about the questions and the unpleasantness there would have been if her father or Bonita had chanced to see her as she fled up the stairs. Would they have believed that she had welcomed Carlos's assault?

Thinking of Carlos had sent a wave of nausea coursing

through her body. Even love, she had thought painfully, did not excuse him. He had meant to dishonor her, and she had little doubt that if Brett had not arrived when he did, Carlos would have raped her. And it would have been rape. Carlos's touch, his hot kisses, his caresses aroused no feeling within her but repulsion, and remembering his seeking hands upon her thighs, the touch of his hardened male flesh against her, she had shivered as she tore off the tattered gown and threw it violently down on the floor of her bedroom. What had possessed him? Had he gone mad?

She almost couldn't believe what had transpired, and yet, staring at the ruined heap that had been her pretty lavender gown, she was forced to face the fact that her friend, the cousin she had known all her life, the playmate of her childhood, had indeed tried to rape her.

Numbly she had gathered up the evidence of his attack and hidden it in the bottom of a pine chest that sat near her bed. She couldn't think clearly right now, but she didn't dare let anyone, especially Bonita, see that ripped and torn gown and ask questions.

Reaction had made her teeth chatter, and with a low moan, she had sought out her bed, burrowing deeply down into the covers, seeking to drive out the chill that seemed to permeate her very bones. She had shut her eyes, Brett's contemptuous face suddenly floating behind her lids. Shivering then almost uncontrollably, she had felt rage rising up through her body. How dare they! Carlos to try such a trick and Brett to blame her!

She was furious with Carlos for his actions and she would never trust him again, but she didn't hate him—there were too many childhood memories binding them together. As time passed, and she gradually calmed herself, she had begun to search for some reason for his actions. She couldn't imagine anything that he could ever say that would wipe out this afternoon's ugly memory, but deep in her heart, she hoped that there *was* some extenuating circumstance that would explain his actions.

As for Brett . . . Her young face hardened. What else should she have expected from him? He had no use for women—except one, according to Tía Sofia—and even though these past days, she had hoped that they were forging a strong new bond, today had showed her how frail that hope had been. He would always believe the worst about any woman, and for that she could never forgive him. Had he really believed that she would respond to him the way she had and then creep out to be mauled and pawed by Carlos? Her mouth had twisted distastefully. What an ugly, tortuous mind he must have, she had thought angrily.

Carlos had betrayed a trust, but Brett's betrayal went deeper. He should have understood, she had repeated savagely to herself. He should have realized, should have *known* I would not be a willing partner to what was going on—no matter *how* it looked! It wasn't very rational thinking, but Sabrina was young and was caught in the painful throes of her first love.

She hadn't known how she was going to react when she saw Brett again, but her heart had given a funny little jerk in her breast when she walked out to join the men at the table and was confronted with his indifferent glance. The face he showed her was politely remote, and remembering the warm smiles they had been exchanging this past week, her eyes sparkled with temper.

As interested as he was in their blooming love affair, it was to be expected that Alejandro would notice immediately the air of reserve and stiff punctiliousness between the two younger people. His eyes puzzled and a little worried, he looked from one set face to the other. What in the world, he wondered bewilderedly, has caused this? And it wasn't until after a stiff, uncomfortable dinner that an inkling came to him.

The long table had been cleared, and fourteen-year-old Lupe, one of the kitchen servants, was bringing in bowls of peaches, green grapes, and cheeses for dessert, when Alejandro said casually to Sabrina, *"Chica,* I hesitate to bring this up . . . but I do not think it is proper or wise for you to be meeting so privately with your cousin Carlos. Brett mentioned to me this afternoon that he had seen the two of you at the gazebo, and I really must insist that if you wish to see Carlos you should do so here in your own home."

Sabrina's face paled, and she stiffened. Tale-bearing was not one of the crimes she would have laid at Brett's door, but obviously she had overrated his scruples. Her voice choked with outrage, her eyes flashing contemptuously, she got out, *"Cielos!* And having seen us there together, he must immediately run to you with the tale! There are words for men like him—ugly words!"

Startled, Alejandro could only stare at her in astonishment. *"Chica,* what is this? Why—"

Sabrina stood up abruptly, and interrupting Alejandro, she said regally, "If you will excuse me, I must leave." Slinging a venomous look at Brett, she added, "The air in here is suddenly foul!"

Open-mouthed, Alejandro watched as she swept from the room, her yellow muslin skirts frothing behind her. He looked over at Brett and muttered, "What in the world disturbed her so? I cannot understand her these days."

The dark green eyes fixed with cold anger on the door Sabrina had just stormed through, Brett threw down his napkin and said in a hard voice, "If you'll excuse me, Alejandro? I would like a word with your daughter!"

Speculation leaping to his eyes, his mouth still open, Alejandro suddenly found himself sitting all alone in the spacious dining room. *"Well!"* he said indignantly to the empty room.

Brett caught up with Sabrina at the top of the stairs leading to their bedrooms. She hadn't been aware that he had followed her, and his brutal grasp of her arm as he swung her around to face him disconcerted her. She gave a small gasp of alarm, and then, when she saw his dark angry face, her heart began to thump painfully.

"Let go of me!" she said furiously, jerking at the arm he held so tightly.

"Not *yet,* your highness! You and I are going to have a private conversation first," Brett snapped.

"I don't want to speak to you! Ever! You have done nothing but slip around and sneak and spy on me since you arrived here—and now you carry tales to my father. You're despicable!"

A muscle in Brett's jaw bunched, and the dark green eyes went nearly black with fury. "I've had just about all of your accusations I'm going to take! Now you shut up and you listen to me!" he said with cold rage, giving her an un-

190

gentle shake. He sent a harassed look down the long hall-way and then pulled her into a small antechamber nearby.

Releasing her arm, he regarded her unkindly as she stood defiantly in front of him, one hand rubbing the place where he had grabbed her. Icily she said, "Since you've dragged me in here, say what you have to say and let me go."

Brett inclined his dark head in mock politeness. "As you command, your highness." Propping himself negligently against the door, he said in a level tone of voice, "I didn't run tale-bearing to your father. I did, however"—an expression of disgust and contempt passed across his lean features—"mention to him that I had seen you and Carlos at the gazebo. I didn't," he went on in an increasingly harsh note, "tell him what you were doing there!"

"And what were we doing?" Sabrina inquired danger-ously, the amber-gold eyes glittering incandescently. "What was it you thought you saw?"

The tanned face full if distaste and scorn, he said bluntly, "You damn well know what I saw! But you can be assured your sordid little secret is safe with me. Not for your sake," he added tightly, "but for your father's! I don't want to be the one to disillusion him about his slut of a daughter!"

Sabrina's hand swung out and cracked against his cheek before she had time to think. And before she had time to realize what she had done, she found herself jerked cruelly up against Brett's hard, long length.

His mouth inches from hers, his warm breath teasing her lips, he snarled thickly, "I think I warned you not to try that again! And since you seem to be passing out your favors, I don't see any reason why *I* shouldn't have another sample!"

Brutally his lips came down on hers, his arms crushing her to him. It was a shockingly carnal kiss, his tongue rav-ishing her inner mouth with frank demand. There was nothing gentle about this kiss, nothing tender; it was full of anger, and yet a strange longing seemed to be there, too. His arms kept her prisoner as he pulled her between his legs, his body supported by the door behind him.

Sabrina was helpless in his embrace, her own desires rising up uncontrollably to meet the spiraling passion she could feel emanating from his muscled body. Crushed intimately against him, she could feel the hardening of his manhood, feel it lengthening and pressing insistently against her own increasingly hungry loins. Unable to help herself, she responded blindly, deliriously, to the fierce demand of his kisses.

Oh, dear God, how very different this was from what she had experienced in Carlos's arms. There was no desire to escape, no feeling of fury or degradation; only passion and sweet need swamped her, driving her to cling to him, her body aching to have his touch upon it. She could stay here forever locked in Brett's savage, oddly yearning embrace, his strong arms holding her a willing prisoner. Hungrily she returned his kiss, her lips opening more fully under the onslaught of his, her tongue daring to touch his as he urgently plundered her mouth.

With a groan, Brett pulled her even closer to him, his hands dropping to her hips and caressing them with a feverish intensity. Sweet Jesus, but it was heaven to have her in his arms, to have those taut, full breasts burning against his chest, to have her warm body arching up next to his.

The embrace was explosive; neither one of them was even aware of what they were doing or how swiftly passion was taking them to a point of no return. Each was lost in the urgent tide of desire that swept over them, their bodies straining frantically together longing for something more.

Suddenly, like plunging into a river of ice, Brett realized how very near he was to taking Carlos's place in her arms.

Smothering a curse, he pushed her violently away from him. The jade-green eyes full of loathing, he snarled, "Oh, no, you don't! I've never taken another man's leavings before, and I sure as hell don't intend to start with you!" His body ached with desire, but stilling the overpowering urge to take her into his arms again, he promised grimly, "I will warn you, though—continue to offer yourself so blatantly, and I might weaken. Next time, sweetheart . . . next time, I'll take you, and the consequences be *damned!*"

192

CHAPTER FOURTEEN

The next day, Tuesday, when the servant appeared in her room announcing that Señor Carlos was waiting to see her downstairs, Sabrina could hardly believe her ears. After what had happened the previous afternoon, she had never dreamed he would seek her out this way.

Angry curiosity brought her down the stairs and out onto the patio where a wary and apologetic Carlos waited for her. The servant had departed for refreshments; so it was that Sabrina was alone with him when they met.

Reluctantly she walked across the patio to where he stood by the iron table, nervously turning his sombrero between his fingers. His expression was suitably woebegone, the black eyes brimming with apparent misery. He looked at her angry, set face and then glanced quickly away. He swallowed with difficulty. His voice almost a whisper, he muttered, "Will you ever forgive me?"

Indecisively Sabrina eyed him, astonished at how indifferent she felt. It was as if the fury she had experienced when Brett had slammed out of the room last night had burned away all her emotions—except the rage that was reserved especially and exclusively for one Brett Dangermond.

Taking her silence for encouragement, he flung his sombrero down on the table, and startling her, he knelt theatrically down in front of her. His hand grasped hers, and he carried it to his lips. *"Querida!* You *must* forgive me! I love you so much that to have you so close to me drove me mad—I could not help myself! I went crazy with love for you! I never meant to harm you or frighten you." He struck his head with his palm. "I do not know what came over me, how I could have acted so despicably, so dishonorably! I am a swine! I am the lowest animal alive!" The

193

black eyes fixed with pleading on hers, he murmured, "Say you forgive me, *querida!* Say that all the years of our friendship are not to be lost to me! I could not bear it, Sabrina—you are too dear to me for me to face the future knowing I have destroyed everything between us." Mournfully he shook his head. "All the years of laughter we shared shattered by my unforgivable actions! I don't think I can bear it!"

Sabrina made a face. Not quite certain how to handle Carlos in this abject mood, she said uncomfortably, "I forgive you—at least I think I do. Now please get up before someone sees you there and wonders what is going on!"

Rising to his feet with alacrity, Carlos reached for her hand once more and covered it with kisses. "You are as good and kind and wonderful as the Holy Mother of God!"

Deeply embarrassed and showing it, Sabrina jerked her hand away from his. Seeing Lupe approaching with a tray of glasses and jug of lemonade, Sabrina hissed under her breath, "Will you *cease!* I said I forgave you!"

While Lupe was present, they both remained silent, but as soon as the girl retreated to the house, Carlos, who was now seated across the table from Sabrina, leaned forward and said passionately, "Sabrina, I can never forgive myself for what nearly happened yesterday. You must believe me—I never meant to harm or frighten you!"

Before yesterday she would have believed him completely, but trust once destroyed does not return easily. She did forgive him because, beyond frightening her, and thanks to Brett's timely interference, nothing *had* happened. But she was wary with him now, wanting to have things as they had been and yet unable to forget that, at least for a moment yesterday, he had taken advantage of their long friendship and would have dishonored her. Awkwardly she muttered, "It's in the past, Carlos. Please put it behind you." Sending him a strained smile, she added, "I have."

"Have you really, *querida?*" Carlos asked shrewdly. "Can you say that nothing is different between us?"

"No, I can't," Sabrina answered truthfully. "Yesterday changed things, but I . . . I . . . I don't hate you, and I wouldn't want our families to be distressed by what happened—or nearly happened."

The black eyes shuttered, he asked carefully, "Does your father know what . . . nearly happened? Have you told him? Did anyone see you when you returned to the hacienda?"

"No, no one saw me," Sabrina replied quietly. "And I didn't mention anything to my father. It . . . it . . . it would have caused complications."

"Complications?" Carlos inquired with a lifted brow.

Sabrina grimaced, her eyes on the glass of lemonade in front of her. "You know very well what I mean. If he knew what had happened, he would either take a bullwhip to you or demand that you marry me—or both! It would make things very unpleasant!"

"I would be honored to marry you, *querida!* As a matter of fact, I have considered telling your father the truth myself and asking your hand in marriage," he confessed softly, the black eyes watching her face intently.

Sabrina's head jerked up at that. "Don't you dare!" she spat angrily. "I love you, Carlos—you are like a brother to me—but I do not want to marry you . . . and I *will* not marry you! Telling my father would only cause a terrible rift between our families and put both of us through a great deal of unpleasantness and pain. I said I forgave you and I do, but speak of what happened yesterday and I'll *never* forgive you!"

There was such grim promise in her young voice that Carlos relinquished the idea immediately. Giving her an attractively rueful grin, he murmured, "I had hoped you would react differently, but . . ." His dark face suddenly serious, he said, "Sabrina, I *am* sorry for what happened yesterday, and I will do everything within my power to earn your trust back." He smiled sadly. "If I cannot have you as my wife, perhaps I can still have you as my friend."

An unexpected lump in her throat at the sadness on his face, she leaned forward impulsively and touched his hands with hers. "You always have my friendship, Carlos. *Always!"*

Friday, Sabrina's eighteenth birthday, dawned hot and

clear, the sun a blazing yellow-orange orb in a blinding blue sky, and she was reminded of the same date last year. Last year. How innocent she had been then. How *unaware*.

Sabrina took a bittersweet enjoyment in the day. She had always delighted in the fuss and frolic that set her birthday apart from any other fiesta, and this year was no different. Bonita had brought in her breakfast tray adorned with the special bouquet of yellow rosebuds as she had for every birthday that Sabrina could remember; the gift this year was a pair of finely wrought silver bracelets that jangled merrily whenever Sabrina moved her slim wrist. Everywhere she went she was greeted and wished well, and she couldn't help basking in the attention.

The day was nearly a repeat of her last birthday celebration, with one notable difference—Brett Dangermond. Everywhere she looked, Sabrina seemed to see him: laughing with her father over breakfast; talking with the guests as they began to arrive; wandering about the grounds with various groups of smiling and gesturing men and women; teasing fat Bonita as she waddled around overseeing the hustling servants, and listening intently as Luis and Alejandro discussed certain business prospects. Against her will, her eyes seemed to follow him, to admire the tall, lean body as he moved with his effortless grace, easily charming anyone who came within his radius. She was angry with herself and irrationally furious with him, because in spite of everything, he still had the power to move her, to make her heart beat faster, to arouse a fierce, inexplicable longing within her. Time and time again she tore her eyes away from the harshly handsome face and threw herself into the festivities that were, after all, in her honor, and yet, not five minutes later, she would find herself anxiously searching the shifting crowd for his dark head.

The bullfight Alejandro had promised Brett was held in honor of Sabrina's birthday; everyone trooped down to watch the various high-spirited young men pit their skills against the magnificent black bulls. Vaqueros and their families lined the makeshift bull ring; the guests viewed the activities from the relative comfort of a hastily constructed grandstand, a canopy of bright yellow material protecting the fair ladies from the blazing sun. Alejandro had considered a bull-baiting and had even instructed his vaqueros to capture a bear to pit against one of the fiercest bulls, but Sabrina had begged, "Oh, please do not, Father! The bull makes such mournful bellows when the bear attacks him, and the poor bear is gored unmercifully. I do not like it!" Alejandro had shaken his head in mystification but had agreed to accede to her wishes.

Narrow-eyed, she had critically watched the young blades display their proficiency with the cape and the sword, and more times than not her sympathy lay with the bull. It was a bloody and perhaps cruel sport, and yet there was something elemental about it, something that stirred dark emotions, something that thrilled as well as terrified. But it wasn't until Brett coolly walked out into the middle of the red-dirt arena, the ground now torn and furrowed from the other fights, small puffs of russet dust rising from beneath his feet, that she knew the full depth of terror. Her heart seemed to stop, and her face went white, her hand unconsciously clenching the lovely scarlet and gold fan Carlos had given her for her birthday.

She gave a small moan of denial, and Carlos, who was sitting next to her and who had not deigned to participate this year in the dangerous amusement, glanced at her sharply. "Is something wrong, *chica?*" he asked.

Forcing herself to relax, trying desperately to hide the utter horror that roiled inside her, she said weakly, "Why, no! What possibly could be wrong?"

"I thought perhaps you might be concerned for the gringo. After all, this *is* a Spanish sport, and big men are notorious for being slow on their feet." Sending her a calculating glance, he finished, "It will be interesting to see if he survives the encounter with one of your father's indomitable bulls."

Numbly Sabrina nodded her head, her gaze fixed painfully on the tall, broad-shouldered man in the center of the arena. The sunlight brought out the hint of blue in the black, thick hair, one lock displaying a tendency to fall across his forehead. He was clothed in Spanish dress, and with one part of her mind, Sabrina admitted it became him wonderfully, the dark green calzoneras fitting snugly

197

across his lean hips and thighs, the gold filigree giving them an elegant air. The white shirt was blinding in the bright sunlit afternoon, the scarlet cape whirling and fluttering in the still air as he made a few practice motions.

Apparently satisfied, Brett nodded to release the penned bull, and with a roar of encouragement from the crowd, a huge nightmare of bone and muscle, of blood and fury, exploded into the arena. To Sabrina, Brett seemed terribly defenseless as the magnificent creature lowered its massive head, the long, wickedly curving horns glinting in the sunlight. Her heart in her mouth, she watched helplessly as, with a spine-tingling bellow, the savage animal charged the still figure with the scarlet cape. To the crowd's delight, Brett proved himself an excellent matador, moving with such precision and artistry that time and time again it seemed the bull must touch him and yet he remained unscathed, stepping gracefully away at the last, vital moment. It was immediately apparent that the tall gringo knew what he was about, and the crowd shouted its enthusiasm as, with elegant skill, Brett imperturbably performed one of the oldest, most classical moves of the bull ring, the *verónica*. The scarlet cape swirled sinuously in the air as he brought it down in front of the charging bull and then swiftly up and around his own body. And when the kill finally came, there was a concerted sigh of pleasure, almost of awe, as the sword found its mark and cleanly made the fatal thrust.

Sabrina had sat like a stone figure throughout the fight, her eyes never once leaving him. And when the agonizing suspense was over, when the bull was only an inert heap in the red dust, to her surprise she discovered that her hands had been so tightly clenched that her fingernails had left deep impressions in the palms of her hands, the skin purple and bruised.

Limp, she had nearly sagged in her seat, only to stiffen when she saw Brett lean down and cut off the ears of the fallen bull and walk straight in her direction. He stopped directly in front of her, his gaze taking in Carlos, who sat next to her. The men exchanged a peculiar look, Brett's dark green eyes glittering with an oddly challenging spark, and then deliberately his eyes switched to Sabrina.

He gave her a long, unsmiling glance, and then impassively offered her the grisly trophy. A trophy won at the risk of his own life.

Sabrina hesitated, her heart beating erratically within her breast. Despairingly she tried to read the expression on that dispassionate, dark face, wondering why he had singled her out this way, wondering with a curious mixture of hope and anger whether he realized the significance of what he was doing. And if he did, whether she dared accept the trophy and all that it might imply.

There was a hushed expectancy from the crowd, every eye on Brett's lean form and Sabrina's slender figure. His actions were almost a public declaration of marriage; at the very least they were a clear indication that he had more than just a passing interest in Don Alejandro's lovely daughter, and everyone waited to see what she would do.

Oblivious to everything but the man in front of her, Sabrina stared helplessly at him, loving him, hating him. Was he merely honoring her birthday . . . or was he staking his claim upon her? Considering the situation between them, one of studied indifference these past days, it was foolish to think this was more than simply a gesture to mark her birthday, and yet, there had been something in the way he had looked at Carlos, something in the coolly determined way he had approached her, that made her breath catch in her throat.

A current of awareness seemed to flow between them, Sabrina so very conscious of the faint sheen of perspiration on his face, of the musky scent of his warm body, of the insane desire to fling herself into his arms and let the world see that she loved him. But she held back, and as the seconds sped by and the tension increased, she was suddenly furious. If she accepted, it would leave them open to avid speculation; if she refused, it would embarrass everyone.

Becoming vaguely conscious of the smoldering anger radiating from Carlos, and of the smile of encouragement that her father flashed her from where he sat on her other side, she moved uneasily. Then, unwilling to prolong the incident, deciding she was making too much of a small thing, reluctantly she reached out and snatched the trophy from Brett's grasp.

"*Gracias, señor.* I am honored," she said stiffly, the amber-gold eyes sparkling with resentment.

Brett sent her a taut smile, a curious expression flickering across the harsh features. "You should be, sweetheart—you're the only woman for whom I've ever risked my hide." He glanced at Alejandro and said coolly, "I'm certain you won't mind if I take my own reward." And under Alejandro's approving grin, and Carlos's naked fury, Brett jerked Sabrina out of her seat and with the crowd hooting and cheering, proceeded to kiss her thoroughly.

Flushed and disheveled, her lips throbbing from the almost brutal kiss, she was rather abruptly set back down in her seat. He gave her an ironical bow, and she watched in absolute rage as he sauntered arrogantly from the bull ring. The onlookers were completely enraptured, and for several moments after Brett disappeared, they continued to clap and shout, some of the more ribald suggestions making Sabrina's ears burn.

After that, the remaining fights were anticlimactic, and Sabrina found herself watching the bull ring with blind eyes. It was with relief that she finally quit the area and began to walk back to the hacienda with the others.

Her relief was short-lived, however, for Francisca and Carlos flanked her, and their comments did nothing for her state of mind.

"What is your father thinking?" Francisca demanded in an angry undertone. "Letting that . . . that *gringo* maul you that way! It was an insult to our family! *Everyone* knows that you and Carlos are to be betrothed, and now this!" Her bosom heaving, the dark eyes full of fire, Francisca said grimly, "Just wait until I have a word with your father!"

Carlos's attitude was much the same but even more venomous. The black eyes cold with an icy fury, he snarled, "How dare he touch you that way! If I didn't want to spare you the indignity of a scene, I would have struck him and challenged him then and there! And as for his ability in the bull ring! Fah! If I had known he was going to make such a spectacle of himself, I would have fought the bulls today and showed him how a true Spaniard kills the bull."

Her face crimson with embarrassment, mortified that

others nearby might overhear the unpleasant conversation, Sabrina said urgently to Carlos, "Oh, hush! It was nothing! Please let it be and do not make it any worse! *Please!*"

Carlos looked at her flushed face consideringly. "Weren't *you* insulted?" His lips curving into a sneer, he added, "Or did you enjoy being publicly degraded by the gringo?"

Sabrina's eyes flashed, and she said hotly, "What I felt is none of your business! Leave the subject alone."

Carlos followed her lead and ceased his questions, but Francisca was not so easily put off, and her eyebrows rising in displeasure, she said sharply, "I notice that you do not seem to be overly distressed. Can it be that you actually *welcomed* the gringo's vulgar attentions? That you were impressed by his coarse skills?"

Holding on to her rising temper with an effort, Sabrina said levelly, "I may not have liked how he chose to celebrate his victory, but I will not allow you to refer to his skills with the bulls as coarse." Meeting her aunt's furious gaze, she said boldly, "He was magnificent! I have never seen *anyone* who is his match in the bull ring."

Francisca's bosom swelled with wrath, and for one tense moment Sabrina thought her aunt would strike her. But Carlos swiftly intervened.

"Magnificent, you say?" he drawled. "You are naive for thinking so, *querida!* Once you have seen the matadors fight in Madrid, you will realize how paltry his skills are. He did nothing but perform a few cheap tricks to dazzle the eyes of these unsophisticated people." And he gave a languid wave of his hand to indicate the other guests who were scattering throughout the grounds near the hacienda.

"And *you* are so much more sophisticated?" Sabrina returned with an edge to her voice.

Carlos shrugged. "I have not buried myself here all my life. I have traveled to Europe, unlike you and most of our neighbors. I have seen things . . ."

If he meant to impress Sabrina, it had just the opposite effect. Her jaw set, she said sweetly, "I hadn't realized how very rustic you found us. And because I am such a thoughtful hostess, I shall not bore you any longer with my *unso-*

phisticated presence! If you will excuse me, there are other, less cosmopolitan guests who will enjoy my naive company." And with that she marched proudly away, leaving Carlos and Francisca to stare after her.

Sabrina sought the sanctuary of her room, and discovering she still held the trophy in her hands, with an exclamation of disgust, she threw the ears down on the floor. Her head was suddenly aching unbearably, and she sank onto her bed, pressing her fingers to her pounding temples. She already regretted the outburst with Carlos, but Brett's actions had jangled her nerves and shattered her composure. What was he trying to do? she wondered uneasily. If the scene this afternoon had happened a week ago, she would have been better able to understand it. Would have been—if she were honest—thrilled and excited, but now? Now, when they barely tolerated one another? When he dared accuse her of being a slut? When he thought she had welcomed Carlos's near-rape?

Unwilling to waste more time in useless speculation, Sabrina finally compelled herself to leave her room. Hiding her turmoil with a smile, she hurried downstairs and rejoined the guests.

Sabrina was not the only one to wonder what Brett had meant by his display this afternoon. Ollie was damned curious about what the guvnor was up to. Naturally, Ollie had his suspicions, but he wanted them confirmed before he made any plans of his own. And Ollie did have plans of his own—little Lupe from the kitchen had caught his eye, and these past few weeks, he had begun to think that if the guvnor was considering getting himself leg-shackled, it couldn't be such a horrible state after all. Besides, he told himself happily as he laid out Brett's clothes for that evening, Lupe was young enough to be properly trained in her duties to her husband. Drifting off into a pleasant dream about a future enhanced by Lupe's dark, nubile charms, Ollie sat holding the boot he had been polishing, a beatific smile on his ugly little face.

It was only Brett's voice asking dryly, "Have you grown particularly attached to the object? Must I wait indefinitely?" that brought him back to reality with a sharp bump.

Ollie hastily handed Brett the boot. "Excuse me, guv-nor—was, um, thinking about other things."

"Obviously!" Brett returned with a teasing glint in the green eyes as he pulled on the gleaming boot. "Other things being that shy, deer-eyed little girl in the kitchen?"

Stunned, Ollie stared open-mouthed at Brett. "How did you?" he began, only to shut his mouth with a snap. How could he have forgotten that *nothing* slipped by the guv-nor? Sheepishly he admitted, "Aye, sir, she's the one."

"Well," Brett said lightly, "that explains why whenever I need you lately, I only have to go as far as the kitchen to find you!" A faintly quizzical expression on his lean face, Brett inquired, "Am I to wish you happy, Ollie?"

Ollie hesitated. "That depends, guvnor," he said uncertainly.

"Oh? On what? Shall I present myself to her parents and vouch for you?" Brett asked mockingly, tying the black silk sash that Ollie handed him snugly about his waist.

"Well," Ollie finally said cautiously, "you could say it all depends on you, guvnor. Especially it depends on exactly what you meant by kissing Miss Sabrina this afternoon. Now if you was considering walking into the parson's mousetrap . . ."

Brett's teasing air vanished, and his chiseled mouth tightened. There was a sudden, grim silence in the room as he shrugged on a black velvet bolero. He made a romantic figure, his scarlet silk shirt a vivid slash of color against the black of his clothing, the gold filigree of the tight-fitting calzoneras glittering in the candlelight of the room. His face was bronzed and vital; the blue-black hair was overlong, waving near his temples, just brushing the collar of his scarlet shirt; and the green eyes were as hard and mysterious as jade as he turned to look at Ollie.

"You have your doubts?" Brett asked silkily, his face devoid of expression.

Ollie swallowed. There were times Dangermond made him distinctly nervous, and this was one of those times. There was an air of suppressed violence radiating from the tall, dark figure, and Ollie had the unpleasant feeling he was facing a keg of black powder with a *very* short fuse.

Uneasily pulling on the lobe of his ear, Ollie confessed

with his usual candor, "Two weeks ago, I would 'ave said no. But these past days . . ." He shot Brett a troubled look. "The thing is, guvnor, you don't *act* like a man in love! Sometimes you act as if you'd like to strangle Miss Sabrina, and lately you've been like a bear. Never seen you like this, and I can't figure it out. Either you love 'er or you don't! And if you don't, why did you act like you did this afternoon?"

"Love has very little to do with marriage, my small friend," Brett said wearily, the dark green eyes bleak.

"A marriage of convenience?" Ollie burst out, shocked.

Brett gave a bitter laugh. "I've thought of nothing else these past few days," he said grimly. "It's all very simple. I admire Alejandro a great deal. Alejandro has a daughter, a daughter who has an unworthy suitor, a suitor who, if successful in gaining the daughter's hand, would make Alejandro very *un*happy. Do you follow me?"

Ollie nodded slowly. Frowning he asked, "But what does that 'ave to do with you marrying Miss Sabrina? You surely ain't the unworthy suitor?"

Smiling wryly, Brett admitted, "No, I don't believe I am. And I'm certain, though he has said nothing, that Alejandro would be delighted if I were to offer for Sabrina." His smile vanished, and his face hardened. "So that's what I'm going to do. At least married to me, Sabrina will have a husband who will not bring her to ruin, nor will Alejandro have to sit by and see everything he has worked for fall into the hands of a wastrel."

Ollie regarded him cynically. Shaking his head, he muttered, "I never thought I'd see the day you'd gammon yourself, guvnor!"

Brett's hand clenched into a fist, and a muscle twitched in his lean cheek. "And I think you're becoming even too impertinent for me!"

"Oh, am I now?" Ollie replied, completely unperturbed by Brett's words. "You know what I think? I think you don't like the truth! If you think you're going to marry Miss Sabrina simply to save her from the likes of that Carlos fellow, or even just because Don Alejandro will be delighted, you're fooling yourself, guvnor! Damn me for a saint if you ain't!"

Brett was silent for so long, his dark face so remote, that Ollie didn't think he had heard him. Then Brett looked at him, the expression in those jade-green eyes so full of tormented fury that Ollie dropped his gaze. Softly Brett snarled, "Don't you think I know it?" and walked out of the room.

CHAPTER FIFTEEN

Sabrina found the remainder of the afternoon unbearably frustrating. Everywhere she went there were misty-eyed, knowing smiles from the women and hearty innuendos from the men. She could have stamped her foot with rage, and when Alejandro came over and patted her affectionately on the shoulder and murmured, "A wise choice, *chica*, a wise choice. It makes me very happy," she could have exploded with fury.

Even Bonita was no help as she fussed and worried over Sabrina's attire for the evening. "It is such a special evening, is it not, my dove?" Bonita murmured, her fat face wreathed in a huge smile.

With an effort, Sabrina swallowed back the scathing reply she would have liked to utter and said instead, "*Sí*, it is. After all, eighteen comes only once—I am very fortunate that everyone has been so kind to me today."

It wasn't quite the reply that Bonita wanted, but she shrugged her plump shoulders. If the little one wanted to hug the not-so-secret love affair to herself a bit longer, who could blame her? To love at eighteen is such a delight. And to be loved by a man like Señor Dangermond . . . Bonita closed her eyes and sighed blissfully.

Despite having found the afternoon an ordeal, as the time passed and she bathed and began to put on her clothes for the evening, Sabrina was aware of a bubble of rising excitement in her chest. Time and time again she tried to quell it, to tell herself that she was going to have a miserable time, that Brett would continue to ignore her as he had after his puzzling display in the bull ring, and yet, as she slipped on a petticoat of frothy lace and fastened the lacings of her satin slippers, she was conscious of an overriding sense of adventure, of a delirious feeling of anticipation.

From down the hall, she could hear the laughter and chatter of the other guests as they, too, changed into their finery for the evening entertainments, and suddenly the last of her anger and confusion disappeared. How could anyone be moody and troubled on a night like tonight?

A full, silvery moon could be seen barely rising above the tips of the trees; the air was warm and soft like silk, the scent of jasmine and roses teasing the nostrils, stirring the senses; and the sultry, throbbing notes of the guitars and marimbas could be heard drifting up tantalizingly from the courtyard. It was a lovers' night, a night that fairly surged with promise, the very air almost pulsating with expectancy.

The amber-gold eyes shining like stars, her cheeks flushed with hectic color, Sabrina dressed with increasing feverishness, eager, impatient to be downstairs—to see Brett. Her gown was a gift from her father, a gorgeous creation of fine silk from Spain. The lavender-blue color was a surprisingly effective foil for Sabrina's red-gold hair and apricot-tinted skin. The neckline was rounded and low-cut, her breasts swelling temptingly above the fabric; a wide sash of deep purple circled her midriff just under her breasts; and the full skirts were trimmed with a narrow flounce of delicate blond lace. The sleeves were very little puffs near her bared shoulders, and gazing at her reflection in the cheval glass, Sabrina gave a pleased gurgle of excited laughter.

Her bright hair fell in natural, wavy ringlets halfway down her back; the candlelight turned it to molten fire as she moved about the room. Bonita's silver bracelets tinkled merrily on her wrists, huge hoops of silver glittered between the strands of fiery hair, and whenever she walked, the faint scent of lemon blossoms lingered in the air. Tossing Bonita a kiss, a smile of anticipation on her full mouth, Sabrina hurried out of her room, eager to face whatever excitement and adventure the night might bring.

And it *was* an evening to remember, Brett looming up suddenly out of nowhere as she reached the bottom of the stairs. For a long, timeless moment they stared at one another, the stunned expression in the jade-green eyes making Sabrina strangely breathless and exhilarated. Those feelings never seemed to leave her that night. Nor did Brett.

He was never far from her side, and though they spoke little, it was as if they communicated without words: a look, a lift of the eyebrow, a smile, and the other seemed to understand. And yet Brett did not monopolize her attention; she was the belle of the ball, and he seemed content to watch her whirl around the courtyard in the arms of her various partners, his gaze never leaving her as he stood near one of the pillars of the archways. The instant the music ceased, he would materialize at her side, making it abundantly clear that while he was willing to share her for the dances, beyond that his tolerance did not go.

Alejandro watched the proceedings with an indulgent smile, and gently he fingered the turquoise and silver bracelet that Elena had given him so long ago. "She will be safe, my love . . . safe and loved!" he whispered softly to himself.

Carlos and Francisca were not so pleased, but even their snide comments couldn't prick Sabrina's bright bubble of happiness. Even when Carlos twirled her around the courtyard and hissed angrily, "He has bewitched you! Listen to me. Follow this course, and it will bring you disaster!" Sabrina smiled vaguely at him, not really caring if disaster did loom on her horizon. She would have tonight!

But Carlos was not one to give up easily, and seeing that his words were having no effect, he said slyly, "I see that Señora Morales is not here tonight. Your doing . . . or his?"

For just a moment, an icy blast seemed to cut through her warm cloak of bliss, and the soft glow that had shone in her eyes faded just a little. "I invited her," Sabrina admitted reluctantly, "but she sent a note declining the invitation. She said she hadn't been feeling well lately."

"And you believed her?" Carlos jeered. "You didn't question why she would avoid one of the premiere entertainments of the year?"

"No, I didn't!" Sabrina retorted stiffly. "And it doesn't matter one way or the other. Leave it be, Carlos!"

"I would like to, *querida,* but I don't want you to be caught in the same trap in which Constanza has found herself," Carlos persisted. "Shall I tell you exactly how your Señor Dangermond has treated her?"

"Hush!" Sabrina said sharply. "I don't want to listen to anything you have to say about him. You don't like him. You are jealous, and you want to turn me against him. I will not listen to you one minute longer!" And leaving others to stare after her open-mouthed, she wrenched herself away from Carlos and left him standing in the center of the courtyard.

His face contorted with fury, he watched as she hurried to Brett's side, and then, aware of the spectacle he was making, of the sly looks and embarrassed laughs of the others, he stalked off the courtyard and disappeared into the night. For Francisca, that was the final affront. Her own features bristling with rage and hostility, she accosted her brother, saying in a low, vicious tone, "I hope you are satisfied now! You have brought my husband to ruin, and now you have shamed and insulted my son in front of all our friends. I will never forgive you for this, Alejandro. *Never!"*

Placing his hand under Francisca's elbow, Alejandro said softly, "You are unduly distraught, my dear. Come, let me find you a place of quiet so that you may recover yourself." And quickly and efficiently, he whisked her into the hacienda.

Once they were alone in the small *sala* at the rear of the hacienda, Alejandro faced his sister, his amber-gold eyes glittering with anger. "I hope," he said grimly, "you have a very good reason for nearly disrupting Sabrina's fiesta this way."

"A good reason!" Francisca fairly screeched. "I should think the humiliation my son has suffered this day would be reason enough! First you allow that . . . that *gringo* to take unwonted liberties with Carlos's *novia,* and now—!" Fury choked her voice, making speech impossible.

Almost wearily, Alejandro muttered, "Francisca, Sabrina is not, nor has she ever been, Carlos's *novia.* It is

209

what *you* long for, but it is not a fact, and you delude yourself in believing that there exists between your son and my daughter anything but friendship." His tone adamant, he finished, "Sabrina does not love Carlos! And I have no intention of seeing her wed a man she does not love. Cease your foolish daydreams!"

It was almost too much for Francisca. The black eyes burning with rage, her hand clenched into a fist as she pressed it dramatically against her full bosom. "You will regret this, *mi hermano!*" she spat. "I have forgiven you much, but this, *this* is unforgivable!"

There was a rap on the door, and with relief Alejandro opened it to find Luis on the other side. His pleasant face full of concern, Luis asked, "Is she all right?"

Alejandro nodded and invited him into the room. Luis hurried to his wife's side murmuring, "My dove, my dove. I know you are upset, but to almost cause a scene! It is not like you. What has come over you?"

Sullenly Francisca regarded her husband. "You can ask?" she managed. "Didn't you see the gringo shame Carlos's *novia* today? Didn't you see what she did to him just moments ago?"

A gentle soul, ruled by his wife, Luis said softly, "It was nothing, *querida.* Our son is not the first young man to encounter the whims of a spirited young woman. He will recover, and no one will think anything of it—*you* are the only one who is making much of it." Throwing Alejandro a helpless look, he added, "As for the other, well, our dream of seeing Carlos marry Sabrina is not to be. And it *was* only a dream, *querida.* Do not be overly distressed that it did not come true." Taking encouragement from her silence, Luis took her hand and dropped an affectionate kiss on it. "Come now, smile for me and make your peace with Alejandro."

That was asking too much of Francisca. Coldly she said, "I have nothing to say to him! He has betrayed me! Take me home, Luis! I cannot bear to remain here longer."

Luis hesitated, but then seeing the implacable expression on his wife's face, he sent Alejandro an imploring glance.

Alejandro met that glance with a commiserating smile. "Take her home, *amigo*. Tomorrow we will talk and find that this has been merely a misunderstanding."

Luis nodded his head, and murmuring coaxingly to Francisca, he urged her away.

His expression thoughtful, Alejandro rejoined his guests, mentioning casually that Francisca had felt unwell and that she and Luis had left.

Unaware of what had happened after she dashed off the dance floor, Sabrina took refuge a short distance away from the hacienda. The music of the guitars floated softly to her, and the lights from the lanterns created a faint golden glow in the silvery darkness of the moonlit night. Her lavender-blue gown rustling gently about her ankles, she rested against the mottled bark of a huge sycamore tree, letting the tranquillity of the night seep into her thoughts.

And such tangled thoughts went through her mind. Brett's attitude was totally incomprehensible to her, and yet she couldn't help responding to him. She wanted to believe that some miracle had taken place, that all the past misconceptions were somehow erased, that the night's actions were a true indication of his feelings. Of Constanza she didn't want to think—she had been almost pleased when Constanza had written declining to attend the fiesta, but now Carlos had destroyed some of her joy. At the moment, she bitterly resented Carlos's constant meddling, but she was also angry with herself for allowing his vexing words to reawaken her own doubts.

A slight sound made her turn her head sharply, and she sighed with a curious mixture of relief and trepidation when she recognized Brett's tall form in the shadows. He was smoking an aromatic cheroot; the pleasing scent of the tobacco drifted on the air as he slowly approached her.

A mocking smile on his mouth, he stopped just inches from her and asked lightly, "The belle of the ball in hiding? Or have I interrupted an assignation . . . again?"

She didn't like the expression in the jade-green eyes when he uttered that last sentence, and a little twinge of anger shot through her. Bluntly she replied, "There is no one else about—you may scour the area if you like. I didn't come out here to meet anyone, and even if I did"—she shot him a challenging look—"it isn't your concern, is it?"

There was silence for a moment as he pensively regarded the tip of his cheroot before tossing it away. Then, leaning his hand on the trunk of the tree near her head, he said softly, "Perhaps I want it to be my concern. What would you say about that?"

Sabrina's throat suddenly went dry, and she was aware of the crazy leap her heart gave. Mutely she stared at him, mesmerized by the potency of his gaze as it roamed over her face.

Gently his other hand moved along the column of her throat, the long fingers caressing the soft skin. Sabrina felt as if she were suffocating—he was so close, and she was trapped by the tree, his powerful body blocking any escape. But escape was the last thing on her mind. Helplessly she closed her eyes, unable to bear his intense scrutiny, afraid he could read what was in her heart.

"Sabrina?" he murmured huskily, his lips barely touching her ear. "No answer? Or am I to take your silence for encouragement of my advances?"

With difficulty she managed, "And if it were?"

A great sigh seemed to escape him, and she felt a feather-light kiss brush across her closed eyes. "If it were, then I would do this." And his mouth closed hungrily over hers, his arms pulling her against him.

He kissed her a long time, a deep, probing, urgent kiss that left Sabrina's wits swimming. She made no attempt to resist him; she couldn't have if her life depended upon it— this was Brett, and she loved him. Passionately she yielded to him, not only pressing herself ardently to him but allowing and encouraging him to deepen the kiss, her lips parting sweetly, her tongue seeking his.

Groaning softly, he tore his lips from hers and muttered into her ear, "This is madness, infant—but I cannot seem to escape it!" He crushed her slender form closer against his tall length, and in an oddly thick voice, he confessed, "I didn't want this to happen. I have fought against it since I held you in my arms that first day in the meadow. It seems

212

it's a hopeless battle that I cannot win—no matter what I do!"

Reveling in his embrace, thrilled by his words, she asked softly, "But it it such a terrible thing? Is there some reason why you should fight against it so?"

He gave a mirthless laugh. An ugly tone to his voice, he demanded, "You ask that of *me?* Me, who has known nothing but treachery at the hands of women?"

"Don't be a fool!" Sabrina said urgently. "Things may have happened in your past that are painful, but they have nothing to do with us! *Nothing!*"

He lifted his head and gazed down at her upturned face. Almost reverently his finger traced her features, lingering on her mouth. "I want to believe that," he said at last. His voice deepening, he muttered, "I *have* to believe it, for I am bewitched by you, Sabrina." He smiled grimly as if some macabre jest had been played on him. "I dream of you—you haunt me, and though when daylight appears I can tell myself it is folly, when night falls . . ." Compulsively his mouth sought hers, all his torment and fury obvious from the nearly brutal way he kissed her. Lifting his lips from her bruised mouth, he murmured, "When night falls, I ache for you. You are like a fever that has entered my brain, and though I try to escape you, though I tell myself I am mad, that nothing good can come from it, that you are like all the others, that you will betray and cause me nothing but pain, in the end I am left with only a gnawing desire to have you in my arms, to kiss you . . . to make love to you."

The last words were uttered so softly, Sabrina barely heard them, but she did, and gently she caressed his dark head, her fingers moving lovingly through the thick black hair. Her own mouth almost touching his, she whispered, "And is that so very bad? So very wrong?"

"Oh, Jesus!" Brett burst out explosively. "I don't know anymore. I only know that when I found you with Carlos, I could have killed him then and there—and strangled you for what you were doing to me. No woman has ever aroused such jealousy within me."

Sabrina started to protest, to explain, but Brett hushed her. Placing a finger on her mouth, he commanded, "*No!* I

don't want to hear anything about what happened there—
it is over and done with and behind us. You said the past
has nothing to do with us, and so even *your* past will have
nothing to do with us!" The dark green eyes glittering
fiercely, he said with barely suppressed savagery, "I want
you. Every instinct I possess urges me to mount my horse
and ride from here as if all the demons in hell were after
me, but I cannot. I find myself deliberately walking into
the web of your spinning." His fingers tightened painfully
on her shoulders, and he gave another mirthless laugh.
"By God, infant, but I *am* mad! I delude myself into
believing that I am doing this to save you from Carlos, but
we both know that is a lie, don't we?"

Unhappily, Sabrina's eyes searched his. For so long she
had yearned to have him confess that he cared for her, but
this wasn't quite the way she had imagined it—nor had he
admitted that he loved her. Wanted her, yes. But love? Of
love he did not speak. But wanting, she thought optimisti-
cally, could become love. Perhaps to a man like Brett, it *was*
love. But there was such tormented fury in his voice, such
bewildered frustration, that her heart ached for him. And
maybe a little for herself—it was obvious that he was a
very reluctant lover. He wanted her, but it was insultingly
clear that it was greatly against his will. Yet she knew
that she could not let this moment escape, that even if he
had not said the exact words she wanted so desperately to
hear, she would take greedily what he had offered. In time
she could prove him wrong, prove that while other women
may have hurt and betrayed him, she never would, that he
would *never* find treachery in her arms. Only love.
And he *would* love her—in time. Time was all she
needed. . . .

When she remained silent, he shook her ungently. The
jade-green eyes narrowing, he asked roughly, "No answer?
No glib reply? No satisfied smile now that you have me
groveling at your feet?"

Inexplicably her mood lifted, and she was filled with a
sudden confidence, a growing certainty that all would be
right. A tiny smile curved her mouth. "Groveling?" she repeated in a teasing tone. "I hardly think so, *querido!* Demanding is more like it!"

He relaxed slightly at her reply, and a mocking light suddenly dancing in his eyes, he murmured, "I have always understood that meek lovers are either fools or fops—I am neither, as you will soon discover!"

A glint of daring in the amber-gold eyes, she said recklessly, "Will I?"

His mouth took on a frankly sensuous curve, and bending closer, he promised huskily, "Oh, yes, infant. *Oh, yes!*" And once again he swept her up into a dizzying embrace, that hard mouth seeking and demanding as it closed over hers.

There was a slight titter of laughter nearby, the intrusive sound of quickly smothered voices, and with obvious reluctance Brett slowly lifted his lips from hers. He sent a smoldering look across his shoulder and muttered with suppressed violence, "I seem to have chosen the wrong place and time for what I want to say." A sleepy fire flickering in his eyes, he added, "And *do.*"

Sabrina laughed breathlessly, the blood singing in her veins, excitement coursing through her entire body at the expression on his face. He *must* love her! And if there had not been the interruption, she was positive he would have admitted it to her. Provocatively she threw him a kiss, and then dancing away from him, she murmured, "But there will be another time . . . won't there?"

He made no move to stop her, and there was almost a tender smile on that chiseled mouth as he drawled softly, "Of *that* you can be certain!"

The remainder of the evening passed in a happy blur for Sabrina. She danced, she ate, and she laughed with gay abandon, the sound of Brett's words a joyous refrain in her brain.

Such was not the case for Carlos. Stalking furiously off the courtyard after Sabrina had left him so summarily, he had immediatedly left the hacienda and ridden to Constanza. Leaving his horse behind her house, he had stomped across the patio only to stop abruptly when he found Constanza sitting there alone.

It was not late, and she had come outside to enjoy the warmth of the night, the house still too stuffy from the heat of the day. A lantern hung nearby, casting a golden pool of light over her; a pitcher of sangría and a glass sat near her hand, and upon seeing Carlos, she murmured, "Shall I call the servant for another glass? Or would you prefer something stronger?"

"Stronger!" he snarled.

Constanza clapped her hands, and a few minutes later, Carlos was sprawled in the chair next to Constanza glaring wrathfully at the amber liquid in his glass. He drank the whiskey in one gulp and then poured himself another from a decanter. His voice surly, he demanded, "Why didn't you attend the fiesta today?"

Constanza smiled faintly. "Because," she said dryly, "I did not want to be as you are now—furious and filled with frustration. Am I to understand that things did not go as you wished?"

"Dios! I have never been so enraged in my life!" Carlos burst out explosively, his black eyes glittering with anger. "I have had to watch the gringo lay claim to Sabrina and have been insulted by Sabrina myself! I could kill them both!"

Her face carefully bland, Constanza asked, "What happened? Nothing you cannot undo, I trust?"

Briefly Carlos gave her a summary of the day's events. When Carlos spoke of the bullfight, of Brett's kiss to Sabrina, Constanza's composure slipped, and her face paled. Noticing it, Carlos smiled nastily. "Disturbs you, does it?" Baring his teeth, he growled, "Think then, how it made *me* feel! *Por Dios!* But I could have slit his throat then and there! As for my beloved *tío* . . ." Eyes narrowing, he said softly, "Some day he will pay for this."

With difficulty, Constanza asked, "You have given up then? You no longer hope to marry Sabrina?"

Carlos laughed, an ugly sound that shattered the quiet night air. "Give up? *Never!* I cannot—without her fortune I am ruined! I *must* have it or be reduced to thieving to keep myself!"

Constanza relaxed. "What do you plan to do? How can you stop what is happening? If Alejandro approves and Sabrina welcomes his suit, what can be done?"

"I could kill him," Carlos offered levelly.

Constanza's dark eyes dilated, and leaning forward, she

said passionately, *"No!* Harm him, Carlos, and I promise you that you shall live to regret it!"

His face tightened, and he demanded in a dangerous tone, "Are you threatening me, *querida?* You will let this gringo drive a wedge between us? We, who have shared so much together?"

Forcing a conciliatory smile on her lips, Constanza said slowly, "I would never threaten you, Carlos . . . but tell me—if I planned to deprive you of Sabrina, wouldn't you try to stop me?"

Reluctantly Carlos nodded his head, a gleam of respect flitting through the black eyes. "So I would, *querida.* So I would." Some of his fury lessening, he said admiringly, "We are so alike. So perfectly matched that nothing will stop us from gaining our goals—Sabrina and her fortune for me, and the gringo and *his* fortune for you!"

The dangerous moment past, Constanza smiled at him, this time more naturally. "You are a rogue, Carlos. Tell me, what do you plan?"

Moodily Carlos stared out into the night. "Bah! I have no plan! I can think of nothing . . . yet." Slanting her a glance, he asked, "Have you thought of something?"

"Perhaps," she began coolly. "But it is going to cost you a great deal of money."

Carlos made a face. "You know that our finances are not overabundant at this time."

"Do you want Sabrina or not?" she asked levelly.

"I want her!" he snapped in reply.

"Then you *will* find a way to give me what I want, won't you?"

"Yes!" Carlos snarled, his mouth tight.

Constanza looked down at her hands as they rested on the pine table. Her voice curiously husky, she said, "We may gain Sabrina for you—she is a woman and can be controlled by her father . . . or guardian. But as for my becoming Señora Dangermond, I rather doubt it. A man cannot be coerced into marriage the way a woman can." She lifted her eyes, and Carlos was startled at the depth of pain he saw there.

Moved, he reached across the table for her hands. "He means so much to you?"

She smiled wryly. "Oh, yes. So much that while I know I cannot have him myself, I cannot bear to see him wed another." Her voice hardening, the fine jaw rigid, she added, "I will do anything to stop him from marrying Sabrina! She has everything—money, youth, and position—while I have nothing! I will *not* let her have him, too!"

"And you have a way to take him away from her? To stop the announcement of their betrothal that is sure to come soon?"

"Perhaps not stop it, but certainly destroy it and make her look at him with loathing, if she is the woman I think she is. . . ."

Carlos regarded her thoughtfully, noting the grim line of her mouth, the unusual hardness of her eyes. "How?"

Constanza smiled. "I will not tell you now. First you must provide me with gold—a great deal of gold, Carlos, for when I am through with your Sabrina, I will not be able to remain here in Nacogdoches. I will have to leave forever, or she will learn the truth and know that we lied to her. And so, when you have given me enough money to pay my passage to Spain, to keep me in luxury for the rest of my life, *then* I shall tell you of my plan."

"We do not have a great deal of time," Carlos persisted. "Something must be done immediately."

A steely smile on her lips, Constanza answered, "It can be done just as soon as you keep your part of the bargain—a fortune in gold. When I have that, I will deliver Sabrina into your arms."

CHAPTER SIXTEEN

It had been hours past midnight before the last guest had left the hacienda and Sabrina had bidden her father and Brett good night. She had laid her lovely gown on a chair near her bed and with a sigh of contentment, had slipped naked into the bed, certain she would fall asleep the moment her head hit the pillow.

Such was not the case. Too much had happened, the future beckoned too alluringly, and there were too many tantalizing moments to remember for sleep to overtake her. She tossed and turned, longing to sleep, to wake and find that it was morning; she burned with eagerness to see what the day would hold.

Eventually she gave up trying to sleep, and after wandering restlessly about her room for several moments, she stepped onto the balcony and stared out into the night. The gleam of the moonlight on the water caught her attention, and suddenly she knew what she wanted to do. She found an old gown, and not bothering with undergarments, she put it on. Quietly she opened her door and with light steps hurried down the silent, darkened hallway to the stairs. Seconds later she was outside, running without a sound on bare feet toward the lake.

The lake was streaked with silver from the moon overhead, and Sabrina gazed at it with wonder as she walked aimlessly along the rippling shoreline, the water still warm from the heat of the day. The night air was calm, not even the cry of an owl breaking the peaceful silence. To Sabrina it seemed as if she were the only person in the world awake, and she found that the night suited her mood, soothing her turbulent anticipation of the morrow.

But Sabrina wasn't alone, nor was she the only person awake. Brett, too, had found it impossible to sleep, and though Sabrina had passed by his room on cat feet, he had heard the slight sound she had made. He had partially undressed, and wearing only his calzoneras, he had been impatiently pacing his room when he heard her pass by. His thoughts had been bitter at that moment; he was unable to believe that he, Brett Dangermond, had fallen in love.

He did not want to admit it, and for weeks now he had deliberately avoided looking into his own heart. To love was weakness and insanity, and like an animal caught in a trap, he was fighting desperately to escape. Tonight he had come dangerously near to committing himself, and he was furiously aware that it was only a matter of time before he *did* commit himself.

It was a painful situation in which he found himself. He hadn't lied when he had said that all his instincts urged him to flee. They did. But just the thought of leaving Sabrina filled him with a black despair, and he knew he was as trapped as any insect in a spider's web. No matter how he struggled, no matter how fiercely he fought, Sabrina's web held him fast, and demons he had forgotten now rose up to taunt him.

The incident with Diana Pardee in London so many years ago had left him particularly sensitive about his own attraction for women. Without conceit, he knew he was a handsome man, an accomplished lover, but were those his *real* attractions . . . or was it his fortune? And not even Sabrina could he acquit of the ugly suspicion that her response to his overtures was because she was even more attracted to his wealth and fortune than she was to him. Repeatedly he told himself that it was a ridiculous idea— the del Torres fortune was probably larger than his own— but his wounds were deep. And there was the knowledge that Carlos was no longer wealthy. If he knew about the de la Vegas' straitened circumstances, it was logical that Sabrina knew about them, too. Had she decided that Brett Dangermond might be a better bargain? It was a persistent thought, and perhaps more than anything, it was what had kept him from declaring himself. If he was to be married, even bitterly conscious that his bride came to him from the bed of another man, he had to be certain that it was not *money* that brought her into *his* arms.

With jerky movements he lit a cheroot, intending to walk downstairs and take a breath of night air before trying to find solace in sleep, and it was then that he heard Sabrina pass by his room. Curious about who might be prowling through the house in the dead of night, he opened his door just in time to see a slight figure disappear down the stairs. Not certain if the form he had glimpsed was Sabrina's but instinctively guessing it was, Brett swiftly shrugged on a white cotton shirt and quickly followed.

He reached the courtyard just as she stepped through the archway in the lattice at the far end of the patio, and in the moonlight he recognized her. Recognized and wondered sickly if she was on her way to Carlos. Disgusted as much as wounded by her apparently insatiable desire for Carlos, he started to turn away, to seek out his room, with every intention of preparing to pack. Tonight. He could not and he would not stay here any longer and let her rip his emotions to shreds. He would think of some excuse to give Alejandro tomorrow for his sudden wish to be gone from this place, but he damn well was *not* staying another night to let that little slut work her wiles on him! But he didn't return to his room.

Instead, telling himself he was all kinds of a fool, he followed her. It was possible, he argued grimly, that he *had* misjudged the situation. And before he condemned her for all time, didn't it behoove him to see the proof with his own eyes? And so it was that Brett stood in the shadows next to the gazebo and watched as Sabrina strolled dreamily near the edge of the lake.

Unaware of Brett's intent gaze, with playful, happy movements Sabrina splashed into the water, laughing softly as it washed over her ankles. Lifting her gown above her knees, with a spurt of childlike glee she ran gracefully along the shoreline, the spray of water from her running feet glittering like diamonds in the night. She stopped just as she came abreast of the gazebo and looked with longing at the placid smoothness of the lake.

Smiling to herself, she stepped back from the water, and giving in to impulse, she recklessly pulled the gown above her head, tossing it carelessly on the ground nearby. For a

221

second she was poised there, her naked body bathed in moonlight.

His breath trapped somewhere in the region of his stomach, Brett stared at the loveliness so unexpectedly presented to him. She was magnificent as she stood motionless at the edge of the water, the moonlight making her a figure of ebony, silver, and ivory, a pagan goddess offering herself to a moon lover. And even as he thought of that comparison, Sabrina raised her arms as if paying homage to the moon.

Her hair hung down her slender back in wild disorder, appearing black in the moonlight, the slim curve of her buttocks a silver arc, the long, lithe legs gleaming like ivory. Her profile was to Brett, and hungrily he stared, entranced by the way the silvery light played across her body, creating tantalizing shadows and mysterious planes. Time and time again his eyes were brought back to the full, tempting thrust of her breast, before his gaze slid appreciatively across the nearly concave stomach and the ivory thighs.

Desire choked him, all the hungry promptings of his dreams rising up full force to conquer his very reason. Like a man in a daze, he threw the cheroot away, heedlessly tossing his shirt in the direction of the gazebo and blindly undoing his calzoneras.

Still thinking she was alone, with a joyous laugh Sabrina slid into the lake, swimming with strong, sure strokes as the water deepened. The water was like silk rushing against her warm body, cooling her, caressing her, making her aware of herself as never before. Playfully she turned on her back, kicking up a large spume of water, and it was then that she saw Brett's tall figure walk out from the shadows of the gazebo.

If the moonlight had clearly revealed her naked state, it did the same to Brett as he slowly, unashamedly walked toward her. Hypnotized, Sabrina was unable to take her eyes away from the sheer masculine beauty of his body. He moved with all the sleek, sinuous grace of a forest animal, a forest lord, she thought giddily, as he neared the water's edge. The blue-black hair glinted with silver lights; the broad chest with its matting of fine, dark curls was intensified in the moonlight; and helplessly Sabrina moved her eyes lower, following the narrow trail of dark hair that grew across his flat stomach down to . . . Shaken by a sudden shyness, she skipped her gaze swiftly to the powerfully muscled legs, and she wondered breathlessly if all men were so superbly fashioned. He looked invincible and very formidable as he stood there, and she was aware of a curling sensation of both fear and longing in the pit of her stomach.

If he entered the water, if he came to her now, they both knew what would happen, and for one timeless moment they stared at each other across the short distance that separated them. Almost as if giving her a choice, Brett demanded thickly, "Do I join you, or do you tell me to leave?"

But there was no choice to be made and they both knew it. Silently, her heart beating frantically in her breast, Sabrina watched as he dived into the lake, his big body cutting cleanly through the water. A few strokes and he was in front of her.

Wordlessly they regarded one another. The water barely covered Sabrina's shoulders, and her wet skin glistened like silver in the moonlight. Her face was clearly revealed, the moonlight caressing the lovely features—the tip-tilted nose, the wide, sensuous mouth—and to Brett there was an ethereal beauty about her. The amber-gold eyes were shadowed, the glory of that red-gold hair muted, and almost reverently he asked, "Are you real? Or only the image of my dreams?"

Brett's face was in the shadows, his back to the moon, and just faintly she could make out the expression of wonderment on his features. It thrilled her and yet touched her, too, and she reached out and stroked a finger across his lips.

"Real," she replied huskily, a smile lurking at the corners of her mouth. "And you?"

Slowly his hands closed around her shoulders, pulling her to him, the buoyancy of the water making the movements light and dreamlike. Sabrina's slender body floated toward his, rocking gently against his as their limbs met, the water rippling around their two bodies. His lips brushed hers, and bringing one arm down to caress her naked buttocks, he brought her even closer to him, making her intensely aware of the heat and full arousal of his lean body. A crooked smile on his mouth, his teeth a brief flash in the darkness, he murmured, "Oh, yes, I am very real!" The smile vanished, and he studied her features intently. "Real and so hungry for you, moon-witch," he crooned the moment before his mouth captured hers in a long, languorous kiss.

Dreamily Sabrina gave herself up to the fierce sweetness of his kiss, her lips opening ardently under his, her entire body tingling as a thousand new and exciting sensations swamped her. Crushed against the wet sleekness of his chest, her breasts suddenly seemed full and heavy, her nipples hardening with a pleasurable ache, and between their bodies she could feel the provocative, insistent pressure of his swollen manhood. Her mouth was full of him, his tongue searching and demanding as it explored, his hands moving with sensuous fascination as they slid down her back to her hips and thighs. It was exquisite torture, the water intensifying the feeling of pagan abandon as it cushioned their locked bodies, increasing the feeling of being lost in a silken, sensual dream.

Sabrina's arms crept around Brett's strong neck, her fingers absently tangling and tousling the thick black hair of his head. She had wanted to be naked against him, and reality proved far more satisfying than imagination, the warmth and power of that steel-muscled body straining so hungrily against hers filling her with a knife-sharp pleasure.

Bracing his feet on the bottom of the lake, his legs wide apart, with demanding hands on her hips, Brett brought Sabrina's thighs between his. When their bodies touched, when her groin brushed delicately against his achingly full organ, he groaned out loud with excitement, his lips moving with increasing urgency over hers, his breathing becoming hard and labored.

He held her still against him, his hands effortlessly spanning her narrow waist, both of them reveling in the sheer delight of feeling the texture and pressure of the other's body. When his lips reluctantly left her mouth to explore her face, to travel like fire along her jawline to her ear, Sabrina's breathing became as difficult and labored as his, desire coiling and writhing almost painfully within her loins. The flick of his warm tongue as it slowly searched her ear was unbearably erotic, and with urgent hands she brought his lips back to hers, kissing him as hungrily as he had her only moments before, her tongue's caress as it searched his mouth driving them both half-mad with a desperate wantonness.

Sensually Brett undulated her hips between his legs, and every time their bodies met, each experienced a shock of raw desire. Sabrina could feel the probing length of his manhood slipping hotly against her thighs, and she gasped with a mingling of excitement and apprehension. He was so strong, so powerful, and the thought of what he would do to her with his lean, hard body was intoxicating and yet faintly alarming. Every inch of her tingled with an arousing awareness of his body, her flesh intensely sensitive, the slightest touch, the lightest movement, sending a shudder of near ecstasy rippling deep within her.

His hands captured her buttocks, cupping them, pulling her up against him as he buried his mouth more passionately on hers, all coherent thought having fled. Mercilessly gripped by the deepest, most powerful desire he had ever experienced in his life, Brett lifted her partially from the water, his lips sliding warmly down her wet chest, hungering for the taste of those sweet breasts that were now exposed to his gently ravaging mouth.

They were like two pagan lovers in the moonlight, Sabrina's skin glistening like silver, small droplets of water gleaming like diamonds on her full, firm breasts; Brett's dark head was bent to her nipple, the steely muscles of his upper back etched by moonlight. Her hands caressed his broad shoulders; her head was flung back in wild abandon as his mouth moved on her breast, his tongue curling tightly over the desire-swollen nipple, his teeth softly grazing the sensitized skin. Sabrina shivered with pleasure, the warm, pulsating feeling in her loins becoming stronger, more demanding. Driven by emotions she had no control over, she pressed her fingers harder into his shoulders, her slender body moving evocatively against him.

225

Brett groaned softly as her movements increased, the blood pounding thickly in his head, and his hold on her hips tightened, his fingers grasping her almost brutally. Her thighs had instinctively found their way around his body, and the touch of her as she pressed against him with wanton innocence was indescribable. The aching, throbbing shaft of his maleness rode up between her buttocks, and Brett trembled at just the thought of possessing her.

Urgently he forced one hand between their bodies, his fingers sliding down her stomach to explore and excite the very center of her being. Breathlessly Sabrina surged up against him as his fingers gently caressed her, her arms clenching around his neck, her lips moving feverishly across his dark hair. Insistently he probed between her legs, arousing a raging storm of carnal emotion within her, and again and again she arched up against his hand, shaking and quivering from the force of the maelstrom his warm, searching caresses had aroused.

Unable to bear the ecstasy that was swamping her body, she moaned aloud, and at the sound Brett could wait no longer. As if guessing what would happen, she returned her lips to his. His hands went to her hips, and impatiently he guided her to him. For a moment she was poised above him, and then with a fierce, fluid movement he thrust himself up within her, pulling her down onto him, the water swelling around them.

Her cry of hurt was muffled beneath his lips but he felt it, as well as the slight obstruction of her virginity, felt her body tense with pain. His eyes snapped open, and he stared at her lovely face with shock. "Jesus, Sabrina," he breathed raggedly, "I didn't mean to . . . I wouldn't have hurt you . . ." He stopped speaking, desire making speech or thought impossible. She was so incredibly warm, so very tight around him, that he closed his eyes with agonized pleasure. His hands caressed her hips, and thickly he muttered, "I can't stop now. I'm eaten up with want of you, and this time I cannot be denied!" With a tender savagery his mouth captured hers, his hands guiding her up and down, his body plunging deeply within her.

For a moment he stayed fully within her, letting her body adjust to this sudden invasion, and Sabrina clung weakly to him in stunned compliance. His very size made her ache, and she was bewildered by the poignant emotions that raced through her. She was a virgin no longer. She hurt physically from that loss, and yet there was such a feeling of rapture, such joy at becoming *his* woman, that soon the pain vanished and she was aware only of pleasure, a pleasure she had never imagined.

Her thighs tightened around his waist, and almost lasciviously she arched up to him, wanting him to do more, wanting to feel him move within her. Brett sighed softly at her movements, and with an odd tenderness he slowly, unhurriedly thrust his body into hers, giving them both ecstasy, taking them with his increasingly frantic movements into the limitless, intensely sensual world shared only by lovers. And when it was over, when ecstasy had been reached, they still clung to each other, unable to let this magical moment end.

Sabrina was so shattered by the pulsating explosion of her own body, by the waves that shuddered through her when at last she reached fulfillment, that it was only when he laid her gently down on one of the cushions in the gazebo that she became aware that Brett had carried her still locked around him from the water. For one tiny moment her mind rebelled that he should bring her here, Carlos's attack still vivid, but then Brett's warm, hard body was lying beside her, his hands touching her breasts, his mouth nipping that sensitive place where her neck joined her shoulder, and she instantly forgot everything but the drugging caresses of the man who lay beside her.

Propping himself up on one elbow, Brett reached for his discarded shirt lying nearby and slowly began to dry her wet body, the warmth of his hands burning through the cotton material. With slow, lingering movements he rubbed her skin, unconsciously arousing her again, the abrasion of the material and his fondling hands equally evocative. When he reached between her thighs, she arched up against the cotton shirt, excited by the way he used it on her body. She thought he smiled at her restless tossings, but she couldn't be sure, and a second later he threw the shirt aside and lay back down beside her.

They touched each other gently, wonderingly, Brett's

227

lips searing a path down to her breasts, his tongue flicking and teasing the rigid nipples, his hands wandering at will over her slender body. Sabrina trembled under his knowing caresses, her own untaught hands moving more slowly, more hesitantly, over his hard muscles. There was an element of astonishment in her touch; she had never realized how soft and downy a man's body hair would feel, how silken the faint strands that covered his legs and arms would be. The mat of curls on his broad chest was thicker, more springy, and with catlike ecstasy, she closed her fingers over them, her nails lightly brushing his nipples.

Brett groaned with pleasure, the sound exciting Sabrina, and with more confidence, she let her fingers continue their explorations, enthralled by the texture and warmth of his skin, delighted at the way his own nipples formed hard little buds as her fingers rubbed across them. With feather-light strokes her hands moved over his body: his arms, his shoulders, the ridges and swells of his muscular back, the surprising firmness of his strong buttocks, and the long length of his powerful legs. Touching him gave her pleasure, and unconsciously she sighed, her hands sliding across his flat stomach and encountering his near-to-bursting manhood. For a second she hesitated, and then, driven by her own needs, she closed her hand around him, and she was elated and shaken by the shudder that rippled through him. She marveled at his size, remembering how it had felt within her, and her hand instinctively began sliding up and down the warm, bulging shaft.

Unable to stand her sweet exploration a second longer, Brett wrenched himself away, gasping for breath. "Not yet," he muttered hoarsely. "I want to make love to you all night. I want to touch you, to taste you, to fill you again with me, but if you don't stop what you're doing, we may both be doomed to disappointment!"

Sabrina's pulse quickened at the naked desire that burned deep within his eyes. Without volition her arms closed around his neck and she offered her mouth to him, wanting him to kiss her, wanting him to continue this wild magic. Instantly he dropped his head, his mouth burning across her face to her lips, but he didn't kiss her. Instead, his lips tantalizing inches from hers, he murmured, "I

228

want to look at you, to burn the memory of this night forever into my mind." And then he shifted slightly, removed her arms from around his neck, and raised himself up to stare down at her body, the moonlight gilding it with silver.

She was beautiful as she lay there before him, her hair spread out like a fan behind her head, her full breasts with the erect nipples illuminated by the silvery light of the moon. Appreciatively his eyes ran down to the flat stomach, to the curly hair between her thighs.

Overtaken by a sudden shyness, Sabrina modestly raised her hands to her breasts, one knee shielding her lower nakedness. An incredibly tender expression crossed his harsh face. "Don't hide yourself from me, Sabrina," he breathed softly, reverently. "You're lovely, and your nakedness is nothing to be ashamed of." Slowly he removed her hands from her breasts and then gently pushed aside her knee. Unexpectedly he lowered his head and pressed a hot kiss where the fiery curls grew between her thighs. Sabrina's body jumped with shock, a fierce, urgent ache suddenly exploding up through her body. With agonizing leisure his lips moved up across her stomach, his tongue leaving a trail of fire wherever it touched. His mouth finally found hers, and he kissed her like a man with a long hunger to assuage, his hand once again at her breast, his thumb gently sliding across the sensitive nipples.

Feverishly Sabrina pressed up against him, the ache in her loins driving every thought but one from her mind. She wanted him. She was consumed by an insatiable need to have him take her again, to know again the rapture only he could give her. This, she thought dreamily, was what being a woman meant, what it meant to make love. Remembering what he had done to her in the lake, remembering the swelling pressure, the magnificent size of him, created a pulsating warmth in her loins, and she returned his kiss with a compelling hungriness.

Startled by the blatant passion of her kiss, Brett glanced down at her, one eyebrow rising quizzically. He fondled her breast, feeling the nipple's tightness. His voice suddenly husky, he asked, "Does this mean what I think it does? What I hope it does?"

Sabrina flushed, but her eyes were bright with unmistakable desire, and Brett laughed exultantly. His lips caught hers, pressing more intimately this time, more insistently. When her mouth opened, her tongue seeking his, it was as if an inferno had been instantly unloosed, elemental desire blinding them to everything but the joy to be found in each other's body. And this time when Brett took her, when he lay embedded deep within her, when his body thrust powerfully into hers, there was no pain, only pleasure, only mindless exquisite ecstasy.

Afterward, passion spent, they sought out the lake again, this time swimming contentedly next to each other, a sweet, companionable silence between them. And then later, when they had dressed, they walked slowly, reluctantly back toward the hacienda, Brett's arm draped possessively across her shoulders, their bodies brushing against one another with every step they took.

Silently, like two conspirators, they entered the hacienda, creeping up the stairs, a slight, breathless giggle escaping from Sabrina. Brett hushed it with a fervent kiss and then, with obvious unwillingness, released her. They regarded each other somberly a moment, and then Brett said roughly, "We'll talk later. After I have spoken with your father."

Mutely Sabrina nodded, a tremulous smile on her mouth. Compulsively Brett traced the outline of her lips with one finger and muttered almost angrily, "You'd better go to your own room, or I won't be responsible for my actions!"

A mischievous grin curved her mouth, and she leaned into him, faintly touching his lean cheek with her warm lips, her slender fingers deliberately touching him below the waist. He groaned and started to reach for her, but with a smothered laugh, Sabrina danced away from him. She blew him an impudent kiss and then disappeared down the shadowy hall.

Brett stood there for several minutes after she had gone, a bemused smile on his harsh face, an oddly tender light gleaming in the dark green eyes. Then, with a light step, he turned away and swiftly entered his bedchamber.

After lighting a candle, he poured himself half a glass of

brandy, holding it loosely in his hands, sipping it with appreciation. He was pleasantly tired, both his mind and body at peace, and yet the thought of bed and sleep were out of the question.

He shrugged out of his shirt, lit a cheroot, and settled down comfortably in a nearby chair to contemplate the events of the night. The candlelight flickered across the room, illuminating the streaks of blood on his discarded shirt where it lay on his bed, and for a long, astonished moment he stared at it. If he had doubted what his own body had told him when he possessed Sabrina tonight, there before his very eyes was tangible proof of her virginity.

He swallowed painfully, a strange sort of savage joy mingling with a sudden, cynical suspicion. Sabrina's cousin had obviously lied about being her lover—but that didn't mean he had lied about *every*thing. It didn't mean that Carlos hadn't been telling the truth about Sabrina wanting the Dangermond fortune or that she hadn't been angling for a marriage proposal from the richer of the two men.

An ugly expression on his handsome face, Brett tossed down the rest of the brandy, hoping the liquor would drive out the sudden nasty taste in his mouth. The memory of Sabrina writhing under Carlos in the gazebo came back with a vengeance to shatter his contented mood.

It was true that Carlos had not possessed Sabrina, but, Brett reminded himself grimly, only because of his timely, or *un*timely, interruption. If he hadn't appeared then, there was no doubt in his mind that Carlos would have experienced what he had tonight.

Filled with an unexpected violence, Brett stood up and poured himself a full glass of brandy this time. Had Sabrina been cleverly playing them off one against the other? And tonight, had she finally decided that he was the better catch? The one to whom she would at last surrender her virginity?

Unemotionally he viewed the past several weeks, the way Sabrina had blown hot and then cold. The way she would charm him one week and then treat him with contempt and indifference the next. Even knowing the supposed reasons behind her capricious actions didn't still the devils that were now fully alive within his brain. Carlos's hints and poisonous words and his own antipathy toward women now joined forces in his mind, awakening all his dormant cynicism.

Had Sabrina calculatingly planned tonight? It was certainly one positive way of wringing a proposal from a reluctant swain. Brett's chiseled mouth twisted. What man, after tasting the delights he had tonight, would, or even could, for that matter, turn his back on an enchantress like Sabrina? He couldn't. Even if she *had* deliberately entrapped him. He wanted her, and he knew that in spite of all the suspicions and doubts that churned in his brain, today, at the first opportunity, he was going to ask Alejandro for Sabrina's hand in marriage.

That decision should have brought him joy, but instead he was engulfed by a feeling of bitter defeat. He would never know the reasons behind Sabrina's actions tonight; there would always be a lingering suspicion that Carlos had spoken the truth, that the Dangermond fortune was what had attracted Sabrina to him.

Revolted and angry with himself for what he was thinking, he pulled on a pair of boots and yanked out a clean shirt from a heavy mahogany wardrobe. He needed to escape the confines of his room, desperately needed to escape his own sordid thoughts.

Dawn wasn't far off when he slipped silently from the hacienda. He wandered aimlessly through the forest, the pink and gold light of the rising sun banishing the murky shadows of the night.

Brett walked for a long time, lost in his own unhappy thoughts. One moment he was positive that Sabrina was the woman he had always secretly hoped would appear in his life; the next, he was equally positive that he had fallen into a trap as old as time, had been ensnared by a scheming, greedy little hussy with all the charms of Venus.

There was, he realized furiously, no simple solution to his dilemma. Unless, of course, he was willing to throw away the precepts of a lifetime. Taking Sabrina on blind trust was his only solution, and that, he admitted acidly, would be insanity. And yet, what other path lay open to him? He had taken her virginity, abused the trust of a man he respected highly, and the only honorable way out of his position was marriage. Besides, he didn't really think he could live without Sabrina. She had come to mean too much to him. For his own sanity and any hope of happiness he *had* to marry her.

But what sort of marriage would they have? he wondered bleakly. One such as that shared by his father and Gillian? Or could they miraculously find the joy that Hugh had with Sofia?

Unhappily Brett sighed. God! What a tangle! And yet, despite all his reservations, he was aware of a reckless disregard rising up through him. Always a gambler, he suddenly realized that in spite of all the odds he was going to marry Sabrina del Torres, that he was more than willing to take the risks, willing to face the possibility of pain and disaster. It might even be worth it, he admitted with a soft smile, remembering Sabrina's sweet mouth under his. She had bewitched him, and for the moment at least, he had no desire to shatter the spell she had woven around him.

The demons momentarily laid to rest, a faint smile on his lips, Brett began to walk swiftly back toward the hacienda. The sun had by now splashed its golden rays through the canopy of the forest, and with pleasure he glanced around him, noticing for the first time the luxurious undergrowth, the myriad vines and young trees and bushes that choked the forest floor. Looking skyward he caught a glimpse of the shiny red and yellow fruit of a Chickasaw plum tree; nearby grew a wild cherry tree, the ripening fruit shining purple-black through the saw-toothed leaves. Flowers, too, were abundant this time of year, providing a rainbow of color—the deep pink clusters of milkweed, the delicate blue of a patch of wild asters, the cheerful yellow of black-eyed Susans, all were scattered here and there. But it was the tall, eye-catching, bright orange wood lilies with their dusting of purple spots that he actually stopped to admire.

A huge clump of the exotic lilies grew near the edge of the forest, and staring at the tall, elegant plants, the slender stalks heavy with vivid orange flowers, Brett was reminded inexplicably of Sabrina. It might have been the bright color that made him think of her glorious red-gold hair; it could have been their very flamboyance, their exotic air, that called her to mind. At any rate, he stood there staring at them, thinking of Sabrina. The petals were velvet soft, and as he gently cupped one particularly beautiful bloom, a whimsical smile twitched at the corners of his mouth. He must have gone mad to compare her with a lily—she was far more like a tigress than a lily! A lily with the spirit of a tiger, he thought amusedly, recalling the day in the meadow when she had slashed his arm with her knife. A tiger lily, he mused slowly. *His* tiger lily.

CHAPTER SEVENTEEN

Sabrina had found sleep no easier to obtain than Brett had, but at least she wasn't driven by the same demons. She did, however, have doubts of her own.

She didn't regret what had happened tonight. And even though she lay sleepless in her bed, her body aching from Brett's lovemaking, a warm feeling of happiness surrounded her. She had become a woman tonight, Brett's woman, and nothing could ever diminish that joy. But in the back of her mind there was a faint, niggling worry, a worry that as time passed became larger and more dominant.

Brett had said he would speak to her father, and it was only natural that she assumed he meant to ask for her hand in marriage. Soon she would be his wife, and while she was flooded with joyous anticipation, she could not entirely banish a persistent feeling of anxiety . . . of foreboding.

At first she suspected it was the memory of all the gloomy things that Tía Sofia had written about Brett that disturbed her. But finally, after much twisting and turning, she decided that it wasn't those letters and what they contained that was behind her sensation of uneasiness. It was Brett himself. She wasn't naive enough to think that he was going to change overnight into a perfect suitor or even husband; she was aware that there were bound to be obstacles in their path to happiness. But if they loved one another . . .

Love. They had made love tonight, wildly passionate love, and she had no reservations about the depth of his wanting—his body betrayed it, and even he had admitted it. But wanting wasn't loving, and not once tonight, even in the throes of his deepest passion, had he mentioned or hinted that he loved her.

Restlessly she turned over in her bed. What did *that* matter? she asked herself rebelliously. *She* hadn't mentioned love either! But I do love him, she thought fiercely. So much so that I cannot even bear to think of life without him. But does he love me?

She wanted to believe that he did. It was incomprehensible to her that he could have acted as he had, done the things he had to her, and yet *not* love her. But he hadn't said so, her brain insisted slyly. He had said he *wanted* her, and men were vastly different from women. They didn't *need* love to *make* love.

Sabrina sat up in bed, and pulling her knees to her chest, she stared blankly through the dawn-filled room. Could she marry a man who didn't love her, who only *wanted* her? And was it only her body he wanted, or did the del Torres fortune have any influence upon him?

Angry for even thinking such a thing, she pushed that unpleasant thought aside. Carlos's suspicions have begun to haunt me, she thought reluctantly. And she wondered, for the first time, what her cousin had meant by his comments about Constanza.

Assailed by the memory of Brett dancing with Constanza, Sabrina was startled at the wave of jealous fury that swept over her. He was hers, and she would *not* share him! But how did one tame such a man, bind such a man so tightly, so strongly, that he would never *ever* wish for another woman?

She didn't know the answer, but with a determined expression on her exquisite face, she made a grim little vow that she would find a solution. There was much, she realized, that she would forgive him, but another woman was not one of those things—his past she could live with, but his future . . .

Suddenly she giggled. She was just going to have to make him want her so desperately, so powerfully, that he would never have a second in which to even think of another woman! And perhaps, just maybe, she could make him love her as much as she loved him—then nothing could ever come between them; their love would conquer any difficulty they might confront in the future.

Satisfied within herself, Sabrina yawned and slid thankfully back between her sheets. She smiled and drifted gently off to dream of Brett, of the wonderful life that was going to be theirs.

That morning, Alejandro was surprised to discover that he would be breakfasting alone. Sabrina, Bonita informed him, was sleeping soundly, no doubt worn out from yesterday's festivities, and Ollie had said that his master was doing the same. Somewhat thoughtfully, Alejandro ate his morning meal. He had been up as late as the others, he was much older than the others, and yet he had found it no trouble to rise by mid-morning. Suddenly he smiled, remembering certain moonlit conversations with Elena during the halcyon time of their courtship. Ah, if only . . .

That lazy afternoon, he was to have his fondest wish come true. A polite note from Brett requesting to meet him in the library at three o'clock sent his hopes spinning wildly, and when at the appointed hour Brett presented himself and formally requested Sabrina's hand in marriage, Alejandro could hardly contain himself.

A wide, affectionate grin splitting his handsome face, Alejandro said joyously, "But of course you have my permission to marry my daughter! It is what I have hoped for, dreamed of since . . ." He stopped and sent Brett, standing politely in front of the sofa where he sat, a sheepish look. A slightly embarrassed flush stained his cheeks, and almost shamefacedly he admitted, "When I sent you the invitation to visit with us, to discuss the planting of sugar, I have to confess that I hoped that you and Sabrina would fall in love and wish to marry. The sugar was only an excuse to invite you." An irresistible twinkle in his eyes, he murmured, "I trust you will forgive you father-in-law-to-be for this deception?"

An answering twinkle in the jade-green eyes, Brett said ironically, "You know, I wondered about that invitation—and your apparently tepid interest in the growing of sugar." He bowed mockingly and added dryly, "You played your cards very close to your chest, I'll grant you

237

that. Remind me to be more wary of you in the future—especially when you send me invitations!"

Even though Brett had told Sabrina he would speak to her father, he hadn't been as certain about the outcome as he would have liked. And as the hour had approached for him to face Alejandro and actually bring up the subject of marriage, Brett had been aware of a feeling of uncertainty and nervousness—he who was always confident and assured and *never* nervous. It had occurred unpleasantly to him that Alejandro might withhold his approval of the match, and he had been shocked at the tight ball of tension that had lodged in his chest when he finally met with Alejandro. Unnaturally relieved to have the business done with, Brett relaxed and allowed himself to be caught up in Alejandro's enthusiasm.

They discussed the possible dates for the announcement, then the possible places and dates for the wedding itself. It was at that point that Brett remembered something of vital importance. A rueful smile curving his chiseled mouth, he said lightly, "I think before we proceed much further, sir, that I had better ask your daughter what she feels about the situation." Wryly he continued, "She could, you know, turn me down."

"Unthinkable!" Alejandro burst out in dismay. Almost beseechingly, he asked, "She won't, will she? You won't let her refuse you?"

Amused, Brett drawled, "I believe you are the one to give me encouragement, not the other way around!"

Alejandro pulled a face. "I know, but with Sabrina I am often helpless." He shot Brett an appraising look. "You know," he said quietly, "it was because I thought you could control her, tame her if you will, that I first considered you as a son-in-law. I wanted someone strong for her, someone she would not lead around like a pet bull." A slight smile crossed his face. "And you, *amigo,* were the only person I could think of. The only man I wanted for my daughter. I wanted her safe and I wanted her loved, and I believe that you will do both—protect her and love her."

Feeling suddenly extremely humble and crass, Brett replied levelly, "I promise you that I shall spend my life doing just that." The enormity of what he had just committed himself to struck him like a blow. Did he love Sabrina? Protect her he certainly would . . . but love her? Love was a word that had never entered his vocabulary. Though he would admit to a powerful attraction, a compelling affinity, he wasn't yet ready to call it love. He wanted her in many ways, not just her body but all the things she was: he wanted to marry her, wanted her as his wife, wanted the right to call her his own . . . but love?

Alejandro was too taken up with his own thoughts to realize that Brett had never actually said that he loved Sabrina, and rising from the sofa, Alejandro walked to the door. Opening it, he motioned to his majordomo, Clemente, who was hovering nearby, and said, "Find Señorita Sabrina and request that she join us, *por favor.*"

A beaming smile on his dark face, Clemente hustled away. That a betrothal was imminent would have been impossible to conceal from the house servants—and after yesterday's scene at the bull ring, the entire ranch was speculating about the situation. Clemente found Sabrina just as she was coming down the stairs, and a benevolent sparkle in his brown eyes, he politely delivered Alejandro's request. He watched her walk toward the library and then immediately rushed to the kitchen, eager to share this tidbit with the others.

Sabrina had taken special care with her toilet this day, and she looked breathtakingly lovely. The red-gold hair tumbled in artless array about her shoulders, framing her bewitching features. There was an expectant glow in the amber-gold depths of her eyes, a soft smile curved her full lips, and her gown of crisp white muslin intensified the golden sheen of her skin. High-waisted in the latest fashion from Europe and trimmed with a profusion of frothy lace at the modest neckline and puffed sleeves, the gown heightened her exotic beauty, the full skirt fluttering delightfully as she entered the room where Alejandro and Brett awaited her.

Brett was conscious of a rush of some indefinable emotion through his body when he saw her, and in that instant nothing mattered anymore except that he *must* have her as his wife. An odd glitter flickered in the depths of those

239

jade-green eyes, not quite tender, not quite savage, and yet wholly devastating.

Almost shyly Sabrina's gaze met his, a becoming flush attractively staining her cheeks at the expression in his eyes. She had forgotten the impact he had upon her, and now, facing him in the sane light of day, seeing that lean, handsome face, remembering the taste of those hard lips on hers, her pulse quickened.

Alejandro observed them with pleased satisfaction, and feeling decidedly *de trop,* he approached Sabrina and took her hand in his. Sending her a smile full of warmth and love, he said softly, *"Chica,* Brett has something he would like to ask you. And like the good father I am, I will leave you alone with him to hear what he has to say. I hope most fervently that you will find his conversation *very* appealing."

Alone with Brett, Sabrina discovered herself to be suddenly tongue-tied. The amber-gold eyes were fixed on the top button of his gaily embroidered waistcoat, and wildly she wondered what to say to him. *Buenos días* seemed an extremely tepid and formal greeting to a man in whose arms one had lain naked and abandoned the previous evening, and yet to blurt out "I love you!" was unthinkable!

Brett found himself to be in exactly the same predicament, although confessing to love wasn't his problem. Sophisticated and urbane as he was, he had never before proposed marriage. Words whirled chaotically through his brain, emotions he had never even guessed at beat frantically in his heart, and yet he was speechless. He was aware of a fierce yearning to sweep her into his arms, to rain soft kisses over her face, to whisper he knew not what in her ear, but he was as helpless and backward as an untried youth.

He should have followed his natural inclinations, but as the silence spun out and grew increasingly strained, he finally said stiffly, "I asked your father if he would allow us to marry—he said it would please him. Would it please you?" It wasn't how he had meant to propose, and silently, bitterly, he cursed his clumsiness.

He had made no move to approach her, and Sabrina didn't realize the effort it had cost him to say those seemingly indifferent words. Numbly she stared at him, faintly conscious of a pain in her heart, a feeling of dismay and disappointment creeping through her. How cold he sounded. How very *un*loverlike, she thought with a flick of temper.

Slowly her eyes searched his shuttered face, pondering the enigma he represented. Where had the impassioned lover of last night gone? Why did he seem so very cold and aloof, almost intimidating? And again it occurred unpleasantly to her that he had never mentioned love. Hadn't even told her that he cared for her now.

Unable to stand the suspense, filled with an alien nervousness, Brett demanded, "Well? Are you going to marry me?" He was aware that he was mishandling the situation, but he was unable to do anything else. Where, he questioned sourly, is my facile tongue? Where are the words that I really want to say? How can I explain what I feel? How do I tell her of the yearnings, the intoxicating sensations, she arouses within me? The pleasure and excitement I feel whenever she is near me?

His proposal struck Sabrina as insulting, and for one brief moment she toyed with the agreeable notion of refusing him. But the reality of the situation held her fast—she wanted desperately to become his wife, and despite his undeniably surly offer of marriage, she knew what her answer would be. But there was a sparkle of resentment in her eyes as she said almost as curtly as he, "Yes, yes, I will marry you."

He felt greatly relieved. A surge of nearly painful joy engulfed him, leaving him strangely light-headed. Fatuously he grinned at her and said devoutly, "Thank God *that's* over with!" And he could have bitten his tongue off the second the thoughtless words had left his lips.

Sabrina stiffened, and her face unfriendly, she started to make a scathing reply, but Brett reached her in one swift stride. Pulling her into his arms, he kissed her warmly, tenderly, almost, Sabrina thought, astonished, apologetically.

Lifting his mouth from hers, his hands lightly holding her shoulders, he said ruefully, "Forgive me, infant! I haven't much practice in offering for a wife."

Not the least appeased, although she did feel a little encouraged, Sabrina sent him a look. "I am not," she spluttered, "an infant! And in the future you would do well to remember it!"

A smile that made Sabrina's hand itch to slap his cheek curved his mouth. "As you say, madame wife-to-be," he replied meekly enough, a mocking gleam in the jade-green eyes.

Trapped between a sudden inexplicable desire to giggle and an urge to smack that infuriating smile from his face, Sabrina stood indecisively in the circle of his arms. A small silence fell, and gradually the smile faded from Brett's lips.

Intently they stared at one another, a powerful, fierce emotion suddenly exploding between them, and with a muttered imprecation, Brett jerked her to him and found her mouth with his. Passionately they clung to one another, their arms locked around each other, oblivious to anything but the sheer, heady rapture that consumed them.

Alejandro's polite tap on the door they never even heard, and after waiting a few seconds longer, he tapped a little harder. Still no response, and impatient to know the results of his matchmaking, he slowly opened the door. Seeing the embracing couple, he sighed happily, an expression of delight crossing his face. He hesitated and then coughed politely.

Reluctantly Brett raised his head and slowly released Sabrina. Looking across to Alejandro, he stated simply, "She said yes."

Alejandro laughed and said merrily, "I assumed so!" And clapping his hands, he ordered, when Clemente appeared, "A bottle of our very best wine—the bottle of claret that I laid down when Sabrina was born." His voice filled with satisfaction, he added, "Your mistress is to be married, Clemente! Wish her well!"

Grinning from ear to ear, Clemente did just that and then raced away to do Alejandro's bidding and to spread the word. Their Señorita Sabrina would marry the handsome Señor Brett! What joy had come to the household of the del Torreses.

Sabrina remained in the circle of Brett's arms, her face glowing with exhilaration. She was to marry Brett! She was to be his wife! Oh, but the saints and the angels had been good to her! The man she adored would be her husband.

Appraising the expression on her face, Alejandro chuckled. "I don't need to ask if you are happy, *chica.* Your eyes give you away."

Sabrina blushed, and she thought she felt Brett's mouth brush her hair the moment before she rushed into her father's arms. Smiling at Alejandro, she confessed, "I am happy! Are you?"

"But of course, *chica!* Didn't I plan it?" he asked with mock affront.

A little frown creased her forehead. "Plan it?"

Alejandro's mouth twisted wryly. "You will not be offended and wreak your wrath on us poor helpless males?" he demanded teasingly. When Sabrina shook her head slowly, he continued, "I wanted a good strong man for you. Someone you could love and respect. Someone who would insure that you had the kind of marriage I shared with your mother. There was no one I could think of until I remembered Brett. And that," he said with a wide grin, "is why I wrote to him and invited him to visit with us. Why I appeared to be so interested in growing sugar."

Sabrina laughed with her father, but there was a hollow feeling in her chest. Was this an arranged marriage then, after all? she wondered tightly. Had her father and Brett arranged things to their satisfaction while she, poor, silly fool, had blindly gone along with their plan, even to the extent of falling in love? Feverishly she thrust the notion away, trying frantically to recapture her euphoria.

It proved to be ridiculously easy to accomplish. The wine arrived, and with Brett's warm, strong arm around her waist, the look in his eyes vanquished her fears as her father offered a toast to them. They drank the toast from the same glass, Brett, his gaze intent upon her face, deliberately placing his lips where hers had touched.

Alejandro was ecstatic, full of plans, full of satisfaction and a strange sense of peace. Lightly he touched the turquoise and silver bracelet Elena had given him. She *will* be happy, *querida,* he promised silently.

Happily he called to Clemente again, insisting that the house servants come immediately and join in the toast. The hacienda was soon full of laughter and excited chatter, the news spreading like wildfire down to the stables, to the vaqueros and their families.

Flushed and jubilant, eventually Alejandro and the betrothed pair found themselves seated on the patio, recovering from the irrepressible outpouring of good will and good wishes the engagement had occasioned. And it was then that Carlos arrived at the hacienda.

That something momentous had occurred was obvious from the animated buzz of conversation he heard when he rode up to the front of the hacienda and dismounted. Clemente's beaming smile and his, "Oh, Señor Carlos! Such good news! But come, come to the patio and let Señor Alejandro tell you!" gave him a further inkling of what was to come.

Carlos hid his fury well. Alejandro never suspected the rage and hatred that churned in his nephew's breast when he called out gaily, *"Hola,* Carlos! Come and join us! If we all seem a trifle giddy, it is because just this afternoon, shortly before you arrived, Brett and Sabrina became betrothed."

The black eyes opaque, Carlos flashed a coldly polite smile to the trio. "My congratulations," he said punctiliously, his voice without warmth or enthusiasm. Fixing Sabrina with an assessing stare, he added, "I trust that you will be happy, cousin, with your choice."

Brett had risen when Carlos appeared, and standing next to Sabrina's chair, he laid a strong hand lightly but meaningfully on her slender shoulder. His dark green eyes full of challenge, he promised softly, "She will be, you have no concern over that."

The hostility between the two men could almost be felt, and Alejandro moved uneasily. With a forced joviality, he said, "Join us, please, in a toast for their future together."

Just short of rudeness, Carlos declined. "I am sorry, Tío," he said coldly, "but I cannot linger. I only came to tell you that the bandits are active again."

"What?" Alejandro demanded sharply. "When and where have they struck?"

Expressionless, Carlos replied, "Last night, as your guests were leaving the fiesta. Apparently they were waiting for them and managed to rob several of our neighbors and friends as they rode toward their homes. No one," he finished remotely, "was harmed, but the ladies were much frightened, and in some cases, family jewels of great worth were taken."

"This is an *outrage!*" Alejandro burst out furiously. "My guests! Robbed as they leave my home!" His cheeks flushed with his emotions, Alejandro rose to his feet, his fist slamming down on the iron table. "Something must be done this time! They must be stopped! No one is safe from them!"

Watching Carlos's face keenly, Brett asked abruptly, "How did it happen? Were they robbed all at once, in a group? Or separately?"

For a second Brett thought Carlos wouldn't answer him, but then the Spaniard glanced at him and said flatly, "Separately. From what has been said, there were no more than three or four bandits and they waited to strike until each family was alone on the road."

"Three or four? Doesn't anybody know how many there were?"

Carlos shrugged. "Some say three, some say four. Who knows? There is such fear and anger over what happened that there could have been a dozen armed men, but the victims cannot remember."

Dismayed, Alejandro looked to Brett. "What is to be done? We cannot let this continue. Now no one will be safe."

Tightly Carlos snapped, "There is to be a meeting tonight at our hacienda. We will devise a plan to trap the bandits then."

Brett said dryly, "I seem to remember something like that last April, but nothing came of it."

Carlos's face whitened. "And do you have a better suggestion, gringo?" he demanded hotly.

Brett nodded his head. "A trap. A trap we three concoct." He slanted a teasing look down at Sabrina, his fingers unconsciously curling one of the silken locks of her bright hair. "We four, rather," he added.

"Bah! You don't know what you are talking about!" Carlos bit out angrily.

"Yes, I do. Have your meeting tonight. But let us now make a plan of our own. A plan that only we shall know about—making it highly unlikely to fail because of wagging tongues." He sent Carlos a level glance. "With only the four of us, five if you count my man Ollie, there is no chance of failure."

Alejandro was nodding his head slowly in agreement, although there was a slight frown on his face. "What do you intend for us to do, *amigo?*"

"Tomorrow is Sunday," Brett began easily. "As usual we will ride into Nacogdoches to attend Mass. But after Mass, when we are talking with all of your neighbors and friends, we will mention that you are most concerned for all the many treasures that are here at the hacienda, Sabrina's jewelry and other valuables. We will tell everyone that you intend to bring them into town on Monday for safe keeping."

"Just like that?" Carlos questioned sneeringly. "No guards? Nothing to protect them from thievery? Do you really believe the bandits are that stupid? They'll know it's a trap!" His lip curled contemptuously, and he added, "If they even know about it!"

Brett's eyes narrowed, but he appeared unmoved by Carlos's statements. "I think you've forgotten precisely how swiftly talk travels in a small community. I would be willing to wager a goodly sum that by tomorrow afternoon, there will be hardly a soul in the Nacogdoches area who doesn't know what was discussed after Mass in the morning."

Alejandro nodded his head judiciously. "That's true. Conversation after Mass is almost as good as a town crier for spreading the news."

"Very well!" Carlos conceded ungraciously. "The bandits will hear of it, but why won't they smell a trap?"

"Because," Brett said smoothly, "Alejandro will tell everyone that he is going to fool the bandits by secreting the jewels and objects in a load of hay he is selling to Señor

246

Gutierrez at the livery stable. That he will be driving the cart himself and will only bring along two vaqueros to accompany it. He doesn't want to be heavily guarded for fear the bandits—and remember, we don't know really how many there are—will guess what he is about and will summon more of their own number and attack him."

"Excellent!" Alejandro said approvingly. "And you and Carlos will be the two vaqueros?"

Brett smiled and shook his head. "No. Carlos, Ollie, and I will be under the hay, armed and ready to strike!"

"You have thought it out well, gringo," Carlos said with grudging admiration.

Brett inclined his head. "Thank you, Carlos." Then, glancing around, he asked, "Are we agreed then?"

The other two men nodded their heads. "*Sí,*" they both replied, and Alejandro rubbed his hands together in anticipation. Only Sabrina had objections.

Her eyes fixed unhappily on Brett's, she asked, "But what if something goes wrong? What if there are more than three or four bandits? You could be hurt!"

"Not a chance, sweetheart!" Brett replied lightly. "There are four of them at the most, possibly only three; there will be six of us, and we will have the element of surprise."

Almost wistfully she muttered, "I wish I could come along, too. I am proficient with the pistol. I could hide under the hay with you."

There was a resounding "*No!*" from the three males, and Sabrina reluctantly put the idea from her.

Carlos left immediately. "There are others I still must see, keeping with the original plan," he said bluntly, and then hurried away.

For some moments after he had departed, the other three continued to discuss the bandits and Brett's plan, but eventually the conversation not unnaturally returned to a more pleasant topic—the wedding that would be arranged within the next few months. Sipping his claret, Alejandro leaned back in his chair and remarked, "It will be lonesome for me once you two are married and you have gone to live at Riverview. I trust you will come back often to visit me?"

Sabrina started to protest that she didn't want to live at Riverview in Natchez, that aspect of being married to Brett not having occurred to her previously, but Brett halted her exclamations by saying calmly, "We won't be living at Riverview."

Alejandro quirked an eyebrow. "Oh? Why not? Since you are heir to the estate, I assumed that you would wish to live there. Someday, after I am gone, you will have to make some decisions about the *rancho*, but that is in the future."

"Far in the future, I hope!" Brett said with an affectionate smile. His face sobered, and he confessed baldly, "I am no longer the heir to Riverview—it is to go to Gordon, my young half brother."

"What?" Sabrina inquired sharply, every suspicion she had ever entertained about Brett rising up before her.

Brett sent her a hooded glance, his face unsmiling. "Exactly what I said. Riverview is not mine—will not ever be mine." An odd note in his voice, he continued, "I have a plantation in the lower Louisiana Territory. It is not Riverview, but you should have no fear that I am not able to provide well for you." Deliberately he made no mention of his other wealth, intensely curious about her reaction to the news that she would never be mistress of his father's elegant mansion and wealthy estate.

The fact that she was a considerable heiress hadn't ever bothered Sabrina. It probably wouldn't have even now if Brett had said he loved her and had explained earlier about Riverview. As it was, she couldn't help but wonder about his proposal, couldn't help but be aware of how *very* little she actually knew about the man she had just consented to marry. Carlos's tale of the knife-slashed girl in New Orleans came back to haunt her, as well as his comments about Constanza, and Sabrina felt slightly sick. If she had been more confident in her love, if Brett had been more forthcoming, more honest about his own emotions and situation, there would have been no sudden doubts, no sudden, unpleasant suspicions running through her mind.

Because she was silent, that the news of his loss of Riverview troubled her was obvious to Brett. That she might be thinking *he* was the fortune hunter never crossed his

248

mind. But then he had never been privy to Sofia's letters about Hugh threatening to disown him, had never realized that there might be some speculation about his reasons for suddenly appearing in the wilds of Spanish Texas. And of course, there was Carlos. . . .

Carlos had done his work well on both of them, the sly innuendos he had flung at Sabrina now taking root, raising all manner of uncertainty in her mind. As for Brett, he had the memory of Lady Diana's disdain, as well as Carlos's ugly statement that Sabrina was vitally interested in his fortune, to arouse demons he had thought he had conquered.

They were both of them appalled at their thoughts, guilt-stricken and horrified that they could harbor such disgusting ideas about the person they had just agreed to marry, and yet, like a tiny sliver under the skin, the suspicions would not go away. Both refused to think about the distasteful subject, and both determinedly thrust the ideas away as nonsense, but the seed had been planted, and they were hampered by their very lack of trust in one another.

The disclosure about Riverview didn't faze Alejandro in the least; he knew the full extent of Brett's fortune. If anything, the lack of Riverview pleased him, and with deceptive lightness he said, "Well, since Riverview has no claim upon you, why don't you consider settling here?" He smiled faintly. "I am approaching the day when I will be relieved to loosen the reins of the Rancho del Torres, and nothing would give me greater pleasure than to see it fall into your capable hands."

It was a tactless remark to have made in front of Sabrina. Completely unaware of its effect upon his daughter, Alejandro sent her an affectionate look and compounded the error by saying, "It has long troubled me, *chica*, the idea of you running the *rancho* single-handedly. A woman needs a strong man to care for her, and now that Brett has undertaken that responsibility, I know that I can rest easy."

Inadvertently made to feel like an imbecile, Sabrina fought down her humiliated anger. Her face stiff and set, the rage and resentment that were stirring in her breast very apparent to Brett—rage and resentment he wrongly attributed to the news about Riverview—she stood up and said tightly, "I didn't realize that becoming betrothed automatically stripped me of the ability to take care of myself! What would you have done, Father, if Brett had not offered for me—put me in a nunnery?" She gave a bitter laugh and sent both men a decidedly hostile look. "Excuse me, I must go and say prayers of thankfulness for the fate I have been spared!"

In shocked dismay, Alejandro watched her sweep regally from the courtyard. Horrified at her reaction, he glanced helplessly to Brett. "She is so young and proud," he muttered excusingly. "I should never have said a word about her needing someone to care for her—she is quite certain that she needs no one, that she is as competent as any man."

Brett's eyes were fixed on Sabrina's departing figure, and almost vaguely, almost to himself, he murmured, "But perhaps it wasn't that which made her angry. Perhaps it was"—his voice hardened—"something entirely different."

CHAPTER EIGHTEEN

༄ Alejandro made his peace with Sabrina that evening, and on the surface everything seemed harmonious. Alejandro was so full of enthusiasm for the match that he never noticed that the two principals seemed a trifle less than wildly ecstatic about the wedding plans. Suspicion once aroused dies hard, and Brett and Sabrina were both fighting their own particular demons—each one wanted to believe in the other, each one wanted the marriage, and yet . . .

Brett's plan to trap the bandits went precisely as discussed. Alejandro's news that he was bringing the del Torreses' valuables into town in a hay cart on Monday found the intended target. And Carlos, Brett, and Ollie were ready when the trio of bandits struck on the dusty red trail that led to Nacogdoches.

The bandits were caught by surprise, but unfortunately, they were not captured alive. Despite being outnumbered two to one, they fought back savagely, and all three died in the barrage of gunfire that was exchanged.

The victors did not emerge unscathed: Carlos was wounded slightly in his left shoulder, Alejandro received a scratch near his temple, and one of the vaqueros suffered a hand wound. But there was such jubilation at having at last rid the district of the murderous rogues that the wounded were indifferent to pain.

Brett's plan was not the only one that would prove to be successful—the instant Carlos had left the del Torreses' ranch on Saturday, he had ridden for Nacogdoches and a meeting with Constanza. His face contorted with fury he had faced her in the privacy of her bedroom.

"It has happened!" he snarled the moment he charged

251

into the shadowy coolness of the curtain-drawn room. *"They are betrothed!"*

Clad only in a shift of white linen, Constanza had sat up abruptly at his entrance. At his words, her face paled and she closed her eyes in pain.

"So," she said numbly. "It has happened—we will now take steps to undo it."

"How?" Carlos demanded furiously. "A betrothal, especially to my *tío*, is almost as binding as marriage itself. Once he makes the announcement, nothing short of dishonor will allow him to retract it."

A rigid smile pinned to her mouth, Constanza replied calmly, "Then we will just have to make certain that there *is* no announcement!"

"Fah! Will this plan of yours work that quickly?"

Some of the color had come back into her face, and languidly she reached for a delicate peignoir lying at the foot of her bed. Shrugging into it, she rose and crossed to a pine wardrobe set against one wall. "Yes," she replied indifferently. "You will arrange for Sabrina to meet privately with me on, say, Tuesday afternoon. I think the gazebo would suit my purposes admirably."

"You don't mean to harm her?" Carlos growled.

Constanza sent him a look that made him uneasy. "Only because I do not want you to kill Brett," she answered finally. Selecting a gown from the wardrobe, she said over her shoulder, "You men are such fools—you think violence is the answer to everything!"

"I want to know what this plan of yours is!" Carlos said dangerously. "You will receive your gold. Now tell me what it is you have planned."

Ignoring him, Constanza said quietly, "On Tuesday you will see the plan yourself." Her lips curved in a mirthless smile. "You must convince Sabrina that it is imperative that she meet with me, that you mean to save her from Brett's wicked scheme to marry her for her money."

Carlos frowned blackly, and grasping Constanza by the shoulders, he shook her cruelly. "Stop playing with me! Tell me! What can you possibly do to make Sabrina change her mind?"

Unmoved by his violence, Constanza stared coolly back

at him, but eventually she said, "Your Sabrina has pride. What do you think she would do if she were faced with a woman carrying Dangermond's child . . . a woman Dangermond had promised to marry but had deserted to pursue her fortune instead?"

Carlos sucked his breath in sharply, his black gaze raking her slender body. "Who?" he inquired harshly. "Not you?"

Constanza's lips twisted. "But of course, *mi amigo!* Who else?"

"You are to bear his bastard?"

An ugly laugh broke from Constanza. "Don't be a fool! Of course not! But your Sabrina will not know it! And with a little padding here and there, my belly discreetly evident, I shall throw myself on her mercy, pleading with her to release him. Begging her to let him marry the one he loves, explaining how he has told me that it is her money he hungers for, that what he really wants is to be with me and our child!"

Admiration filled his face. "It will work," he murmured, slowly. "It *will work!*"

Because of the wound he had suffered in the battle with the bandits, it had been decided that Carlos would spend the night at the del Torres hacienda, so it was easy enough for him to have a private word with Sabrina on Monday evening. He sought her out at dusk as she stood near the stables watching a pair of young colts scamper and race around in a paddock with their mothers.

They spoke quietly for some minutes of the events of the day, and it was only when conversation began to languish that Carlos was able to broach the subject uppermost in his mind. Watching Sabrina's lovely profile in the gathering shadows, he said softly, *"Querida,* I must speak to you about this betrothal—there is something that you must know."

She turned to look at him, her face shuttered and guarded. "What?" she asked flatly.

Carlos appeared reluctant and uneasy. Regretfully he began, "I know that you do not trust me as you once did, but you must believe that I have only your best interests at heart." A wry expression flicked across his face. "You

253

know that I love you, but I could happily see you married to another if I knew that he loved you as you deserve to be loved."

Sabrina froze, her gaze locked painfully on his. "What do you mean?"

Carlos glanced away and hesitated. Gravely he said, "As you are aware, I have known Constanza Morales a long time—I visited with her Saturday evening, and . . ." He stopped, and then, as if the words were dragged out of him, he said heavily, "You must meet with her, Sabrina. There are things she must tell you about the man you have promised to marry."

An icy chill swept through Sabrina. In a low voice she demanded fiercely, "What things? Why can't you tell me? And why should I meet with her?"

He sent her a pitying look. "It is not for me to say. It is her secret, and only she can tell you. She has asked me to implore you to meet with her tomorrow afternoon at the gazebo by the lake—secretly. Most of all she doesn't want Brett to know that she is seeing you."

"Why not?" snapped Sabrina.

Again Carlos sent her that pitying look. "Have you forgotten the girl in New Orleans? Constanza is afraid of what he might do to her if he were to learn that she wishes to see you."

Sabrina was silent for a long time. Meeting with Constanza was the last thing in the world that she wanted to do, but Carlos had touched upon painful subjects—the girl in New Orleans and Brett's failure to mention love.

During the past two days, she and Brett had had little time together and none of it in private. She was badly in need of reassurance, needing Brett's strong arms about her, needing to hear that he loved her, but this had been denied her. Her betrothal to the man she loved, instead of bringing contentment and peace, seemed to have created more dissension and uncertainty within her. One moment she was filled with joy, the next full of misery and suspicion. She despised herself for being so mean and small as to suspect Brett of having ulterior motives for seeking her hand in marriage, and yet she was unable to ignore that possibility.

Brett had not helped matters either. He was strangely aloof, and on more than one occasion lately, she had glanced up to find his assessing eyes on her. Whatever she had thought being betrothed to Brett Dangermond would be like, she had never imagined it would be this painful, this full of agonizing ambivalence.

Perhaps she should meet Constanza, she thought wearily. Conceivably it would clarify things in her own mind. Certainly it couldn't add to the painful battle that was now being waged in her heart. Dully she said, "Very well. I'll meet her. What time?"

"Two o'clock?" Carlos suggested, the elation he felt carefully hidden.

Reluctantly Sabrina nodded her bright head. Brett and her father were approaching, so further conversation was impossible. The afternoon's events were mentioned, and for the next several minutes the four of them talked of nothing else.

"It is a shame that they all died!" Alejandro said slowly. "Now we will never know where they have hidden their spoils. There wasn't time enough for them to have disposed of the valuables stolen the night of Sabrina's birthday. Their cache must be nearby . . . but it could be anywhere."

Brett grimaced. "That was the one flaw in the plan—we made no allowances for trying to recover the stolen objects." He hesitated, his eyes shadowed. "I didn't believe they would fight to the death like they did. It wasn't until Carlos killed that last one that I realized that the others were dead, too." He looked rueful. "I suppose I thought we would capture them and be able to question them."

Carlos shrugged indifferently and then winced as his wounded shoulder made itself felt. "I think most people will be satisfied with the way things turned out. Granted they would all like to recover their valuables, but everyone will rest easier knowing that those thieving devils are no longer alive."

"What you say is true," Sabrina murmured quietly. "But it is so sad that our friends and neighbors lost so many objects that meant so much to them." Her fingers brushed against the huge gold hoop earrings that hung near her cheeks. "I would pay three times what these are

255

worth to recover them if they were stolen. Bonita gave them to me, and I treasure them."

"I know what you mean," Carlos said seriously. "Yesterday, after Mass, Señora Galaviz, the trader's wife, could do nothing but bemoan the loss of the lion's brooch that had belonged to her mother."

"Oh, no!" Sabrina cried distressfully. "Not her lion's brooch! I remember it so vividly—as a child when we would go into their store, she would show it to me, pointing out the tiny emerald chips for the eyes and the ivory for its teeth." Mournfully she added, "It was so lovely, so beautifully designed, the gold so wonderfully wrought. I shall never forget it."

Glancing beseechingly across at her father, she asked, "Isn't there any way we can find the stolen things?"

Slowly, regretfully, Alejandro shook his head. "No, chica. Wherever the bandits hid their treasures, that location would be known only to them—and they are all dead. Trying to find their hideout, if they had one, would be impossible in this wild, untracked area. Someday someone might stumble across it, but not in our lifetime, I would wager."

Sabrina still appeared unhappy, and Carlos said, "At least they are dead—they will rob no one else."

It was small comfort, but Sabrina took it, and the conversation wandered on to other more pleasant subjects. Shortly thereafter, Brett firmly detached her from the others, saying lightly, "You will excuse us? I have not had a chance to talk alone with my novia since we became betrothed, and I wish to discover if she is still of the same mind as she was then."

Sabrina blushed, her heart suddenly pounding in her breast. Alejandro laughed, and waving them away, admonished teasingly, "Do not be gone too long—I may be an old man, but I remember what it was like to be young and in love."

Carlos kept his features carefully bland as Brett and Sabrina walked away, but he glanced down at the ground lest his eyes reveal his murderous rage. Tomorrow, he thought savagely, cannot come soon enough.

Breathlessly Sabrina allowed Brett to guide her into the

concealing arms of the forest where it grew near the hacienda, and there, under the leafy branches of a gnarled oak tree, he pulled her next to his warm body, his mouth hungrily finding hers. He kissed her urgently, compulsively, his lips hard and demanding on hers.

Pressed tightly against him, she kissed him back eagerly, their bodies straining together, her arms creeping around his strong neck, and all doubts and suspicions fled. It was such heaven to be in his embrace, to feel his passion rising up hard and powerful between their locked bodies.

Eventually he raised his head. "I've been mad with longing to do that since Saturday," he muttered huskily, "but something or someone kept getting in the way. I couldn't wait another moment. I either had to have you to myself or do something violent."

Shyly she replied, "I wondered if you had changed your mind."

"Not a chance, sweetheart! I want you too badly." His eyes met hers gravely, a curious intentness about him. "I wondered perhaps if *you* might have changed your mind." An odd smile twisted his chiseled mouth. "Women have been known to do so."

With mocking affront Sabrina surveyed him. "Not *this* woman!" She was strangely light-headed, full of a warm, burgeoning ecstasy. All she had needed to banish her unhappy thoughts was to be in his arms, and dreamily she curled next to him, offering her mouth to him.

Groaning, Brett captured her lips, kissing her more deeply, even more passionately this time, his hands caressing her back and hips. The blood thundering in his brain, he reluctantly pushed her slightly away from him. "We keep this up," he said with a frankly sensuous cast to his mouth, "and I'm afraid I'll compromise you again—a dozen times before we are married."

Possessed of the same driving, elemental needs, she said daringly, "And would that be so very terrible?"

His eyes darkened with desire, but with an effort he resisted the lure of her tempting mouth and body. Ruefully he admitted, "No, except that even if I didn't make you pregnant the other night, if we make love too many times before marriage, Alejandro is definitely going to be very embarrassed at the arrival of his first grandchild an indecently short time after our wedding."

Startled, Sabrina stared at him. "Pregnant?" she breathed blankly. "Me?"

"It's possible," Brett said with a strangely tender smile.

Wonderingly Sabrina glanced down at her slim stomach, a wave of intense pleasure surging through her. "Our child," she said reverently.

"Mmmm, yes," Brett agreed softly, pulling her gently next to him, resting her pliant body against his. His lips brushed her temple, and he murmured, "I'm afraid I didn't take any precautions that last night—all I could think of was you. A child would please me, but selfishly, I don't want to start sharing you too soon!"

There was a companionable silence between them, both lost in their own happy thoughts of the future, each completely unaware of how closely those thoughts paralleled the other's. Sabrina's head rested on Brett's shoulder, his arms were about her waist, and for the moment there was no passion between them, only an engulfing sensation of tenderness, a sweet promise of what would come.

Night slowly enveloped the forest, and suddenly becoming aware that Alejandro was calling them from the hacienda, Brett stirred and shouted back a reply. He stared down at Sabrina's face in the gloom, thinking he had never seen a more lovely, entrancing sight in his life. The fiery hair was muted, tumbling in gorgeous disarray around her bewitching features, and the look in those dreamy amber-gold eyes made his breath catch painfully in his chest.

Almost as if mesmerized, his lips slowly found hers again, kissing her with such tenderness and gentleness that Sabrina felt tears sting her eyes. He must love her! He could not act as he did and *not* love her!

Arm in arm they walked slowly back toward the hacienda, and it was only when they neared the entrance to the courtyard that Brett spoke. "About the date of our wedding," he said abruptly, a slight frown creasing his forehead. "I think that in view of what happened the other night, we had better not have a lengthy betrothal. You could very well be pregnant, and if you are, we shouldn't delay too long in marrying." He suddenly grinned. "Be-

258

sides, I don't know how long I can behave myself where *you* are concerned!"

Engulfed in a warm, hazy glow, Sabrina drifted dreamily through the following hours. And it was only the next afternoon, as two o'clock drew near, that some of the glow left her. Wishing now that she had never agreed to meet with Constanza, she almost decided to send a note to the gazebo stating that she had changed her mind. But her conscience would not let her.

She had just risen to her feet from the chair she had been sitting in on the patio when Brett and Alejandro appeared. Brett held a piece of paper in his hand, and from the expression on both men's faces, she knew that something was wrong.

"What is it?" she asked instantly. "Is something wrong?"

"Well, it is not good news," Alejandro said quietly. "But it could have been worse."

Brett lifted his eyes from the paper, a curiously speculative gleam in his gaze. "This letter from my agent in New Orleans just arrived. It appears that in June a hurricane leveled my plantation in Louisiana."

A gasp of dismay escaped Sabrina. "Leveled? Can nothing be salvaged?"

He shook his head, a waiting air about him.

"How dreadful for you!" she exclaimed helplessly, deep sympathy for him rushing through her. "What will you do? What *can* you do?"

Brett shrugged negligently. "I suppose I could sell it. Or, with enough money, a lot of money, I could probably bring it back into production again."

"Oh!" Sabrina said in a small voice.

Watching her closely, trying to gauge the effect of his news on her, Brett said slowly, "It is not a complete disaster. The plantation was in deplorable condition when I first acquired it, but I made it productive once and I'm certain I shall do so again. The crop was destroyed, it is true, as well as several outbuildings, but apparently the levees held, although the house itself was badly damaged."

"Well, I wouldn't worry about it now," Alejandro said

heartily. "Besides, when you marry Sabrina you gain the Rancho del Torres—you may never want to do anything about that piece of property but sell it. For selfish reasons, it would delight me if you settled here. As far as I'm concerned, the destruction of the plantation in Louisiana could be quite a blessing."

Sabrina smiled sickly, and Brett's eyes narrowed, her reaction not going unnoticed. Conscious of a fierce urge to throw caution to the winds, wanting desperately to reassure her about their future, about his own wealth, Brett almost blurted out the truth about his finances, but pride stilled his tongue. That and suspicion. Was she already having second thoughts about marrying him? he wondered with a queer feeling. Could he bear it if she proved to be false and treacherous? He didn't think he could, suddenly realizing with a frightening intensity that Sabrina meant more to him than anything else in the world.

Feeling as if she were being driven mercilessly toward conclusions that were only going to bring her pain and misery, Sabrina couldn't look at Brett. Instead she glanced at her father and with over-bright eyes, muttered, "I feel a little faint. If you don't mind, I'll leave you two to discuss this unsettling news." And then, not waiting for a reply, she bolted from the courtyard.

Constanza was waiting for Sabrina at the gazebo, and still distressed and shaken by the uncertainties that were battering at her fragile peace, Sabrina was totally unprepared for the older woman's assault.

Sabrina had run through the forest when she left Alejandro and Brett, and consequently she was a little out of breath when she entered the gazebo. Constanza had her back to the door, and when she heard Sabrina's entrance, she glanced over her shoulder.

"You came," Constanza said simply.

Mutely Sabrina nodded, wishing she were anywhere but here, wishing she were back at the hacienda, wishing Brett were holding her in his arms. She was suddenly afraid, afraid of this woman, afraid of what Constanza would tell her.

And a moment later she knew she had good reason to be afraid; Constanza's condition was evident the instant she turned to face Sabrina. Numb, her mind frozen, Sabrina stared at Constanza's gently swollen belly, saw the pity and misery in the dark eyes that watched her so intently.

She became aware that someone was crying. At first she assumed it was she, but then she realized with a shock that it was Constanza. Constanza was weeping softly, heartrendingly, the tears sliding dolefully down her cheeks, and despite the sharp agony that was clawing its way through her own body, Sabrina was moved by the other woman's misery.

"Don't cry," she begged. "Please stop. Tell me what is troubling you."

"Brett Dangermond," Constanza said sadly. "I carry his child. He promised to marry me—I would never have given myself to him otherwise. I trusted him—he told me he loved me, and yet not three days ago I hear he is to marry you." Mournfully she added, "What is to become of me? Of our child?"

Pain like she had never imagined pierced Sabrina's heart. She had known of his involvement with Constanza, but the reality of it had never hit her. It did now, agonizingly, shatteringly. This woman had lain in Brett's arms, had known his caresses, and now she was carrying his child. . . .

Sabrina was barely aware of Constanza standing in front of her, didn't see the calculating expression that crossed the other woman's face before Constanza threw herself to her knees and sobbed, "You must give him up! You must! If it weren't for your fortune he would marry me. I know he would! He said he would! It is your money that is keeping my child from having a father; your money that is keeping the man I love from me."

"What do you mean?" Sabrina asked dully.

Her sobbing reduced to a pitiful hiccuping, Constanza begged, "Promise you will never tell that you saw me? Promise you will never let him know what I have said? He would beat me if he knew."

Tiredly Sabrina nodded her head.

"He said that he wants to marry me, but that he needs your fortune more—that with your fortune he would better be able to provide for me and our child. Your money

261

doesn't mean anything to me, but he is obsessed by it."
Constanza's voice was filled with pleading as she implored, "Oh, please give him up! If you refuse him, he will marry me. I know he will. He loves *me*—it is only your money that he wants. Please, you *must* release him."

Possessed by an odd serenity, Sabrina gently touched Constanza's shoulder. Nothing mattered anymore; she felt nothing, only a blessed numbness. "I will," she promised simply. "You have nothing to fear. I will not marry him"— her voice shook slightly—"not now."

Vaguely Sabrina realized that it wasn't that Brett had made love to Constanza that she found so unforgivable—he was a sophisticated man, and there were bound to have been many women in his past, even his most recent past. But to seduce Constanza with promises of marriage, to father a child and then refuse to do the honorable thing because he wanted *her* fortune, *that* she could not forgive! Earlier in the year, when he had been seeing Constanza, she had been jealous when she'd had no real right to be, but she had thought that their association had been finished for some time. To discover that such was not the case, that these past weeks when she had been falling deeply in love with him he had still been seeing another woman, still promising love to Constanza, was shattering.

How she returned to the hacienda Sabrina never knew; one minute she was unconsciously patting Constanza's shoulder and the next she was in the courtyard. Alejandro and Brett were still there. They were seated at the iron table; tall glasses half-filled with liquid sat in front of them.

Both men looked up when she appeared, and Alejandro called out, "Ah, there you are! I wondered where you had disappeared to. We were just discussing different dates for the wedding. Your *novio* is an impatient man—he wants the wedding before the end of the month!"

The amber-gold eyes were empty, the beautiful features strangely lifeless, as Sabrina said flatly, "I've changed my mind. There will be no wedding. *I will not marry him.*"

Throughout the emotional, exhausting scene that followed her startling announcement, Sabrina remained unmoved, wrapped in an icy shell. Nothing seemed to matter to her anymore. Confusion, disbelief, and finally anger washed over her, not touching the tranquil emptiness that kept her from feeling anything but mild indifference to Alejandro's reactions. That Brett said nothing, his hard face dark and unrevealing, didn't even arouse a twinge of interest within her. He belonged now to Constanza—he was nothing to her, meant nothing to her . . . would *never* mean anything to her.

If she had been more aware, she might have seen the spasm of pain that had flitted swiftly across his face, might have recognized the brief flash in his eyes as bitter disillusionment. But as the moments passed, he seemed to retreat within himself, seemed to become a different man. Certainly he was no longer the man who had held her in his arms the night before. Now he was a stranger—an enemy, if the cold, hard glitter in the jade-green eyes mirrored his feelings.

When Alejandro finally stopped shouting, when he realized that nothing he could say would change her mind, Sabrina inclined her head politely and murmured, "If you will excuse me now? I have other things to do."

Helplessly Alejandro glanced from one set face to the other. Almost angrily he demanded of Brett, "Haven't you anything to say? Aren't you going to try to persuade her differently?"

"Why?" Brett returned curtly. "The lady knows her own mind. If she won't listen to you, I doubt anything I say will change her feelings."

Sabrina felt something stir deep within her. Objection? Pain? She couldn't tell, and she didn't want to know; she wanted this comforting emptiness to continue.

Alejandro threw up his hands in despair and marched away, leaving an oppressive silence behind him. Against her will, Sabrina's eyes strayed to Brett's still figure, and the icy shell that had kept emotion at bay slipped just a little.

Ah, God, she thought painfully. Is that the deceitful face I loved? The lying mouth that set me aflame?

He looked very large and virile as he stood there staring at her, his harsh features seeming as if carved in stone, and Sabrina was powerless against the storm of emotion

263

that suddenly shattered the shell she had erected around herself. Pain and fury, revulsion and rage, came sweeping through her body, and unable to trust herself, afraid she would fling herself scratching and clawing at his face, she spun away, intent upon as much distance as possible between herself and Brett Dangermond.

Two steps was all she took. For a big man, Brett moved like lightning, and his hand curved bruisingly around her arm, jerking her back to face him. "Don't run off so quickly, sweetheart," he drawled in a dangerous voice. "I think you and I have a little talking to do. Like why you've suddenly changed your mind."

Barely in time she remembered her promise to Constanza not to say anything about their meeting. Taking refuge in fury, she spat, "I don't have to explain myself. Certainly not to you!"

His eyes narrowed. "Wrong, sweetheart. *Especially* to me!"

Futilely she clawed at the hand that kept her captive. Panting slightly from her efforts, she hissed, "Let me go! I don't want to talk to you—*ever!*"

He gave a bitter laugh. "No, your kind never does, do they? They just play with a man's emotions, and then, when they grow weary of the game, they destroy him." He loosed his hold on her arm and caught her chin between his strong fingers. The dark green eyes, black with some indefinable emotion, bored into hers. "And to think I believed in this lovely face—to think I almost trusted you, tiger lily."

His fingers hurt where they pressed brutally against her jaw, and her hands came up in an attempt to break his hold. "Don't call me names!"

"Why not?" he taunted. "Tiger lily is a lot nicer than some of the other names I have in mind for women like you. Names like . . . jade, cheat, and lying slut!"

Sabrina gasped with outrage, her fingers digging into the hand that held her jaw. Brett only smiled, a cold, mirthless smile that didn't touch the hard eyes.

"You almost fooled me," he snarled softly. "Almost had me believing—" He stopped abruptly, his mouth twisting. "What does it matter? You were an illusion after all."

PART THREE

PRIDE AND DESIRE

Spring, 1806

> Revenge, at first thought sweet,
> Bitter ere long back on itself
> recoils.

John Milton
Paradise Lost

CHAPTER NINETEEN

April of 1806 was a lovely month in Nacogdoches. Everywhere Sabrina walked in those warm, golden days, she saw signs in the meadows and woodlands that life was renewing itself. Spotted fawns trotted daintily alongside their watchful mothers, the demanding cheep of newly hatched birds filled the forest air, and once during her lonely walks Sabrina surprised an elegant tawny puma sunning herself while her two furry kittens slept nearby.

Along the stream banks and in the marshes the fragrant white swamp lilies bloomed, and in the forest and meadows other spring flowers burst forth in bright hues. Scarlet and lavender "prairie pointers," wild blue phlox, and delicate tulip-shaped pasqueflowers sprang up everywhere. Even the trees were covered with blooms—the creamy white flowers of the dogwood, the bright pink of the redbud, and the pale yellow clusters of the small sweetleaf tree were vivid patches of color against the many shades of green of the forest.

Seated in the gazebo this particular day in mid-April, Sabrina was aware of a heaviness of spirit, a gnawing depression that was at odd variance with the lovely season. She should have been happy, feeling at one with the season, but instead she found herself withdrawing from it. But then, she admitted glumly, it was normal for her to feel this way this particular time of year. She felt this way every April. Every April since Brett Dangermond had come into her life six years ago.

Six years, she thought with a start. Could it really have been that long since that day in the meadow when he had surprised her . . . and kissed her? With an unfortunate flash of pleasure, she also remembered that she had stabbed him.

Incredible to realize that six long years had passed since that time, six years in which so much had happened. Not only to her but to the world. Napoleon was emperor of France; Spain and her possessions were a mere pawn in the new emperor's hands. Louisiana was no longer Spanish. It wasn't even French anymore—Napoleon had seen to that! Now it belonged to those brash Americans. Those gringos, Sabrina thought with a curl of her lip. England and France were still at war, a war that encompassed most of Europe and that was, many believed, inexorably dragging the fledgling United States into its conflagration. Thomas Jefferson was in his second term as President of the United States, and it was hoped, despite the impressment of seamen from American ships by the British and the disastrous effect the war in Europe was having on American trade, that he could steer his country unscathed through these perilous times.

There was an even more immediate danger that faced Jefferson closer to home, though: the Spanish had not been pleased with the way Napoleon had sold the Louisiana Territory, and they were even more displeased that the United States had had the temerity to declare that the western boundary of the territory was the Rio Grande River, that the United States in fact owned all of Texas. Spain insisted angrily that the boundary was the Sabine River and that they were in fact prepared to defend the lands west of the Sabine River with force. The threat of war hung in the air, and for weeks now, Spanish troops and supplies had been pouring into Nacogdoches. Daringly the Spaniards had been sending their troops across the Sabine River into American territory, and the situation between the two countries was tense and volatile.

But somehow all of those events seemed a long way from Sabrina on this beautiful day in April. There were other occurrences, painful incidents, that had marked the passage of time since Brett had ridden so suddenly into her life six years ago. And ridden just as suddenly from it, she reminded herself savagely, ignoring the curious twist of pain in the region of her heart.

He had left within the hour, had gone before Sabrina even realized it, and she had told herself fiercely that she was glad. Glad that she didn't have to look again on his treacherous, lying face. But she knew that she lied. Sometimes during the past six years, when her spirit was low, when she was aware of a crushing loneliness, she would think that it might almost have been worth it to marry him, knowing what she did, rather than live without ever seeing him again.

The days following Brett's abrupt departure, except for the period following Elena's death, had been the most miserable of Sabrina's life. Her situation was made even more painful this time because, when her mother had died, she and her father had at least been able to comfort one another. Not so after the ending of her exceedingly brief betrothal to Brett Dangermond. Alejandro was deeply upset with her and perhaps just a little hurt and bewildered that she could act so capriciously. A dozen times she nearly blurted out Constanza's secret, but the promise she had given the older woman sealed her lips.

Her father did not reproach her, he didn't berate her, he merely shut her out, his displeasure obvious from the very way he kept her at a distance, the cool way in which he met her attempts at reconciliation. Even the servants seemed to radiate disapproval, Bonita saying forthrightly some two weeks after Brett's departure, "I do not understand you, *chica!* What were you thinking of to act as you did? It was disgraceful and unkind!"

Torn between anger and resentment, Sabrina had glared at Bonita, the promise to Constanza stilling the furious words that choked her throat. But she could not let the comment pass, and sharply she demanded, "Why does he have everyone's sympathy? Why does everyone believe that it was *all* my fault? Haven't any of you thought that perhaps I might have had good reason to act as I did?"

"Did you?" Bonita had asked in a softer tone, her brown eyes shrewd and considering.

"I thought I did," Sabrina had said flatly.

Bonita had looked thoughtful, and after that, Sabrina had noticed that there was a slight lessening of the disapproval that had seemed to follow her. Alejandro, too, unbent somewhat, love for his daughter overcoming his own disappointment. He had appeared puzzled and hurt, but gradually some semblance of their old relationship had been re-established, although it was never quite the same again. Sabrina had had too many secrets to be able to act as she once had, and Alejandro had been aware that some barrier lay between them.

The news that Constanza had left the area had been relayed to Sabrina via Carlos. Three days after Brett had left, Carlos had arrived at the hacienda, and finding her alone, had mentioned casually that Señora Morales had suddenly packed up everything she owned and had departed for New Orleans. At least, he had *thought* it was New Orleans—she had once stated that she longed to go to Spain, and he wondered if that might have been her ultimate destination. Of course, Carlos had said, she could have gone *any*where, with anyone. . . .

After Carlos had left, Sabrina had run away to the gazebo, and there she had wept bitter, angry tears, hating Brett for being what he was and hating herself for loving him in spite of it.

The knowledge that she might be carrying Brett's child had kept her vacillating between terror that she was pregnant and the equally fervent hope that one day she would hold their child in her arms. But then, some ten days later, proof that she was not pregnant had appeared, and with a strange blend of regret and relief she had begun bleakly trying to gain some control over her life.

At first she had had little success, the wound too new, too deep, too raw to heal easily. Reminding herself over and over again of Brett's ugly duplicity hadn't helped at all, and she had learned painfully that love is an obstinate, unpredictable emotion and that one cannot, despite the best intentions, always love wisely.

A great deal of the time in those first painful days she had spent alone, much of it at the gazebo, and it was there nearly five weeks later that Ollie Fram had found her. She had been staring moodily out at the blue waters of the lake and had watched with open-mouthed astonishment as Ollie had ridden up to the gazebo.

Her heart had been beating with heavy, uncomfortable strokes, but she had managed to say with credible calm, "Why, Ollie, what are you doing here?"

Ollie had sent an oddly furtive glance around and then had slid from his horse. He had handed her an envelope and had muttered, "The guvnor said I wasn't to let anyone but you see me. Said you was to 'ave this and that I was to wait for your answer."

The missive was curt and short:

If there is to be a child, tell Ollie that your answer is yes. If it is yes, I will return at once and marry you.
    Brett

For one tiny, weak moment, Sabrina had wished passionately that she could say yes, but then Constanza's tragic face had risen up before her and her mouth had twisted. Deliberately she had torn the note to shreds, the amber-gold eyes hard with purpose. Coldly she had said, "You can tell the 'guvnor' that my answer is no!"

Ollie had been obviously disappointed. His brown eyes had fixed hopefully on hers, and he had asked, "You won't change your mind?" When Sabrina had remained icily silent, he had gone on more forcefully, "Miss, these past weeks have been—well, I'll not wrap it in clean linen— they've been bloody awful. I don't know when the guvnor has been more cast down and yet so ripe and ready for trouble. Never know what is going to set him off! And I can't say that I've liked the accommodations we've 'ad across the river either!" Speculatively he had eyed her. "Why he insisted we stay there is beyond me! But every time I've suggested we move on, he's thrown me one of those black looks of his and growled something about 'unfinished business' with you. Said once I delivered this note and returned with your answer, we'd be moving—one way or the other."

Sabrina had supposed she should have been touched that Brett hadn't left her to face the aspect of a child alone, but she wasn't. The knowledge that he hadn't thought anything of leaving Constanza alone in the same condition had eaten like acid in her heart. And to know that all these weeks when she had been suffering so dreadfully, wondering where he was and what he was doing, he had been just across the Sabine River in the small outpost of Natchi-

271

toches in the Louisiana Territory hadn't sat well with her. Stiffly she had said, "You can tell him I'm sorry he's had an unpleasant time of it—especially since it was so needless. But it doesn't change my answer."

Disgustedly Ollie had stared at her. He had shaken his head and said gruffly, "I'll never understand you gentry! 'Ere's the guvnor pretending that he don't give a fiddler's damn, that you mean nothing to him, and 'ere you are doing the same, when it's plain as the nose on your face that you're both lying through your teeth!"

Sabrina had drawn herself up angrily. "You're impertinent!"

Ollie had grinned. "That I am, miss, that I am! But it seems to me that someone 'as to take a 'and in this affair, and being as 'ow no one else seems to be doing it, I thought I'd best take a stab at it."

He had spoken with such disarming sincerity that Sabrina had felt herself unbending. A small, sad smile had flitted across her face, and she had said softly, "Ollie, it won't do any good. My answer is still no. Tell him."

Ollie's grin had faded, and his brown eyes had searched her face intently. What he had seen there must have convinced him that his case was hopeless, for he had sighed heavily and had said glumly, "Very well, miss." He had turned away and had remounted his horse. Gnawing nervously on his bottom lip, he had suddenly said with a rush, "Miss? Would you be so kind as to pass on a message to Lupe for me?"

"Lupe?" Sabrina had repeated dumbly.

Nodding his head vigorously, Ollie had said rapidly, "Lupe Montez. She works in the kitchen."

"Oh, yes, of course—Bonita's godchild," Sabrina had answered, curiosity in her expression. "What do you want me to tell her?"

"Only that I wasn't bamming her when I said the things I did," Ollie had muttered shyly. "Tell her to wait for me. I might be gone only a year, it might be ten, but if she feels the way I hope she does, she'll be waiting for me when I do return. And I will." He had stopped speaking, his monkey-face troubled and unhappy. "I don't want to leave her, but the guvnor needs me more than he ever did. Tell her that just as soon as I get the guvnor settled I'll be back for her—*I swear it!*"

Without a further word, he had wheeled his horse about and disappeared. For a long time after the sound of his horse's passage through the forest had ceased, Sabrina had stood there staring blindly into space.

Looking back on it now, Sabrina realized that it was then that she had begun to face reality and had stopped yearning for the illusion that had been her love for Brett Dangermond. She laid it to rest like a cherished dream that had become a nightmare, and with a fierce vigor she picked up the scattered threads of her former life.

She had relayed Ollie's message to Lupe, and seeing the faint glow in the younger girl's big dark eyes, seeing the soft flush that lit her cheeks, Sabrina had been aware of envy. Lupe at least had hope.

But delivering Ollie's message to Lupe had also brought the girl to Sabrina's attention, and some months later, when Bonita had broached the subject of training someone to take over some of her tasks, Sabrina had found herself casually suggesting Lupe. Bonita had been pleased, and Lupe, a sweet, gentle girl, had proved to be clever and quick to learn what was expected of her.

As Sabrina thought of Bonita, her face clouded. Had Bonita known that her time was limited when she had wanted to begin training someone to one day take her place? Had she guessed that in less than a year, in late 1801, she would die of one of the many outbreaks of fever that swept through the area?

Fate, Sabrina thought with a wry grimace. Fate did such strange things. Had it been fate in the fall of 1804 that had arranged for Tío Luis to be gored and killed by one of the bulls he had just purchased from her father?

Sabrina shuddered remembering that dreadful day. Poor Tía Francisca! Who would have thought that Tío Luis's death would change her so drastically? Gone was the domineering, outspoken harridan who had ruled the de la Vega household with an iron hand. In her place had been left a pitiful, broken woman.

The de la Vega ranch had greatly shrunk over the years, and upon Luis's death, Carlos had decided to sell the hacienda itself. His dark eyes shuttered, his mouth in a grim line, he had said to Sabrina, "Why should I keep it? It means nothing to me—especially since the woman I love will never share it with me." Sabrina had turned away, depressed that after all this time, he still seemed to care deeply for her.

Alejandro had been greatly distressed not only by Luis's death and the tragic change in his sister but by Carlos's decision to sell his birthplace. There were many long, not always friendly, discussions between the two men, but eventually Alejandro had told Sabrina, "Carlos is, perhaps, wiser than I thought. He does not want to be in debt to me, though I have explained repeatedly that he is not to worry about it. But as he pointed out, with the sale of the hacienda and several hundred acres, he can pay me back and begin anew with fresh capital. I cannot blame him for wanting to be clear of debt and to manage the remaining lands his own way. It may be that Luis's death will be the making of him."

Francisca and Carlos had moved in with Sabrina and her father after the de la Vega hacienda had been sold. It had seemed at the time to be a logical situation, but Sabrina had never quite gotten used to sharing a house with her aunt and cousin. Particularly since Francisca did little to hide her resentment of Alejandro and Carlos made no secret that he still harbored hopes of one day winning Sabrina's hand.

It was strange, Sabrina thought gloomily, how the passage of time since Brett had departed seemed marked by death. First Bonita, then Tío Luis, and finally, just over a year ago, in January of 1805, her father. . . .

Choking back a small sob, Sabrina buried her face in her hands. Would the pain of his death never leave her? Would she always think of him and feel this sharp ache to see his beloved face one more time? To tell him that she loved him? That despite all their differences, he was the best father a girl could ever possess?

Time was supposed to lessen the hurt and the pain, but Sabrina, feeling as she did, doubted it ever would. She still grieved for her father, still felt rage for him—and against him.

Alejandro's death had been sudden and violent—he had been riding home one day from Nacogdoches when, it was presumed, a lone bandit had accosted him. There were signs in the dust near his body of a struggle, a struggle Alejandro had lost, a pearl handled stiletto driven through his heart. His valuables were gone, including the dearly prized turquoise and silver bracelet that Elena had given him.

Sabrina had been in a state of shock when Francisca had told her, unable to believe that her father would never come home again, unable to believe that she would never feel his comforting arms around her, never hear him call her *"chica"* in that teasing, affectionate tone of his. And once the shock had worn off, she had been like a wild woman, possessed with the savage desire to find her father's killer, to extract the most awful vengeance possible. But though the del Torreses' vaqueros had scoured the area, though Sabrina had offered an exorbitant sum as reward for the killer of her father, Alejandro's assailant had never been found.

Francisca and Carlos had been her bulwark in those first weeks following Alejandro's senseless death. They had been kind, exceedingly so, and Sabrina had been pathetically grateful, feeling real affection for her aunt. For a while the two women had grown close, both having lost the most important men in their lives within months of each other, but after several months, Sabrina had found Francisca's constant dwelling on death suffocating and morbid.

Sabrina lifted her face and stared blankly at nothing in particular, wondering morosely if she would ever feel true happiness again. Ever feel as young and lighthearted as she had before Brett Dangermond had come into her life. Ever feel free of the oppressive air that seemed to hang over her.

She glanced down at her black silk skirts, her slim fingers idly toying with the rich material. The year of mourning for her father was past; she could, if she wished, now begin to wear colors again, but somehow that seemed to be too much of an effort.

Where was her spirit? she wondered drearily. Her zest

for life? Was she simply going to fade away into a sad, spineless spinster?

Francisca's dark, depressing presence wasn't conducive to laughter, or even pleasure, Sabrina mused slowly, and she suddenly wished that her aunt and Carlos didn't still live with her. She suspected that left to her own devices, she wouldn't have barricaded herself away from their friends and neighbors. Without Francisca and Carlos sheltering her to the point of isolating her, she probably wouldn't be still wearing black, still brooding over the injustice of fate, still mourning this deeply her father's death and his unexpected betrayal. . . .

A bitter gleam lit the amber-gold eyes, an angry flush staining her cheeks as she remembered the ghastly day when the enormity of his betrayal had been made clear. It had been almost a year ago when the stunning contents of Alejandro's will had been disclosed to her.

Even now, just thinking about it jarred her from the apathy that seemed almost a natural part of her. Her mouth tightened, and her jaw set. How could he have done that to me? she thought furiously.

Alejandro hadn't disowned her, but occasionally, when anger got the better of her, Sabrina almost wished he had. *Any*thing would have been better than what he had done!

Reviewing it rationally, she really shouldn't have been so stunned—at least a hundred times before he died, Sabrina had heard Alejandro complain bewilderedly, "It would have been such a wonderful match! I just don't understand you, *chica!* He would have been so good to you, been such an exceptional husband!"

She smiled grimly. Well, he couldn't force her to marry Brett, but he had done his best to see that Brett would hang around her neck like a slave chain for the rest of her life. She had been her father's only heir, and listening to the lawyer's precise voice that day, Sabrina hadn't been surprised to discover that all Alejandro's belongings had been left to her. It was the codicil to the will that had caused the furor and left her so resentful and furious with Alejandro—Brett Dangermond had been named as her sole guardian. Like some prized filly, she had been handed over to him to do with as he pleased. *Everything* was to be in

Dangermond's control—until she married. The problem was, and this infuriated Sabrina almost as much as the guardianship, Brett had to approve of her husband. If he didn't, the entire del Torres fortune, except for a modest annuity for her, became his.

Sabrina's teeth gritted together. *Dios!* How angry she had been that day! Francisca's fury, though, had been frightening, and to this day her aunt could not speak Alejandro's name. Carlos had been as stunned as Sabrina, but though he had ranted and raved after the lawyer had departed, of the three of them, he had accepted Alejandro's will most quickly. When Sabrina had taxed him with it several weeks ago, he had shrugged his shoulders and muttered, "What good does it do to rail against that infamous will? *I* cannot change it. We have to live with it. Besides, you've made it clear you don't intend ever to marry me—so what does it matter to me that Dangermond is your guardian?"

Sabrina had looked at him dismayed. "It doesn't bother you that I am left in his complete control? That he practically *owns* me?" she had asked with puzzlement.

Carlos had drawn her into his arms, his lips gently touching her hair. "Of course it bothers me, *querida!*" he had murmured softly. "But until Dangermond makes some move, I can do nothing." He had tipped her head back and asked quizzically, "Unless you've changed your mind and will make me the happiest man in the world by saying you'll become my wife? Together, I'm certain we could break that damned codicil."

Sadly Sabrina had smiled at him. "If I could love you that way, I would. But you are my friend, my cousin . . . not my lover."

"I could be," Carlos had said thickly, "I could be, if you would let me."

Warily Sabrina had regarded him, that terrifying day in the gazebo far away but not forgotten. "Carlos, you will always be my friend. Nothing more," she had said gently.

He had sighed and released her. "It is just as well that I leave for Mexico City tomorrow." A teasing glint in his eyes, he had murmured lightly, "Perhaps there I shall find

277

a red-haired beautiful heiress to take your place in my heart."

Sincerely Sabrina had replied, "Oh, I *do* wish you would! How happy it would make me!"

Carlos had grimaced and turned away. The next day he had left on his long journey to Mexico City to sell a sizable herd of del Torres and de la Vega cattle.

Sabrina guessed that part of the reason she was so moody today was because she missed Carlos. During the months since Alejandro's death they had tentatively reestablished their bond. Left alone with only Tía Francisca, she discovered that she longed for Carlos's easy companionship. At least with him around there was the occasional moment of laughter.

But it wasn't only Carlos's departure that preyed on her mind. The vexing, infuriating problem of the guardianship had begun to loom larger and more frighteningly before her. In the weeks following the reading of the will, Sabrina had waited with fury and impatience to hear from Brett; she had received only a polite letter from a lawyer in New Orleans informing her that her guardian was currently out of the country and would, as soon as he returned, take up the duties of his guardianship.

For a moment Sabrina frowned, remembering an odd incident the past October. She had been in the gazebo, lying on the cushions, when she had heard the sounds of an approaching horse. She had raised herself up slightly, and her heart had literally stopped when she had glimpsed through the concealing gloom of the forest the tall, dark figure astride a bay stallion. The rider's features had been hidden by the pulled-down brim of his hat, the lower half of his face completely obscured by a heavy black beard, but for one strangely ecstatic moment, Sabrina had been positive it was Brett. Something about the arrogant way he sat on the horse, the breadth of shoulder, the proud carriage . . . For a timeless second, man and horse had seemed to freeze as she slowly rose to her feet, making her presence known within the gazebo. And then, like a ghostly apparition, they had disappeared into the murky shadows of the forest, leaving Sabrina to wonder if she had dreamed the entire sequence.

Sighing, she pushed the unsettling memory away, knowing that it couldn't possibly have been Brett. If it had been, he would certainly have done more than simply stare and then ride away, she thought with a twisted smile.

Her initial rage about the guardianship had abated, even some of her resentment against Alejandro, but the knowledge that Brett Dangermond would one day ride back into her life hung over her head like a death sentence. She could only wait . . . and wonder.

Drawing her knees up against her chest dispiritedly, she rested her chin on her legs. Why? What had her father been thinking of when he had written that wicked codicil? For a second, she remembered the last time she had seen Brett Dangermond, remembered that inimical glance. *Dios!* And he was now her guardian!

Some of her old pride and fiery spirit came rushing up. Well, she certainly wasn't going to let him find her beaten down! She would show him that Sabrina del Torres was equal to anything he could send her way.

Suddenly feeling much better, better and more like her old self than she had in years, Sabrina stood up. She looked down distastefully at the black silk gown she wore. It was time, she decided resolutely, to put aside her black and begin to face the world—Alejandro would have wanted it.

She arrived back at the hacienda a few moments later and was just crossing the rear courtyard when Clemente appeared. "Señorita Sabrina," he said with a faint frown, "there is someone to see you."

"Who?"

He looked puzzled. "I don't know. A young man. He has asked to see you. He seems familiar, and yet . . ."

Her interest sparked, Sabrina swiftly went to the front of the hacienda. A horse was tied to the wooden hitching rail, a tall, slender young man standing beside it. The pair of them had obviously come a long distance.

Her curiosity evident, she walked up to the young man. "Yes?" she said when she was near enough to speak. "What is it?"

The young man turned and stared at her, his not-quite-handsome face vaguely familiar. She had the feeling that

279

she had met him before. Consideringly her gaze ran over him, taking in his wiry six-foot frame, the dark brown hair, and the knowing brown eyes.

"Do I know you?" she asked at last. "You remind me of someone."

"Damn me for a saint if I don't!" the stranger said. "I told you I'd come back, didn't I, miss?"

"Ollie?" Sabrina gasped.

CHAPTER TWENTY

It was indeed Ollie! He had grown considerably in stature during the past six years, and now at twenty-five he stood several inches taller. No longer did his facial features resemble those of a wise little monkey. His once nubbin nose was now a quite respectable size and shape; his chin had squared, his jawline firmed, and his forehead broadened, making him a surprisingly handsome young man. Only those too-wise, button-bright brown eyes remained unchanged. That and his cheeky, impudent grin. It spread from ear to ear as he said, "When me and the guvnor finally arrived home last summer, I told him then and there that it was time I kept my promise to Lupe. It took me *months* to talk him around!" Ollie winked broadly at Sabrina. "And besides, now that he's decided to cease his wanderings, he'll need me and Lupe to run his household proper for him."

Astonished by his unexpected arrival and the change in him, Sabrina could only nod her head bemusedly. A dozen questions trembled on her lips, but she couldn't think clearly; she was only aware of a feeling of intense, almost painful excitement surging up through her. Laughter suddenly springing to her eyes, she said warmly, "Oh, Ollie, how good it is to see you again!" Teasingly she murmured, "But I mustn't keep you . . . I am sure there is someone else you would rather speak to right now."

Ollie's brazen air instantly vanished, and he blushed bright red up to the very roots of his brown hair. He swallowed and appeared to be attacked by a severe case of nervousness. Fiddling with the tied reins, he got out uncomfortably, "Um, is she . . . ? I mean, did she . . . ?"

"Is Lupe still here, is that what you are wondering?" Sabrina asked lightly, a smile lurking at the corners of her mouth. At Ollie's vigorous nod, she added, "Of course she is! She has become my maid. But I'll not tell you anything else—you'll have to speak with Lupe yourself."

Taking the suddenly shy Ollie firmly by his arm, Sabrina urged him across the front courtyard. Inside the hacienda, to the hovering Clemente she said, "It is Ollie Fram come back to visit us! But first he has something important to talk about with Lupe. Please send her to the small *sala.*"

Maternally Sabrina watched Ollie as he prowled nervously about the small room, his hand going again and again to his neck as if his shirt had suddenly become too tight. When there was a timid knock on the door a few minutes later, he went white and threw Sabrina a look of utter terror. "Miss," he hissed under his breath, "she hasn't married someone else?"

Sabrina smiled mysteriously. "That is something you'll have to discover for yourself!"

At Sabrina's command, the door opened slowly, and Lupe stood there framed in the doorway, her dark eyes wide and expectant. Not seeing Ollie immediately, Lupe asked softly, *"Señorita,* is it really true, my Ollie has come?"

There was a strangled sound from Ollie, and Lupe's eyes went instantly in that direction. "Ollie, *querido,* is that you?" she breathed, taking in his height and handsome face.

Ollie nodded dazedly, his eyes traveling hungrily over Lupe's slender form, the delicate bones of her face, memorizing, assimilating the changes that six years had wrought on her. She had been a mere child when he had last seen her, and now here she was a lovely young woman. Great dark eyes clung to his, heavy black hair framing her features, her full lips half-opened with astonishment as she, too, took in the change in him.

For long, timeless seconds the two of them stared across the short distance that separated them. Sabrina left the room quietly.

They never even knew when she departed, Lupe moving like a creature in a dream from the doorway toward Ollie as Sabrina brushed past her. Just before she shut the door,

Sabrina turned, intending to make some encouraging comment, but the sight of Lupe's small hands tenderly exploring Ollie's besotted features, the soft glow in Ollie's eyes as he stared down into Lupe's upturned face, brought a lump to Sabrina's throat, making speech impossible. Quietly she shut the door behind her, and slowly, thoughtfully, she made her way to the inner courtyard.

The initial pleasure of Ollie's unexpected appearance was fading slightly, and with it came a deep sense of uneasiness. Did Ollie carry some message from Brett? Would there at last be an end to this terrible limbo?

She hadn't expected Francisca to be happy about Ollie's arrival, but Sabrina hadn't been prepared for an outburst of hatred and fury. She was seated under the pine tree at the iron table in the courtyard when Sabrina approached, and the black eyes murderous with rage, Francisca demanded, "Is it true? That the gringo's companion is here? That you allowed him to enter this house?"

"Yes, it is true," Sabrina replied levelly. "And yes, I did invite him in—after all, it *is* my home."

Francisca's mouth thinned. "Only if that devil-gringo, Dangermond, decrees it is so!" she spat venomously. It was the last really coherent thing she said—from there her comments evolved into the usual nearly insane monologue of rage against Alejandro and Dangermond.

Sabrina listened wearily for a few minutes, and then, unable to stand it any longer, she said sharply, "Cease! The situation is unpleasant enough without you making it more so! And insulting my father's memory does neither of us any good!"

Francisca's outburst effectively banished Sabrina's enjoyment of Ollie's arrival, and, her fists clenched in anger, she strode swiftly away, seeking the solitude of her room. But in her room she found no peace, her thoughts going immediately to speculation about what Ollie's presence might mean to her. That Lupe, whom she held in an affectionate high regard, might be leaving her never even entered her mind. Nor did it occur to her that Lupe's reluctance to desert a much-loved mistress might cause trouble between the newly reunited lovers.

But one look at Lupe's stormy face, half an hour later

283

when the girl marched into the room, alerted her that something had gone wrong. Very wrong.

Rising up from the stool on which she had been seated, Sabrina asked with concern, "Lupe? What is it? Why do you look so unhappy? Your Ollie has returned, and after listening to you moon over him for years, listening to your worries that he would find someone else, that he would never come back for you, I would have thought you would be ecstatic."

Lupe's big eyes filled with tears. "Oh, *señorita*, I *was* so happy! And he has grown into such a man that I knew my heart had been right in waiting for him"—she glanced miserably across at Sabrina's worried face—"but he wants me to leave you! To come back with him to New Orleans." Her face crumpled, and sobbing, she ran to fling her arms around Sabrina's waist. "I love him so much!" Lupe cried. "And I have waited and hoped so long for his return, but now I am torn in two! I cannot bear to leave you, my family, my friends, everything I have ever known, and travel so far away with a man I barely know. I love him," she said earnestly, "but I don't *know* him."

Sabrina's face twisted with pain. So she had loved Brett Dangermond, but she hadn't known him either. Sighing, she gently disengaged herself from Lupe's embrace. "Don't cry, my dear. I'm sure that Ollie will understand if you explain everything to him. Besides," she continued with a slight smile, "nothing has to be decided immediately, does it? We must plan your wedding, and that will take time. Don't worry. When you marry your Ollie everything will be just fine."

Sabrina wished she were as confident as she sounded, but her words must have convinced Lupe, because the tears dried instantly. "Oh, *señorita!* I *knew* that you would understand! And that you would have the solution."

Smiling wryly, Sabrina turned away and asked, "Where is Ollie now? You didn't send him away, did you?"

Lupe looked horrified. "Oh, no! I could not send him away when he has just arrived; it would not be kind! Besides, he has said that he will not leave without me!"

Ollie repeated that statement some minutes later when Sabrina came downstairs and met him in the small *sala*

284

where he was waiting for her. "Miss," he said bluntly, "I'm not leaving here without her." Bewilderedly he added, "I just don't understand her! Here she is happy as a lark to see me, promises to marry me, and then when I mention living with the guvnor, she turns all Friday-face. *Women!*"

Finding it a bit strange to act as a lovers' peacemaker, Sabrina said soothingly, "Give her time, Ollie. Your arrival has been a great surprise for all of us."

"But I said I'd be back!" he protested. "And she must have believed it, because she's waited all this time."

Sabrina nodded her head slowly. "I know. But it's one thing to dream of something, to long for it with all your heart, and another to have it presented to you. We Spanish have a proverb—'Be careful what you ask God for . . . He may give it to you.' Don't you understand, you must give her a little time to get used to you again—she was a child when you left."

"Not *that* much of a child!" Ollie retorted darkly, his resentment at this turn of events obvious.

Smiling fondly at him, Sabrina coaxed, "Come now, do not look so surly. Tomorrow, after you have rested and you and Lupe have had more time to talk, you will feel much better. You'll see."

Ollie grumbled something under his breath, but he seemed willing enough to concede the point. "Very well, miss, I'll do as you say." Changing the subject abruptly, he went on, "Clemente said I was to have the room I used when I was here before, and if you have no objections, I'd like to start settling in." His face gloomy, he ended with, "It appears I'm going to be here longer than I figured."

Amusement dancing in her eyes, Sabrina asked demurely, "Did you really expect to arrive one day, after a six-year absence, marry Lupe, and depart by the next?"

A sheepish grin curved his long mouth. "Not really," he admitted reluctantly. "But guvnor said . . ." He stopped, his face almost comical with dismay.

"What is it?" Sabrina demanded.

"Afore God, miss, I plain forgot!" Ollie burst out, embarrassed. Excusingly, he added, "In the excitement I just fair forgot to give you his letter."

285

Sabrina's face paled, but she said calmly enough, "I'm certain that it's understandable."

"Always knew you were a bang-up article, miss!" Ollie said admiringly as he fumbled under his shirt for the letter. Finding it, he handed it to Sabrina, a troubled expression on his face.

"Miss," he began hesitantly, "I don't know what went wrong between you two, but it hit the guvnor hard. He's never quite been the same since, and these past years . . . well," he went on more strongly, "these past years have marked him, changed him. He was always a hard man, but now, except with damn few people, he's like cold steel. Now I don't know what's in that letter he's written to you, but I will tell you this: he wasn't best pleased when he found out about your father's will." Ollie stopped, his face filled with a sort of reluctant awe. "When he heard about being your guardian and everything, he swore like nothing I've never heard before. Right off he declared he would have nothing to do with it. That someone else could be your damned duenna, but it sure as hell wasn't going to be him!" Ollie shook his head. "But then, after he thought about it a bit, he said he owed it to your father. Said for Alejandro's sake he'd do his duty by you." Ollie pulled on his ear, distinctly uneasy with the situation and Sabrina's increasingly frigid expression. Aware that he had overstepped himself, he scowled unhappily. "I just thought you ought to know."

"Thank you," Sabrina replied with icy politeness. "Now if you will leave me alone with my letter . . . ?"

"That I will, miss!" Ollie answered swiftly. But then, as if noticing her black garb for the first time, he added quietly, "Miss? I'm sorry about your father—I meant to say something just as soon as I saw you." His brown eyes full of sympathy, he added, "Don Alejandro was a good man; I'm certain you miss him badly." He hesitated, as if uncertain whether to continue, but then, taking a deep breath, he said, "Miss, the guvnor took your father's death real hard. He was angrier than I've ever seen him, and he swore that someday he'd find your father's killer. He was damn grim and silent for days afterward, and then, just all of a sudden, he disappears, left me in New Orleans with orders to mind my manners and stay put!" Ollie shook his head. "If I didn't know better, I'd say he'd gone looking for your father's killer, but then, just as sudden as he went, he shows back up, acting as if nothing had happened. I figure he had to take himself off somewhere private-like to work out his grief. He doesn't let much show, but I know he grieved for your father."

Ollie's words rang in her ears long after he had left the room. The letter in her hand, Sabrina sat down behind her father's old pine desk and stared blindly into space for several minutes. Sighing, she pushed aside the sad thoughts and looked at the sealed envelope in her hand.

Her face set in grim lines, she opened the letter and read it. Ollie had, she realized, tried to warn her, and she supposed she was thankful to him. But nothing could have controlled the fury that suddenly erupted up through her when the full import of Brett's letter hit her. *Dios!* What an arrogant swine!

There was no salutation, no mention of condolences, not one personal word. Just hard facts and cold, unfeeling commands. He would, Brett had written, in the following weeks be taking complete control of every facet of her fortune. Decisions concerning where she would live and how would be made soon. The same held true of who she would be allowed to associate with and when. Alejandro's business agent in New Orleans had already informed him of the current state of finances, and the family agent in Mexico City would be sending along his report just as soon as possible. In the meantime, she was to remain precisely where she was. . . .

There was such an insulting tone to the letter, such a haughty assumption that she would meekly obey his every whim, that Sabrina choked with fury. Did he really believe that he could treat her this way? She would show him!

Gone was the lethargy of the past months. Gone was the feeling of helplessness. Furiously she ripped his letter to bits. She glared at the scraps of paper, wishing she could destroy Brett Dangermond as easily.

In that mood, it was difficult to remember that once she had loved him, that once she had lain in his arms and had

287

known the ecstasy of his lovemaking. That, she thought with a scornful toss of her bright head, was all in the past.

When she announced to her startled household a few minutes later that she intended to leave for New Orleans within the week, there was a stunned silence. Then a babble of voices rose, some full of objections, some expressing excitement. Whatever their opinion, from the set of her jaw and the look in her eyes, it was abundantly clear that the *señorita* would not be swayed—she *was* going to New Orleans!

Francisca's objections couldn't be dismissed as effort-lessly as those of the servants, but they had as little effect. Her face implacable, Sabrina said decisively, "I'm sorry, Tía, that you don't like the idea, but I am going. I'm deter-mined to fight Dangermond. The money doesn't even mat-ter that much; it is his arrogant treatment of me that I will not tolerate!"

Further argument by Francisca proved fruitless, and seeing that nothing would sway her niece, Francisca pro-posed angrily, "At least wait until Carlos returns from Mexico City. He is due back any day. You cannot travel to New Orleans without a duenna—it would be unseemly!"

Her amber-gold eyes unnaturally bright, Sabrina re-plied grimly, "If you like and if it will make you feel better, you may come with me to New Orleans." A hint of irony in her voice, she murmured, "I doubt I could find a stricter duenna."

Uncertain whether to take offense or not, Francisca stared hard at her for a moment. But then she nodded her head. *"Sí!* I shall come with you. Until Carlos returns and follows us to New Orleans, I shall protect you!"

Sabrina's decision to travel to New Orleans only strengthened Ollie's insistence that he and Lupe be mar-ried immediately. At first Lupe stubbornly resisted, main-taining that he was being unfair, but she loved him, she knew, and she allowed herself to banish her doubts.

Their marriage was hastily arranged, but Sabrina thought on Wednesday afternoon, as she watched them re-cite their vows before the priest in Nacogdoches, that it was wonderful. There was such an air of happiness, such warmth and good wishes enveloping the newly married young couple, that she felt tears sting her eyes.

Much to Francisca's disgust, the departure for New Orleans was delayed a few days because of the wedding. The delay didn't trouble her, but the reason for it did. "They are just servants," she had sniffed, and at Sabrina's look of surprise, had added, "You pamper them far too much. Why, at the Rancho de la Vega I would never have allowed a mere servant to disrupt *my* plans!"

Wisely Sabrina bit her tongue, wondering how she was going to endure the long, uncomfortable journey to New Orleans. It will teach me patience, she told herself virtuously the night before they were to leave. Patience and control and restraint and forbearance and . . .

The journey proved to be almost enjoyable. The weather was good, there were no mishaps or accidents, and they were left unmolested by bandits and robbers who lurked along the trail.

For Ollie and Lupe, the trip to New Orleans was a unique adventure. Newly married, falling more and more in love with each other by the hour, they found the long days spent riding slowly through the untracked, almost tropical wilderness a lovers' delight. And the nights . . .

Sabrina tried to still the faint twinge of envy that she felt, watching moodily as Lupe moved blissfully about, helping to repack the items that had been taken from the wagon for the night. Ashamed of her unworthy emotions, Sabrina turned away, wondering if her face would ever wear such a contented, ecstatic expression. Probably not, she decided coldly, particularly if Brett Dangermond remained in control of her future!

The closer they came to New Orleans, the more highstrung Sabrina became. She snapped at Lupe, was curt with her aunt, and made Ollie stare at her in surprise on more than one occasion. She was always instantly contrite, mortified that she had so little control over herself, but nothing seemed to be able to still the inexorable tension that built within her. She was a mass of taut nerves, anger and resentment battling with a queer, insistent feeling of excitement and anticipation. That the thought of seeing Brett again could arouse such violent, contradictory emotions only increased Sabrina's feeling of helpless rage.

What am I to do? she wondered savagely a few days later, just as the travelers began to cross the last deep bayou that barred their way into New Orleans. In a matter of hours, perhaps less, she would be face to face with a man she had once loved passionately, a man who had showed himself to be a scoundrel and a liar, and a man who had no reason to think kindly of her—a man full of wrath. Well, she was prepared to take the battle right into his camp, she thought with a grim sort of pleasure.

But it wasn't the idea of war with Brett that disturbed her so, it was the bitter knowledge that in spite of everything, he still held a sinister fascination for her. She feared that fascination, and yet she was powerless against it, wanting to see him, eager for the sight of that once-beloved face, and yet knowing full well that those handsome features hid a selfish and ruthless nature.

And how was he going to react to her sudden, unexpected appearance in his life? With anger and fury? Or would he attempt to charm her again? To woo her into blind, loving obedience as he had almost done six years ago? Sabrina's mouth tightened, the amber-gold eyes glittering angrily. Never! He would never be able to make her forget the past, never again dupe her as he had then. *Never!*

She had his measure now, and she was prepared to fight him, fight him for what was rightfully hers. But could she win? her mind asked slyly. Could she win when confronted with that dark charm of his? Remembering the way he had kissed her by the lake that moonlit night, remembering how it had felt to lie in his arms, she trembled, suddenly wishing that she had remained safely at the ranch, safely away from the danger he represented to her foolish heart. But then angrily she pushed the traitorous thoughts aside—she was no coward. She would never run from a fight, and she would face the future proudly, defiantly. Besides, she reminded herself harshly, he is far more likely to greet me with open warfare than open arms!

Brett's town house in New Orleans was in the more settled area of the city east of Dauphine Street, not far from the Mississippi River. Taking the lead, Ollie guided them directly to the rather elegant three-storied house that from its envied position on Condi Street, commanded, for the present, a glimpse of the powerful river that had brought the French here to settle in 1718.

Recalling that six years ago Brett had been on the edge of ruin after the hurricane destroyed his plantation, Sabrina stared disbelievingly at the size and grandeur of the stuccoed, slate-roofed house. Escorting them efficiently to the side of the house, Ollie quickly herded the straggling party through a pair of delicate wrought-iron gates that guarded the carriageway.

Following Ollie through the gates, Sabrina discovered that she was inside a wide, covered passageway that would bring them, she suspected, to the stables and garden area at the rear of the house. About halfway down the carriageway, Ollie reined in his horse, and turning around to her, he said simply, "You ladies can dismount here." Nodding toward another, smaller gate set in the walls that enclosed the carriageway, he added, "Go on through there. A servant is bound to be about and will show you into the house."

Her legs suddenly weak, her heart beating at a frantic rate, Sabrina slowly slid out of her saddle. Why had it seemed so important to bring herself face to face with Brett Dangermond?

Furious with herself, the moment her booted feet hit the ground she squared her slim shoulders. She would not allow herself to be intimidated by the mere thought of seeing him again! She was strong, strong and wise enough not to be affected by his disturbing presence. And besides, she reminded herself spiritedly, he should never, never have written her such a cold, arrogant, insulting, overbearing . . . *contemptuous* letter! He was going to discover that by law, and for the moment, she might be his ward, but she was not going to let the matter rest there for long!

A faint hint of color staining her high cheek bones, with a determined step, she pushed through the gates, stopping in sheer appreciation of the beauty that met her gaze.

She found herself at the edge of a spacious courtyard. The house formed three sides of it, the walls of the carriageway making the fourth. Square in shape, the flag-stoned courtyard was attractively decorated with massive pottery tubs of gorgeous flowers and exotic foliage: scarlet and white geraniums, orange hibiscus, pink azaleas, sprawling feathery ferns, and small palmettos all vied for the visitor's eye. Two large magnolia trees, their leathery dark green leaves contrasting wonderfully with the creamy white cup-shaped blossoms, provided spreading pools of welcome shade.

There was an air of repose, of graciousness, in this enchanting place. Several balconies overlooked the courtyard from the second and third stories of the house, and their lacy, wrought-iron railings were festooned with more subtropical vines and flowers. Fanlight windows and graceful arched doorways all faced the courtyard; the soft ocher of the walls of the house was exceptionally pleasing to the eye. It was, Sabrina thought with astonishment, a lovely place. An elegant place.

Even Francisca was impressed. "Well!" she said sourly from behind Sabrina, "it would appear that the gringo was not the fortune hunter that we believed. Unless, of course, it is *your* money that has provided him with all of this."

Slowly Sabrina walked across the courtyard toward a pair of French doors set in the main part of the house. Her stomach was fluttering uncomfortably, an odd sense of dread and anticipation driving her forward.

As she drew nearer, she became aware of a flight of wide wooden stairs that were situated a little distance from the French doors and that seemed to disappear as they angled upward into the second story of the wing to her right. A few feet from them she stopped, uncertain whether to knock on the French doors or go up the stairs.

At her side, Francisca sniffed contemptuously. "How rude of the gringo! No one is here to meet us! He may have the trappings of a gentleman, but it is apparent he hasn't the manners! *Some*one should have greeted us before now!"

Defensively Sabrina replied, "We *are* unexpected, Tía! It is possible that none of the house servants are aware of our arrival."

"After the racket we made riding through the carriageway?" Francisca inquired acidly. "Don't delude yourself! This is just another insult!" Her shoulders rigid, Francisca marched angrily forward and rapped imperiously on one of the French doors.

Except for the lazy drone of the bees and the occasional cry of a bird, there was silence. Francisca's lips thinned, and she turned to Sabrina, but in that instant they both heard the opening and shutting of a door somewhere near the top of the stairs. Francisca stepped back from the French doors and craned her neck upward.

The upper portion of the angling staircase was hidden from view, but hearing the firm tread coming downward, Sabrina suddenly felt her mouth go dry. She was conscious of a clamminess in the palms of her hands, and again she wished she had stayed in Nacogdoches—it was far better to meet the enemy on familiar ground, and she realized that she had inadvertently given him an advantage by coming to New Orleans. Now the battle would be fought on *his* ground.

Her eyes were fixed painfully on that flight of stairs, every nerve in her body frozen as the sound of the footsteps came closer. A booted foot appeared first, then another. The gleaming russet boots were of fine Spanish leather, the workmanship exceptional, and Sabrina swallowed with difficulty. No servant would wear boots like those.

Almost as if he were deliberately prolonging the suspense, the man on the stairs continued to move down the steps with an infuriating lack of speed, one booted foot after the other. More of his body came into view, the buff pantaloons clinging like a second skin to the powerful calves and thighs, a wide brown leather belt encircling the lean waist. His upper body still hidden in the shadows of the house, the man stopped, one strong, tanned hand resting lightly on the railing. The faint hint of tobacco teased Sabrina's nose, and she glimpsed a smoking cheroot in his other hand before he raised it to his mouth.

He moved lower down the stairs, the white linen shirt with its flowing sleeves and cuffed wrists hiding nothing of the muscled body it clothed. It was open at the neck, the strong column of his throat appearing dark against the whiteness of his shirt. Indolently he continued on his way downward, the obstinate chin, the hard jawline, and that chiseled mouth instantly recognizable to Sabrina.

Her heart was beating so frantically she thought she was going to choke, and when at last the sunlight fell full upon those handsome, arrogant features, she was almost relieved. The worst, in a way, was over; they were face to face.

The past six years were distinctly stamped on that strong, masculine face: attractive creases radiated out faintly from the corners of the jade-green eyes, and cynical grooves were apparent in the lean cheeks. With a start Sabrina realized that he would be thirty-four now. The thick blue-black hair gleamed in the sunlight. A light, *very* elegant dusting of silver could be seen near his temples, and startling her by its intensity, she knew an impulse to reach out and touch, to caress those few silvery hairs that grew there.

With his predatory grace, he came down the few remaining stairs, the expression on his face unfathomable as he took another drag on the cheroot, the emotion in those hooded jade-green eyes hidden by his ridiculously long eyelashes. Reaching the bottom of the staircase, he stepped onto the flagstone courtyard and stopped just a few yards from Sabrina.

Slowly, insolently, those dark green eyes moved over her, and she was instantly aware of her dusty, travel-stained riding habit, of her hair that had been plaited into one long braid that lay across her left shoulder. A slightly worn beaver hat with a very narrow brim protected her head from the hot sun, her boots were scuffed and dirty from the journey, and she was miserably conscious of her untidy state. Suddenly annoyed with the situation, she tightened her grip on the small leather quirt she carried, and she lifted her chin pugnaciously.

Brett noted the movements, and he smiled sardonically. Walking closer, he reached out and touched the bright braid of fiery hair. In a motion that was both a caress and a threat, he tugged at the braid and murmured with an odd note in his voice, "My ward. My sweet, obedient ward come to visit her wicked guardian."

Sabrina glanced at him sharply, the angry retort dying on her lips at the cold indifference in those hard green eyes. She started to jerk away, but his hand tightened on her braid. In a silent battle of wills, they stared at one another, Sabrina's eyes full of defiance, Brett's enigmatic. He smiled again, not a nice smile, a smile that never reached those expressionless dark green eyes. "My win this time, tiger lily," he said dryly.

CHAPTER TWENTY-ONE

✥ Hours later, comfortably situated in a set of elegantly appointed rooms, Sabrina wondered how she had kept from striking him with her quirt. Maybe it had been the knowledge that Francisca was there behind her; maybe it had been the cold promise in those dark green eyes. She didn't know; she only knew that she was still angry and seething with resentment.

She might have held her tongue, but Francisca certainly hadn't, and remembering her aunt's furious tirade, she half-smiled. Brett was definitely not going to find things all his way, if her aunt had any say in the matter. And Francisca had made that very clear. Not only that, but her displeasure with Alejandro's infamous will, Brett's total unsuitability as a guardian of her niece, and finally, the completely unacceptable way he ran his household. Brett had listened to Francisca's scathing commentary impassively, but there had been the icy edge of steel to his voice when he had said, "May I remind you that you are my guest? That whether you like it or not—whether you approve or not—Sabrina *is* my ward, and that if I so choose, my house will be closed to you?"

Francisca had gasped with outrage, but she had read the threat in those dark green eyes and had subsided . . . for the moment. Brett had turned away, calling for servants, and from there events had moved rapidly. Two Negro women had instantly appeared, almost as if they had been waiting just out of sight for his command, and had immediately ushered Sabrina and Francisca up the staircase that Brett had descended only moments earlier.

The suite of rooms that Sabrina had been given overlooked the courtyard and possessed an ironwork balcony like those she had noticed initially. A pair of French doors led to the balcony, and with an irritated motion, she flung them wide.

It was early evening now, and the courtyard below her was in pale shadows, the glory of the vivid colors dimmed by the falling darkness. But it didn't matter to Sabrina that all was shadows below her; she was too busy prowling the small confines of the balcony, thinking of seeing Brett again, dreading yet eager for that next meeting.

She felt better able to deal with his unsettling presence now that the difficult hurdle of that first meeting was behind her. A long, soothing bath had somewhat calmed her disordered emotions, and attired in a sophisticated gown, a low-cut, bosom-clinging creation of black silk with charming bell-shaped sleeves that ended at the elbow, she was now ready to open the next salvo.

If Brett's features revealed the changes that six years had wrought, so did Sabrina's, and in many respects those changes were far more noticeable on her than they had been on him. She had been a child-woman when last they had met; now the arresting face that Sofia had once thought Sabrina would possess was fully evident. And it was an arresting face, just missing being truly beautiful. Her jawline was a trifle too strong for the soft, ethereal features so admired by the poets, and her mouth was just a little too full, too wide, to be perfect, but her nose was classical, and the high cheekbones lent a patrician cast to her features. With that glorious hair and those striking dark eyebrows and incredible amber-gold eyes, Sabrina would always cause a stir.

Always tall, fully grown she stood just an inch under six feet, and she had all the physical grace and the full-figured body of a Valkyrie as well as the fierce spirit that went with those mythical maidens of Odin, the Norse god of war. Yet despite her almost voluptuous shape, there was a deceptive slenderness about her, the full, proud bosom and gently swelling hips complementing her shapely, long-limbed body.

But there were also other changes in her, not just those brought on by the maturing of her face and figure. The pain and unhappiness that she had suffered during the past six years were apparent to the discerning eye: the faintly

297

vulnerable curve to the full mouth, a mouth that had been fashioned for laughter and loving; the shadows in the amber-gold eyes, eyes that should have been bright and smiling; and the wall of reserve that she had carefully erected around her.

Once the darling of a beloved father, the pride of the Rancho del Torres, she had been full of joy, eager and confident of her future, innocent in so many ways of the reality of life. But that was true no longer. Betrayed by the man she loved, orphaned by her father's death, this Sabrina was a very different young woman from the one Brett had met that long ago spring in Nacogdoches. And yet, underneath, waiting impatiently to break free of the gloom and sadness that had enveloped her was an entirely new Sabrina, a Sabrina who would combine the best of the two people she had been—the girl-child who had become a woman in Brett's arms, and the woman who had suffered the devastating loss of both father and lover.

Sabrina wasn't aware of all the changes in herself, but she had been conscious for some time now of a growing feeling of impatience with her situation. Guilty impatience that she couldn't continue to grieve as deeply as did Tía Francisca; resigned impatience that Carlos continued to pursue her, despite all her protestations; angry impatience with the unfair shackles put on her by Alejandro's will; and finally, eager impatience to join the battle with Brett.

And at the moment that last emotion was the dominant one, the need to see him again, to make it clear that she was *not* going to be the obedient ward he might have wished for, driving her off the balcony and into her room. She strode swiftly across the large room, stopping for a moment in front of a tall cheval glass.

Telling herself that it was only natural to check one's appearance before leaving the privacy of the bedchamber, she took a quick glance at herself, satisfied with the coronet braid that circled her head primly, in direct contrast with the generous swell of bosom that rose so temptingly above the low-cut gown. A heavy necklace of black onyx and gold adorned her neck, and studs of the same design and color were at each ear. The black silk of the gown was extremely effective against the creamy whiteness of her skin, increasing her air of fragility and vulnerability.

Staring at herself, at the conflicting image she presented, Sabrina suddenly smiled. The hair was prim and proper, the gown, while in the very best of taste, was decidedly . . . sophisticated, she thought slowly, her smile mischievous. The word *wanton* also had occurred to her, but she much preferred to ignore that particular description. She supposed that unconsciously she had been striving for just the look she had—that of a demure sybarite! Pleased with the result, she gave a gentle twitch to the full skirts, and then, her eyes sparkling, she left her rooms.

She found herself in the middle of a long, wide hallway that ran the entire length of the wing. About halfway down it was the staircase that led to the courtyard, and a bit farther on from there was another staircase, a graceful, beautifully designed affair that spiraled downward toward what Sabrina assumed was the main part of the house.

She was correct. Descending the interior staircase, she was soon standing in a spacious foyer. The floor was of pale green marble, the walls only a few shades lighter in color. Gilt sconces lined the entranceway, tall beeswax tapers revealing that Brett did not stint on household requirements.

Several doors opened off the foyer; the pair of wide, skillfully carved ones that were at one end of the hall probably led to the street, Sabrina concluded as she stood there indecisively, wondering behind which of the other doors she would find Brett. Fortunately she didn't have long to wait. A second later, a door to her right opened and a servant in black and white attire came out.

Seeing her standing there, he bowed politely and asked kindly, "May I help you, miss?"

Her stomach instantly filled with butterflies, she replied breathlessly, "Yes. I am looking for Señor Dangermond. Do you know where he is?"

"In here, miss," the man answered, motioning to the room he had just departed. He started to say something else, but Sabrina, not giving herself time to consider the wisdom of what she was doing, swept regally by him. An impatient flick of her wrist and the door swung open; two deceptively confident strides took her beyond the door. The soft sound of it shutting behind her gave her the unnerving impression that her one avenue of escape had just been shut off, but wrapping her reservations in outward bravado, she continued on her way.

The room she had just entered was obviously the library, the scent of leather that came from the neat rows of books that lined every wall pleasantly teasing her nostrils. A marble-manteled fireplace interrupted the flow of books in one wall of the long room, a russet and green carpet lay upon the floor, and several comfortable chairs of dark green velvet were scattered about the area. Satinwood drum tables stood near the chairs, and an elegant cream and green silk sofa divided the room in half. Beyond the sofa and the fireplace was apparently where Brett had his office; an impressively large desk of mahogany dominated that end of the room, a few wing chairs done in green leather faced the desk, their backs to Sabrina, and from where she stood, she glimpsed the top of a marble table behind the sofa.

Again she was struck by the discreet display of wealth that met her eye, and again she wished that Tía Francisca had not planted the ugly seed of suspicion about the source of Brett's unexpected wealth. But before she had time to let her thoughts wander too far, she was brought back sharply to the present by Brett's voice saying mockingly, "Ah, Sabrina, there you are. I wondered how long it would be before you appeared."

Her jaw clenched, and with determined steps she approached him as he rose with languid grace from one of the wing-backed chairs. Her approach was momentarily halted, though, when another tall, dark-haired man rose from the other chair and turned to face her. She stopped abruptly, a faint flush staining her cheeks. "I didn't realize that you had a visitor," she said stiffly. "I'll come back later."

"Don't be silly," Brett drawled infuriatingly. "Morgan is not just any visitor, and I would like you to meet him." The dark green eyes hard and unfathomable, he walked up to her, and taking her hand, brought her over to face the other gentleman. "Sabrina del Torres, I would like to pre-

300

sent Mr. Morgan Slade. He is one of my oldest friends, and you will find him a frequent guest in my home. Morgan, *this* is my sweet ward."

Angry and resentful at his tone of voice, Sabrina sent him a fulminating glance, but then her gaze turned to Morgan Slade, and she muttered politely, "How do you do. It is a pleasure to meet you."

A pair of twinkling sapphire blue eyes met hers, and Sabrina felt some of her annoyance with Brett's provoking introduction fading. Bending over her hand, Morgan Slade murmured lightly, "The pleasure is all mine, Señorita del Torres. And do not mind half of what your wicked guardian says—he delights in being particularly aggravating upon occasion . . . and I should know, having had the misfortune to grow up with him!"

Sabrina's eyes widened. An enchantingly shy little smile upon her lips, she uttered softly, "Why, I remember you! We met when I attended Tía Sofía's wedding to Señor Hugh. Don't you remember me?"

Morgan's handsome face creased into a startlingly attractive smile. "I remember a big-eyed child with red hair, but certainly not the delightful young lady you have become."

Liking this tall, broad-shouldered gentleman with his laughing blue eyes and easy manners, Sabrina relaxed slightly. Morgan appeared to be much the same age as Brett, although his black hair showed no sign of silver. He was a very handsome man, his features perhaps more classically perfect than Brett's uncompromisingly arrogant face, although Sabrina gained the distinct impression that in spite of Morgan's generously curved mouth and merry eyes with their thick, dark lashes, he could be as hard and ruthless as Brett if need be.

To Morgan's light comment, she replied. "You are very kind, *señor*."

"And *very* married," Brett interjected dryly. "Leonie, his wife, is at their plantation, the Château Saint-André, awaiting the birth of their second child."

Morgan's face changed magically at the mention of his wife's name, his love for her obvious. Smiling across at Sabrina, he said, "All he says is true. And I'm afraid I must

301

confess that beautiful as you are, my heart is firmly held by a little honey-haired spitfire who would cheerfully have my liver for breakfast if she ever even just thought I was looking too long at another woman." Grinning at her, he added, "You do understand my position?"

Sabrina did. It was very apparent to her that Morgan Slade adored his wife much the way Alejandro had loved Elena, and she found that knowledge comforting. Her expression teasing, she said, "I would like very much to meet this fierce lady. Do you think I could?"

"I'm certain nothing would give Leonie greater pleasure —except the healthy and speedy arrival of our child," Morgan returned promptly. "But I would suggest that we postpone that occasion until after the birth of the baby. She is in her last weeks and is very uncomfortable at times."

"Oh, of course!" Sabrina said quickly. "And I will look forward to the day when we do finally meet."

The conversation was desultory for several minutes, and when Sabrina next suggested that she leave the gentlemen to finish their conversation, Brett agreed with unflattering alacrity. His face unrevealing, he walked to a velvet rope pull in one corner, and giving it a brief tug, he said coolly, "I'll have Andrew, my butler, show you about the house. After all, it is going to be your home, too."

There was something about the way he said those seemingly innocuous words that gave Sabrina an odd shiver down her spine. Delight or fear?

Andrew turned out to be the servant who had first directed her to the library, and with an obedience that dismayed her, Sabrina found herself meekly following Brett's orders. A warm, polite smile curving her mouth, she bid Morgan good-bye and then swiftly preceded Andrew from the room.

There was a moment of silence after she had left, and then Morgan said thoughtfully, "I wonder if you realize what you are doing?"

Brett snorted. Walking over to the marble-topped table that Sabrina had glimpsed behind the couch, which served as a liquor cabinet, Brett poured them both a snifter of brandy. Turning back to face Morgan, he handed him one of the snifters and muttered, "Where that particular little witch is concerned, I never realize anything except that she drives me half-mad!"

"And yet you accepted the guardianship?"

A peculiar expression flitted across Brett's dark face. Not quite cruel and yet not exactly *un*kind. He seated himself in the wing-backed chair before answering Morgan's question. Staring at the amber liquid in his snifter, he said quietly, "Yes, I did. And even I'm not certain of either the wisdom of having done so or the reasons why I did. I know the most acceptable one is because I feel compelled, in view of the respect and affection I bore Alejandro, to carry out his final wishes, but the others . . ." His voice trailed off, that strange expression once more crossing his features.

"Revenge?" Morgan suggested softly, well aware of the bitter, disillusioned state Brett had been in upon his return from visiting Spanish Texas six years ago.

Brett looked at him, the dark green eyes suddenly hard, the chiseled mouth with a ruthless slant to it. "That, too," he admitted harshly.

Picking his words with care, Morgan said dryly, "Be careful of revenge, my friend. It can harm you as well as pleasure you."

A mirthless laugh came from Brett. "Sabrina may have caught me once in her lovely claws, but never again—I know her for the greedy jade that she is!"

Morgan looked at him a long time. "Brett," he began slowly, "I'm not going to argue which one of us has suffered the most at the hands of a woman, nor am I about to suggest that you forget the past. However, I *am* going to say that not all women are vipers . . . and things are not always what they seem. Look at Leonie and me, for God's sake! I was certain she was a scheming littly hussy, and she was equally certain that I was a blackguard out to steal her dowry . . . and we were both so very wrong about the other."

Brett sent him a level glance. "And love makes fools of all of us—especially reformed misogynists!"

Morgan smiled wryly. "Perhaps." Deciding it was futile to argue further with his friend, he changed the subject. His voice taking on a more serious note, he said, "This letter you received from Eaton really troubles me, Brett."

And frowning suddenly, Morgan reached across Brett's desk and picked up the letter in question.

Again he read its contents and then turned to Brett. "How well do you know him?" Brett started to reply, but Morgan held up his hand. "I already know that 'General' Eaton, as he is styled, has been made much of in powerful circles in Washington; I know that he has served our government well in the war with the Barbary priates; but I also know that some consider him a drunkard and a braggart. So, aware of all that, can what he writes in this letter about Aaron Burr, our ex-Vice-President, be trusted?"

Thoughtfully Brett regarded the tip of his polished boot. "I can't deny that Eaton has his detractors, or claim that they are completely mistaken in what they say about him; I do know, however, that I trusted him enough last spring to join his ragtag crew near Arab's Tower in Egypt and that I willingly followed him across the Desert of Barca for the attack on Derna on the coast of the Mediterranean Sea." Brett sent Morgan a hard look. "It wasn't a pleasant journey, and the battle for Derna won't figure as one of my favorite memories—but we took Derna in spite of the odds against it and probably would have captured Tripoli if hostilities hadn't ended so abruptly. Eaton got us out of Derna alive when we learned that there was not going to be any naval support."

Momentarily diverted, Morgan asked exasperatedly, "What in the hell were you doing in Egypt anyway? And why go traipsing across the desert with a band of cutthroat Arabs and Greeks to fight in a war that meant little or nothing to you?"

"Boredom?" Brett offered hopefully, an imp of mischief flickering in the jade-green eyes.

Morgan snorted, but he desisted his probings. He knew too well from past experience that seemingly guileless expression on his friend's face—Brett obviously didn't want to talk about his adventures in northern Africa, and it was apparent that any further questioning would bring forth only glib, mocking replies.

His eyes strayed again to the letter under discussion. "This is a wild tale," Morgan said slowly. "A tale one would tend to put down as the mad ravings of a lunatic."

Dryly Brett said, "Eaton is not a lunatic—peculiar and given to exaggeration—but not a madman. And if Eaton writes that Burr plans to raise a force of men and invade Washington, kill President Jefferson, and seize ships to sail to New Orleans, I would believe that there is some substance to it."

"The entire thing is sheer lunacy! You met Burr last summer at Stephen Minor's ball for him in Natchez and again here—did he strike you as a maniac? An assassin?"

There was silence as Brett stared blindly at his boots, his thoughts running backward to his meeting with Aaron Burr last summer in Natchez. On the surface Burr certainly didn't resemble the sort of man to be associated with the wild schemes that Eaton wrote of—Burr was charming and agreeable, perhaps a little too charming and agreeable. And he could be quite persuasive when he wanted to be, Brett mused with a slight smile, thinking of the conversation he'd had with the former Vice-President at Minor's house.

It had happened that he and Burr had strolled out for a moment of air, and as they walked amicably through the lantern-strung grounds next to the house, Burr had said casually, "You realize, of course, that I have deliberately manipulated this private talk between us."

Brett had nodded his head. He had glanced down at his much shorter companion, noting the thin mouth, the almost voluptuous chin, and had wondered idly what it was that drew men to Burr. The ex-Vice-President had smiled at him just then, and for a second Brett had basked in his charm.

"I need young men like you," Burr had murmured easily. "Young men willing to take desperate chances . . . young men ripe for great adventure . . ."

Brett's thick brow had arched. "Oh? And tell me how the innocent settling of the de Bastrop tract on the Washita River is going to do that?"

Burr had waved an airy hand. "The de Bastrop tract is for those who wish to be settlers." He had eyed Brett speculatively, almost as if gauging how much he could say. "But you, my friend, would never want such a mundane thing . . . I have heard of your adventures in Derna." When

305

Brett had remained silent, Burr had gone on. "Throw your lot with me, and I can give you adventure and riches you never dreamed of—you could be part of a new and grand empire."

Carefully Brett had asked, "An empire? Where?"

Burr had smiled slyly and had shrugged negligently. "Who knows? Perhaps west of the Sabine River? Mexico even? If there were a war with Spain, many opportunities could await a clever man."

Brett had allowed a flicker of interest to appear in his eyes, and seeing it, Burr had bent forward eagerly, the dark hazel eyes flashing with intensity. "I have a plan, a great plan, and already it is taking shape." He had glanced around as if making certain that no one was near. "On my way here, I met with General Wilkinson at Fort Massac on the Ohio River, and we talked of many things . . . things a young man seeking adventure would find interesting." That had been as far as Burr would reveal himself, and Brett had discovered that Burr was extremely adept at sizing up people and wooing them to his side with whatever tale he thought would appeal most. For some it had been the offer of the de Bastrop lands, for others the possibility of invading Mexico, but no one had heard the same tale—and now there was another tale—one of murder, betrayal, and treason. . . .

Looking across at Morgan, Brett finally shrugged and said soberly, "An assassin? No, I don't think so, but then what does either of us really know about the man? He is a facile charmer, but there is also an unclean odor about him. For God's sake, look at how he almost took the Presidency from Jefferson in 1800! Look at that duel with Alexander Hamilton—there were indictments for murder out on him! Not a pretty character I would say."

"All you say is true, but that doesn't mean that he plans to do anything as radical as murder the President of the United States!" Morgan said impatiently. He shot Brett a sharp look. "What is there about Burr that fascinates you so? Last summer when we met, you implied it was because of Burr that you were in the city, something about Burr and our good Commander of the Army, General James Wilkinson."

"You don't find the way Wilkinson and Burr seemed to be connected interesting?" Brett inquired lightly.

Morgan made a helpless gesture. "I don't know, Brett. I know Wilkinson is rumored to be in the pay of Spain, but that doesn't make a conspiracy of this magnitude. Everything seems to be conjecture; no one so far has been able to come up with anything tangible to use against either man. It's like trying to capture a handful of smoke."

Standing up and placing his empty snifter on the corner of the desk, Brett prowled restlessly between the desk and the chairs. There was silence for a few minutes, then he suddenly stopped his perambulations and asked abruptly, "Are you aware of the habit President Jefferson has of employing certain civilians to do, strictly speaking, governmental tasks for him? Using gentlemen of good family to carry private messages for him, to sometimes, in effect, spy for him?"

Morgan went very still. Staring hard at Brett, he demanded, "Is *that* why you were in North Africa? And that's why you're so dogmatic about this Burr-Wilkinson affair—Jefferson's doing?"

Reluctantly Brett nodded his head. "I'm not betraying any secrets by telling you this, but yes, that's why I ended up in Derna. Jefferson wanted a report of the situation on the Barbary Coast, but he didn't want it from a government official or military man. He wanted it from someone with no political ties, but someone he could trust, who would act as his private agent."

"You?"

Brett nodded his head again. "He'd heard from my father some months previously, late in 1804, that I was coming home after several months in India but that I would probably be off for God knew where within a short time." Brett smiled faintly. "After that it was a foregone conclusion that I would be Jefferson's man."

"Does Jefferson suspect something definite of Burr?" Morgan asked abruptly.

"I don't know that he actually knows of any specific plot . . . I gather that the President is just mistrustful of Little Burr," Brett answered dryly. "When Jefferson learned, last summer, that I was going to cease my wanderings and

307

settle here, he asked if I would mind keeping an eye out for any suspicious activities by Wilkinson *or* Burr in the Territory of Orleans. What could I say?"

It was a rhetorical question, and Morgan made no reply, merely nodded his head in understanding of the position. Reflectively he said, "Well, at the moment I don't have anything to add to your information—this letter of yours from Eaton is the first I've heard of Burr in months."

"Your friend Jason Savage has intimated nothing?"

"Aha!" Morgan replied dramatically, a glint of laughter in the blue eyes. "I *knew* that there was some ulterior reason for you to write and request that I come by and see you on my next visit to town."

Brett looked at Morgan with annoyed amusement. "That wasn't the *only* reason! But I did want your opinion of Eaton's letter, and I was curious whether Savage had written any news to you about Burr—or Wilkinson for that matter."

"I've not heard from Jason since last fall when he and his family came to visit us at Château Saint-André. But I can write to him and tell him of Eaton's letter, and ask that if he has heard of anything he write you with the information."

"I'd appreciate it," Brett said simply. After refilling his snifter, they drank in companionable silence for several moments, each man lost in his thoughts.

Heavily Brett finally admitted, "I've done a lot of thinking about the situation, or lack of it, trying to figure out what would make a man desert and betray his country. And precisely what a man intent on doing that would need to accomplish his task." Holding up his lean hand, finger by finger, Brett ticked off the necessities. "It would take a desperate man, a man with nothing to lose. Yet, in order to convince others to follow him, this man would need to possess charm and persuasiveness. Burr seems to fit all of those requirements. But he needs more than just desperation and charm—he would need money, men, and arms . . . an army." Brett leaned forward, his harsh face somber. "He's had meetings with our good General Wilkinson, highly secret meetings, and what was discussed is at present something that can only be guessed. But whatever

308

Burr plans, whether it is the invasion of Mexico as is rumored, or the establishment of a rival government in the lands west of the Allegheny Mountains, he is going to need a large force and arms." He stopped for a moment then added slowly, "I can't get the thought out of my head that Wilkinson, with his penchant for intrigue, is the more dangerous of the two. Being the Commander of the United States Army gives one all sorts of power—with Wilkinson's help, Burr could precipitate a war with Spain without having to wait until the situation came about naturally. And with Wilkinson's control of the Army, if Burr did intend to take New Orleans, he would have all the men and arms he needed to establish himself before anyone realized what they were about."

"But why would Wilkinson do such a thing? He's the highest officer in the land—possibly receiving money from Spain. Why would he betray both?"

Brett appeared faintly sheepish. "There you have me," he admitted ruefully. "My little plot hangs together rather well until I reach that point, but after that . . ."

Morgan snorted. "I think you spent too much time in the desert with Eaton!" he remarked with the brutal candor of long friendship.

"Perhaps," Brett agreed readily. "I just wish I knew more of Wilkinson—I have reached the place in my musings where I feel that Wilkinson more than Burr is the man to watch. Burr may plot and plan, but Wilkinson is the one with the position and power to make things happen."

Morgan left shortly thereafter, promising to write Jason Savage. He also reminded Brett to bring Sabrina to the Château Saint-André once Leonie had been delivered of their child. Brett looked sardonic, but he agreed.

Left alone in the library, Brett wandered aimlessly about, slowly sipping his brandy and speculating further about Wilkinson and Burr. There were a lot of things he knew about both men that he hadn't mentioned to Morgan, some of the information so nebulous and unconnected to the present as to make *him* wonder why he even considered it.

A knock on the door and Andrew's information that the

309

ladies were awaiting his presence in the blue salon prior to dining finally ended, for the present time, Brett's unprofitable speculation. Tossing down the remainder of his brandy, he set the snifter down on his desk and proceeded to join Sabrina and Señora de la Vega.

Entering the elegant blue and gold room a few moments later, he was greeted by a frosty Señora de la Vega, who, observing his casual dress—he was still wearing the same clothes he'd worn when they arrived—sniffed and said disdainfully, "I see that while you have a home worthy of a gentleman, your manners do not match—only the lower classes do not change for dinner."

Francisca was seated regally on a long, low sofa of pale blue velvet, her gown of black satin spreading out like an ink stain around her plump form. A black lace mantilla covered her dark hair, and several chains of gold rested on her prominent bosom.

Sabrina was standing silently near an empty fireplace, one slim hand resting on the cream-colored mantel, and she bit her lip and turned away, uncertain whether to applaud her aunt's speech or cringe with embarrassment. But more importantly, she wondered how Brett was going to take her aunt's decidedly rude comment.

Brett's eyes narrowed, and crossing to where Francisca sat, he stood before her and said levelly, "I think we had better get one thing straight, señora. You may be my guest, and as such I will give you hospitality and reasonable courtesy. I will not, however, be dictated to by you, nor will I change the manner in which I live to suit you. If you don't like it, you may leave. And continue in the vein in which you have begun, and you won't have a choice about leaving—I'll demand it! Now, if you will excuse me, I'll go change for dinner." He slanted her a sardonic look and added, "I was about to do so, but thought it only proper to first explain the reason for my absence." Turning on his heel, he strode from the room.

CHAPTER TWENTY-TWO

🙠 Dinner was not a pleasant affair, despite the fact that Brett played the polite host to perfection. Suitably attired in a pair of black satin breeches and a jacket of dark blue velvet, he looked very handsome and vital as he presided over the long, gleaming mahogany table in the commodious dining room. It was a very English room—the furniture was made by Sheraton, the carpet was a Savonnerie in pleasing shades of gray, the walls were hung with pale gray silk, and at the long windows that were at each end of the room hung drapes of burgundy velvet. A huge pair of silver candelabra graced the dining room table and a magnificent silver tea service was set on the mahogany sideboard. Their meal was served in crystal goblets and on delicate china.

Francisca ignored Brett as best she was able, her chagrin after their exchange in the blue salon effectively silencing her. Sabrina had little to say, the thought of her coming interview with him making the expertly prepared food she was eating taste like dirt. But Brett seemed unperturbed by the uncommunicativeness of his two guests. With a mocking light in his eyes, he inquired after their comfort. Were their rooms adequate? Were their needs being met? Were his servants making themselves useful? Being met by monosyllables didn't deter him in the least, and by the end of the meal, Sabrina was positive that if he asked just one more question in that hateful, sardonic tone about her well-being, she was going to fling her goblet of wine at him.

The amber-gold eyes flashing with resentment, she glared at him, wishing he didn't look quite so damnably attractive, the starched white cravat at his neck making his skin appear darker, the candlelight intensifying the blackness of his hair, creating hollows and angles in his features that made him seem at once more handsome than she remembered and yet infinitely more dangerous, too. As if aware of her gaze, he glanced at her, their eyes meeting. The expression in those jade-green depths suddenly made her throat feel dry, her breath freeze in her breast.

Dios! she thought with furious bewilderment, how dare he look at me that way, as if he hated me, as if I were the one beneath contempt! She had guessed that he might harbor bitter feelings against her—after all, she *had* confounded his nefarious scheme to marry her for money—but that he would view her with such hostility and scorn had never occurred to her. And why scorn? she wondered uneasily, why that expression of undisguised contempt?

Francisca spoke up then, demanding Brett's attention. *"Señor,"* she said bluntly, "my son will be arriving some time within the next few weeks. He would have come with us, but"—and she shot an annoyed look at her niece—"Sabrina would not wait for him to return from Mexico City. I assume that you will have room for him here when he reaches the city."

Leisurely Brett lifted his crystal goblet and took a drink of wine. Setting the goblet down, he looked directly at Francisca and said deliberately, "No, I'm afraid that won't be possible. There are several inns and hotels nearby, and I am sure he will find comfortable quarters for his stay."

Francisca swelled up like a toad, venom in her black eyes, but prudence, for once, stilled her tongue. She had clashed with the hated gringo twice now, and each time she had come off the loser. But her anger was too great to be contained easily, and rising to her feet, she threw down her linen napkin and snapped, "If you will excuse me? I find your company less than congenial."

A tense silence suddenly filled the air, and Sabrina wished violently that her aunt had not deserted her so precipitously. But determined to show her mettle and to make it plain that she wasn't the *least* intimidated by him, she said forthrightly, "Surely your home is large enough to accommodate another guest. After all, he is her son and my cousin, not a stranger."

Gently Brett replied, "But you see, it is *my* home, and I don't wish to have him here."

Sabrina flushed at the deserved rebuke. It *was* his home, and she could understand his position. Curiosity, however, prompted her to ask, "Why don't you want him here?"

The jade-green eyes hooded, he suggested lightly, "Because I don't trust him?"

Sabrina frowned. "Why ever not? What has he done to you that makes you think he is untrustworthy?"

His long fingers toyed lazily with the crystal goblet, the dark face revealing little as he said unemotionally, "He told me lies—lies that were and are unforgivable."

Her frown increased, and unaware of how lovely she looked, the candlelight casting its golden glow across her creamy bosom and arms, the red-gold of the coronet braid on her head heightened by the flickering light, she persisted seriously, "What lies? Are you certain? As long as I have known him, he has never told me, or anyone I know, a lie. It would be dishonorable of him, and Carlos is basically an honorable man."

Sabrina might have been oblivious to her own charms, but in spite of his best intentions, Brett was not. Against his will, his eyes strayed over her, lingering with cynical appreciation on the slim shoulders and the smooth, tempting flesh that rose above the black silk gown. He remembered instantly the taste of her, the texture and scent of her skin, the feel of her soft mouth under his, and an intense, almost painful surge of desire hit him. Cursing himself for giving way to emotions he had thought long conquered, he stood up abruptly, furiously willing his body not to betray the state he was in. Walking swiftly across the room to the door, he said harshly, "I doubt that either one of you knows the meaning of the word *honor,* and in any case, I don't wish to discuss it now. If you will excuse me, I have business to attend to."

Startled at the lightning change in manner, she stared at him from across the room, her eyes puzzled and yet angry, too. "Wait!" she cried helplessly as he flung open the door and prepared to leave. Standing up, she hurried around the end of the table, crossing the room to where he stood.

She stopped inches from him, suddenly realizing that she didn't know what she wanted to say—she only knew she didn't want this unsatisfactory conversation to end this way. Attacked by an unexpected wave of shyness, she dropped her eyes from his hard face and muttered the first thing that came to her mind. "You can't have business this time of night . . . and besides, I wish to speak with you." She risked a glance at him, and not at all reassured by the unyielding features, she stammered, "A . . . a . . . a . . . about th . . . th . . . the guardianship."

Brett stiffened. Flatly he said, "There is nothing to discuss—I am your guardian, and you are my ward; those are the terms of your father's will, and I intend to abide by them."

Angrily Sabrina retorted, "Don't be ridiculous! You can't possibly want me for your ward."

Insolently the jade-green eyes wandered over her, and Sabrina felt as if she had just been stripped naked. A curious note in his voice, he drawled, "If I find the duties of guardianship wearing, I'm certain I shall find some *other* benefit from the arrangement. . . ."

Her face pale, she demanded jerkily, "What do you mean?"

He smiled cynically. "Oh, come now, my dear, you can't be *that* unsophisticated!"

Without conscious thought, she slapped him, hard, the sound of her palm striking his cheek ringing out like a pistol shot in the room. A deathly silence fell, and for a second they stared at each other, the astonishment reflected in both faces making it clear that neither had quite expected such a violent reaction to his provoking words.

Brett recovered himself first, and with something between a snarl and a curse, he slammed the door furiously behind him. His broad shoulders resting against the panel behind him, blocking any escape, he regarded her with narrowed eyes. "I do believe," he began silkily, "that I once warned you not to be so quick with your hands."

Very aware that she had crossed over into dangerous territory, Sabrina bravely tried to hold her ground. Chin lifted belligerently, she said warily, "I don't know what you're talking about!"

He smiled, a smile that didn't reach those cold green

eyes, and replied almost gently, "Then I'll just have to show you, won't I?"

His statement both thrilled and terrified her, and with one part of her mind, she miserably acknowledged that she had known exactly what would happen the instant she slapped him. It also, belatedly, occurred to her that Brett, too, had known precisely what reaction his insulting words would draw from her and that he had deliberately created their situation. She didn't have time to explore that fascinating avenue of thought, because in that moment, his hands closed painfully around her shoulders and she was jerked unceremoniously up against his hard form.

A shiver of something akin to ecstasy rippled uncontrollably through her at the touch of that well-remembered muscled body against hers, and when his mouth descended as she know it would, her lips were upraised, strangely eager and yet equally unwilling for his kiss. His mouth took hers with a savage intensity, almost as if he wanted to hurt her, his arms tightening powerfully around her, pulling her closer to him, allowing no room for resistance or escape.

But Sabrina was without fight. It didn't matter just then that he was kissing her for all the wrong reasons; it didn't even matter that it was almost a brutal kiss, a punishing kiss, his lips moving with a cruel urgency against her. All that mattered was that she was in his strong arms again. With a soft moan of part denial, part pleasure, her arms crept around his neck, her swelling breasts crushed between their locked bodies, her legs straining against his.

Brett kissed her like a man with a fierce, insatiable hunger to appease. His lips were everywhere—her brows, her cheeks, her earlobes—but compulsively he found her mouth again and again, his tongue plunging deeply, insistently, between her lips, driving every thought but one from his mind. It was as if the six years between them had never been, as if they had parted just yesterday, and only the memory of pain and the savage hunger that ate at him were reminders that so much time had passed since he had last held her in his arms. So much *wasted* time, he thought bitterly, the arms that pressed her close constricting possessively around her.

315

Sabrina gave a breathless murmur of surprise at the power of his embrace, desire like sun-warmed honey flowing in her veins, making her oblivious to everything but the man kissing her. Even when his hold on her slackened and she felt a questing, impatient hand at her breast, she couldn't bring herself to utter a protest, couldn't make a move to break the chains of passion that bound her to him. She could feel him forcing her gown lower, feel the warm fingers caressing and pulling at the nipples he had freed, and she trembled with a force of emotions those knowing fingers created. And when his head bent, his tongue curling around those stiffened coral nipples, his hot mouth hungrily suckling at her breast, Sabrina knew that she could deny him nothing. Nothing. She knew then that the dark fascination she had always feared still possessed her, knew that in spite of everything, she still wanted him. Wanted whatever he was willing to give her —and if it was only his body for now, at this moment, she would be willing to settle for just that.

Six long years she had denied wanting or needing him, but it took only a moment in his arms to know that she had lied to herself. Her body was aflame with desire; she ached to be naked against him, to have him possess her as he had on that warm, moonlit summer night, and feverishly she arched up against him, her hips moving in a motion as old as the universe. Exultantly she heard his muffled groan at her breast, and she was made unbearably conscious of the rigid staff of his manhood standing up between them as his hands captured her hips and guided her closer against him.

Blindly his mouth sought hers, his hands staying on her hips, controlling her movements, keeping her pressed tightly to him. Sensually he moved against her, sending little shocks of pleasure exploding along her body every time the swollen length of him brushed erotically across her stomach and upper thighs.

A sudden knock on the door broke them apart, and his eyes fever-bright, his voice thick, Brett snapped, "Yes, what is it?"

Andrew's apologetic words came muffled through the door. "Oh, excuse me, sir, I didn't realize that you were still in the dining room. I'll come back later to clear the table."

Straightening his cravat, instantly in icy control of himself, Brett said crisply, "Come back in five minutes and the room will by yours."

There was a polite reply from Andrew and then silence. Cynically Brett stared at Sabrina's flushed features and murmured, "I trust you know now what I mean. And sweetheart, any time you want to slap me—go ahead. I have my own far more pleasurable form of retaliation."

He watched with interest as her fist clenched, and then, after bowing mockingly, he strode arrogantly from the room.

Tears of pain and rage pricking behind her lids, like a wounded animal, Sabrina sought refuge. There was no gazebo by the lake here to offer her sanctuary, but the small balcony of her room gave her the impression of protected isolation, and with relief she made her way there, thankful that she met no one as she did so.

It seemed she'd had good reason to fear the fascination Brett held for her, and woefully she stared down at the dark courtyard, wondering wretchedly how she was going to make it through the next few days.

It was useless to pretend that she felt nothing for him, that she could deal with him unemotionally. Useless to tell herself that what had happened tonight would never happen again—he had only to touch her and she was clay in his hands, willing, no *eager*, to be molded in whatever fashion pleased him. Angry and ashamed at how easily she had responded to him, Sabrina bitterly faced the fact that in spite of all her denials, she *did* still feel something for him. Not love, she told herself fiercely, but the memory of love. The memory of what she had felt for him before that horrible conversation with Constanza. The memory of what it had felt like to be in his arms, to feel that for the moment he was hers and hers alone.

Somewhere behind all the arguments she presented to explain her motives, Sabrina knew that she was deluding herself. That behind the anger, behind the hurt, behind even the passion, perhaps even the reason for the passion, was love. But for tonight she convinced herself that love had nothing to do with the situation between her and Brett Dangermond, that it was only desire that had prompted his actions and that it was only her own foolish clinging to what had once been that had allowed her to act as she had.

Ironically, Brett used the same arguments on himself, arriving at much the same conclusion. Only in his case there was never any question of love being involved. He did *not* love her! he vowed furiously to himself once he had reached the privacy of the library and poured himself another snifter of brandy. He hadn't admitted to loving her six years ago when he had offered to marry her, and he sure as hell wasn't going to admit it now! It would be the height of insanity to love a woman who had made it so painfully clear that her only interest in him was the size of his fortune.

Even now, with the distance of nearly six years between the events, he could remember vividly the pain and bewilderment that had eaten at him, the black rage that had consumed him, as he had waited those nerve-racking weeks in Natchitoches, one part of him longing unbearably for her to indeed be pregnant, another part of him ready to saddle his horse and leave the greedy little jade to her fate. And not even to himself would he admit the crushing disappointment that had knifed through him when Ollie had returned with her answer. Secretly he had hoped that some miracle had taken place since he rode away, that she had discovered, child or not, that she had been too hasty in rejecting him, that there had been another emotion besides greed that had prompted her to surrender to him, that the same unacknowledged yearnings that had possessed him had urged her to accept his proposal of marriage in the first place. Obviously such had not been the case, he thought dryly, as he took another sip of his brandy. Not once in the ensuing years had there been any hint that she had changed her mind—Alejandro's few letters to him had been carefully empty of any but the most mundane references to his daughter. They also, Brett reminded himself ruefully, had not contained one hint of what Alejandro had added to his will.

God! but he had been furious when he learned of the trick Alejandro had played upon him, and his fury had initially deadened his pain at the news of Alejandro's death. His first impulse had been to reject the guardianship out of hand, to refuse to accept it or anything to do with Sabrina del Torres.

When he had ridden away from Natchitoches that September of 1800, he had taken a bitter contempt and cold fury for Sabrina with him. And after the pain had lessened, after months had passed and he could look back on the situation without an aching wrench in his gut, the unfortunate need to seek revenge had gradually taken hold in his mind. He wanted with a ruthless intensity to teach her a lesson that she would never forget, teach her brutally that men were not playthings to be toyed with and then carelessly tossed aside when it suited her. Night after night he had dreamed of ways of wreaking vengeance upon her, of having her completely in his control, forcing her to answer to his every whim. That his vengeance usually entailed her being bound to him for life and that much of his punishment involved having her in his arms and making violent love to her never quite occurred to him. But the fact that Alejandro's will made her almost his virtual prisoner for life dawned on him within hours of hearing the news.

His fury against Alejandro had vanished in an instant, and even suspecting that Alejandro had probably had far different objectives in view when he had added that codicil to his will, Brett had been exultant that at last his moment for revenge had come. And at present he was oddly content just to know that she was in his power . . . that he could do with her what he wanted and that there was no one to gainsay him.

For months now he had savored the thought of this meeting, dreamed of it, planned it, and he was vaguely uneasy that it wasn't going exactly as he had envisioned. He hadn't expected to feel a stirring of those disturbing emotions he had thought dead and forgotten—seeing her standing there travel-stained and faintly defiant this afternoon in the courtyard, he had been assailed by a fierce need to sweep her into his arms, to kiss those dream-fashioned features and hold her. He had also been appalled and shaken by the wave of joy that had swept through him

319

at seeing her again; appalled and shaken by the knowledge that there was no thought of revenge in his mind, only delight at the changes in her, pleasure that she was here in his home at last. He had damned Francisca's unwanted presence in those first bittersweet seconds, but later he had been bleakly thankful that she had been there—at least he hadn't betrayed himself, revealed that he was still vulnerable. . . .

Infuriated that he would even consider such a ridiculous notion, he swallowed the remainder of his brandy and with a jerky movement, slammed the empty snifter down on the desk. He was *not* vulnerable! he snarled grimly to himself. And certainly not vulnerable to a woman's wiles. *Especially* not Sabrina's! She was just a greedy little jade who had gotten under his skin once, but she wasn't going to get the chance to do so again. No. This time the cards were all in his hands, and he intended to take full advantage of the situation. *She* would suffer this time. Not him! And a slightly cruel smile curved his chiseled mouth as he recalled this evening's scene after dinner.

He hadn't planned it, but from the moment Francisca had left the dining room, he had become intolerably aware of the intimacy of the situation, the *opportunity* of the situation. Sabrina had always been overpoweringly attractive to him, but tonight she had looked particularly fetching, the barbaric necklace of gold and black onyx gleaming against her warm creamy skin, and he had wondered idly how she would look with that glorious fire-red hair tumbling wildly about her shoulders, wearing nothing except that necklace. . . .

The argument that sprang up between them had been unpremeditated, and he *had* been astonished when she had slapped him. And yet deep inside he knew he had deliberately provoked her, wanting an excuse to take her into his arms, to kiss her thoroughly, to taste again the sweetness of her lips. And her charms had been everything that he had remembered, everything and more, the feel of her against him, the warmth that had enveloped him, the perfume of her skin driving coherent thought from his mind.

He didn't regret what had happened—if he regretted anything it was his butler's untimely interruption, and he smiled ruefully, imagining the scene if Andrew had knocked just a few minutes later. And if Andrew hadn't knocked at all . . . to his amused dismay, he felt his body harden at the thought of what might have happened.

His mood lifted slightly, and in a better frame of mind, he wandered aimlessly about the library, coming to stop eventually in front of the fireplace. Putting one polished boot on the empty grate, he stared blankly down at the shining brass andirons, his thoughts roaming restlessly.

Who would have imagined that years later he and Sabrina would once more be housed under the same roof? That he would have all the powers of a husband except one, and that that one right would be his if he chose to abuse his guardianship? An odd expression came over his lean face. There had been a time in his life when such an idea would never have crossed his mind, no matter what the urgings of his body, no matter how desperately he may have wanted to do so. But then, that had been a different time, a different man, and the years in between had changed him, carved him into a man whose cynical view of life Alejandro wouldn't have recognized, and Brett wondered, if Alejandro had been aware of that, whether the codicil to the will would have been made.

Ollie had told Sabrina that Brett had changed, and he was right. Colder, harder, more cynical and disdainful of the rules that other men abided by, he was a law unto himself, and regrettably, he had the fortune and charm to gain whatever he wanted. There were few places in the world he hadn't seen, and there were few things he hadn't done.

When he had arrived back at Natchez after the ugly parting with Sabrina, he had stayed only a few days and then had departed on a restless search for relief from the agony that was with him always. In those first months he hadn't really cared about anything but wiping out the memory of a forest nymph with flame-colored hair and amber-gold eyes. No excess had been too much for him, no debauchery too base, and he had drunk heavily, sometimes not drawing a sober breath for days, spending his time trying to pave his own private road to hell. Finally though, there had come a day when he had realized the futility of his actions, and sickened and disgusted by himself,

321

slowly, painfully, he had fought his way back to cold sanity. Unable to settle down, he had taken to wandering again, his travels leading him all over the world—to the wilds of South America, the mysteries of darkest Africa, and the opulence of India. Every wild, dangerous scheme that had caught his attention, he had thrown himself into with reckless abandon, little caring whether he lived or died.

It had been his ceaseless and wide-ranging travels that had first brought him to President Jefferson's attention, and from there it had been simple enough for the President to suggest that Brett might like to travel to Eygpt and perhaps take in the Barbary Coast. . . .

Brett smiled, remembering how cleverly the President had broached the subject. How delicate had been his probings; how carefully he had aroused Brett's interest and then magnanimously *allowed* Brett to spy for him.

Brett had enjoyed his travels in Eygpt and other parts of the world that few white men had seen, but when he had arrived home early last summer, he had known that he was finally weary of traveling aimlessly across the face of the earth. He wanted a home. Further than that he wouldn't think.

The stunning disclosures of Alejandro's will had seemed to set the seal on his plans. If he was to be a guardian, he had thought sardonically, it was only proper to provide an adequate home for his ward.

He had long owned the house in New Orleans, and it had always accorded him a place to deposit his souvenirs from all over the world, as well as acting as a base from which to plan other forays. The plantation, Fox's Lair, in lower Louisiana, had been salvaged at no little cost, but it was now, and had been for a number of years, productive and adding to his already sizable fortune. The house at the plantation had been a total loss, and knowing he would seldom be there, he'd had a smaller though quite spacious dwelling erected for his use whenever he wished for the country life. It had been little used during the last five years. Of course, he reflected grimly, all of that would change, now that he had a ward. . . .

CHAPTER
TWENTY-THREE

~~~ Surprisingly, Sabrina slept soundly that night and woke the next morning in unaccountably high spirits. The bed had been delightfully comfortable, especially so since she hadn't slept on a proper mattress for days; the sun was shining brightly through the French doors that led to the balcony; and a smiling Lupe greeted her with a pot of rich, fragrant coffee and a plate of hot, buttery pastry. It was impossible to be gloomy or downcast.

A long, luxurious bath, the red-gold hair washed and washed again, and Sabrina began to feel that last night hadn't really been so momentous after all. Brett had kissed her, and she had liked it—liked it immensely. But what did *that* prove? That he was an attractive man and that she was merely a normal young woman? Of course! It was all very simple when one viewed it from the proper perspective. She had been tired last night, excited and slightly apprehensive, and when he had kissed her she had overreacted, and that was *all*—nothing to alarm one, nothing to depress one, or make one downcast.

Satisfied with her reading of the incident, clad in a silk wrapper of brilliant blue, she wandered out onto the balcony and standing in the warm spring sunlight, slowly brushed the long flame-colored hair. The heat from the sun rapidly dried the thick, wavy mass of hair, small tendrils curling softly about her temples and forehead, and like a child seeking a kiss, she lifted her face to the yellow sunlight.

From his own balcony on the third floor directly across from Sabrina's, Brett watched her movements with something akin to bittersweet pleasure. Thinking herself unobserved, she had let down all her barriers. She laughed at the antics of a hummingbird, and Brett found himself smiling in instinctive response to that happy sound. When she turned her face again to the sun's kiss, he found that he envied those shining rays that wandered at will over that slim, lissome body. . . . With an effort he turned his mind to other things, and unwilling to let her intrude into his thoughts, with cool deliberation he walked back into his own rooms.

Ollie was busy laying out his clothes for the day, and sending Brett a cheeky grin, he said, "She's a pretty sight, ain't she?" Adding slyly, "And with that fortune of hers, I don't imagine you'll be saddled with being her guardian for long . . . once the local beaux get a glimpse of her, the house will be full of them. You'll just have to take your pick of her suitors, then fast as Jack-be-Quick, you'll be rid of her."

A muscle throbbed in Brett's lean jaw, and he sent his interested valet a decidedly black look. "I see," he began sardonically, "that marriage hasn't taught you the wisdom of holding your tongue . . . yet."

"There are no secrets between Lupe and me," Ollie returned immediately. "And she doesn't care what I say as long as I say I love her!" His almost handsome face becoming serious, he said shyly, "Lupe and me want to thank you for the fine quarters you assigned us and for giving us that tract of land near Fox's Lair."

Brett grinned at him. "Now that you are a staid married man, you must think of your future and not be such a harum-scarum scamp as your disreputable employer. Besides, what else could I do if I intend to keep you in my service, which I most certainly hope to do!"

Ollie looked thoroughly scandalized at the idea that he might ever possibly work for someone else. "Guvnor! Damn my eyes! You don't think . . . Why I would never!"

Affectionately Brett ruffled Ollie's dark hair. "No, I don't suppose you would, and I apologize for even suggesting such a thing." His eyes softening, he added, "I'm pleased that you and your bride are happy with the gift."

Lupe had been ecstatic with both the rooms she would call home and the gift of land, and a few minutes after the

conversation between Brett and Ollie, her dark eyes sparkling with delight, she told Sabrina, "Oh, *señorita!* Señor
Brett must be the kindest man alive! He is so good to my
Ollie and me! We have three whole rooms to ourselves—it
is almost like having our own home. And"—her eyes
getting bigger—"he gave Ollie a hundred acres of fine land
near his plantation. Just think, my husband is a landowner!" Sending her mistress a fond glance, she added,
"You are so lucky that he is your guardian—he is such a
kind man!"

Sabrina nearly strangled on the sharp reply that sprang
to her lips, but hastily she turned away. In the days that
followed, there were many adjectives Sabrina could have
used to describe Brett, but the word *kind* was never among
them. Mocking, arrogant, infuriating, and derisive, but
definitely *not* kind!

For reasons best known to herself, Sabrina decided upon
a waiting game—she did not, as she had originally
planned, immediately launch an all-out battle to escape
from the galling authority of Brett's guardianship. Instead, she convinced herself that there was no reason to begin hostilities *instantly*. Besides, she needed a little time to
orientate herself in this new situation. She needed time to
decide upon a lawyer and seek his advice. Time to prove
that she was *perfectly* capable of handling her own affairs
and that she certainly did not need or want Brett Dangermond to have *any* say in her life!

Having come to these conclusions, she was ready to treat
Brett with cool politeness during the first difficult days.
Unfortunately, a curt request that she meet with him in
the library before lunch unsettled her slightly and had her
approaching that room at the appointed time in a mixture
of trepidation and aggression.

Shoulders squared, chin held high, and gowned in a
plain, practical black muslin frock, she entered the library. Reaching the area where Brett lounged carelessly
on one corner of his desk, she glanced dismissingly at him,
and then, deliberately fixing her eyes somewhere above
his dark head, she inquired haughtily, "You wanted to see
me, *señor?*"

A faint smile curved Brett's full mouth at her attitude,

325

and softly he drawled, "Infant, I have no intention of talking to someone who won't even look at me."

Her gaze flew to his, a slight flush staining her cheeks, and the amused mockery in the jade-green eyes made her palm itch unbearably to smack his dark face.

"Now that I have your attention," he murmured, "I thought we should discuss some of the, shall we say, more mundane aspects of our regrettable relationship."

Aware of him in ways that she wished she weren't, Sabrina refrained from objecting to his choice of words and instead replied stiffly, "Whatever you desire, *señor.*" And could have bitten her tongue at the derisive smile that instantly flicked at the corners of his mobile mouth.

"Desire, my dear, has nothing to do with this conversation," he said lightly, and before Sabrina could think of a suitable reply, he added casually, "I have arranged for a sum of money to be at your disposal at a bank here in New Orleans. And that same amount will be deposited quarterly until such time as I decide it is inadequate for your needs"—his voice grew silky—"or you marry."

Wisely Sabrina kept her mouth shut. After a second Brett continued, naming a generous sum of money, explaining carelessly that it would be her allowance for any feminine trifles that she required. Naturally she would not be expected to pay for her room and board; he, as her guardian, would see to all her household expenses—servants, horses, and equipage were, of course, included. He had also set up accounts at some of the best-known modistes and millineries in the city, and as long as—said with a sarcastic inflection—she didn't attempt to bankrupt him, those bills would be sent directly to him.

Sabrina hated every moment of this somehow humiliating interview. Brett's terms were generous, but there was something in the way he looked at her, something in his tone of voice, that made her writhe with embarrassment. What he was proposing was little different from the way her father had seen to things, but she bitterly resented Brett's authority over her, and his insolent manner did nothing to still her sense of injustice. It was an offensive situation, all the more so, she reminded herself viciously, because the money he was so lavishly doling out was *hers!*

326

He had no *right* to dictate to her—no matter what Alejandro's wretched will stated!

She had a very expressive face, and watching the angry flash of her eyes and the way her soft mouth tightened, Brett almost felt sorry for her. Almost. It was time she learned a little humility, he thought cynically. Learned that possessing great wealth gave her no divine right to play with a man's emotions, to play with his heart. . . .

Annoyed that he had allowed his attention to wander, he said more crisply, "I have no objections, at least at the present time, if Señora de la Vega acts as your duenna, and as for your amusements and friends—as long as I meet them and approve and your social engagements are appropriate, I shall not interfere unduly . . : unless, of course, I deem your activities unsuitable."

That was too much for Sabrina. Forgetting that she was not to lose her temper, forgetting that she was determined not to let him disturb or ruffle her, she glared at him and spat, "How dare you! Since when have *you* become such an arbiter of fashion? Since when does a black-hearted rogue like you decide what is proper or improper?"

His face hard, the jade-green eyes dark with fury, he snarled, "Since your father so unwisely named me guardian of you in that blasted will!" Unaccountably enraged by the situation, he said thickly, "Believe me, I have no wish to have you on my hands—and the sooner you find some poor, besotted fool to marry you, the happier I shall be!"

Hurt and not certain why—after all, she wanted to be free of him, didn't she?—Sabrina stared angrily at him. Her magnificent bosom heaving, the amber-gold eyes glittering brightly, she retorted instantly, "Have no fear—I'll marry the first eligible man who crosses my path! Marriage to *any*one would be better than having to suffer your guardianship a day longer than necessary!"

Skirts swirling behind her, she wheeled about and marched toward the door. But, her hand on the knob, she stopped abruptly, something that had been bothering her instantly coming to the forefront of her thoughts. Turning back to look at him, she frowned and asked sharply, "How is it that you have all these arrangements made? I only arrived yesterday afternoon. You told me to stay in Nacogdoches—you can't have known that I was coming to New Orleans against your express orders."

Once again lounging on the corner of his desk, his arms folded negligently over his chest, Brett smiled slightly. "Wrong, my dear. Unfortunately, being somewhat acquainted with the tortuous mazes of the feminine mind, I knew that if I requested politely that you come to New Orleans, nothing short of an army would pry you loose from Nacogdoches." His smile widened. "Ah, but if I demanded, and in the most rude manner possible, that you *stay* where you were—then, of course, being female, you would race to New Orleans with all possible speed."

For a long moment Sabrina stared at him, chagrin and fury churning in her breast. *Dios!* but he was diabolical! Then, suddenly, her anger fled and amusement glimmered in her eyes as she realized how correctly he had judged the effect of that contemptuous letter upon her. Rueful appreciation of his tactics caused a wry smile to curve her full mouth, and without rancor she said simply, "It is indeed your win, *señor.*"

The door shut softly behind her, and Brett gazed transfixed at the spot where she had stood only a second before. From fury to amusement in an instant, he thought with bafflement, the memory of her smile making his hard features soften. Shaking his head, he stared down at the rug. Women! Would he ever understand them?

Oddly enough, after that clash in the library, the following weeks went by without incident, Sabrina and Francisca gradually settling into the routine of Brett's household. Acquaintances were made and renewed. From previous trips with Luis, Francisca knew many people. Alejandro, too, with his many business connections in the city, had known several families, and these, not unnaturally, presented themselves to his sister and daughter. Some of the people Sabrina had met as a child when she had traveled with her parents; others she knew of from her father's letters and conversation. At any rate, she and Francisca, despite the definite stigma of living with an *americano,* were soon absorbed into Creole and Spanish society.

It often puzzled Sabrina as the days passed that her

aunt seemed content with the present situation. Francisca made few complaints about their circumstances, and regardless of the venom that flickered occasionally in the black eyes, she managed to rub shoulders with the hated gringo without breaking into open warfare.

Perhaps, her niece thought slowly on a warm, muggy day in mid-May, Tía is waiting for Carlos to arrive. Or else, Sabrina decided with an impish smile, Tía is so pleased with all the lovely new things Brett is so generously paying for that she has thought it prudent to hold her tongue in his presence.

And Brett was being generous to Francisca. Without a murmur he accepted and paid the older woman's bills when they were sent to him along with Sabrina's purchases. Francisca's bills were considerable, for as she had exclaimed to Sabrina more than once, she needed *some* compensation for having to put up with him!

Sabrina, too, was ordering new gowns, shawls, shoes, bonnets, and all manner of delightful fripperies. It was such a pleasure to shop for colors after nearly two years of wearing black that she threw herself into an orgy of buying, telling herself frequently that she didn't really need to worry about expenses—after all, it *was* her own money! And yet there were times when she was distinctly uncomfortable knowing that her bills were sent directly to Brett. Buying clothing was such a *personal* task, and she blushed when she thought of all of the delicate, intimate bits of silk and frothy lace that she had purchased, imagining the sardonic lift of those black brows when he read the descriptions on the bills.

Brett's manner completely bewildered Sabrina. She had been prepared for him to extract a certain measure of vengeance from the situation in which they found themselves, but beyond the first evening when he had kissed her, his manner had been precisely that of a guardian . . . well, not exactly, she thought with a slight frown. There was a look in his eyes, something about the way his gaze would sometimes travel over her, that made Sabrina remember vividly what it felt like to be held in his arms. Yet at other times, times when he was being his most sarcastic and provoking, she would find it hard to believe that once his derisively curved mouth had plundered hers, that once those strong arms had been locked passionately around her, his big, hard body joined with hers.

It was peculiar, Sabrina reflected with wonder, how quickly she and Francisca had settled down to living with Brett. They had come here determined to fight him to the bitter end, but here it was already the middle of May and they were comfortably, if not ecstatically, established in his home. A faint smile crossed her lips as it occurred to her that one of the reasons for the apparent tranquillity was the fact that Brett was seldom at home—occasionally he had joined them for breakfast, and a few times he had dined with them, but for the most part, they went about their daily life as if he didn't exist.

Sabrina grimaced. Francisca might be able to pretend he didn't exist, but she herself was always very aware of him, even when he wasn't around, very aware that once he had been her love—her lover. At the strangest times— brushing her hair in the morning or seemingly absorbed in the selection of material for a new gown—she would find herself thinking of him, visualizing the way his thick black lashes could hide the expression in those jade-green eyes, the way his mouth would quirk with sardonic amusement, and regrettably, the way her heart would plummet to her toes every time she glanced up and found his eyes upon her.

Restlessly she stirred on the stone bench where she was sitting beneath one of the magnolia trees in the courtyard. She didn't want to think about Brett, didn't want to acknowledge that the idea of challenging his guardianship was growing less and less desirable, becoming less important. . . .

Angrily she brought herself up short. Of course she was going to fight for what was hers . . . eventually. Naturally this situation couldn't be allowed to continue. After all, he *was* a blackguard! A conniving, scheming scoundrel who had utterly hoodwinked her father!

The truth of the matter, though, was that Sabrina was finding it harder and harder to whip up the righteous indignation she had once felt so deeply. She had forgotten nothing, not the terrible pain she had experienced when

330

she had faced Constanza and realized the full extent of Brett's villainy, nor the fury she had known when Alejandro's will had been read. Yet it all seemed so long ago, so removed from *now,* that entire days would go by without her ever thinking of the guardianship or what had happened six years ago.

She sighed heavily, conscious that she no longer really even held her father's will against Brett. She might have ranted furiously at first, too stunned to think clearly, but her own sense of fairness had reasserted itself, and she was willing to admit that Alejandro's will hadn't been Brett's fault—he'd made it abundantly clear that being her guardian was the *last* thing in the world that he wished. No, she couldn't blame him for her father's stubborn determination to bring them together again, and she more than Brett, perhaps, was aware of precisely what Alejandro had hoped would happen if they were forced into each other's company.

A sad little smile flitted across her lips. How wrong could her father have been? But then, he hadn't known the truth, hadn't known the real reason Brett had wanted to marry her, hadn't known of Constanza. And, Sabrina admitted miserably, it wasn't just that Constanza and Brett had been lovers that had caused her to reject him. *That* she could have forgiven him, if he had loved her, if his affair with the other woman had been over with before he had asked her to marry him. She had known that he was no monk, knew that there were bound to have been other women in his life; she had even been aware of the affair between him and Constanza—Carlos had been so very kind to point it out—but Brett's past hadn't mattered to her— provided it *was* his past. To discover that after he had made love to her, had asked for her hand in marriage, he had still been seeing Constanza, still been making promises to the other woman, had in fact seduced and ruined Constanza—that type of reprehensible conduct could not be borne.

And yet . . . and yet, while she could and did, for the most part, bury the past, bury her pain and disillusionment deep in her mind, the memory of the love she had once felt for him would not be banished along with the other ugly memories. She was shamefully aware that time may have blunted her anguish and rage, but it had done nothing to lessen the shattering impact his very nearness had upon her.

Her expression bleak, Sabrina stared down at her clenched hands. How *could* she possibly feel anything for such a man? How dare her heart continue to long for such a wicked creature! She was no fool, no silly, naive child falling in love for the first time. She was nearly twenty-four years old, a woman who should know better. Yet she felt as foolish and deluded as any female who had ever yearned for a handsome, unscrupulous rogue, knowing full well that if she persisted upon this mad course, the future would only bring pain and humiliation.

Which was why she could not allow herself to drift any longer, she thought painfully. Coming here, seeing him again, was the most ridiculous and unwise thing she could have done. She would have been far better off if she had never seen him again, never subjected herself to his powerful lure. For a second tears stung her eyes. What a weak, maudlin creature she was! Surely she had more control over her actions than did the poor besotted moth, fascinated by fire? Or was she doomed, like the moth, to be consumed by the beckoning flame?

Her chin lifted slightly. She must speak with Brett. Must make her escape while there was still time. While she could still think clearly, still clearly see the pitfalls that lay in front of her. Things must be settled between them before her own treacherous emotions betrayed her, before they blinded her to everything but the craving need to accept him on *any* terms.

She started to rise, to go in search of Brett immediately, but then, with a sigh, half-impatient, half-relieved, she sank back down, remembering that he had left five days ago on business and that he wouldn't be back until evening. That would be soon enough, she reflected slowly. She would leave word that she wished to speak to him, and she would carefully plan what she would say. And pray God that she could convince Brett, the guardianship aside, that it would be best for all of them, if she returned to Nacogdoches.

It was unusual for Sabrina to find herself with this much time all her own, but today there had been nothing planned. No fittings. No shopping trips in town. No visiting with Tía Francisca's friends—her aunt was currently nursing a mild indisposition and was resting in her rooms. Tonight, too, was free—no amusements, no soiree, no opera or theater to attend. Nothing.

It was actually her first opportunity since she had arrived in New Orleans to sit down and think, to examine her own emotions and to realize how effortlessly she was falling under Brett's spell once again. The first time she'd had to speculate about him, to wonder about his actions . . .

He was a complete enigma to her. He could have made things very unpleasant, and she had every reason to believe that he would do so, but he hadn't. Of course, he hadn't made them precisely pleasant either, she thought with a twist to her sweet mouth. He treated her with an infuriating sort of detached, friendly contempt that she found difficult to accept or understand. But then there were times, precious few, when for long moments she would catch dizzying glimpses of the Brett who had so fascinated her, moments when he would completely disarm her Yet, a second later, almost as if realizing that he had lowered his guard, his face would close up, his smile fade, and she would be left with the caustic indifference that he usually accorded her. He did well at keeping her confused and unsettled, at never letting her totally relax in his presence. And yet, more perturbing than anything else, she had the uncomfortable sensation that behind the detachment, behind the sardonic manners, he was merely biding his time, playing with her, waiting for something. . . .

For what? she wondered uneasily. For her to lose her temper and lash out at him? Was that why he acted so provokingly at times? Because he was deliberately driving her in a direction of his own devising?

Well, what did it matter now? she asked herself wearily. She would see him tonight and convince him, somehow, that she no longer wished to remain in New Orleans. That she belonged in Nacogdoches and that, as soon as was practical, she should return to her home. It was the wisest thing to do.

What her servants and Francisca were going to think, she didn't even want to speculate on. First she had dragged them willy-nilly to New Orleans, and now, with almost as little warning, she was preparing to drag them back to Nacogdoches. She shook her head at her own folly. What a fool I am! But at least, she told herself grimly, fool or not, I know when to retreat!

Her mind made up, Sabrina would have liked to have proceeded instantly with her plans, but the arrival of a note from Brett informing his household that he would not return until well after midnight this evening delayed her meeting with him. It also gave her a long and restless night in which to struggle with her thoughts, to question her own wisdom, to speculate on what his reaction to her request would be, and to rehearse again and again in her mind the cool, mature way in which she would counter any arguments he might put her way.

She had left word with Ollie that she wished to see Brett at the first possible time the following day, but she was considerably surprised when Ollie knocked on her door at eight o'clock the next morning and said gaily, "The guvnor says that if you *must* see him today, now's the time. Otherwise it will have to wait indefinitely."

Sabrina muttered something uncomplimentary under her breath. She wasn't prepared to see him this early in the morning—her hair had just been brushed and was tumbling about her shoulders, and she was gowned only in a simple frock of apple-green muslin. She looked very young and innocent, certainly not the cool, collected woman she had planned to present to him. For a second she hesitated, torn between the desire to have the meeting behind her and the equally strong desire not to give him any advantage. But if it meant waiting indefinitely . . .

Swallowing her dismay, trying to gather her flying thoughts, she walked beside Ollie as they made their way to the wing where Brett's rooms were located.

Brett's voice came muffled through the doors in response to Ollie's knock. Stepping aside, he motioned her to enter. An impish grin on his face, he said, "I expect you and the guvnor want to talk private-like."

Sabrina nodded her head, and then, her heart thumping uncomfortably, she pushed open the door and entered Brett's bedchamber. She had never been in this wing of the house, much less his personal rooms, and curiously she glanced around.

She was in a spacious antechamber. A brilliant green carpet lay upon the floor, several comfortable chairs covered in a rich brown leather were attractively arranged throughout the room, heavy marble-topped tables sat here and there, and at one end a massive, intricately carved sideboard of Spanish design caught her eye. The polished top had several neatly arranged objects on it—crystal decanters and glasses and various leather-covered boxes. A huge gilt mirror hung above the sideboard.

A wide archway separated the antechamber from Brett's actual sleeping quarters, and through it Sabrina glimpsed a large satinwood armoire and a balloon-backed chair covered in velvet. Unwilling to move farther into an area she considered dangerous, she stood uncertainly just inside the double doors. Clearing her throat nervously, she called out, "Are you there?"

Even expecting his answer, she was startled by his sudden appearance in the archway. He was clad in flesh-clinging nankeen breeches and calf-hugging boots of umber leather, and was in the process of slipping on a white cotton shirt. His state of undress didn't concern him in the least, but it increased Sabrina's agitation. His black hair was ruffled and damp, and she guessed that he had just come from his bath. He made no move to finish fastening his shirt, and hastily she averted her eyes from the bronzed, muscled chest.

Embarrassed and uneasy, she muttered, "I can come back later if I have arrived at an inconvenient time."

Brett shrugged. Walking farther into the room and approaching the sideboard, he lifted the lid of one of the boxes and reached for a cheroot. Lighting it, he looked at her. "Your message was that you had to talk to me right away. 'Right away' is either now or next week—take your choice."

335

It wasn't an auspicious beginning. Sabrina wished passionately that she weren't so aware of his potent masculinity. Her mouth dry, trying not to let her eyes stray in his disturbing direction, she stated baldly, "I want to return to Nacogdoches."

Dead silence greeted her words. She waited tensely for some reply, and when none was forthcoming, she finally risked a glance at him.

He was regarding her thoughtfully, the cheroot clamped between his teeth. He inhaled deeply, and then with a maddening slowness gently blew out a stream of smoke. Almost idly he asked, "Why?"

Sabrina had been dreading that question, unable to simply say, because I'm afraid of you, afraid you'll destroy my own self-respect, afraid you'll reduce me to pleading for whatever of yourself you could give me. Helplessly she stammered, "B . . . because it's m . . . m . . . my h . . . home."

Brett shook his dark head. "Not anymore."

"I beg your pardon?" she replied breathlessly, a little spurt of angry fear shooting up through her.

"Your home is where *I* decide. And I've decided it is here."

Determined not to lose her temper, Sabrina strangled back the hot retort that sprang to her lips. Clasping her hands tightly in front of her, she said distractedly, "I am unhappy here. I . . . I . . . I think it would be best, for both of us, if I returned to Nacogdoches."

A mocking smile on his handsome mouth, Brett cocked a thick black eyebrow. "Best for both of us?" he drawled. "Why, my dear ward, whatever do you mean?"

The beast was enjoying this, she thought furiously, and unable to resist his baiting manner, she burst out angrily, "Oh, stop it, damn you! This is ridiculous! You never wanted to be my guardian, and I don't wish to be your ward! The only solution is for us to have as little as possible to do with each other." When he remained unmoved, his eyes fixed on her flushed features, she said tiredly, "I don't want to fight with you, Brett—and while we've managed to brush through the last few weeks without any clashes, it is only a matter of time until . . ." She stopped, the words dying in her throat as he slowly walked toward her.

The cheroot tossed accurately into a brass spittoon nearby, he stopped inches from her. His smoky breath caressing her face, he prompted, "Until?"

Sabrina swallowed convulsively, his tantalizing nearness driving coherent thought from her mind. All she could think of was the warmth that emanated from that powerful form, the pleasure she had found in his arms, the sweet ache that was spreading irresistibly through her own body. Humiliated by the betrayal that was going on inside her, and unable to bear the intense scrutiny of his eyes, she said huskily, "Until you push me too far."

He gave a harsh little laugh. "Until *I* push you? Sweetheart, you are far more likely to push me!"

Still too aware of him for her own good and unwilling to speculate on precisely what he meant by *that* statement, she said with far more calmness than she felt, "Which only proves my point—it would be better if I were not here in New Orleans, if we didn't see each other very often."

As if bored of the game, Brett turned around and flung himself down in one of the leather chairs. The expression in his eyes hard to define, he asked coolly, "How badly does this guardianship bother you?"

Surprised by the question, Sabrina stared at him. "A . . . a . . . a g . . . great d . . . deal," she got out almost on a whisper, wishing frantically that she knew what he was thinking.

"Only a great deal?" he questioned sardonically. "It doesn't chafe at you? Infuriate you? Madden you to know that I have complete control over you—and your *much-prized fortune*?"

There was a note in his voice when he mentioned her fortune that made her frown slightly. A note of contempt and distaste. Now why . . . ?

Brett's voice broke into her thoughts. "Doesn't it?" he demanded grimly.

A little angry at the whole conversation, Sabrina replied fiercely, "Yes, yes, it does! Sometimes it is intolerable!"

"Only sometimes?" he jeered, a considering gleam in the jade-green eyes.

"All the time!" Sabrina snapped, and carried away by frustration and the heat of the moment, she said rashly, "I would give *anything* to be free of you!"

Something that looked unpleasantly like satisfaction crossed his lean features, but he only said quietly, "You always surprise me, Sabrina."

Her puzzlement showing on her expressive face, she demanded, "What do you mean? Surely you knew that sooner or later I would fight against your restrictions."

"But what restrictions have I put in your way?" he inquired mildly.

"None!" Sabrina retorted uneasily. "But that doesn't change anything—I don't want to live here in your home, and if you force me to, I shall seek to have my father's will thrown out in a court of law."

"Ah, I see," Brett murmured. "I can remain your guardian as long as I let you do as you wish." His voice hard, he added, "And that's been your trouble from the beginning—your father indulged you, spoiled you beyond belief, and made you into one of the most self-centered individuals I have ever had the misfortune to meet!"

Deeply hurt and mortified, Sabrina turned her head, blinking back an unexpected sting of tears. It was unjust. She had been indulged, even she would admit it, but she had never taken advantage of that fact. Before she could betray how badly his words hurt, however, pride came to her rescue, and stiffly she said, "You have no right to sit in judgment upon me—you don't even know me!"

"Thank God for that!" he growled, and rising up, he walked over to where she stood with her back against the door. "But I can sit in judgment upon you—your father gave me that right, and in the future I intend to exercise it to the fullest!"

Tears gone, her face set, she glared at him. "I hate you, Brett Dangermond! And I *will* do anything to overset this despicable guardianship!"

He smiled cynically. "You know, sweetheart, I thought it would take us months to reach this state." His hand sliding with an odd possessiveness down her throat, he continued carelessly, "Of course, I was certain I would have to play the heavy guardian a few times first—really enrage

338

you and make you so angry by my actions that anything I suggested would find instant favor with you." Mockery in his eyes, his voice a velvet purr, he asked, "You did say *anything*, didn't you?"

Suffocatingly aware of his tall body so near hers, the heat of his hand upon her throat scorching her flesh, and feeling as if some just-noticed deadly trap was opening up beneath her feet, Sabrina nodded her head. And driven to hide any weakening on her part, she declared unwisely, "Yes! Anything!"

The jade-green eyes moved slowly over her, deliberately lingering on the full mouth and then sliding appreciatively down her slender form. Huskily he muttered. "Then I think we can come to a satisfactory arrangement."

His mouth gently touched the corner of hers, and helplessly Sabrina felt her body respond. She couldn't think straight with him this close, with his hand slowly caressing her shoulder, his mouth tantalizingly brushing hers, and on a shamed little whisper she got out, "What sort of arrangement?"

He lifted his head, and she was chilled by what she saw in his face. "A simple arrangement, tiger lily," he said thickly. "You become my mistress for six months, and at the end of that time, I sign all rights to your damned fortune over to you." Cynically he added, "I think that's a fair enough price to pay for six months' use of that delectable body of yours, don't you?"

CHAPTER TWENTY-FOUR

It took a moment for the enormity of his suggestion to sink in. Dumbly Sabrina regarded him, and then she stammered incredulously, "M . . . m . . . mistress? You want me for a mistress?"

His expression enigmatic, he replied bluntly, "I want you. I always have. I offered you marriage once, but it seems that it wasn't enough, at least not enough when I was the only thing that came with it." He smiled wryly. "So this time I'm not so foolish, although I suppose my fortune is far larger than it was then. However," he continued harshly, "I'm no longer in the market to *buy* a bride. A mistress, now that's another thing. . . ."

How she kept from clawing his eyes out, Sabrina never knew. Perhaps it was the promise of retaliation in his eyes, or it could have been the instinctive knowledge that he wanted her to react that way, that he was only looking for an excuse to take her into his arms. And if he touched her, if he kissed her . . . Sabrina momentarily closed her eyes in angry despair—if he kissed her, there wouldn't be any decision to make.

Turning her head away, desperately fighting against the need to be in his arms, she said huskily, "I need time to think."

It wasn't what she had meant to say. She had meant to throw his insulting offer back in his arrogant face, but somehow the words had come out all wrong.

"As you wish," Brett said with apparent indifference. He pushed away and walked toward his bedchamber but then stopped and glanced back at where she stood frozen by the double doors. "I think you should be aware," he said softly, "that I'm an impatient man, a *very* impatient man— after all, I've waited six years for this moment, and I don't intend to wait much longer. And sweetheart, something else for you to consider—I've been very kind to you these past weeks, I've actually even surprised myself, but don't make the mistake of thinking that if you turn me down, I'll continue to be so benevolent." His chiseled lips tightened. "Believe me, I won't—I'll *enjoy* acting the wicked guardian!"

He *would*, Sabrina thought miserably as she almost ran down the hallway toward the sanctuary of her rooms. He was capable of making her life such a hell that his insulting, degrading proposal would seem like heaven. Reaching her own rooms, she threw herself down on the bed, tears of hurt and shame trickling down her cheeks. Ah, dear God, she felt as if her heart would break. And how much easier, how much simpler her decision would be, if she didn't love him so. . . .

A muffled gasp of angry shame came from her. She couldn't *love* him! Surely he had killed any feeling but hatred within her? A derisive smile curved her mouth. No, unfortunately, she did still love him, and she wasn't going to pretend otherwise, no matter how humiliating the admission. It was love that had driven her to seize the first excuse to see him, love that had been behind her need to come to New Orleans; otherwise, she would have tossed his letter aside and set about breaking the will from the comfort and security of Nacogdoches. And it had been love that had delayed her these past weeks, that had stopped her from immediately seeing a lawyer and beginning to fight Alejandro's will.

Her tears drying, Sabrina turned over on her back, staring up blindly at the white canopy overhead. All right, so she was foolish enough to still love him. That didn't mean that she had to allow him to manipulate her, to dominate her and turn her into a fawning, adoring slave. She might love him, but he wasn't ever going to know it! He didn't deserve her love—he didn't deserve *any* woman's love! What he deserved was to be hanged, or drawn and quartered, or boiled in oil, or . . . For several pleasurable moments she considered all the lovely ways in which she would like to torture him, but eventually she stopped, realizing that while it made her feel a little better, it wasn't solving her problem.

And she did have a problem. Oh, it seemed so simple on the surface. She loved him, she wanted him, wanted him desperately with every fiber of her being, and he wanted her—for six months. A soft little groan of despair broke from her. If she accepted his infamous proposal, she would have six months of ecstasy, six months in which to try to make him love her. . . . But if she failed, if at the end of six months he terminated their relationship as coolly as he seemed prepared to enter it, she would have nothing but memories, memories that would turn bitter and ugly and leave the pain of shame and degradation forever within her.

Sabrina took a deep breath and sat up, a bleak expression on her exquisite face. Dare she risk it? Dare she say yes and hope that . . . A harsh little laugh escaped her. Hope for what? That he would suddenly change? That he would fall so madly in love with her, that miraculously he would become a different man? An honorable, faithful man who would want to marry her?

And if she didn't accept his proposal, what then? He had made it abundantly clear that the pleasantness of the past few weeks would cease. What could he do to her? she wondered uneasily. Lock her in an attic with bread and water? She could bear that, but she suspected that Brett's idea of a wicked guardian would take a more original form. A more painful, humiliating form. A form that could conceivably bring her to his bed without the guarantee that he would release his control of her body and fortune.

Dios! What was she to do? There had to be a solution! Some other way out of this coil. Suddenly feeling as if she were suffocating, Sabrina sprang up and, grabbing her reticule, started out the door of her rooms. She got five steps down the hall before she became aware of Ollie lounging near the staircase. His expression was determined but unhappy, and Sabrina's steps slowed.

They gazed at one another, then Ollie's eyes dropped from the suspicion in hers. Pulling nervously on his ear, he said uncomfortably, "I don't like it any better than you do, miss. But the guvnor says I wasn't to let you out of my sight." Ollie cleared his throat. "Says you should be aware that trying to run away from him is one of the options that ain't open to you."

"I see," she said calmly enough, despite the rage that burst through her. Smiling grimly she asked, "Are you very good at spying on people, at creeping around behind their backs?"

Ollie flushed slightly. "Yes, miss, I am," he answered steadily. "I'm not so good in the forest, as you should know, but there ain't no way you could get out of New Orleans without me or the guvnor knowing it. And miss, you should know that the guvnor is *very* good at tracking in the forest, so don't think if you escape from me that you can escape from *him!*"

Sabrina swallowed tightly and nodded her head. Dejectedly she turned away, walking slowly back toward her rooms. What was the use of leaving the house? Ollie's presence would be a constant reminder that she was no longer really free.

Inside her rooms, she wandered lethargically around, her fingers idly brushing first one object then another, her steps as aimless as her unhappy thoughts. What did it matter, she finally wondered tiredly, if she accepted Brett's proposal or not? He held all the cards, even one he didn't know about, her love for him. Whether she agreed or not, sooner or later, he would gain his way.

Facing that fact squarely, Sabrina realized that there really was only one choice left to her. Escape appeared out of the question. Even if she could evade Ollie, how would she live? Where would she go? Not home, that would be the first place Brett would look for her. Besides, how would she get there? She had no doubt that he had taken precautions against her simply saddling up and riding madly for Nacogdoches.

So, she thought dryly, if she was to find herself in his bed one way or another, she had better strike the best bargain. And the best bargain he had offered was to release her at the end of six months. Her features hard, she stared out at the balcony. At least, she told herself bitterly, she had a little time. She didn't have to give him the satisfaction of an immediate capitulation. And just maybe, just maybe, in

343

the short time that she had, some other solution would come to her. . . .

Somehow she had expected Brett to act differently after their conversation of that morning, but to her confusion, he continued to behave as if nothing important had passed between them. That evening when he greeted her in the blue salon before dinner, his manner was the same as it always had been—mocking, slightly derisive, and unfortunately, totally fascinating.

Francisca had recovered somewhat from her indisposition and was up to joining them for dinner, for which Sabrina was inordinately thankful. She didn't think she could have gotten through the meal if her aunt had not been present, and even more importantly, Francisca's conversation with Brett covered any silence on Sabrina's part.

It was unusual for Brett to join them for dinner, and Francisca couldn't help commenting on it. "Well, *señor*," she said snidely, "this is an honor to have you with us this evening."

Brett smiled slightly. "I'm so happy that you are aware of it," he replied dryly, a little gleam of mocking amusement in his eyes.

Francisca's mouth thinned, but determined not to be roused, she said less unpleasantly, "You have been gone for several days and seem to be very busy of late. Does it have anything to do with my niece's affairs?"

Taking a sip of his wine, Brett answered easily, "Yes, as a matter of fact, it does."

Francisca waited for him to continue, but when it appeared that no more information was forthcoming, she demanded impatiently, "Explain, if you will." Brett looked at her, and she muttered, "Please."

"Since you asked so politely," he murmured, "I have been seeing that Fox's Lair, my plantation some miles south of here, is made ready for our removal there."

"Removal?" Sabrina repeated sharply.

Brett glanced at her. "Yes. Surely you know that it is the custom to retire to one's plantation for the summer months? The city is only agreeable for the winter time. But before we can leave, there are necessary alterations to be made to the house"—he flashed a charming smile to

344

Francisca—"before it is suitable for such delightful visitors."

Francisca was not the least charmed. "I do not think that this is a good idea! We have no intention of leaving New Orleans! " she stated firmly.

But before she could continue further, his face implacable, Brett said coolly, "It really doesn't matter what you think, *señora*. By the first of June, Sabrina and I will be living at Fox's Lair—if you wish to accompany your niece, do so. If you don't"—his voice grew silky—"I'm certain you can find other accommodations here in the city."

Sabrina watched with appalled fascination as Francisca's hand tightened around the knife she was holding, and for one terrible second Sabrina feared that her aunt would not be able to resist the impulse to bury it in Brett's chest.

Eyes narrowed, Brett waited, his body poised for action, but then, as if regaining control of herself, Francisca smiled sickly. "You must forgive me, *señor,*" she muttered thickly. "I am not used to having my wishes held in such little regard."

Brett made some polite reply and then went on to talk of Fox's Lair as if nothing unpleasant had ever occurred. The awkward moment was past, but Sabrina really wasn't surprised when Francisca refused the strawberry glacé for dessert and excused herself early. Left alone with Brett, Sabrina started to rise, saying hastily, "I'm not hungry anymore either. I'll leave you to finish your meal in peace."

"Sit down, Sabrina," Brett commanded dryly. "I don't intend to attack you, so don't run from me like a frightened doe."

Indignantly Sabrina gasped, "I am *not* frightened! I just thought—"

"You just thought you'd better go soothe your aunt?" he asked with a sardonic lift of his brow.

"Well, you were rather rude to her!" she said defensively.

"No more than she was to me," he stated wearily. Looking at her, he demanded, "Do you really think I like being so impolite? And do you really think I am not aware of her resentment and bitterness? That I don't see the black looks

345

she sends my way, or know that she'd really have liked to use that knife on me?" He snorted. "Your aunt hates the very sight of me, and she is the last person I would want standing near me if I were at the edge of a cliff."

A small, rueful smile curving her lips, Sabrina murmured, "It is very hard for her, Brett."

Brett made a wry face. "It probably is—and if she would try meeting me with just a little politeness of her own, I could rise to the occasion and return it."

Strangely at ease with him, the chill that had been around her heart melting just a little, Sabrina asked softly, "Are we really removing to your plantation by the first of June?"

He toyed with his wine glass a second. Then his eyes met hers and he said quietly, "Yes, we really are. I think you'll enjoy it there. Château Saint-André where Morgan lives is not too far away, so you will have your opportunity to meet his beloved Leonie."

Sabrina nodded her head slowly, bewildered and amazed that they were having this perfectly civilized conversation. Brett was smiling faintly, a hint of warm laughter lurking in the depths of his jade-green eyes, and she felt her heart swell with love. It was times like this, and there had been far too few of them, that she treasured most. His cynical, sarcastic manner was gone. He was talking to her as he used to in Nacogdoches, beguiling her as he had then, the careless charm washing effortlessly over her, and she almost felt that there was hope for the future. That somehow, someway, the future would be good for them.

They talked enjoyably for some time, Brett explaining the changes he was making in Fox's Lair, making Sabrina smile at his enthusiasm for the place. But then, all too soon, as if he had just remembered the situation between them, his face changed slightly, and he said in that sardonic tone of his, "Well, my dear, I believe that I have bored you long enough with my tales of the trials of a poor planter."

His mood shift was too quick for Sabrina, and still basking in the warmth of his charm, a teasing smile on her lips, she waved her arm around, indicating the room, and murmured, "Surely not *poor?*"

Brett stiffened, and with dismay Sabrina knew that this friendly interlude was over. He had withdrawn from her, and the cold, infuriating creature she so disliked was once more in command.

His eyes icy, he drawled, "No, certainly not poor!" His face grim, he added deliberately, "But then, I never was poor—something you should have discovered before you so summarily threw my marriage proposal back in my face."

Furious that he had given so much away, Brett stood up abruptly. "If you will excuse me, I will leave you now."

Open-mouthed with astonishment, Sabrina stared speechlessly as he walked quickly across the room and disappeared through the doorway. Frowning, her thoughts in a turmoil, she, too, rose and left the dining room.

Sleep did not come easily to Sabrina this night. There was too much to think about, too many confusing, contradictory things to reflect upon.

This morning she hadn't really taken in much of what he had said beyond the statement of wanting her for a mistress, but now, lying wide-eyed in the darkness of her room, she slowly reviewed that unsettling confrontation. There had been the distinct implication, now that she thought of it, that six years ago she had found him wanting, or rather, that she had found his fortune wanting. She frowned. But that was impossible! She had loved *him,* and his money or lack of it had never entered into her emotions. But then, why was there always that jeering note in his voice whenever he mentioned money, especially *her* money? What had he called it once—her *much*-prized fortune? And now, tonight, again the implication that she might not have terminated their bethrothal if she had known the true state of his financial affairs.

Her frown deepening, she sat up in bed, knees against her chest. Oh, it was ridiculous! He can't have thought that she was after his fortune? A guilty flush covered her face as slyly the question crept through her brain—why not? You thought he was after yours! She wiggled uncomfortably, shame crawling within her. But I had good reason! she protested weakly. Good reason? her mind jeered. *What* good reason could make you believe such a thing of the man you professed to love? But Sabrina knew the answer to that question even if she wished she didn't. Carlos and Constanza, she whispered into the darkness. And that effectively ended her argument with herself. It was true that Brett himself had never given any indication that her fortune held any particular allure for him, but even if she could have brushed away Carlos's comments about Brett being a fortune hunter as jealous barbs, there was no possible way she could refute Constanza's far more damaging confession that terrible afternoon in the gazebo. For just a second, she was conscious of a spurt of outrage at the callous way Brett had apparently abandoned Constanza to her fate. But then, sighing heavily, Sabrina lay back. What good did it do to torture herself this way? That query was unanswerable, but there was an even more puzzling and disturbing question to ponder—if Brett had been after her fortune as Carlos and Constanza claimed, and she had no reason not to believe them, then why did he appear to he laboring under the misapprehension that she had only been interested in *his* fortune?

There was no answer to that question either, and eventually she fell into troubled sleep, but even her dreams gave her little comfort. All through the remainder of the night, she was doomed to dream the same dream over and over again: her heart so full of love it felt it would burst from her breast, she was running joyously toward Brett where he stood by the lake, his arms outstretched to catch her near. His face was warm and welcoming, love clearly shining out of those jade-green eyes as she approached. But then, without warning, a heavy fog came between them and she was enveloped by a smothering sense of foreboding. That terrible feeling of suffocating foreboding increased when out of nowhere Carlos and Constanza suddenly appeared and began to clutch her wrists, stopping her progress as she fought to reach Brett. She cried out, but no sound seemed to permeate the thick mist, and she struggled futilely to free herself. Through the ghostly vapors, she could barely see Brett's tall figure, but she knew the instant his face changed, knew when it became hard and contemptuous, knew when his arms fell listlessly to his sides. Frantically she increased her efforts to escape, but it was fruitless. Tears sliding unheeded down her cheeks, she watched helplessly as Brett finally disappeared into the concealing mists.

Not unnaturally, she woke tired and depressed, barely able to force herself out of bed. The dream was still vivid, and she was unhappily conscious of a feeling of resentment against Carlos and Constanza—if only they hadn't interfered! But then she pushed that thought aside. Their interference didn't change anything—Brett hadn't loved her.

Brett, too, woke tired and depressed—a most unusual state for him. The fatigue he could put down to the hard work he had been cramming into every spare moment of the past few days, seeing that Fox's Lair was made ready for Sabrina's arrival. But the depression troubled him—surely after yesterday's confrontation with Sabrina he should be elated . . . shouldn't he? After all, he had her precisely where he wanted, didn't he?

If all of that was true, why did he have this nagging feeling of dissatisfaction, this depressing feeling that something was missing, this increasingly annoying sensation that his quest for vengeance wasn't giving him quite the pleasure he had thought it would? He should have woken this morning with a feeling of eager anticipation—Sabrina might not give him the answer he wanted immediately, but there was no doubt in his mind that before too long, she would humble that arrogant pride of hers and consent to his unscrupulous proposal.

His face twisted. Was that the root of his depression and dissatisfaction, the knowledge that he was acting dishonorably and unscrupulously?

With a sort of baffled rage, he glared at the elegant furnishings of his bedroom. Surely, having dreamed of this moment, having *planned* to put her in this position, he wasn't having second thoughts . . . wasn't allowing his resolve to weaken? Or was he?

No, he decided coldly. He wasn't having second thoughts —Alejandro had been a damned romantic fool to have added that codicil to his will! And if the man he had chosen to act as his daughter's guardian took advantage of the powers given him, it was Alejandro's own fault!

Moodily Brett got out of bed and splashed some water in his face from the pitcher that sat on the marble-topped washstand near his bed. Honor, he argued, had *nothing* to do with the situation. She deserved to suffer at his hands—hadn't she made him suffer? Hadn't she hurt him more deeply, more painfully, than anyone ever had in his entire life? Heartlessly and cruelly tossed him aside simply because his fortune hadn't been large enough to satisfy her greed? Wasn't it only justice that he gain a certain amount of satisfaction from the handful of aces that Alejandro had so foolishly dealt him?

Ruthlessly he told himself that the answer to all of those questions was a resounding yes! Unfortunately, that decision didn't help his state of mind and didn't lighten his black mood. He suspected that some of his heaviness of spirit had to do with the affection and respect that he had borne Alejandro—it went against the grain to betray a man's trust . . . even a dead man's.

Alejandro's death had hit Brett hard, almost as hard as losing his own father would have. And to learn that Alejandro had been basely murdered had filled him with such a vengeful fury that he had finally not been able to contain it. As Ollie had speculated, he *had* gone to Nacogdoches late last summer, intent upon finding Alejandro's killer. But by the time he had arrived in the small Spanish outpost, whatever trail had existed was cold. Disguised by a thick beard, a slouch-brim hat, and rough clothing, he had spent several weeks quietly, unobtrusively asking questions, sifting through what little information was available, savagely determined that just one tiny clue would emerge. In the end, however, he had known his quest was hopeless, and so, with a bleak heart, he had ridden away from Nacogdoches . . . but not before giving in to the impulse that had been eating at him since he had first crossed the Sabine River—perhaps since he had ridden away so furiously that summer of 1800. It had been folly, sheer madness, to ride by the lake, to stop and look at the gazebo where he had made love to Sabrina that moonlit night so long

350

ago. And when, through the open arches of the gazebo, he had seen her suddenly rising up before him, a knife-sharp sense of pleasure had cut through him. Only for a second, only for a moment, his guard had been down, before he had viciously throttled the powerful emotions that had sung through him. Not ready to see her again, unwilling to trust his own reactions, especially in this evocative place, he had sharply reined his horse aside and stoically ridden for New Orleans, envisioning the sweet revenge he would take upon her.

So now, why, when everything was working out precisely as he had planned, did the idea of victory leave him so dissatisfied and depressed? His desire to possess her was unabated—too many nights of late, he had slept restlessly, his body aching to know the ecstasy of hers, and he had only to conjure up her image in his mind for physical proof of his desire to be instantly noticeable. The need for revenge was just as strong and powerful as ever, or rather, the desire to teach her a lesson was just as strong, but he had the unsettling conviction that forcing her to become his mistress wasn't necessarily going to teach her the lesson that he wanted her to learn—nor was it going to ease the incessant pain that had been with him since she had so summarily terminated their betrothal nearly six years ago. . . .

His face tightened, one hand closing into a fist, the knuckles gleaming whitely. He would just learn to live with the pain, just as he had in the past, and in the meantime . . . In the meantime, he would have her in his bed, he thought caustically, and his body would have relief, if not his heart!

Dressing swiftly, he left his rooms minutes later and was on his way to the stables when Ollie, an envelope in his hand, stopped his progress. With resignation, Brett noticed that the envelope had been opened, and dryly he asked, "Am I ever to receive *any* missive that you don't peruse first?"

Ollie grinned. "Now, guvnor, you know you can't teach an old dog new tricks! And I've been opening your letters for so long now that I don't think I could ever stop!" Brett

351

snorted and quickly made himself cognizant of the facts of the letter. It was from Morgan. It read,

> Dear Brett,
> When I returned home, coincidentally there was a letter from Jason waiting for me. He and his family are planning to come to New Orleans in late July, early August, and so, instead of writing to him, if it meets with your approval, I suggest we simply wait until he arrives and then I shall arrange a meeting for the three of us, perhaps here at the Château—that way, Sabrina and Catherine can visit with Leonie while we gentlemen discuss matters to our satisfaction. Agreed?
>
> Morgan.

Glancing at Ollie, Brett said, "Write a reply for me, telling him that I am agreeable to whatever he arranges, and have one of the servants deliver it to the Château Saint-André, please. Oh, and while I think of it—before I leave, I'll write a letter to my father, and I'd like you to have a servant carry it to him personally." He smiled. "Otherwise, Hugh might not get it for weeks."

Ollie nodded and started to turn away, but Brett's voice halted him. "I'm leaving you in charge of everything while I'm at Fox's Lair—I've already told Andrew and the other servants that they are to look to you for their orders," Brett said slowly. "I should be gone about a week to ten days this time. I'll write you, giving you a more definite return date later, but when I get back, I'd like the household ready for removal to Fox's Lair."

Sabrina took the news of Brett's absence rather well, almost with relief. There was time yet before she had to make her fateful decision, and she could only hope that in the pitifully short time allotted to her, some other resolution to her dilemma would present itself.

But even with the uncertainty of the future hanging over her head, despite her anger and resentment at the path he was forcing her to follow, she found that she missed Brett's vital presence dreadfully. The atmosphere within the house seemed so dull, so boring, so listless, without him, and to her horror she found herself counting the days until he would return.

Much to Francisca's delight, Carlos arrived one sunny afternoon after Brett had been gone for about five days. Sabrina, however, viewed his arrival with decidedly mixed emotions, and she discovered that she wasn't as elated to see him as she could have been. His presence was only going to complicate matters further. Her uneasiness grew when Francisca insisted that he stay the night with them and arrogantly ordered that a suite of rooms be prepared for him. The initial greetings and current news had already been exchanged, and the three of them were seated in the tree-shaded courtyard, seeking relief from the humid warmth of the day, when Francisca made her wishes known. At her aunt's brazen disregard of Brett's views on the subject, Sabrina stiffened and somewhat stiltedly said, "Tía, I don't think that would be such a good idea. Señor Dangermond—"

Haughtily Francisca interrupted. "What do I care what he thinks! He is not here; we *are!* Besides," she added smugly, "now that Carlos is here, things will be changed."

Her expression suspiciously meek, Sabrina asked, "Oh? How is that?" And she glanced questioningly at Carlos, who was sprawled comfortably in a cane-backed chair.

Carlos regarded her thoughtfully, aware that her greeting had not been as welcoming as it could have been. And he was very much aware that while she was willing to visit politely with him and offer refreshments, she definitely didn't want him staying here. Slyly he drawled, "Is there some reason why I shouldn't abide in the same house as my mother and dear cousin? Especially since *your* money probably bought it!"

"We don't know that!" Sabrina flashed back angrily. Her color heightened, she said more calmly, "And until we do, this is his home." Looking Carlos squarely in the eye, she finished with, "Señor Dangermond has expressed the wish that you *not* stay here with us. It is un-

353

fortunate that he feels that way, but I think it is best if you find another place to stay during your visit here in the city."

Francisca was outraged. Sending her niece a glance of scathing dislike, she spat, "And just who do you think you are to make such a decision? I am your aunt, and you *will* obey me! I say that my son stays here with us where he belongs! How dare you side with that gringo!"

Carlos watched Sabrina's set face carefully, wondering what she was thinking. It was obvious that these few months apart, while he had been gone to Mexico City, had badly damaged his relationship with her. She was friendly, but he sensed a barrier between them. The gringo? A jealous glitter in his black eyes, he searched her features for a clue.

Despite everything, Carlos had never given up hope that one day he would marry Sabrina and at last gain the two things that had always eluded him—the woman and the del Torres fortune. Doggedly he had pursued both, confident that one day he would win Sabrina. Alejandro's will had nearly been the death of his dreams, but during the long ride back from Mexico City, he had decided that he would make one last effort—it was foolhardy to hold his hand much longer. Bitterly he had acknowledged that after this length of time, Sabrina wasn't ever going to love him as a husband, and so he had cold-bloodedly begun to plan a way in which to force her hand in marriage. There was only one way, he had finally conceded to himself—to make her pregnant.

A slightly cruel smile had crossed his dark face. It would give him great pleasure to get her with child. It wouldn't matter that she would hate him; shame alone would force her to marry him. And once married, from the security of Mexico City, he was certain he could break Alejandro's will. After all, their common relatives in Mexico were rich and powerful, and Carlos never doubted that they would join in the battle to wrest control of Alejandro's fortune from an outsider.

He'd had it all plotted out—even the place where he would keep Sabrina prisoner until she was pregnant and had learned who was her master. He hadn't been best pleased when he had arrived at Nacogdoches and had discovered that he had left things almost until too late. But then, Constanza had warned him that might happen. . . .

For a second his eyes narrowed. Who would have thought that Constanza Morales would be in Mexico City? Or that they would meet? His mouth thinned. Or that she would be contentedly married to a wealthy Spanish grandee? A tall, handsome man who reminded him infuriatingly of Brett Dangermond. Even now he couldn't believe it. Couldn't believe that the glowing, comfortably plump woman at the side of the visiting aristocrat at his Tía Ysabel's grand house in Mexico City was indeed Constanza Morales. Only she was now Constanza Ferrera, happily married and the doting mother of two young children—two fine sons, ages three and four. He had been thunderstruck. Not only to meet her there in Mexico, but to find her so changed, so *greatly* changed. Gone was the scheming, unhappy woman who would have done anything to gain her way. Marriage and security had softened her, molded her into a creature he hardly recognized.

When, at last, he had contrived a moment alone with her, when he would have re-established their intimacy, she had gently but firmly rebuffed him. Her liquid dark eyes full of pity, she had said, "You haven't changed at all, Carlos, *mi amigo.*" Her voice husky, she had added, "But I have—and those days of careless, selfish passion are behind me. I am shamed when I remember them." Love evident with every word she spoke, she had continued, "I am married to a *good* man, the kind of man I dreamed of but never expected to find! God has blessed me abundantly these past years since we parted—with my husband and my sweet babies. There isn't an hour that goes by when I don't send up a silent prayer of thankfulness for all the wonderful things that have happened to me since I met Jorge." Her eyes shadowed, she had finished with, "I don't deserve any of it . . . especially since I gained all I have at the expense of innocent people—a pair of young lovers who were separated because of me."

To Carlos's utter amazement, she had been sincere. It

had been patently obvious, from the expression in her eyes when she spoke of her husband and children to the way she very honestly *pitied* him! Angrily he had snarled, "It is all good and well when one has everything one ever desired to sit in judgment on others. There was a time when you didn't feel this way—when you used every means at your disposal to get what you wanted!"

Constanza had looked away. Her voice thick with remorse she had whispered, "All of what you say is true, and if I could undo it, I would." Tears swimming in the large dark eyes, she had said painfully, "I have often thought of writing to Sabrina and explaining my part in what we did—"

"No!" Carlos had shouted, fear shooting through his body. It was imperative that Sabrina continue to trust him. Whatever plans he made for the future were pivotal upon that one fact.

Constanza had stared at him, and hastily he had improvised, "It doesn't matter anymore what we did—she never really loved the gringo. She told me so." He had forced a pleased smile on his mouth. "When I return, I have hopes of marrying her. Of late she has given me certain indications . . ."

Thoughtfully Constanza had regarded him, and he had been aware that she was trying to decide if he was telling the truth. She must have decided that he *was* telling the truth, because a tense second later, she had murmured lightly, "Then you should not tarry here too long—your Sabrina might escape you."

How prophetic Constanza's words had been! He shot Sabrina a calculating look. His task was going to be much harder now—it was glaringly apparent that her opinion of the guardianship had altered drastically since she had arrived in the city. He noticed that there had been no outward signs of resentment against the gringo, and it was also obvious that she was a little aloof from his mother and even himself. Then there was the problem of finding a place to keep her, once he had kidnapped her. . . . Mentally Carlos shrugged. He would think of something. He always did.

PART FOUR

THE PROMISE OF LOVE

Alas! how light a cause may move
Dissension between hearts that love!

Thomas Moore
Lalla Rookh, Part VIII, The Light of the Haram

CHAPTER TWENTY-FIVE

Having decided that it would gain him little to insist on staying in Dangermond's house, Carlos had immediately set about soothing his mother and at the same time teasing Sabrina into relaxing. He had convinced both women, and it was true, that he had no intention of staying there. He would be nearby if they needed him, but for the time being he thought it best to find his own lodgings.

Sabrina had thrown him a grateful smile, and her parting with him was much warmer than her greeting had been. It wouldn't have been, however, if she'd had any inkling of what was going on in Carlos's mind. Upon leaving the Dangermond house, he had instantly repaired to the room he had hired at an inn near the center of the city. Dangermond's being gone was a stroke of luck, he decided thoughtfully that evening as he sat alone in his room. But he would have to work quickly if he meant to take advantage of it.

By the next afternoon, his plans were in place. He had secured a small, isolated cottage, five miles from the city. It was a dilapidated but sturdy little building that would suit his purposes. There were no neighbors nearby, and it was well concealed by the rampant undergrowth that characterized the uncultivated portions of the country. A swamp nearly surrounded the abandoned building, and Carlos had no doubt that it would be difficult to find. But even if Dangermond were eventually to track Sabrina to this place, it would be too late. Carlos smiled—it took such a little time to rape a woman. That she would be pregnant within days, if not hours, of his forced possession was a foregone conclusion in his mind.

Having found the place of captivity so quickly, Carlos

was dismayed when his plans suffered a setback, in that Sabrina proved to be damnably elusive. He had come to call on Wednesday suggesting that they take a ride along the river, but Sabrina had demurred politely. She had excuses for declining every outing he proposed, almost as if she realized that her safety lay in the confines of the Dangermond house.

Sabrina didn't suspect Carlos of anything; she was just conscious of a growing feeling of unease whenever she was in his company. She knew that Brett was going to be furious when he returned and discovered that Carlos was running tame throughout his home, but that wasn't what kept her from accepting any of Carlos's invitations. It was something about the way Carlos looked at her. Something that gleamed in the back of those watchful black eyes that made her unwilling to be alone with him for longer than a few minutes. Something that made her remember his attack on her in the gazebo . . .

That and the dreams that had begun to haunt her at night. The dream of Brett at the lake came back often, but now it took an even more sinister turn. Constanza would fade away, and she was left alone with Carlos, but a Carlos she didn't recognize. Instead of the handsome, smiling visage of her childhood companion, his face changed into a malicious mask of evil. It frightened her, and while she was not superstitious, she couldn't shake the instinctive feeling that perhaps she shouldn't disregard her dreams. The memory of the gazebo, coupled with the nightmares, made her particularly skittish in his company. And then there was the fact that Brett had said that Carlos had lied. About what? she wondered frequently, but the moment to ask her cousin hadn't presented itself, and she resolved to ask him the next time Francisca left them alone for a moment.

Carlos's arrival had momentarily pushed the indecision about Brett's disgraceful proposal to the back of her mind, but by the time Carlos had been in New Orleans a few days, Sabrina knew that she could hide from it no more. She was going to accept Brett's ultimatum. Accept it and hope and pray that sometime within her six-month period of grace a miracle would occur . . . that Brett would fall in love with her.

It was a bitter decision. Made all the more so by the knowledge that she was actually aching to be in his arms, yearning to have him kiss and caress her as he had that moonlit night. She hungered for him, not just for his body, but for everything he was—arrogant, kind, cruel, generous, sardonic, fascinating, infuriating, hated, and dearly beloved, all at the same time.

Yet once the decision was made, once she had admitted that she loved him, that *any*thing was preferable to not having him, she discovered a queer sense of confidence. That someway, somehow, she was going to make him love her—that the six months would stretch into a lifetime and that one day she would be his wife.

Perhaps it was the relief from the uncertainty that made her careless, that made her not think twice about attending the small soiree that was being held some distance from the city at the plantation of the Robleses, friends of Francisca's. Francisca was also going, so Sabrina felt no qualms that night when she stepped into the carriage with Carlos and his mother. The coach was Brett's, as were the servants who drove it, Ollie being one of them, and that, too, may have added to her feeling of security.

She enjoyed the soiree, and gowned in a sumptuous creation of icy green satin with a gauzy overslip of wispy white chiffon, her hair pulled back in an elegant chignon decorated with a fine silver net, she attracted all eyes. Her height as well as her graceful carriage made her instantly recognizable, and given those qualities and her warm smile and laughing amber-gold eyes, it wasn't surprising that there was usually a crowd of eager, flamboyant young Creole and Spanish gentlemen surrounding her.

Carlos was not one of them. Determined to take advantage of both the distance from the city and his mother's doting devotion to him, he had laid his plans accordingly. An important part of those plans was not to frighten off his quarry.

About halfway through the evening, when one of the older couples was preparing to leave, Carlos said casually to his mother, "Why don't you ride back to town with the

361

Correias?" A coaxing note in his voice, he added, "It would give me an opportunity to be alone with Sabrina."

Francisca had looked at him and smiled fondly. "But of course, my son." She had shot him an arch glance. "You will use the time to woo that silly girl, *sí?*"

Carlos smiled. "Yes, you could say that." He dropped a light kiss on his mother's forehead. "And *mamá*—don't worry if Sabrina doesn't come home for a few days."

Francisca was shocked at first, her eyes troubled. But then slowly she nodded her head. "I do not approve of this, but it may be the only way to force the gringo to release control of her," she said heavily.

Carlos nodded. "Exactly."

Making certain that Sabrina was occupied with her group of gallants, Carlos escorted his mother to the Correias' carriage, and once the carriage had pulled away, he walked over to the Dangermond coach. Idly he glanced around. Most of the servants were at the rear of the plantation house enjoying a little festivity of their own, and seeing that he was unobserved, he quickly wrenched loose the axle nut that held one of the rear wheels in place.

Throwing the nut over his shoulder, he smiled. There was a sharp curve in the road, about three miles away . . . and two tethered horses were waiting a short distance off the road in the underbrush. The wheel should stay in place until then, and once it came off and he had sent the servants after help . . . His smile widened as he re-entered the house.

Francisca, too, was smiling as she entered the Dangermond house a short while later. At last, she thought exultantly, her dream of seeing Carlos and Sabrina wed was going to happen. True, she wasn't pleased that it had taken this long or that it would be a runaway match, but she comforted herself with the knowledge that it didn't matter *how* it came about. All the insults she had put up with from the gringo would have been worth it—especially when, as she was certain would happen, the codicil to Alejandro's will was declared invalid.

She smiled happily, envisioning the things she would say to the gringo, and there was a proprietary gleam in her eyes as she glanced around the handsome foyer. Soon, all of this would be hers.

Her smile faded, though, when she suddenly spied Brett's tall form lounging in the doorway of the library. "What are *you* doing here?" she demanded angrily. "You were not expected until Tuesday!"

Displaying far more calmness than he felt, Brett moved away from the library door and said coolly, "I didn't realize that I had to give notice before returning to my own home."

A mottled flush stained Francisca's cheeks. Her black eyes not meeting his, she muttered, "I was surprised to see you. When did you arrive?"

"About an hour after your little party left for the Robles plantation," he drawled lightly. "It was the Robles soiree that you attended, was it not?"

"Sí!" Francisca replied, thinking furiously of some way to conceal the current state of affairs. It would never do for the gringo to decide to ride out to the Robles plantation and escort Sabrina home. And certainly she must delay him until Carlos and Sabrina had made their escape. Hastily she said, "You must wonder why Sabrina is not with me?"

His eyes narrowed and watchful, Brett answered, "I think you could safely say that was the case. Where is she?"

The dark face gave nothing away, but something about the set of his jaw made Francisca decidedly uneasy. Did he know that Carlos was here in the city? That Carlos had escorted them to the soiree? And how was he going to take the news that Carlos was apparently escorting Sabrina home alone?

It was rather an awkward moment for Francisca. She would have preferred to dismiss the gringo, to refuse to answer his questions, yet on the other hand, she was aware of the need to be conciliatory—it would never do for him to go tearing out of the house in pursuit of Sabrina. She was also conscious that after the many ugly skirmishes between them, he wasn't about to be disarmed by a sudden charming manner. Quite the contrary, she thought sourly. It would far more likely alert him that something was afoot.

363

Brett watched her carefully, then, weary of the game, he demanded flatly, "Where is she? With that son of yours? Is he escorting her home?"

There was nothing to be gained by not admitting that much, so Francisca shrugged. "Yes. I was tired, and they were having such an amusing time, I left them and came home with the Correias."

He had expected something like that since the moment he had arrived home and had been informed that Carlos had accompanied the ladies to the soiree. And only the knowledge that Ollie was one of the servants with the coach had kept him from saddling his horse and riding to the plantation. But even suspecting that Carlos and Sabrina would take advantage of his absence for a tête-à-tête didn't lessen either the bitter disappointment that she still seemed to be dallying with her cousin or the unexpected jolt of fierce jealousy that ripped through his body. His voice clipped, he said, "You don't seem to take your duties as duenna very seriously. I would have thought it highly improper to desert your charge so far from home and this late at night."

Francisca drew herself up scornfully. "You dare to chastise *me?*" she asked incredulously. She flicked a disdainful glance up and down Brett's still form. "You forget yourself, gringo! Sabrina is my niece, Carlos, my son and her cousin; there is nothing the least improper in my actions!"

She had a valid point, but it did little to ease the anger and blind jealousy that was clouding his judgment. Dimly he realized that lashing out at Francisca would accomplish nothing. He gave her a mocking bow and murmured sardonically, "How kind of you to instruct me in etiquette."

Francisca glared at him, but although her hand clenched whitely over the handle of her black lutestring reticule, she said nothing. She would not let him goad her into foolish action. Stiffly she nodded her head and muttered, "If you will excuse me, I wish to seek out my bed."

"By all means," Brett returned with suspect affability. "I shall wait up for my ward alone." His eyes narrowed. "And *señora,* if she is not home here within a reasonable time . . . you and I shall have another little talk."

With an insouciance she was far from feeling, Francisca

nodded her head and almost scurried up the stairs. That swine! she thought viciously as she reached the safety of her rooms. Who did he think he was? And how dare he threaten her! But she was a trifle apprehensive, especially when she remembered the look in his eye. And what, she wondered uneasily, was she going to tell him when Sabrina did not appear?

Deciding that retreat was the better part of valor, she cautiously opened her door and peered down the deserted hallway. Just as cautiously she slipped down the hallway to the staircase that led to the courtyard. She was *not* remaining here to be bullied and insulted by the gringo! She would take refuge with the Correias for the night. A more confident smile on her thin mouth, she hurried across the darkened courtyard toward the carriageway entrance. Ha! Let the gringo wonder where they had all disappeared to! And for a second she allowed herself the pleasure of picturing his expression when Carlos and Sabrina returned a few days from now as man and wife.

Unaware that Francisca had left the house, Brett wandered back to the library, his thoughts not pleasant ones. The situation was rather ironic, he mused a few minutes later. Like a romantic fool, he had spent the past ten days acting almost like a bridegroom preparing a bower for his bride. For a second he looked down at his calloused hands, a cynical smile curving his mouth. Even to the point of building a latticed gazebo near a secluded corner of the estate with his bare hands, so that his sweet ward would have something that reminded her of home.

A bitter growl of laughter escaped him. What folly! Extensive and expensive alterations had been made at Fox's Lair—bare walls were now silk-hung, fine carpets covered the planked floors, elegant furniture from New Orleans had been arriving by the wagonload, and he had even harried his workmen to create a small courtyard that was reminiscent of the one at Nacogdoches. The gazebo had been his own personal, private contribution, and he had taken pride and pleasure in the hard work of constructing it, trying to visualize Sabrina's reaction to it, boyishly hoping it would please her and make her more resigned to staying here in Louisiana. He could not create a lake, but he had situated the gazebo in a spot that overlooked a tranquil stretch of the Mississippi River, and he hoped that she would find it an acceptable substitution.

During the days he had been gone, Brett had done a lot of thinking, a lot of looking at his own emotions, and he didn't like what he saw. It was the idea of Sabrina's forced surrender that gave him the most displeasure, that caused him to turn restlessly night after night. He wanted her, but he wanted her to come to him of her own free will—for it to be like it had been the first and only time they had made love. And the thought of releasing her at the end of six months was intolerable. Just thinking about a life without her created an aching emptiness deep within him, for which he knew there was no solace. . . .

His mouth twisted. What a damning admission for a cynic like him to make! He, who prided himself on being above the emotional entanglements that made such fools of the sanest men. Slowly he poured himself another glass of brandy. Well, Sabrina would just have to be his concession to the follies that men commit over women, he thought sardonically as he drank his brandy.

He was deliberately avoiding thinking about Carlos alone with Sabrina on the long ride back to New Orleans in a closed, private coach. . . . It was a futile battle, mental images of Sabrina in Carlos's arms, her mouth pressed sweetly against the Spaniard's, driving him half-mad with jealousy. With grim resolve he tried not to let that fierce jealousy burst out of control, tried with a cool desperation not to dwell on what might be happening. But as the time passed, as the decanter of brandy grew lower and lower, the tight check he kept on his emotions began to slip. . . .

Sabrina wasn't alarmed when Carlos informed her that his mother had left early, but she was dismayed. She didn't relish the seven-mile journey back to New Orleans in Carlos's company. Not when they would be cloistered in the closed coach. But there was nothing she could do about it, so resignedly she allowed him to help her into the carriage, hoping that he would continue to be charming and polite.

As the coach slowly pulled away, there was silence between them. Determined to take advantage of the forced tête-à-tête, Sabrina blurted out the question that had been on the tip of her tongue for days. "What did you lie to Brett about?"

Carlos was caught by surprise only for a moment, and when the implications of what she was asking sank in, he was conscious of a terrible burst of fury. In the darkness his fist clenched, and it was all he could do not to reach across the short distance that separated them and strike her and call her the slut she was. There was only one lie that he had ever told the gringo—that he and Sabrina were lovers—and there was only one way the gringo could have known that he had lied. . . .

It was as well that Sabrina couldn't see his face. If she had, all the nebulous fears and doubts that had plagued her would have crystalized into certain knowledge of his nefarious actions. As it was, though, Carlos's manner put her on guard, and for the first time in a long time, she wished that she still wore the blade of fine Spanish steel that her father had given her.

A sneer very evident in his voice, Carlos replied, "Why don't you ask the gringo? I'm certain he would be eager to vilify my character to you."

Sabrina bit her lip. Wishing there was light to see his expression, but not liking his tone of voice, she confessed, "I did, but he wouldn't tell me."

"Then you'll just have to wonder about it, won't you?"

Doggedly she persisted. "He said you told him unforgivable lies when he was staying at our home. Did you?"

Maniacal fury erupting up through him—that and the knowledge that soon it wouldn't matter whether she knew the truth or not making him careless—he leaned over and grabbed one of her wrists in a cruel hold. His face only inches from hers, his teeth a gleam of white in the darkness, he snarled, "*Sí!* I lied to the gringo! I told him that we were lovers. That I had long been your lover." His fingers crushed her wrist more brutally, and he gave her a rough jerk, nearly spilling her off the seat onto the floor of the coach. "And just think, my sweet *whoring* cousin, there is only one way he can have known that I lied. Only one way—*puta!*"

Blazingly angry, so angry she couldn't think straight,

367

not even feeling the pain from his vicious hold on her wrist, she struck him with the open palm of her free hand. He had *lied,* poisoned Brett against her, and now he had the audacity to condemn her!

The slap stung for Sabrina was no simpering miss, and for one second Carlos almost lost sight of his objective, almost gave in to the impulse to put his hands about her slender throat and strangle her. Instead he drew in a ragged breath and laughed harshly. "And to think that all this time I thought you were an innocent virgin! To think of how I have controlled myself! Tried to woo you gently! Tried to win your trust again—and all the while you were nothing more than the soiled leavings of a damned gringo!"

Aware of the dangers of this situation, but too angry to care, Sabrina demanded icily, "Let go of me, Carlos! Let me go before I scratch out your eyes and tear out your wicked, lying tongue!"

Carlos laughed again, an ugly sound that sent a shiver coursing down Sabrina's spine. Thickly he muttered, "You won't be doing anything to me; it is *I* who will be doing to you!"

Unerringly his cruel mouth found hers, and he kissed her brutally. Furiously Sabrina struggled to escape from his touch, but it was useless. She was pressed back against the seat of the coach, and the hold on her wrist was merciless. Too angry and revolted to be frightened, she closed the fingers of her free hand over several strands of his hair, and savagely she yanked his head back, away from her mouth.

Carlos let out a growl of pain, his other hand reaching up to capture hers, but Sabrina was ready for him, and moving like a striking snake, she hit him with the heel of her hand under the chin. His head snapped back, and her wrist was free. Breathing heavily, they regarded each other in the darkness, and in that instant the coach went around the corner and the wheel came off.

There was a mad lurch, a bone-jarring thud, and the coach stopped. A babble of voices was heard from the coachmen, and a second later, the door to the coach was wrenched open.

With heartfelt relief, Sabrina met Ollie's worried eyes. "Miss!" he exclaimed. "Are you all right? Damn my eyes! I near swallowed the spider when that wheel came off!"

Shaken more by what had happened with Carlos, Sabrina gratefully took Ollie's hand as he helped her down from the disabled vehicle. From the light of the coach lantern on the side, Ollie could see that she was white, and softly he whispered, "You all right? You look pasty."

"She's perfectly fine!" Carlos said sharply, following immediately behind Sabrina. Sourly he surveyed the damage and then ordered arrogantly, "You two men walk back to the Robles plantation and have someone bring up some sort of transportation."

Ollie looked at Carlos with dislike. "I ain't leaving Miss Sabrina," he said flatly. Then, glancing across at the driver, who had come to stand beside them, Ollie muttered, "Well, Joel, do you think we can fix it?"

This wasn't how Carlos had planned things, and impatiently he snapped, "I gave you an order! Now go back to the plantation and see about transportation."

The sound of approaching hoofbeats suddenly broke the silence, and ignoring the seething Spaniard, Ollie walked to the center of the dirt road and began to slowly wave one of the lanterns from the coach. A moment later, a second vehicle came into view, a stylish coach carrying its occupants from the very soiree that Sabrina had attended earlier. In no time, the situation was explained, and much to Carlos's helpless fury, a ride back to the city was warmly offered.

Sabrina was fervent in her thanks when at last she was deposited in front of Brett's house. She hadn't exchanged a word with Carlos during their ride home, but now, conscious of Ollie standing a short, watchful distance away, she said frostily, "It was an enlightening evening, cousin. I'll not thank you for it, and I would appreciate it if you don't ever—"

She got no further, for the front doors suddenly flew open, slamming loudly back against the walls of the house. Brett stood there in the doorway, such an air of menace radiating from him that Carlos took a nervous step backward.

369

The candlelight from the foyer streamed out into the dark street from behind Brett. To Sabrina he looked very large and forceful, and her heart gave an unexpected leap at the sight of him. His features were in shadow, the white shirt he was wearing undone nearly to the waist, exposing glimpses of the hard, sleek muscles of his chest. Black breeches were molded to his long, elegantly muscular thighs, and his thumbs were loosely hooked into the wide black belt around his lean waist as he stood there blocking the entrance to the house.

Silence fell, and Sabrina was very aware of the sudden frantic pounding of her pulse. She had done nothing to be ashamed of, but she had the lowering feeling that Brett was in no mood to be reasonable.

She was right, he wasn't. A dangerous glitter in the jade-green eyes, he drawled, "Well, well. If it isn't my little ward and her escort, finally come home."

Ollie looked at him sharply and then whistled silently under his breath. The guvnor was fair-foxed, and that made him all the more unpredictable and lethal. Only to someone like Ollie who knew him well were the signs obvious that Brett had been drinking heavily—the very careful way that he held himself, like a tiger on eggs, and the faintest slur to his speech, almost undetectable unless one was listening for it.

Certainly neither Sabrina nor Carlos was aware of it, although both were uneasily conscious of the spine-prickling feeling that they were faced with a potentially explosive situation. For Carlos, the wisest course was to retreat. His plans had gone dreadfully awry, and nothing could be salvaged at that moment. He needed to rethink his strategy, and he knew that after tonight's debacle, Sabrina would be even harder to capture. Under his breath, he cursed for the hundredth time the inopportune arrival of the other coach, but most of all, he cursed the fury that had allowed his tongue to wag so foolishly—at least, he thought savagely, he hadn't exposed his ultimate plan, and there was a chance that he could explain his actions away. Jealousy? Could he convince Sabrina that he had been so consumed with jealousy that the reason he had lied to the gringo six years ago had been to protect her? Maybe. But for now, the

370

most important thing was to escape from this unfortunate circumstance as unscathed as possible.

Politely Carlos said, "How kind of you to wait up for us. We would have been home much sooner, except that our coach threw a wheel and that delayed us for a little while." He pasted a sickly smile on his thin mouth. "Fortunately the Fourniers' coach was right behind us, and they gave us a ride back to town."

Brett fixed Carlos with a bone-chilling stare and then after a second, glanced at Ollie. Ollie nodded his head, and Carlos was conscious of rage that the gringo so obviously had not believed him and had sought confirmation from a mere servant. If it weren't imperative to leave without creating more of a scene, he'd have liked to strike the gringo's arrogant face, but as it was, he merely sighed and said sarcastically, "You see, I am telling the truth."

"This time," Brett murmured softly, his eyes cold and unblinking. Ignoring the fury in Carlos's face, he crooked a finger at Sabrina and said flatly, "Inside with you. And wait in the foyer for me—I want a word with you after I've spoken with your cousin."

For just a moment Sabrina considered refusing, but there was something so menacing about his stance that common sense and a very real desire to avert something ugly and dangerous prompted her to obey immediately. And it was those same feelings that kept her waiting in the foyer when she brushed past him a second later and he shut the door behind her. What, she wondered uneasily, was he saying to Carlos? And more to the point, what, dear God, was he going to say to her? She had done nothing wrong, and she was furious with Carlos, but Brett's attitude made it very clear that he viewed the evening far differently. And of course, he didn't know how she now felt about her cousin.

Outside, Brett and Carlos faced each other. Carlos was the first to make a move. "Well," he said with a false heartiness, "now that Sabrina is safely home, I shall bid you good evening."

Brett nodded and said with a dangerous softness, "I particularly hope that you enjoyed this evening, Señor de la Vega—it was your last with Sabrina." The jade-green eyes

371

hard with the promise of violence, he continued, "I won't deny you access to your mother, but remember this. Sabrina is my ward, and I won't have her subjected to the company of men of your ilk—liars and bullies."

It was a deliberately brutal speech, and Brett waited with a curious sense of savage anticipation—he hoped that the Spaniard would take offense at his words, almost *willed* Carlos to fling a challenge back in his face.

But Carlos was not to be goaded. Controlling himself, he replied thickly, "I understand you well, gringo. But remember this: Sabrina and I have known each other since childhood, and you cannot *command* her affection and loyalty." With great cunning he continued, "I may have lied to you about the situation between us once, thinking to drive you away from her—but do you really think that in all the years that have passed, I have not finally gained what I have always wanted—Sabrina, warm and responsive in my arms? Do you honestly believe, while you may have awakened her to passion, that these past years I have not taught her even more of physical love than you?" Sneeringly Carlos ended with, "You may claim her as your ward, but I lay claim to both her heart and body!"

There was a roaring in Brett's ears, and blindly he hurled himself down the few steps to the pavement, his one thought to stop the ugly, stabbing words that Carlos shot at him. A part of him was screaming in silent anguish, lies, lies, *lies!* But the cynical part of him was not surprised by the Spaniard's words. Either way, he couldn't stem the murderous rage that consumed him.

Brett's steel-muscled body met Carlos's with a thud that made Ollie wince, but he made no move to interfere. Even half-drunk and in a blind fury, the guvnor could whip two of the Spaniard, he thought confidently.

Ollie's summation of the fight was correct, Brett's iron-honed fists connecting again and again with Carlos's increasingly battered face. Only one or two of Carlos's punches managed to land on their mark, but beyond an annoyed grunt from Brett, they seemed to have no impact.

This evening would not figure pleasantly in Carlos's memories; first the realization that Sabrina and Brett had been lovers, then the helpless impotency as his well-laid plans were easily circumvented, and now *this!* His body aching from the beating he was taking, Carlos searched desperately for a way out. Unwilling to retreat ignobly and yet full of a savage desire to inflict some measure of pain upon the gringo, he swiftly reached for the knife he always carried. Stepping out of range of Brett's punishing fists, he warned, "Gringo, come closer and I will split you from throat to groin!"

Brett halted, his eyes narrowed. "Do you really think that is going to stop me?"

Carlos nodded, the black eyes wary but full of determination. He'd have liked to skewer the gringo, and for the first time the thought of what Brett's death would mean crossed his mind. With the gringo dead, the guardianship would be ended. With no guardian, Sabrina would be at his mercy. . . . Suddenly he smiled and taunted, "You are so brave with your fists, but it changes nothing, gringo—the woman is still mine, and there is nothing you can do about it! She loves me, and this time I do not lie when I say we will be married!"

The night air was full of dark enmity, and slowly the two men circled one another, Ollie watching uneasily now. The guvnor was unarmed, and nervously Ollie fingered the pistol in the inner pocket of his coat. Should he stop the fight? It was one thing to let a bare-fisted fight run its course, another to let the guvnor wind up dead!

But the decision was taken from him, for in that instant, like a lion leaping from ambush, Brett's arm shot out and captured Carlos's wrist. Brutally his fingers tightened and he gave a vicious little twist that brought a moan from Carlos; the knife fell unheeded to the road below. Deftly Brett twisted Carlos's arm behind his back and gave him a contemptuous shove that sent the other man sprawling in the dirt of the road.

His breathing revealing hardly any sign of exertion, Brett snarled softly, "Next time, *señor,* I will kill you! And if I find you within twenty feet of Sabrina, I'll make certain you take a long time dying."

Carlos rose slowly from the dirt and angrily brushed off the black, loamy soil that clung to his once-elegant breeches. His voice full of hatred and fury, he growled,

"You have won, tonight, gringo, but the battle is not over."

Brett shrugged, the dark green eyes cold and hard. "It is as far as any plans you have of marrying Sabrina," he retorted icily.

Carlos had to content himself with a vicious glare, and then he turned around and walked stiffly away. Brett watched him go with a curious mixture of frustration and resignation. Impotently his hands clenched and unclenched, and he longed fiercely to call the Spaniard back, to settle the matter between them once and for all. But with the part of his brain that was still rational, he understood the folly of it. Besides, he asked himself caustically, why should he risk his hide further for a flame-haired, avaricious little spitfire? And in that instant, unfortunately, Sabrina became the focal point of the situation and of all his bottled rage.

Turning to Ollie, he said in a velvet tone that didn't fool his valet at all, "I'll bid you good night—we'll talk in the morning." He started up the stairs, adding in that same dangerously velvet tone, "But for now I want a word with my ward."

Thoughtfully Ollie watched him disappear inside. Bloody eyes! Ollie muttered to himself. He wouldn't be in Miss Sabrina's shoes tonight for all the spice in India!

CHAPTER TWENTY-SIX

Looking at Brett's face when, with an unnerving quietness, he shut the door behind him, Sabrina rather wished that she weren't in her shoes, too. Her first feeling of overwhelming relief and delight that he was unharmed had vanished the instant she saw his face. It was apparent that nothing good had come of the talk with Carlos, and half-angrily, half-apprehensively, she wondered what *other* lies her cousin might have told him. She had hoped that they would not come to blows, but with a sinking heart she noted the signs of battle that were on Brett—the faint smear of blood near the corner of his mouth and the bruised, skinned state of his knuckles. She knew a nearly irresistible urge to fly across the room, to offer comfort, to touch and see for herself that he was not really hurt, but she knew at that same moment that he wouldn't take kindly to her ministrations.

Her heart aching with an odd mixture of love and anger, she watched him as he slowly walked toward her. His hair was disheveled, falling forward across his forehead, his shirt was gaping open all the way to his lean, narrow waist, the bronzed skin gleaming through the silky strands of black hair that grew there, and Sabrina was suddenly assailed by an unexpected surge of sexual awareness.

Swallowing convulsively, trying helplessly to ignore the nearly overpowering animal virility that exuded so naturally from him, she blurted out, "Are you hurt? What happened out there? Is Carlos all right?" After what had happened tonight, what had been revealed to her, she didn't give a damn about Carlos, but it was easier to ask after him than it was to let Brett's sheer magnetism blind her to everything but the compelling need to be in his arms, to touch him, to love him. . . .

Brett cocked an eyebrow at her. "Such concern!" he mocked. And lifting a bloody scraped knuckle, he murmured, "Will you kiss it better for me, sweetheart?"

There was something in his voice, as well as the look on his face, that made her increasingly uneasy. He was, she realized with a start, furious. Violence seemed to fill the very air where he stood, and there was a reckless glitter in the jade-green eyes.

She was very lovely as she faced him across the short distance that separated them, the candlelight turning the red-gold hair to fire, the icy green of her gown with its gauzy overslip giving the illusion of some ethereal fairy creature. But Brett knew that she was no ethereal creature, knew that she was full of fire and passion, his body remembering the heat and warmth of her skin, the fire that consumed him at her mere touch. It was a fire that he longed to burn in for an eternity, and he knew in that moment that he loved her. That he had always loved her and that he would be a double-damned fool if he allowed *anything* to come between them this time.

Nothing mattered anymore to him but that he have the right to call her his own. That money meant more to her than he did didn't even matter now. Carlos's words he dismissed with a sort of defeated disdain. Even that didn't matter. He had come to her experienced, so why should he cavil that she, too, had known other lovers? Not *loves!* he thought savagely. There had been no other loves in his life. Women, yes, he couldn't deny, but he had taken them in the same manner that a thirsty man would gulp water. There had never been emotion involved, only a physical response, never any caring—until Sabrina. And having known that exquisite feeling once, having known the joyous ecstasy of lying in the arms of the loved one, he wondered that he had survived these past years without her. He couldn't even deny that there had been other women since that night nearly six years ago—celibacy was not one of his virtues—but oddly enough, there had been no women in his life since he had returned from Derna. It was almost as if he had known that he had come back to Sabrina, as if he had realized the futility of seeking solace in other arms. Here was the only pair of arms he ever wanted around him, the only mouth he wanted to kiss, the only woman he would ever love.

It was a galling admission. The important women in his life had never treated him kindly; the pain of his mother's rejection was still buried deep within him, and the blow inflicted by Diana Pardee was an ugly scar on his emotions. But it was Sabrina's rejection of him that had gone the deepest, and yet here he was six years later, ready to walk once more into the silken trap that would bring him as much pain as it brought him joy. He faced that fact realistically, knowing that life without her would be far more unbearable than the pain she was certain to cause him.

But although he had admitted to himself that he loved her, it was an admission that brought no joy. If anything, it filled him with a furious impotency. He hated loving her, believing as he did that money would always mean more to her than his love, and he vowed fiercely that she would never learn that he loved her. It was too powerful a weapon to place in the hands of a greedy woman, and he cursed a fate that had made her the one woman in the world who had captured his heart. Why her, he wondered with a dull fury, why couldn't he have fallen in love with some sweet, innocuous little creature who would love him in return? Why did his fancy have to fall upon this bewitching, mercenary, flame-haired virago?

At least, he told himself viciously, he would have the pleasure of her body . . . and the pleasure of taming her to his bed. A pulse suddenly beat in his temple, and he was conscious of a demanding, hungry desire stirring in his blood at the thought of Sabrina lying naked in his arms. And once desire struck him, there was no denying it, his body responding instantly, his eyes darkening with passion, his full mouth taking on a sensual curve.

Sabrina had been staring mesmerized at the hand he had extended, longing to do just as he had proposed, kiss it better. There was nothing that would have given her more pleasure than to rain healing kisses all over his hand, his mouth, his body. . . . Realizing where her willful thoughts were taking her, with an effort she wrenched her eyes from his hand and met his gaze. Her breath caught in her throat, for there was no mistaking the look in his eyes, and treacherously she felt her body responding to it. She dropped her eyes, trying to ignore the sweet ache that was curling deep in her belly. Her gaze accidentally fell upon the lower half of his body, and her eyes widened at the clear sign of his arousal beneath the tight-fitting breeches. A smothered little gasp broke from her, and almost accusingly she glanced back up at him.

An odd little smile twisted his lips. Deliberately he walked closer to her. "A man," he breathed huskily, "can't hide what he is feeling. Women," he muttered against her mouth, "however, can. And a man only knows what effect he is having upon a woman by touching." With a leisurely movement, his hand cupped her breast, the thumb moving with an aching slowness across the nipple. Her nipple hardened instantly, and brushing a feather-light kiss at the corner of her mouth, he whispered, "Like that."

Helplessly Sabrina fought against the wave of insistent desire that washed over her. She mustn't. It didn't matter that she had already decided to accept his infamous bargain, this was different somehow—this, she realized sickly, was reality, and she couldn't bear to turn the love she felt for him into something so sordid as a trifling medium of exchange, her body for her freedom. She mustn't let him do this to her, mustn't let him touch her this way, mustn't . . . Oh, but it was so sweet, so wonderful, to have him touch her, and the fiery ache within her flowed ravenously through every part of her body. But drawing strength from some hidden reserve deep inside her, she stammered, "N . . . n . . . no. Y . . . y . . . you s . . . s . . . said you would give me time to consider the bargain."

For a second Brett stared at her, not understanding what she was referring to. Then his mouth twisted, and he shook his head slowly. "Sorry, sweetheart," he murmured thickly, "but there will be no bargains between us. Not anymore." His hands caught her shoulders, and he jerked her up next to his hard length. His mouth skimming hers with a burning heat, he muttered, "Not now!" And then his lips trapped hers in a hungry, demanding kiss.

With a small whimper of part pleasure, part defeat, Sabrina surrendered. What did it matter? *This* was what she wanted. And even when he swept her up into his arms and swiftly carried her up the stairs, his mouth urgently searching hers, she made no protest. She loved him. He wanted her, and for the moment she was content. Later she would worry about the consequences. Worry about her shame and her pride. Much later, she thought hazily as Brett kicked open the doors to his rooms and carrying her quickly across the outer chamber, deposited her on his huge bed.

His breathing was irregular, and sliding down beside her, a thread of amusement in his voice, he said, "God knows, you're a perfect Venus, but next time, sweetheart, I'll make certain my bed isn't so far away."

For just a second the sensuous mood was broken by his words, but before Sabrina could register them or gather her scattered wits, his mouth came down demandingly on hers and there were no thoughts in her mind but those of Brett. Heedlessly she returned his kiss, her defenses totally demolished by the cravings of her own traitorous body.

His kiss was ecstasy itself, those firm, knowing lips moving with a tender urgency across hers, his tongue seeking and finding the inner warmth and sweetness. There was a languid quality about his movements, as if he had been waiting a long time for this moment and didn't want to rush it. Slowly, lingeringly his fingers wandered through her hair, finding and discarding the silver net that held the chignon in place, gently letting the wavy, silky strands of red-gold hair slip through his fingers as he splayed it out across the pillows of the bed. His mouth kept hers a willing captive, the warmth and heat of his lips, the lazy, erotic probings of his tongue making Sabrina even more aware of how much she wanted him, how much she had hungered for him to do exactly as he was doing.

There was no question of stopping him, no thought of trying to escape the inevitable, and with a cat-sigh of pleasure, she let her hands slip up along his hard chest, over his shoulders, delighting in the touch and texture of his skin—skin that felt like sun-warmed, heavy satin. Her fingers curled sensuously through the thick, springy hair, and instinctively her body arched up nearer to his, seeking closer contact.

Even lost in his own world of sensual gratification, Brett was still conscious of a bittersweet satisfaction. She was in his arms, in his bed where she belonged, and dimly he knew that he was never going to let her go. That he could not. She was *his*, and before this night was through, she would know it, too.

As they lay there kissing, Brett's body half on hers, Sabrina became vaguely aware of other things: the yielding softness of the bed; the coverlet beneath her, warm and sleek, not velvet, not satin, but extremely voluptuous against her bare shoulders; and the faint flicker of candlelight across her closed lids. But then his hands stopped their wanderings through her hair and slid down to her shoulders, caressing and kneading the soft skin before insistently slipping the icy green gown farther down her body, laying bare her breasts and midriff, and Sabrina lost consciousness of anything but Brett.

The touch of his hand on her breast made her tremble; the ache that was building deep within her became more and more intense, more and more persistent as his fingers fondled and stroked her, his thumb teasingly circling her nipple, driving her half-mad with longing. Needing desperately to touch him, to caress him as he was caressing her, with impatient hands she pushed his opened shirt off his shoulders, pleased when he helped her by shaking free of the garment. Almost purring with satisfaction, she let her fingers explore the expanse of flesh now available to her, the lean length of his back, the broad shoulders, and the hair-covered muscled chest. Her fingers lightly circled his nipples, imitating what he was doing to her, evoking an unexpected response from him.

His teeth lightly caught her bottom lip, and he muttered in a muffled voice, *"Don't!* Not yet. I want you so badly, I've waited so long for this, that if you touch me now, I shan't be able to control myself."

But she had waited a long time, too, and frustratedly, not even aware of what she said, Sabrina mumbled, "But I want you, too. I want to touch you, too."

Her words were as potent as the strongest aphrodisiac,

and with a groan Brett sought out her mouth again, kissing her with an odd fierceness that only made the hungry yearnings in her loins more voracious. And when his mouth left her lips and scorched a trail of fire to her breasts, Sabrina's entire body leaped with pleasure. His mouth was warm and moist over her breasts, and the flick of his tongue as it curled around her hardened nipples, the gentle grazing of his teeth as he pulled on them, had her arching up eagerly against his mouth. Her hands moved restlessly over his dark head at her breast, and she was filled with a wondering tenderness. I love him so much, she thought helplessly. So much.

When Brett raised his head a second later, she gave a small moan of protest, not wanting the intoxicating sensations he was arousing to stop. Then his hands were at her waist, tugging at her gown, and with the slight sound of ripping cloth, she felt it sliding down her body, leaving her naked on his bed.

There was silence in the room for a moment, and then Brett's husky "Oh, Jesus, Sabrina, but you are lovely—not even memory could compare to reality."

Shyly she opened her eyes and found him kneeling on one knee beside her, the other leg resting on the floor. The flickering light from a candle on the small table near the bed danced over his naked chest, the bulge in his tight breeches even more pronounced now, but it was the expression in those jade-green eyes that suddenly made Sabrina breathless. Oh, there was passion and desire to be sure, but there was also another emotion glittering in the depths of those dark green eyes the second before he dropped the concealing lashes, and that emotion had her reaching blindly for him, sheer joy surging through her body.

But gently Brett brushed her arms aside, and he said thickly, "I want to look at you. I've dreamed of you here so often. . . ."

For the first time, Sabrina became fully aware of her surroundings, of the luxurious black velvet that draped the canopied bed, of the barbaric splendor of the huge tiger skin upon which she lay. Her eyes full of wonder, she touched it, marveling at the rough silkiness of the fur, her

381

eyes dazzled by the vivid orange and black stripes, by the very size of it.

Brett moved nearer to her, and bending low, his breath warm on her ear, he muttered, "When I killed it, in India, I always pictured you as you are now upon it . . . pictured *us* together on it."

A thrill shot through her, and her eyes swung to his. Mesmerized, she watched as he slowly, deliberately slid out of his breeches, his manhood springing free and proud before her. There was no embarrassment in his movements; it was almost as if he wanted her to look at him, to see the power and majesty of his naked body.

He was a magnificent animal, all sleek, hard muscles and beautifully proportioned size and strength. Wide shoulders tapered down to narrow hips and long, powerful legs, but Sabrina's eyes were locked on that harshly handsome face, that beloved face, willing him to look at her as he had a moment ago, willing him to come to her with love in his heart.

Possessively his gaze traveled over her, resting briefly on the swollen coral nipples before moving on down her slender length. Sabrina could feel the heat of his look, and when his eyes stopped at the junction of her thighs, it was as if he had touched her there, caressed her there . . . kissed her there. She swallowed agitatedly, incredibly erotic images flashing through her mind, and afraid he could see her thoughts, she closed her eyes.

Wordlessly Brett stared down at her, the blood pounding hotly in his veins, his whole body throbbing with the fierce compulsion to take her now, immediately. Her flame-colored hair was spread out wildly across the tiger's pelt, her slim, lissome body pale gold against the more vivid orange and black stripes, and he had never seen anything quite so achingly lovely in his entire life. She had been fashioned for loving, the full bosom lush and tempting, the slender waist and gently flaring hips perfection, the long, shapely legs flawlessly formed.

With a groan, he slid down on the bed beside her, gathering her hungrily in his arms, his mouth half-savagely, half-sweetly plundering hers. His legs entwined with hers, and he crushed her next to his hard body as if he meant to absorb her into his very being.

His skin felt hot against hers, the roughness of his embrace startling her momentarily, but then, sighing deep in her throat, she eagerly offered herself to him, returning his kiss fervently, her body yielding sweetly to the force of his. Her arms locked lovingly around him; she arched closer to him, delighting in the feel of him against her, the hair on his chest rubbing sensuously against her nipples, the heat and hardness of his manhood caught between their bodies.

Leaving her mouth, he found her nipples again, but only for a moment before his lips slid lower, exciting and alarming her as they traveled down across her belly to the triangle of soft red curls at the top of her thighs. Sabrina gave a small moan when his searching mouth moved even lower and she felt his tongue seeking that most intimate part of her. She stiffened in shocked pleasure when he opened her gently and that warm, invading tongue began to explore her thoroughly there where she had never imagined.

Frightened by the powerful emotions that were surging through her body, she clutched at his dark hair, wanting him to stop, certain she would die if he did stop. A shamed little gasp of ecstasy broke from her as he kneaded her breasts with his hands, his mouth moving carnally against her, his tongue creating havoc with her as again and again he tasted and explored the hot sweetness he had found between her thighs.

The sensations were incredible, like nothing she had ever dreamed, and mindlessly she writhed on the tiger skin, her fingers moving helplessly over his head and shoulders, her body shaking. A sensation, not quite pain, not quite ecstasy, suddenly seemed to focus under Brett's warm, probing tongue, and Sabrina found herself pushing up frantically against his mouth. It was as if every nerve in her body was centered there, and she heard herself sobbing aloud, begging for release, and just when she thought she could bear it no longer, there was such an intense burst of pleasure, such a piercing, sweet throbbing radiating out from her, that her entire body went limp with ecstasy.

She had never felt such pleasure, such incredible contentment, and for several seconds, she lay there, basking in the afterglow of the wonderful things he had done to her. She felt boneless, so exhausted she was certain she could hardly hold her eyes open, but then she felt Brett sliding up across her body, and her pulse jumped.

He raised himself slightly and looked down at her, noting the dilated iris, the soft sheen of perspiration upon her body, and with a slight groan of satisfaction, he parted her thighs with his knees. His eyes were fever-bright and his voice was husky when he said, "This time we'll share it together; this time I want to see your face. . . ."

He touched her lightly with his hand between her thighs, and to her stunned astonishment, she felt passion stir, felt her body responding instantly to his caress. Without volition her arms closed around his shoulders, her eyes fixed dreamily on his.

Brett could stand it no longer; he had held back as long as he could, had managed to momentarily suppress his own hungry desires, but his control was now gone. Sighing deeply, he cupped her buttocks and thrust himself into the warm, satiny sheath of her. She was so tight, so smooth and hot around him, that he gasped for breath, frightened he would spill himself in that instant. His body shook as he gained control, his breath coming in hard little gasps, and then his eyes closed as he moved upon her, delirious bursts of pleasure rippling through his big body.

It was heaven here in her arms, heaven and more to have her with him, to know again the rapture only she could give him, only she had ever given him. He didn't want it to end, didn't want reality, suspicion, and the world to intrude into this warm, wonderful Eden they had created as slowly, tantalizingly he thrust himself into her. She was silken fire beneath him, her fingers warm and encouraging as they caressed his broad shoulders and back, but the pleasure was too much, and almost frenziedly he began to move against her.

Sabrina met his every thrust, her body arching and surging up against his in sensuous rhythms, her long legs tightening around his hips, possessing him as he possessed her. To her amazement she could feel the now familiar sensations that heralded another mind-spinning pleasure peak, and her body stiffened as the first wave lazily surged through her.

Brett felt her response, and opening his eyes with an effort, he stared down at her face and muttered, "Look at me, Sabrina . . . look at me and let me see your pleasure."

Helplessly she did as he commanded, her amber-gold eyes drowsy with passion. His face was tight, the black hair spilling over his forehead, the mobile mouth curved sensually. The jade-green eyes were black with the force of his emotions, and she found it oddly exciting to watch his face as he fought to stave off the incredible physical gratification they both knew was only seconds away.

Suddenly Sabrina couldn't bear it any longer. Pleasure like a sweet shaft of fire cut through her, and helplessly she moaned her joy, her body arching up uncontrollably against his. She could hide nothing beneath his intent gaze, her eyes dilating as the pleasure flowed throughout her entire body, her features softening as the passion ebbed.

The expression on her face was his undoing. His control broke, and he buried his head in her neck, his teeth lightly nipping that sensitive place where her neck joined her shoulder. Ecstasy erupted hotly through his big body. He growled low in his throat, his body thrusting deeply into hers, and then with a sigh he slumped against her.

They lay there a long time together, their bodies entwined, each one unwilling to be the first to break the sweet spell that had been woven around them. And throughout the remaining hours of the night, they spoke of nothing, their bodies saying what neither dared speak aloud as time and time again they sought and found that special joy that comes from knowing the possession of the loved one.

Minutes before dawn, Brett stirred again and looked down at her passion-exhausted face, cursing the years that he had denied himself the ecstasy he had known this night. But never again, he thought grimly. Never again will I let her go. *She is mine!*

Sabrina stirred, as if feeling his intent gaze upon her, and opening her eyes, she caught for one brief, dizzying moment the expression on his face. But he hid it quickly, so quickly that she almost thought she had imagined what she had seen, for the features she looked upon now were once more guarded and sardonic. And for the first time since he had swept her up in his arms, she was suddenly shy. Suddenly aware of her nakedness upon the rumpled tiger skin, suddenly hideously embarrassed at the things he had done to her, the things she had done to him . . . and a delightful flush spread across her face.

Brett smiled faintly at the sight of it, and his voice oddly tender, he said, "A blush, sweetheart? Where is the tigress who has shared my bed all night? The fierce tigress who begged me incessantly to 'please, *please*, please me.' Hmmm?"

Sabrina's flush increased, and she glared at him, tugging futilely at the edge of the soft pelt to cover her nakedness. Brett only laughed and dropped a light kiss on her indignant mouth. "Don't worry," he said huskily, "I won't tease you further." His face changing, a slight frown darkening his brow, he added, "I will, however, see that you are found in your own bed." He flashed her a mocking smile. "Can't have the servants talking."

Confused and uncertain, she watched him as he stood up and casually walked naked across the room to pick up the breeches where he had discarded them last night. The faint light that was stealing into the room kept his body in shadows, but Sabrina needed no sight to know what he looked like. For all time, that magnificent body was imprinted in her brain, imprinted on her own body. . . .

He dressed quickly and then just as quickly gathered her torn gown and other things and tossed them carelessly at her. Before she had time to react, she was scooped up, tiger skin and all, in his strong arms.

Brett glanced down at her, at the red-gold hair, tousled from his lovemaking as much as from the little sleep they had shared, and at the full mouth, swollen a little from his bruising kisses. Her eyes were still languid from their lovemaking, and one naked coral-tipped breast peeked out from the concealing tiger skin. Amazingly, passion stirred through him, but with grim determination, he turned and began to walk out of the bedroom.

More awake now, reality unfortunately beginning to intrude, Sabrina wiggled in his arms and demanded, "Where are you taking me?"

"Where you should have been last night," Brett replied dryly as he kicked open the double doors to the hallway. "To your own bed."

Slowly Sabrina digested that statement, dismay spreading through her. Was he sorry about last night? Did he regret making love to her? *Had* she imagined those expressions on his face that had given her such hope? Such joy?

There was silence as they traveled down the hallways to her room. The servants were beginning to stir in other parts of the house, but none was as yet in these areas, and they met no one on the way.

He pushed open the doors to her own rooms and unerringly made his way to her bedchamber, and unceremoniously dumped her on the pristine coverlet. With a swift flip he jerked the tiger skin out from underneath her, spilling her clothes haphazardly about her. Grinning, he watched as she scrambled to gather them against her nakedness.

Angry and bewildered, the amber-gold eyes glittering dangerously, she half-sat, the remains of the icy green gown clutched to her bosom, and asked furiously, "What do you think you are doing?" She hadn't known what to expect in the morning, hadn't given the morning any thought, but certainly she hadn't been prepared to be treated like a sack of grain!

Brett stared down at her, his hands on his hips, an odd smile playing at the corners of his mouth. "It was either that, sweet madame, or make love to you again."

"Oh," she said in a small voice, pleasure and embarrassment both flooding through her. Unable to look at him, she glanced away and asked in a low voice, "After last night . . . after what . . ." She stopped and then got out bravely, "You said no bargains. What happens now?"

His smile faded, his features becoming hard and grim. Bluntly he said, "We marry."

CHAPTER
TWENTY-SEVEN

Her heart jostling wildly in her breast, Sabrina stared at him speechless. "Marry?" she finally croaked, still not certain she had heard correctly.

The jade-green eyes narrowed and fixed intently on her face, Brett nodded. "Yes. Marry."

In all her wildest dreams, she had never really thought that he would ask her to marry him. Hoped, prayed, longed for, but never had she truly believed that it would come to pass. And while one part of her rejoiced at his words, she was very conscious that there had been no mention of love. . . . She risked a look at his hard features. No, he didn't resemble a man in love to her. A determined, implacable man, yes, but no suitor seeking his beloved.

For a second Sabrina closed her eyes. Oh, dear God, what to do? This moment might never come again; she might never have the chance to reach out and snatch at the dizzying opportunity offered to her. Love, on his part, appeared to have nothing to do with his proposal, but as his wife, wouldn't she have ample time to *make* him love her? And wouldn't it be far better to be his wife than his mistress? She glanced at him from beneath her lashes, and her heart twisted. He was so handsome, so dearly beloved, and yet so *unknown!* Memories of Carlos's tale of the girl in New Orleans and that dreadful interview with Constanza flashed through her mind. Was he really that kind of man? A brutal bully and coldhearted, calculating rogue? Or was he the lover she had known last night? The sardonic and yet generous man she had known these past weeks? She hesitated, torn between the promptings of her heart and the very real fear that she might wake up and find herself married to a monster. Dare she chance it? her mind wondered. Dare she not? her heart demanded.

Fencing for time, as well as trying to understand his motives, she asked huskily, "Why?"

An amused little smile flickered across his face. He stepped nearer the bed, and one hand reached out and lightly traveled down her cheek. "You can ask that, after last night?" he murmured.

It wasn't what she wanted to hear, but it seemed to satisfy something within her. He wanted her. He had never made any secret of that, and she decided grimly that his apparent passion for her body could be a powerful weapon in her hands. He *would* love her! she vowed fiercely. Someday he would love *her* as much as he seemed to want her body, but in the meantime . . .

Brett's voice broke into her thoughts as he said dryly, "I didn't expect you to fall on my neck with joy, but on the other hand, I didn't realize you found the idea of marriage to me to be such a shock." Gently he tipped up her chin, his eyes holding hers. "Once you were willing to marry me. Why the hesitation now?"

"Have you forgotten that I broke off my betrothal to you?" she flashed.

His face tightened, the hold on her chin becoming slightly painful. "I've forgotten *nothing*," he suddenly snarled, anger slashing through him. "Neither that you couldn't decide whether my fortune or Carlos's was the largest, nor that you spurned me when you decided that my fortune wasn't adequate for you!"

Sabrina's jaw would have sagged open in astonishment if Brett's fingers weren't holding it captive, but her eyes did widen dramatically, the shock she felt clearly visible. Only Brett wasn't in the mood to notice her reactions; all the old pain and fury were surging up through him, blinding him to what was before him, and jerking his hand away from her, he said harshly, "But none of that matters now. What matters is that your father put me in charge of you, and I have decided that the best way to discharge my unwanted duties is to marry you." His mouth curved bitterly. "It's what Alejandro would have wanted, and"—his voice hardened—"it's what will happen."

Sabrina started to speak, but hands on his hips, the lean, dark face dangerous, he demanded thickly, "Which will it be? Marriage or mistress?"

Stunned by his earlier statements, infuriated by his current attitude, Sabrina was torn between the desire to split his head open and the equally strong desire to shout yes before the chance was wrested from her. She desperately needed time to think, needed to sort out the astonishing things she had learned in the last twenty-four hours, not the least of these Carlos's damning confession in the coach last night, but it was obvious that Brett wasn't going to give her any time. Angered and frustrated by his manner, she sent him a sparkling look, the amber-gold eyes glittering with rage.

Brett noted the look and raised a mocking eyebrow. "Well?" he inquired coolly. "Am I to have an answer or be treated to a tantrum?"

Nearly choking on the hot wave of anger that swept up through her, Sabrina clenched her hands into fists, and she uttered furiously, "You'll have your answer, you arrogant beast! But be warned—I'll make you a terrible wife! You'll learn to regret forcing me this way, I promise you."

Relief surged through him, but hiding it, sternly quelling the leap of joy his pulse gave at her capitulation, he said with apparent lightness, "Threats, sweetheart? And after such a loving acceptance of my proposal? It was," he added innocently, "an acceptance, wasn't it?" It cost him an effort to treat the matter so casually, but it was either that or betray how much he wanted her to be his wife.

Temper riding her, forgetting her naked state, Sabrina thrust aside the torn garments that partially covered her, and bounding up furiously in front of him, she spat, "Damn you! Yes, the answer is yes!"

Their eyes locked, and her anger evaporated as for one giddy moment, she glimpsed something in the depths of those jade-green eyes that made her joyously eager for their marriage. But only for a second, then his eyes dropped from hers to travel lingeringly down the length of her body. "Good," he muttered, and dragged her into his arms, his mouth closing firmly over hers.

Sweet, hot desire fused their bodies together, Sabrina

390

fervently returning his kiss, her body tingling with anticipation as she felt him swelling against her. But despite his
clearly evident arousal, Brett had no intention of going
further. Grimly he promised himself that when they came
together again, it would be as man and wife. Reluctantly
he lifted his mouth from hers and put her a little from him.
A crooked smile curved his chiseled lips. "You are too
tempting, sweetheart." His gaze caught by the impudent
thrust of her breasts, he added roughly, "Far too tempting." And swinging on his heels, he walked away. At the
doorway he stopped and over his shoulder said, "I'll see the
priest today. The banns can be called on Sunday, and we
will marry within three weeks."

He was gone before Sabrina could reply, not that any
reply was expected or forthcoming, she thought light-
headedly. Dumbly she stared at the torn and scattered
clothing, her mind reeling from the events of the past evening. Had it only been twelve hours since she had left for
the Robles soiree? Only twelve hours in which so much had
happened?

Dazedly she moved about the room, picking up the
scraps of clothing and absent-mindedly stuffing them into
the back of the satinwood armoire that held her gowns.
Lupe was sure to find them and ask embarrassing questions about their state, but at the moment it mattered
little. There were far more important things to think
about.

Walking back to her bed, she lay down, curling up in the
tiger skin he had left behind about her. It reminded her
vividly of Brett—sleek and warm, rough and gentle at the
same time. And in three weeks she would marry him, she
thought with a shiver of half-joy, half-apprehension tingling through her. But then a little smile played across her
full mouth. Oh, but she would make him love her! And her
heart beat faster as she remembered the look in his eyes
before he had kissed her only moments ago. Had it been
love that had flickered there for such a tantalizingly short
time? And last night, just before he had come to her on his
bed, hadn't that same emotion been revealed?

She hugged the tiger skin closer. Could he possibly love
her? Dear God! It was an intoxicating thought. For a long

time she drifted off into a heavenly dream of Brett loving her, of the future that would be theirs, but then, like a serpent in Eden, another thought shattered the dream.

Carlos. Carlos had lied to Brett. And he was condemned by his own admission. It was difficult for her to accept that fact, to realize that a person she had loved and trusted for as long as she could remember had deliberately tried to destroy her happiness. And with a sickening lurch of her stomach, it occurred to her to wonder if Brett had been the only one he had lied to. . . . It was, she admitted painfully, entirely possible, no probable, that Carlos had lied to her, too. That he had abused and taken advantage of the trust and affection she had borne him.

He had confessed that he had told Brett that they had been lovers, and from what Brett had revealed tonight, he had also planted the ugly seed in Brett's mind that she had been more interested in their respective fortunes than in Brett. If he had done that to Brett, why should she doubt that he might have done the same thing to her?

It was an unsettling thought. One which once she would have pushed unceremoniously aside, but not now. Not when she coupled it with Carlos's never-forgotten attack on her in the gazebo and his actions last night. There had been a note of real venom in his voice, and she had sensed a dangerous violence about him.

It had been Carlos, she mused unhappily, who had first sown in her mind the disquieting idea that Brett was a fortune hunter. Carlos who had continually harped on the notion that Brett was only out for money. That not only was he taking advantage of her, but of her father, too.

Sabrina sighed miserably, her thoughts tumbling backward to those days when Brett had suddenly reappeared in her life. If she were honest, she supposed that at first she had used the idea that he might be a fortune hunter to put a protective barrier between them, to give her time to adjust to his dangerously exciting presence. Tía Sofia's letters had certainly not led her to believe that he was a paragon of virtue! she mused defensively. If anything, they predisposed one to be suspicious of him! But it hadn't been until Carlos had recognized him as Devil Dangermond . . .

Her mouth quirked wryly. *Carlos* again. It was still difficult to believe that he had so cruelly set her and Brett
against one another, and yet it was obvious he had. But
had he done it out of malice or out of a misguided attempt
to protect her? Had he honestly believed that Brett was a
fortune hunter up to no good? She sighed again. She was so
confused—and absolutely furious with Carlos. It really
didn't matter *why* he had done his manipulating, all that
mattered was that he had deliberately created mistrust
and suspicion. But even if that were so, even if Brett
hadn't been a fortune hunter—and she no longer believed
that he had been—it still didn't explain his actions with
Constanza Morales.

Honest and forthright herself, Sabrina found it incomprehensible that Carlos and Constanza might have conspired together. She could accept, albeit painfully, that
Carlos had lied to Brett and to herself, but beyond that she
couldn't think. Constanza had been noticeably with child,
and she had named Brett as the father. But like a welcome
ray of sunlight in a dark, frightening maze, Sabrina remembered that it had been Carlos who had told her that
Brett and Constanza were lovers. . . .

Tiredly she rubbed her forehead. Am I so blindly in love
that I will grasp at anything to exonerate him? she wondered dully. Oh, God! but I am confused. All I know for
a certainty is that Carlos is not to be trusted and that I
love Brett Dangermond and will marry him within three
weeks. For now I can look no further.

She slept after that, soundly and deeply, not awakening
until it was late afternoon. Still slightly dazed by all that
had happened, she lay there, staring blankly at the canopy
overhead for several seconds. Then sounds and smells
gradually permeated her tangled thoughts.

Rising up, she noted a tray of coffee and flaky croissants
sitting on the table near her bed. From the aroma and
wisps of steam that came from the silver coffee pot, it
had obviously been placed there only moments before.
Through the door that led to her dressing room, she could
see that the bathtub had been set up and that Lupe was
busily filling it with hot water.

Groggily Sabrina sat up, and after dragging on the robe

that had been placed at the foot of the bed, she poured herself a cup of coffee and called out, "Good morning, Lupe. How are you today?"

"Morning!" Lupe exclaimed with a smile as she walked into the bedroom. *"Señorita,* it is past four o'clock in the afternoon!" Shyly she added, "I would have let you sleep even longer, but Señor Brett said that it was time you got up—he has invited several friends over this evening to drink a toast to your coming marriage." Then, forgetting all her training, she impetuously threw her arms about Sabrina's waist and said excitedly, "Oh, *señorita!* How happy Ollie and I are for you! We have often talked of the situation between you and Señor Brett, and your marriage is what we have wished for these past weeks! It is wonderful, *sí!* We are so happy for you both!"

Lupe's good wishes flowed warmly over Sabrina, but she was a little disturbed at the swiftness of Brett's actions. There were so many barriers yet between them, so much still unknown and unsaid, and Sabrina couldn't help feeling a trifle uneasy at his haste. If only she knew the truth about the past, if only she were certain of what she thought she had glimpsed in his eyes. . . .

Unwilling to spend more time in useless speculation, a happy smile on her mouth, she thanked Lupe for her congratulations. By the time Sabrina had bathed and slipped on a confection of gold silk with amber lace at the demure neckline and short puffed sleeves, she was completely caught up in a rosy dream of the future.

There was a soft glow in the amber-gold eyes, a becoming flush on her cheeks, as she made her way down the inner staircase. The fashionable golden gown enhanced her vivid coloring, and with the flame-red hair artfully arranged in short ringlets over her forehead, the remainder coiled elegantly at the back of her slim neck, she was incredibly lovely.

Brett certainly thought so as he caught sight of her. His heart gave an unruly leap, and he was suddenly flooded with a fierce surge of love. She *was* going to be his bride, and at the moment he didn't really care that his tactics in gaining her hand were questionable. All *is* fair in love and war, he thought cynically.

He had been very busy since he had walked out of Sabrina's bedroom before dawn that morning. The priest had been seen, and the calling of the banns had been arranged, the time and date of the wedding ceremony also. Friends had been notified by quickly scrawled notes delivered by his servants, and this evening a small party had been arranged to introduce Sabrina as his betrothed. He was staking his claim clearly and publicly.

He grimaced. Of course, Francisca and Carlos were bound to cause trouble, but that couldn't be helped, and he was rather certain most people would put their animosity down to spite. And they would be right, he conceded with a slight smile, the memory of this morning's confrontation with Francisca crossing his mind.

He had just returned from seeing the priest when Francisca had arrogantly swept into the library, where he had been busy writing notes to his various acquaintances in the city. He had been surprised that she was still gowned in the clothes of the evening before, but it had taken but a very few minutes for everything to be made clear to him. It had also been obvious that she hadn't talked to her son.

Francisca had been very confident, very arrogant, as she stood there before him. The black eyes full of spiteful glee, she had stated regally, "By now you must know that Carlos has run away with Sabrina. You must also know that I outsmarted you last night and did not spend the night here—I thought you should learn of the elopement and your temper have time to cool before I returned."

When Brett had remained unmoved, Francisca had frowned and demanded, "It doesn't disturb you that my son has run away with your ward? That soon they will be married and"—her eyes swept greedily around the room—"you will have to leave this house and give it back to us."

How he kept his features controlled Brett never knew. Black fury and bone-sagging relief both had thudded through him at the import of Francisca's unguarded words. So. It seemed that last night was to have been an elopement. But had Sabrina been a party to it? he had wondered slowly. Somehow he didn't think so. She had returned to the house, for one thing, and for another, Ollie had been with her. Sabrina was many things but stupid was not among them, and she would have known that Ollie would have had to be eluded for any elopement to be successful. For just a second his gaze had dropped as he had tried to recall the scene last night when he had thrown open the doors and found Sabrina and Carlos there on the banquette below him. He had been too blind with rage to consider the situation then, but now, from a distance, he was certain that Sabrina had been angry with Carlos and that Carlos had been visibly upset. . . . Upset because Sabrina had escaped him?

A little smile had curved his mouth. Carlos must have miscalculated badly, and almost affably Brett had asked Francisca, "Now why do you think I will leave my home and give it to you?"

"Why, because it is ours! Because you must have used Sabrina's money to buy and furnish it," Francisca had replied smugly.

Even now Brett was surprised that he had been as restrained with her as he had, but still there had been a stinging bluntness about his words, and he had quite, *quite* clearly explained the situation to her. Not only his own financial security, but also that she had made a gross mistake about the elopement between Carlos and Sabrina. Mocking amusement glittering in the jade-green eyes, he had murmured, "You really should have been certain of your facts first, *señora*, and I'm positive that as soon as you see your son you will discover your error. As for my ward, she is, I assure you, currently upstairs sleeping, and when she awakes we will be announcing our engagement." He had moved from behind the desk where he had been standing, and meeting Francisca's stunned gaze, he had added coolly, "As her closest relatives, you and your son are naturally invited to attend the small gathering I have arranged for this evening, but under the circumstances, I'll understand if you decline."

Francisca had been utterly chagrined. She had been even more so when it was made chillingly clear that the hospitality of his home would no longer be extended to her. "I'm certain," he had said dryly, "that you will be much happier staying with your friends. The Correias, perhaps?

After all, they took you in last night and are so much more worthy of your company than a mere gringo!"

Her face had been full of fury, and a mottled flush had darkened her skin, but Brett gave her credit. Pride in every inch of her bearing, she had nodded her head haughtily and sailed from the room. Within the hour, she and all her belongings had been gone from his house.

After Francisca had left, he had spent several minutes staring blankly at the top of his desk, wondering if he weren't being a bullheaded ass. Did he honestly believe that Sabrina had been against a runaway match with her cousin? That she had been innocent of any plotting? Or was he so helplessly in love with her that he would grasp at any excuse to exonerate her? No, he didn't think so; he knew that he was remarkably hardheaded but that his instincts seldom failed him, and instinct told him that in this case, at least, Sabrina had not had any knowledge of what had been planned.

That assurance had warmed him a little, until it had occurred to him that it didn't prove she had changed—that his fortune might still be the only reason she had consented to become his wife. In the weeks that she had been here in New Orleans, she had had ample opportunity to realize that she had misjudged his wealth six years ago, and it was entirely possible that she was now intent upon rectifying the earlier error.

A painful little smile had flitted across his harsh features. He didn't believe that, couldn't believe it after last night. She had been too warm, too sweet and yielding in his arms, to be that sort of cold-blooded, calculating creature. There had been an odd innocence about her, and he would have sworn that no other man had ever touched her as he had—that Carlos had lied . . . again.

For a moment, something deadly and dangerous had entered those jade-green eyes. Brett had already caught Carlos out in one lie—Sabrina's virginity that first night they had made love proving that Carlos had deliberately tried to vilify her to him—and he suspected that the other man had been trying to do exactly the same thing last night. Carlos obviously made a habit of lying, and suddenly Brett had remembered the look in Sabrina's eyes when he had snarled out that morning that she had spurned him because his fortune hadn't been large enough. She had been, he would have sworn on his life, genuinely stunned. Was it possible, he had wondered with an unexpected leap in his pulse, that she hadn't broken their original engagement because of money? That it had been some evil lie of Carlos's that had torn them apart?

It was only logical that if Carlos had lied to him, he could just as easily have lied to Sabrina—and Sabrina would have trusted her cousin. Brett might have disliked Carlos on sight, but from things that Alejandro had said, it was obvious that Sabrina had a great deal of affection for her cousin. How very easy, Brett had admitted thoughtfully, it would have been for Carlos to have planted suspicion and mistrust in her mind. Created discord where there should have been none. . . .

Like a man blinded by a heavenly vision, Brett had stood frozen in the middle of the library, a look of dawning hope on his hard face. Might all their differences have been for naught? Might some plain speaking on his part six years ago have saved him all the pain and sorrow he had suffered? It was a heady thought, an intoxicating one, and it had been all he could do to keep himself from tearing from the library and bounding up the stairs to Sabrina's room and pouring out his heart to her. But inbred caution had held him back. He had seen the suffering his father had gone through and knew that loving the wrong woman could be a nearly fatal mistake. Instinct told him that Sabrina was *not* the wrong woman, but fear and wariness counseled him to tread softly. Besides, he was making a lot of sweeping assumptions, and there were things that the possibility of Carlos having lied to Sabrina didn't explain—like the time he had found them making love in the gazebo. . . .

A knock on the door had scattered his thoughts, and throughout the remainder of the day, there had been no further time for introspection. But now, as he stared at Sabrina as she finished her descent, all the pitfalls of their situation came rushing back to him. Was he acting the fool? Was it sheer folly to hope that she felt something for him? That her ardent response in his arms last night had been because she, too, felt the powerful emotion that drove him?

Intently his eyes swept over her, and he could hardly control the violent urge to sweep her into his arms and demand that she love him, but deliberately he forced himself to merely take her hand and drop a light kiss on the inside of her perfumed wrist. "You are very lovely, my dear," he murmured softly, longing to say something less prosaic but oddly bereft of his usual ready tongue.

Her heart beating erratically, Sabrina returned his greeting in a low voice. She was suddenly shy with him, and sending him a look from beneath her long lashes, she found it incredible that only last night she had lain naked in his embrace, known the magic of his possession.

He was very elegant this evening. The black, unruly hair with the attractive sprinkling of silver was brushed and gleaming, the gold and black brocade jacket he was wearing fit his broad shoulders superbly, and the black satin breeches displayed the muscular length of his well-proportioned legs. But it was the expression in those jade-green eyes that increased the already erratic beat of her heart, an expression that gave her hope, that had her smiling radiantly at him.

Brett was dazzled by that smile, dazzled and completely enchanted. The hard features softening, he muttered thickly, "I promised myself to act like a proper suitor these few weeks before our marriage, but if you smile at me like that, I don't think I'll be able to withstand your charms."

Flushed with pleasure, a sweet joy bubbling in her veins, Sabrina smiled even more dazzlingly and teased daringly, "But *should* you?"

Brett threw back his head and laughed. "Witch!" he murmured appreciatively. A smile as brilliant as hers curved his mouth, and for a timeless moment they stood there staring at one another, all the uncertainties of the ugly past forgotten, each one basking in the warmth and charm of the other. But then Brett seemed to shake himself, and, a serious note in his voice, he said bluntly, "Sabrina, I had to ask your aunt to move out of the house this morning. I hope that you will realize that it had to be done . . . especially under the circumstances."

Her smile faded, and she searched his face keenly. She wasn't greatly surprised at his news, nor, if she were honest, very distressed by it. It would be such a relief not to have to listen to her aunt's sly insinuations and grievances about Brett. Hesitantly she asked, "Did you tell her about us? About our coming marriage?"

Brett nodded, a little thrill running through him at the ease with which she had said "our marriage."

"Was she very upset?" she asked, dismayed.

Brett shrugged his broad shoulders and said lightly, "Let's just say that she has even *less* love for me now than she did in the beginning!"

Sabrina made a little face. She hated discord and she wished that Tía Francisca hadn't taken Brett in such violent dislike. "Where did she go?" she questioned unhappily, and glancing at him, added appealingly, "You do understand that I can't just abandon her? She is my aunt, and she was very kind to me when my father died."

Suddenly aware as never before of the deep sense of loyalty Sabrina had for her, unfortunately, unpleasant relatives, Brett bit back the blunt comment he would have liked to make. Quietly he said, "She is welcome to visit you whenever you wish, and I certainly have no objections to you seeing her—I'm no jailer, sweetheart, but I don't want to guard my back for the rest of my life either." He smiled faintly and added, "But to answer your question, she is, I believe, staying with her friends, the Correias."

Sabrina noted that he made no mention of Carlos being welcome, which suited her perfectly, and nodding her head, she said softly, "Yes, of course she would go to them —they are old acquaintances of hers, and I'm positive she will be happy visiting with them, once she gets over the chagrin at being asked to leave your house." She glanced across at him and asked with a twinkle of amusement in the amber-gold eyes, "Were you awful to her?"

Brett looked suspiciously innocent. "No more than I had to be," he answered smoothly.

Sabrina snorted. "Which means you were probably beastly!" she retorted dryly.

He smiled and drew her arm within the crook of his. "But all for a good cause, darling, all for a good cause. And lest you worry, I have already found a new duenna, the widowed sister of my business agent, Mrs. Bonnel, a most worthy woman, I am told. She is waiting in the blue salon for us, and before our guests arrive I would like to introduce you."

Strangely lighthearted, loving him to distraction, Sabrina grinned at him and murmured impishly, "You are, I can see, going to be a *very* managing husband!"

The sweet accord that had so unexpectedly sprung up between them remained through the evening that followed. A soft glow in her eyes, a scintillating smile on her lips, Sabrina was the very vision of a young woman in love as she moved about the blue salon greeting their guests. Brett was little better than Sabrina at hiding his feelings and as the guests left, there wasn't one who wasn't convinced that here was a true love match. Only the two most intimately involved had any reservations, and both were blind to what was so clearly evident to everyone else. Yet if Brett couldn't see that Sabrina was plainly a woman in love, and if Sabrina didn't recognize him as a man obviously besotted, one who was falling deeper and deeper in love with every passing hour, there was a growing sense of peace within them, an increasing hope, a burgeoning, exhilarating anticipation of the future.

Time flew by after that evening, and there existed a tacit agreement between them not to disturb the fragile optimistic mood that prevailed. They avoided all talk of the past, both seeming to draw back from any conversation or comment that would arouse any of their sleeping demons.

The certainty that Carlos had been the root of the disastrous ending of their first betrothal had grown in both of their minds. But Sabrina was conscious that even knowing Carlos's lies had set her against Brett, that still didn't explain Constanza. It troubled her greatly, but she was too much in love to let it stop her from marrying him.

As for Carlos . . . Carlos not unnaturally made several brazen attempts to see her, but Sabrina would have none of him. She didn't want to see him or talk to him just now, afraid he might spread more of his poison and equally afraid that when she saw him, she would forget all the good memories she had of him and allow the contempt and anger she now felt for him to rule her.

There was only one really ugly incident to mar her growing happiness, and that was the unpleasant interview she had with her aunt about a week after the announcement of her betrothal to Brett. Sabrina sought out her aunt when it became apparent that Francisca was not going to accept the inevitable. Calling at the Correia house one afternoon in the first week of June, Sabrina was relieved when Francisca consented to see her.

Relief quickly turned to anger, however, when it became obvious that Francisca had agreed to see her only so that she could heap her fury and bitterness at the situation upon Sabrina's head. Francisca was nearly hysterical with her rage, and it was then that Sabrina learned of Carlos's intention to elope with her the night of the Robles soiree. Appalled by Francisca's blind fury, disgusted and further disillusioned by the ugly knowledge of Carlos's deplorable tactics, Sabrina knew then that her sincere desire to mend the breach with her aunt was fruitless. Rising gracefully from the sofa, she pulled on her lacy gloves and prepared to depart.

Malevolently Francisca stared at her. "Leave the gringo," Francisca said suddenly. "Leave the gringo and marry Carlos, and all will be well. My son loves you, he still wants to marry you." With a desperate intensity, Francisca added, "It was his profound desire to marry you that drove him to even consider a runaway match. You must know that he adores you and would do anything within his power to make you happy."

It was as well that neither Sabrina nor Francisca knew the full extent of what Carlos had planned, but as it was, Francisca's plea didn't sway Sabrina from her path. Sadly she shook her head and said gently, "I cannot, Tía."

Furiously Francisca spat, "If you leave here today, if you refuse to do what I ask, I will never willingly have you in my sight or presence again! Take your choice—your family or the gringo!"

"There isn't," Sabrina replied steadily, "any choice to make."

CHAPTER
TWENTY-EIGHT

The arrival of Brett's parents the following week banished Francisca and Carlos from everybody's minds. Sabrina was delighted to see her aunt after all these years. Sofia was just as delighted to see her only niece, and throwing her arms about Sabrina's neck, she exclaimed, "Oh, my dear! How could we have let so much time pass? Seventeen years! It is unbelievable! And you are just as lovely as I always knew you would be! Come now, tell me *everything!*"

Hugh and Sofia both were absolutely thrilled with the match. "It is what I have always wished for!" Sofia had informed Sabrina that first evening in New Orleans. Her dark eyes sparkling, Sofia had added, "Just think, now you will be not only my beloved niece, but also my best-loved daughter-in-law!"

Time had changed Sofia little. Only a few years from being fifty, she was just a bit plumper than Sabrina remembered; the silky black hair had a few silver strands in it, and the laughing eyes and enchanting smile were exactly the same. She reminded Sabrina vividly of her mother, and spontaneously Sabrina burst out, "You look precisely as I remember Madre."

They were upstairs in the suite of rooms that had been set aside for the senior Dangermonds, and Sofia's smile softened and she walked over to where Sabrina was sitting on a velvet stool. "Dear child, what a lovely thing to say to me!" Her expression a little sad, she added, "If only she were here with us, and your dear father, too—how happy they would be for you!"

Fighting back a sudden impulse to weep, Sabrina nodded her bright head. "I know. I feel it—sometimes, lately, I have felt that they are very close to me and that they are smiling."

Dressing for dinner on the eve of her wedding, Sabrina was reminded again of that conversation, and for one spine-tingling moment, she was certain she heard her father's voice saying, "It is good, *chica,* it is what I wished for you. Be happy."

And later that evening, as they were all sitting around enjoying a glass of wine, the sensation that Alejandro and Elena were nearby was suddenly very strong within her. Oh, but they *would* have been delighted, she mused with a bittersweet pang.

Almost as if sensing her thoughts, Brett stood up, and raising his wine glass high, he said softly, "I would like to offer a toast—to Alejandro and Elena del Torres." His eyes locked on Sabrina's, he added, "May my marriage to their lovely daughter be as full of joy as theirs was."

It was as close to declaring the love he felt for her as Brett could come for the moment. He still had demons to contend with, but like Sabrina, he was putting his trust in the future. In time, he had told himself fiercely, night after night these past weeks, in time, we will be able to speak of the past, and then there will be no shadows between us.

The remainder of the evening passed in a rosy mist for Sabrina, and before she knew it, they were all saying good night and departing for their various bedrooms. Sabrina had thought she would find sleep impossible, but such proved not to be the case. The instant her head hit the pillow, she drifted off into a delicious dream of the wonderful time-to-come that awaited on the horizon.

The wedding was necessarily small, but it didn't matter to Sabrina; she had eyes only for Brett as he stood tall and handsome beside her in the quiet coolness of the St. Louis Cathedral. The priest's words flowed sweetly over her, and softly her responses echoed through the cathedral, Brett's deeper, more ringing tones almost overshadowing hers.

They made a handsome couple, Brett resplendent in a dark blue frock coat of superfine and buff pantaloons, Sabrina glowing in a gown of pale yellow, an overskirt of

404

ivory lace gently billowing out whenever she moved. The cream-colored mantilla that her mother and her aunt had worn at their weddings was draped attractively over her fiery curls. As they slowly walked from the cathedral, now man and wife, Sabrina was reminded of the questions she had asked her aunt on that long ago day when Sofia had married Hugh. *Was* she as lovely a bride as Sofia had been?

Back at the house, where the guests who had been invited to attend the ceremony and the informal luncheon that would follow were gathered, Sabrina had her question answered. Sofia surged up to her and clasping her about the waist, cried out gaily, "You see, my dear, I once said you would make a lovely bride—and oh, pigeon, you *have!*"

Hugh walked up more slowly, relying a little on his silver cane. The black hair was now nearly completely silver, but he was still a very handsome man, and looking down at Sabrina, he said sincerely, "My dear, I am so happy for you. . . ." And glancing across at his son, who stood possessively by her side, he continued half-seriously, half-teasingly, "And I almost regret that I let this young rapscallion talk me into changing my will—you would have made a lovely mistress for Riverview some day." He winked at her and added lightly, "You'll have to watch him—he already gave the family plantation to his younger brother, Gordon. Make certain he doesn't, in one of his wild moods, give away the roof over your head!"

How Sabrina kept her mouth from falling open she never knew. It had been *Brett* who had not wanted Riverview, not Hugh who had disinherited him! She swallowed painfully. Oh, *Dios!* Here was more proof that she may have terribly misjudged the situation all the years before. But I have a second chance, she thought with relief. A second chance to *trust* my love.

Morgan and Leonie Slade joined them just then, and Sabrina had no time for further speculation. Proudly Morgan presented his wife, and Sabrina felt herself immediately drawn to the small, honey-haired young woman. Sea-green eyes reflecting her own instinctive liking, Leonie said warmly, "It is a pleasure to meet you, Madame Dangermond, and I want to extend my most sincere wishes for your happiness."

Shyly Sabrina thanked her and then added, "And you? Am I not to offer congratulations, too?"

Leonie beamed. *"Mais oui!* Our sweet *bébé,* Suzette, is now almost six weeks old and simply adorable!" Leonie instantly blushed and contritely added, "I should not say such things about my own daughter, but I cannot help it!"

They talked happily for several moments, and before Leonie and Morgan moved on, the invitation to visit them at Château Saint-André was issued again. Morgan's blue eyes glinted with amusement as he said to Brett, "Fox's Lair is only a day's ride from us—and now that your wanderings are over, you have no excuse not to come and visit."

Brett grinned and murmured, "You will allow me time for a honeymoon first?" His arm had slid around Sabrina's waist, and looking down at her, he said huskily, "I've waited a long time for this moment, and I'm afraid I'll want my wife all to myself for quite a while."

Sabrina flushed, and everyone laughed. Laughter seemed to be the order of the day, everyone enjoying themselves immensely.

It had been decided that Sabrina and Brett would leave for Fox's Lair in the morning. Hugh and Sofia would remain in New Orleans for a bit longer before joining the newlyweds, and her gaze mischievous as she helped Sabrina prepare for bed that night, Sofia said, "Entertaining your in-laws on your honeymoon is not what I would have wished for you, pigeon, but we will not stay long, and then in the fall, perhaps you and Brett will come up to visit us in Natchez, *sí?* As for now, I will leave you—your husband awaits you!"

Sabrina nodded, and with a mixture of apprehension and anticipation, she watched Sofia sweep out of the room. Left alone in Brett's bedroom, she moved aimlessly about, her heart catching in her throat when she heard the outer doors open.

Nervously she pleated the delicate gossamer silk of the enticing lavender peignoir she was wearing, wondering about the night to come. Would it be as wonderful as the other nights she had lain in his arms?

Brett suddenly appeared in the archway, his emerald-green robe intensifying the color of his eyes. For a timeless moment they stared at each other, and then, with a smothered groan he dragged her into his arms. Their mouths met, and when at last they parted, they were both breathless. Thickly Brett muttered, "How I've stood these past weeks, I'll never know, sweetheart. But no more now, sweet tiger lily, you're mine . . . my wife." Sweeping her up into his arms, he carried her to the bed, and all through the long, passionate night that followed, Sabrina learned explicitly that this night was every bit as wonderful as the others. More so, she thought dreamily as she lost herself in the joy of his embrace—he was her husband now, she his wife, and nothing was ever going to come between them again. *Nothing*.

Fox's Lair, Sabrina discovered two days later, was, as Brett had warned her, not a large house. It was two-storied, only the center-pedimented portico, supported by four fluted columns, saving it from being plain. The second-floor gallery had wrought-iron railings, and dark green shutters graced the many long windows of the pristine white house.

Tall oaks draped with gray-green Spanish moss grew nearby, and the long drive leading to the house had been lined years ago with more of the sprawling trees. Despite the unprepossessing facade of Fox's Lair, Sabrina wasn't the least disappointed. If Brett had wanted to sleep on the bare ground, she would have been happy to do so.

His arm around her waist, he escorted her up the stairs to the house and said almost hesitantly, "I know it's not much to look at right now, but I intend to change all that. We can add on a wing or two, and you can make whatever alterations you like. . . . I want you to be happy here."

Sabrina smiled mistily at him. "I will be," she promised softly, and Brett felt a tight knot of fear disappear within him. He had been afraid she would summarily dismiss the house, the stubborn suspicion that she coveted wealth not quite banished.

Fox's Lair might have had a plain exterior, but Brett

had richly furnished the interior—silk-hung walls, velvet drapes, and luxurious carpets had been used throughout the house. Gilt-edged mirrors, sofas done in fine silks and tapestries, marble-topped tables, and elegantly crafted chairs and other furnishings were tastefully arranged in the various rooms. But it was the latticed gazebo that made Sabrina exclaim out loud with delight and joy.

Her eyes sparkling with pleasure, she impulsively flung her arms about his strong neck and cried, "You remembered!"

"How could I ever forget?" he asked roughly, hugging her to him, his mouth compulsively seeking hers.

The past still lay between them, but they were each unwilling to destroy this magical spell. And it was a magical spell. Hugh and Sofia's visit to Fox's Lair came and went, the days that followed their departure passing Brett and Sabrina by in a dreamy haze.

In early July, however, news reached them that created a little cloud on their happy horizon. The Spanish were once again crossing the Sabine River into American Louisiana and had occupied the post at Bayou Pierre, near Natchitoches. The threat of war between the two countries was in the air. Brett had learned of the worsening situation in a letter from a friend in New Orleans and had mentioned it to Sabrina. Remembering the men and arms that had been massing in the Nacogdoches area for months before she had left that spring for New Orleans, she asked worriedly, "What will happen? Do you really think that Spain and the United States will go to war?"

Brett pulled her into his arms and resting his head on the top of hers, said soberly, "I don't know. I just don't know. It could come to that—certainly many people here think that it will." His mouth quirked. "Some probably even hope so."

It was a terrifying thought, and Sabrina shivered. "Would you go and fight?"

Brett shrugged. "Once I might have, but now . . ." He tipped her head back. "But now I have too much to live for . . . ."

The subject was dropped, but it stayed in the back of Sabrina's mind. Was she just to have found her love, only to lose him in a senseless war? Any loyalty she might have harbored for Spain vanished. She was Brett's wife, and Spain and all it stood for could disappear in a cloud of smoke! In fact, she decided tautly, she hoped that the potentially dangerous situation on the Sabine River would do just that!

A note from Leonie inviting them for a visit during the first week of August pushed aside thoughts of war. Sabrina looked forward to strengthening the feeling of friendship she had experienced upon meeting Leonie. The news that another couple, Jason and Catherine Savage, would also be visiting and were looking forward to meeting Brett and Sabrina had her impatient for the journey to Château Saint-André.

Château Saint-André was situated near a bend in the Mississippi River, some miles below New Orleans, and Sabrina thought the immaculate, stately house was absolutely lovely. An elegant horseshoe-shaped staircase swept gracefully up to the second floor of the house, and Brett and Sabrina's little cavalcade—the gig in which they were riding and the small wagon occupied by Ollie and Lupe and the various necessities for a stay of several days—had hardly reached the beginning of the circular driveway when Morgan, Leonie, and the Savages appeared, coming down the stairs to greet them.

The next few minutes passed in a flurry of greetings and introductions. Shyly Sabrina acknowledged the Savages, slightly in awe of the tall, emerald-eyed gentleman with the hawklike features and the flawlessly beautiful black-haired woman who was his wife. But Catherine's warm smile and sweet nature soon disarmed her completely, and Jason's utterly charming manner had her relaxed and laughing within seconds.

The remainder of the day passed by pleasurably. Brett and Sabrina were shown through the house and over the grounds. And then, of course, there were the children. . . .

Just before changing for dinner, the women gathered upstairs in the airy nursery that had only recently been constructed, and Sabrina was completely enchanted by the children. She fell helplessly in love with Justin Slade on sight. At six years of age, he looked very much like his father, Morgan, except he had Leonie's great sea-green eyes, and Sabrina suspected that in another dozen years or less he would be breaking hearts. If Justin looked very much like his father, young Nicholas Savage, approaching two and half years of age, was a miniature of Jason. Except when he smiled, his entire little face changed and there was no doubt that Catherine was his mother. That fact was especially true in the case of the younger Savage son, Randall, just over a year old. Randall had smoky purple eyes, not quite the clear shade of violet of his mother's, but the generous curve of his baby mouth and the stubborn line of his small chin were definitely inherited from Catherine.

Almost with envy, Sabrina watched the three boys play on the floor with some wooden soldiers, and she was aware of a sudden fierce hunger for a child of her own. Catherine caught the unguarded expression and said softly, "Next year, my dear, you will probably be proudly showing us *your* offspring."

"Oh, I do hope so!" Sabrina breathed, and it suddenly occurred to her that since she'd married Brett, she hadn't . . . A look of delighted wonder crossed her face. Was it possible? That already?

Leonie, with the baby, Suzette, in her arms, laughed and murmured, "Ah, but which shall it be—a handsome son, or a beautiful daughter? Now come and see my petite Suzette."

Suzette Slade was the most exquisite little thing Sabrina had ever seen—fine, delicate features, a rosebud mouth, petal-soft skin, and a tiny head covered with wispy black curls. Nearing three months of age, Suzette was undeniably adorable, and Sabrina sighed with longing. Oh, if only her sudden suspicion were true!

Dinner that evening was thoroughly enjoyable, and afterward, the gentlemen remained in the dining room savoring their cigars and brandy while the ladies retired to the front salon to discuss the plans for the morrow. It was then that Brett was able to have his long-awaited conversation with Jason.

The three men talked aimlessly for several minutes, but eventually Morgan, seated at the head of the long linen-covered table, observed forthrightly, "This is a very friendly, pleasant conversation we're having, but shouldn't we be talking about the one thing that interests us the most—the current state of affairs between our country and Spain?"

Jason grimaced, and Brett smiled ruefully. "I suppose," Brett said slowly, "we've simply been putting off the inevitable—not wishing to spoil a lovely day."

Morgan snorted. "It won't be a lovely day for any of us if war comes!"

Thoughtfully Jason toyed with his brandy snifter. "It is going to be very interesting when Wilkinson confronts the Spanish, I'll wager you that. The Secretary of War, Dearborn, ordered him posthaste to the Sabine River area weeks ago, but our good General seems intent upon taking his own sweet time leaving his headquarters at St. Louis." He glanced across the table at Brett. "What's your opinion? Morgan told me about your letter from Eaton." He smiled wryly and added, "And about Jefferson—remind me to tell you one day of the 'mission' the President sent me on to England a few years ago."

Brett grinned back at him. "I'd like to hear of it—at least you went to a civilized place!" But his grin faded a little, and he said heavily, "If you gentlemen will indulge me a bit, I'd like to present a theory to you." He shot Morgan a slightly mocking look. "Morgan has heard part of it before, but I'm certain he would like to again, just so he can point out how ridiculous it is."

Morgan raised his snifter and murmured, "Go ahead—fairy tales have always enchanted me!"

Ignoring Morgan's comment, Brett glanced at Jason, who was watching him intently. Briefly, keeping events in as much of a sequence as he could, Brett told of the conversation between himself, Wilkinson, and Hugh on that stormy night in November of 1799. "That," he admitted with a little smile, "was when my interest was first aroused." Taking a deep breath, he plunged on, telling about Jefferson's request last year that he keep an eye on Burr and Wilkinson; of the conversation with Burr the night of Stephen Minor's ball in Natchez; and lastly, of the persistent rumors that circulated in dark places that Wilkinson had murdered Gayoso and that an important piece of paper had disappeared the night the Governor had died. . . .

Apologetically, Brett looked at the other two. "Having bored you with all that, I'll now present my theory, and you'll see the connection with the events on the Sabine River."

"Before you do," Morgan said with a frown, "I'd like a word with Leonie—it could have some bearing on what you have told us so far." He walked from the room, and finding Leonie with the other women, he smiled politely to Catherine and Sabrina and asked, "May I steal my wife for a few minutes?"

In the foyer, Morgan turned to Leonie and asked softly, "Would you mind telling Brett and Jason about being at the governor's mansion the night Gayoso died?" He smiled at her warmly, a teasing glint in the dark blue eyes. "You don't have to tell them about us!"

Leonie frowned for a moment, then shrugged her shoulders. Love shining in her gaze, she murmured, "If it pleases you."

Leonie's tale of sneaking into the Governor's mansion all those years before held Brett and Jason spellbound. An embarrassed flush staining her cheeks, she said fiercely, "You do understand that it was only to get my grandpere's gaming vowels? I am no thief!" Both men nodded instantly, neither wishing to insult her, and once the tale was told, Brett asked eagerly, "Leonie, when you were watching through the window, did you see the fat man, Wilkinson, take anything from the Governor's desk?"

Leonie's forehead creased in thought, trying to remember an event that had happened almost seven years before. "They were angry with each other . . ." Her face suddenly cleared, and she added excitedly, "Oh! I never saw Wilkinson take anything, but at one point, the Governor had a piece of paper in his hand and he thrust it toward the General. The General seemed fascinated by that paper and frightened by it at the same time, too, I think."

"Anything else?" Morgan prompted gently.

"There was something about a report to the Viceroy . . ." Her lip drooped. "I didn't see or hear very much

412

because I was so terrified of being seen," she admitted forlornly.

Brett smiled encouragingly at her and asked curiously, "But in what you did see, was there anything that struck you as strange, anything that made you wonder?"

Leonie stiffened as if just suddenly remembering something. Her eyes widening, she muttered, *"Mon Dieu, oui!* I had nearly forgotten—when I had to slip past the doorway that separated the two rooms, I risked a glance inside. The Governor was acting strangely—his face was all contorted as if in pain, but the General didn't seem to be concerned. If anything he seemed pleased. . . ."

They all looked at each other, and Morgan said hastily, "Thank you, my love. I'll explain all," he promised with smile, "later. But for now, would you mind if we continued our speculations in private?"

Leonie made a little face. "For now," she agreed reluctantly.

There was silence in the room for a second after Leonie left. Then Brett said aloud the thought that was in each of their minds. "Poison! The bastard poisoned Gayoso! It had to be!"

The other two nodded their heads in agreement, Jason saying slowly, "It certainly sounds that way."

It was Morgan, however, who asked dryly, "But what does all that ancient history have to do with today?"

"Since I can postpone the evil moment no longer, I'll tell you," Brett said grimly. "I believe that there *was* a map drawn by Nolan and meant for Wilkinson's eyes alone, only somehow it ended up in Gayoso's hands, and Wilkinson murdered him for it." He looked at the other two, and seeing their interest, he continued, "Let's say that the map led to a treasure," and when Morgan snorted, Brett added warningly, "You have to remember Wilkinson's reactions to my father's idle comment about Aztec treasure—he nearly jumped out of his skin! He and Nolan were going to go after the treasure, but before their plans were fully realized, the Spanish killed Nolan."

Vaguely Brett was aware of the muscles tightening in Jason's face, and he had the definite impression that speaking of Nolan's death brought the other man pain. He

413

hesitated, but Jason sent him a twisted smile and said, "Nolan was a good friend to me—a mentor in my misspent youth. But go on with your tale."

"Theory," Morgan said with affection.

Brett sent him a look of friendly exasperation, but not to be sidetracked, said doggedly, "After Nolan's death in the spring of 1801, the Spanish were especially skittish—they didn't want any foreigners in their territory, and it would have been impossible, with the way they were watching the borders, for anybody to get into Spanish Texas to retrieve the treasure. Besides, if Wilkinson is in the pay of Spain, he'd have to be willing to completely sever a profitable association. He could afford no mistakes. And with Nolan dead—Nolan, his most trusted tool and, incidentally, the only man who really knew the country they would have to travel through—I think Wilkinson got cold feet and decided not to risk it . . . until now."

"Why now?" Morgan asked, his interest piqued.

"Because now and for the past year or so, the threat of a war with Spain has been in the air. . . . And then there is Aaron Burr and the rumors that he means to invade Mexico. Burr and Wilkinson, an unholy pair if there ever was one."

Jason nodded his head. "I think I begin to see what you're getting at—Wilkinson is never out in the open with his schemes; there is always someone for him to hide behind, first Nolan and now Burr. He'll let Burr be the figurehead, let Burr make his plans, appear to totally support whatever Burr says, but behind Burr's back, Wilkinson will be weaving his *own* plans. . . ."

Thoughtfully Morgan mused, "By letting Burr be the figurehead, the good General also has the option of deserting Burr at any time things look too risky."

"Precisely!" Brett said harshly. "If Burr can gather the men and arms he really needs to make a successful invasion of Mexico, then Wilkinson will throw his lot in with him—and seek out the treasure in the wake left behind. Or even if Burr fails in his scheme, then there is the current situation—war with Spain and the invasion of Spanish territory by United States troops. All Wilkinson has to decide is which way will benefit him the most. I think the reason

414

he is lingering in St. Louis is simply that he's waiting to see which way to jump. Once he positions his troops along the Sabine River, he'll have no choice but to attack the Spanish, and he probably doesn't want to do that until he is absolutely certain that he can get his hands on the treasure. Then whatever relationship he has with Spain won't matter anymore."

"There is only one thing that bothers me," Morgan protested seriously. "Your entire theory rests upon the notion that there *is* a treasure out there. We have no proof."

"Yes, we do," Jason said abruptly. And at the expression of surprise on the other two men's faces, he stood and slowly began to roll up the sleeve of his fine linen shirt. "I told you that Nolan had been my mentor. What I didn't reveal was that on a horse-trading trip we made to the Palo Duro Canyon area about fifteen years ago, we stumbled across a treasure, an Aztec treasure." His shirt sleeve pushed up nearly to his shoulder, Jason pointed to the heavy gold and emerald arm band that encircled his muscular upper arm. "And *this* is proof that the brandy hasn't gone to my head." His face sad, Jason muttered, "Nolan had the twin to it . . . and I think now that it was probably what he used to convince Wilkinson the treasure existed, and I *know* that it was what got him killed." He could not speak of Davalos, the Spanish lieutenant who had once been his friend and who had killed Nolan, nor of what Davalos had cost him and Catherine, but his voice hardening, he added, "The treasure does exist, believe me."

Brett whistled softly under his breath, and Morgan stared dumbly at the gold and emerald arm band. Finally, in a contrite voice, Morgan said, "I owe you an apology, Brett."

"Yes, but how can we prevent Wilkinson from using his quest for the treasure to start a war with Spain, or just as bad, to encourage Burr to invade Mexico?" As soon as he said the words, Brett knew the answer. His jade-green eyes narrowing, he growled, *"The map!* If we get the map, Wilkinson would have no reason to support Burr or, just as importantly, to provoke a war with Spain. There would be nothing for him in Spanish Texas."

"I agree," Morgan said immediately, "but it isn't going to be easy. The instant one of us shows up nosing around, he's going to be on his guard. Besides, where to look? He must have it well hidden."

Jason smiled widely. "Everything you say is true, but I think, Morgan, you have forgotten someone."

"Who?" Morgan asked with a frown.

"Blood Drinker!" Jason said with satisfaction. "He can get into Wilkinson's camp, and remember, he was with me on the trip when the treasure was discovered. He would recognize the map, and there is *nowhere* Wilkinson could hide the map that he wouldn't find it!"

"Who is Blood Drinker?" Brett demanded immediately, his eyes moving from one man to the other.

It was Jason who answered. "Blood Drinker," he said softly, "is a Cherokee, a blood brother to me. We share much together, and our thoughts about a war with Spain are the same. But more importantly, he doesn't like the idea of *anyone* disturbing that treasure site. He says it is a bad place and should remain hidden." Jason smiled slightly. "And for our purposes of getting the map, he is perfect—who pays any attention to an Indian? And Blood Drinker is *very* adept at concealing himself. No one would ever even notice him, and I'm certain that he's the only one who could find that map for us."

They discussed the situation for several more minutes, agreeing that Jason would see Blood Drinker and have him strike out instantly for Wilkinson's camp. Reluctantly Brett said, "I hate leaving it in someone else's hands, but I think it is our wisest course."

"It is," Jason replied seriously. "Trust me, Blood Drinker will get the map."

They left the dining room after that, joining the ladies in the front salon. The decision to send Blood Drinker in search of the map lifted a weight from Brett's mind, and he found himself relaxing completely for the first time since news of the Spanish crossing of the Sabine River. Now if only Blood Drinker was every bit as good as Jason implied . . .

CHAPTER TWENTY-NINE

The visit at Château Saint-André proved to be so enjoyable that it was mid-August before Brett and Sabrina returned to Fox's Lair. The place was beginning to feel like home, and recalling all the unhappy events that had taken place at the ranch near Nacogdoches, Sabrina realized that Fox's Lair was where she wanted to live forever. She had found happiness here, and though the dark murky bayous with their knobby-kneed cypress trees, knife-sharp palmettos, and reed-lined banks, the acres of tall sugar cane and the moss-draped oaks and leathery-leaved magnolia trees that dotted the land near the house bore no resemblance to the area she had grown up in, Sabrina found that the region had a charm all its own. A lazy, primeval charm that drew her and brought a strange peacefulness. She had found happiness here, her husband was here, and her child would be born here. . . .

The startling thought that she might be pregnant had become a certainty within her as the days passed, and by the time they returned home, she was positive that already there would be outward signs. With disappointment she had looked at her naked body in the cheval glass that was in her small dressing room, the morning after their return from Château Saint-André. Surely her breasts would be fuller, her waist thickening, and her stomach rounding by now? Then she giggled. She couldn't even be two months pregnant yet, but she was impatient for the signs of her impending motherhood to appear.

She hadn't told Brett of her wonderful discovery, an odd sense of shyness flooding her whenever she thought about it. What would he think? Would he be happy? Displeased? Indifferent? She sighed. Even though they had been married for almost two months, there were still many barriers between them.

Brett was still a stranger to her in many respects in spite of their intimacy. He was an ardent lover, and while they had separate bedrooms, there had been no night since their marriage that he hadn't spent at least part of the night in her bed. Except during Hugh and Sofia's visit and the visit at Château Saint-André, Brett was seldom around during the daylight hours. He was often gone at sunrise, supervising the men who worked the huge sugar cane fields, and some days, the only time she saw him was when he came to her bed late at night. There were days, however, when she had his undivided attention, days when he took her over the plantation, proudly showing her the sugar mill, the plantation gardens, the wharf he was having built at the river's edge, and the lands that were being wrested from the swampy wilderness by a series of levees. She treasured those days, but she was also aware that there was a part of him that he kept aloof, a part of him that she could not share. There were times when she would surprise an odd look on his face, a questioning look, almost as if he didn't quite believe she was everything she appeared to be, and she longed to reach out and touch him and ask, "What is it? Why do you look at me so?" But she was afraid to, afraid that she would shatter the bond between them.

There was a deep core of reserve within her, too, and though she tried to hide it, she was conscious that she didn't fool Brett all the time. Too often when she had withdrawn from a particular topic of conversation, she had seen his eyes narrow, seen speculation leaping in those jade-green depths.

Able to look back on the past with new eyes now and armed with her new knowledge of Carlos, Sabrina understood how effortlessly her cousin had practiced his duplicity. He had told Brett one thing and her another, had fanned her uncertainties, had spread vicious lies to Brett; it wasn't surprising that they had parted as they had. But had Carlos lied about the girl in New Orleans? And had he had *anything* to do with what Constanza had told her?

She was bitterly conscious now that she should have

418

faced Brett with what she had been told, should have given him a chance to defend himself, instead of blindly trusting in Carlos. And her stomach crawled with humiliation whenever she thought about revealing how gullible, how mistrustful, she had been. But it was one thing to want to believe that everything that had happened had been a base plot of Carlos's and another to know it without a doubt. And it was as much shame at her earlier crass actions as the fear buried within all the lies, that there was some measure of truth about what had happened that kept her from forcing a confrontation with Brett. Painfully she acknowledged that she was a coward—if he was innocent, she didn't want him to look at her with disgust and contempt for being so willing to condemn him unheard, and if he was guilty, she didn't want to know that he had cravenly deserted Constanza and his own unborn child.

The fact that he had never mentioned love to her also preyed on her mind. He had never made any secret of wanting her physically, but though there were intriguing, heart-fluttering hints in the things he said and did, he had never said, "I love you." Was it only passion for her body that drew him to her? It was a dismal thought, and unhappily Sabrina turned away from the cheval glass and reached for her robe.

She was very quiet that morning at breakfast, and Brett sent her a quizzical glance. "Is something wrong?" he asked quietly.

She hesitated, wondering what his reaction would be if she suddenly said baldly, "I want you to tell me about Constanza. I want to know if you really loved her and if you did indeed abandon your unborn child." But she didn't, and ashamed at her own cowardice, she said the first thing that came to her mind. "What will happen to the Rancho del Torres now that I live here with you?"

"What do you want to happen to it?" Brett inquired warily. A faint note of reserve in his voice, he added, "I know that Fox's Lair isn't nearly as grand, although I do have plans to build a larger house in the future." He watched her face closely. "Would you prefer that we live at the ranch?"

That note in his voice bothered her, reminding her viv-

419

idly that there were still dangerous pitfalls in their relationship. Somewhat stiffly, she answered, "I think that if you wish to live here, we should put a competent overseer in charge of the *rancho* or sell it and buy more lands here in Louisiana."

She hadn't quite answered his question, and Brett was aware of an angry impatience within himself. Why, because she had asked a perfectly ordinary question about her old home, did he have to immediately assume it was because she had found the home that he had provided wanting? Why, after all these weeks, did he still look for some sign that material things meant more to her than he did? Because there is a part of her that I cannot touch? Because, though I have her in my arms, I feel that I do not have all of her? Because I don't know for certain what she really feels for me?

Frustration eating at his gut, he finished breakfast silently, not tasting one bite of the spicy grillades that had been so expertly prepared for him. The fact that he had ramrodded Sabrina into marriage with him, that he had not actually allowed her to make a choice, had begun to take on immense significance in his mind. As the weeks passed and he fell more and more in love with her, realized how very much she meant to him, had *always* meant to him, instead of becoming more confident and complacent about their relationship, he grew more and more tense and intolerant of the situation.

This morning was the first time that either one of them had mentioned Nacogdoches, and for one moment he actually toyed with the idea of asking her bluntly why she had broken her engagement with him six years ago. Had it been because of lies spread by her damned cousin or had it been because she had really thought he had no prospects at all? His fists tightened, rage billowing through him. If he found out that Carlos had indeed been behind her actions, he really didn't think he could deny himself the pleasure of killing the other man. But Brett wouldn't allow himself to speculate further on this particularly painful subject. He had told himself it didn't matter, but he had found it did, and he knew that soon he was going to demand some an-

swers from her. He *had* to know the truth about the past;
the uncertainty was tearing him apart.

During the next few weeks, instead of the tension that
had sprung up that morning lessening, it seemed to increase. Brett was aware that something new had entered
their relationship, but he couldn't put his finger on it. Sabrina seemed more introspective, more removed from him,
and he became both angry and concerned about it. Feeling
as if she were slipping away from him, as if a widening
chasm were separating them, Brett was aware of an icy
lump forming where his heart should be. Had he come this
far only to inexplicably lose her in the end? Lose her to an
enemy he couldn't see? Couldn't fight?

Sabrina wasn't deliberately shutting Brett out, but lost
in the wonder of the exciting changes that were happening
within her, she inadvertently put him at a distance. The
baby was a precious secret she hugged to herself, longing
to tell him and yet . . . What if he didn't share her joy? Babies, like the past, were things they hadn't discussed.

September proved to be especially hot and humid, and as
the sugar cane ripened in the fields, so did Sabrina's body.
With delight she noted her fuller bosom, her thickening
waist, and at the oddest times an enchantingly satisfied
little smile would flit across her face. That smile infuriated
Brett for some reason. It was as if she had some private secret, and he found himself eaten up with jealousy. What
was she thinking when she looked like that?

As the month waned, the sugar cane took on a purplish
tinge, and Brett knew that the crucial season was near.
The Big Grass, as it was called, never fully ripened here in
Louisiana, and Brett was very aware that he could delay
only so long before harvesting—it was an annual race between the weather and the planter's judgment. And once
the order had been given, the plantation became a hive of
activity, cutters, loaders, and haulers beginning the hard,
back-breaking work of clearing the cane.

October came and the work continued, Brett returning
late at night almost exhausted, too exhausted even to seek
Sabrina's bed. She took to waiting up for him, making certain that a hot bath awaited him no matter what the hour
and that a plate of bread, meat, and cheeses was prepared

for him. The third week of October, while there was still much to do, there was an easing of the tension that always accompanied harvest time. The sugar mill was running almost twenty-four hours a day, and in spite of this being a time of long hours and little rest, there was a crackling vitality in the air. The slaves liked it—it brought the promise of extra reward, of drinks and songs and at the end a grand ball.

Returning home very late one night, Brett tiredly walked up the stairs to his room, a pleased smile on his face. He was going to sleep the day away tomorrow. One day, at this stage, wouldn't make a difference.

Entering his room, he was surprised to find Sabrina still waiting for him, and tossing aside his wide-brimmed, sweat-stained white hat, he murmured, "You should have gone to bed. I didn't think you would still be awake."

She smiled at him, noting the lines of fatigue on his face. Softly she said, "I never get to see you these days except for now, and I wasn't about to be cheated."

Stripping off his shirt, he glanced over at her as she stood by the big brass tub that had been set up for his bath. She was wearing a gauzy nightdress and peignoir, the candlelight on a table behind her silhouetting her body, making him instantly aware of the soft, yielding flesh they covered and how long it had been since they had made love. Sabrina turned just then, presenting him a sideview, and his breath caught in his throat.

She was four months pregnant, and the rounding of her belly that she had so impatiently looked for two months previously was now clearly evident. Brett was conscious of a sudden, dizzying rush of blood to his head. His voice almost a whisper, he croaked, "Why didn't you tell me?"

For a second Sabrina didn't know what he was talking about, but then she noticed that his eyes were locked on her gently protruding stomach, and she said breathlessly, "Because I didn't know how you would feel."

"How I would feel?" he repeated dazedly as he walked toward her. Then he gave a delighted little laugh and scooping her up in his arms, whirled her about the room. "Oh, God!" he muttered. "I don't know how I feel—pleased, excited, perhaps a little afraid."

"Afraid?" she asked with surprise. "Why?"

"What if something goes wrong?" There was naked fear in his eyes as he said thickly, "What if something happens to you?"

Sabrina smiled reassuringly at him, suddenly feeling so much stronger and wiser. Her arms were about his neck, and she kissed him on his chin, the stubble of the day's whiskers pleasantly scratching her lips. "I am strong as a horse—look at Tía Sofia. There'll be no trouble, I promise you."

He hadn't said that he loved her, but his obvious fear for her safety wrapped a warm little glow around Sabrina's heart. That and his obvious delight in the news. And he *had* been delighted.

Depositing her gently on his big bed, he kissed her with a sweet restraint, as if she were very fragile. Wonderingly he said, "I've never thought of being a father before, but I find the idea suddenly greatly appealing." An endearingly uncertain expression crossed his face. "Will I be a good father, do you think?"

Sabrina giggled, loving him so much. "An exemplary one," she replied gravely, a twinkle in the amber-gold eyes. It was times like this that she had no regrets, no fears for the future, times like this that banished any reservations about the past.

Lying next to her, Brett's hand moved possessively down to her stomach, gently caressing it. His eyes warm and tender, he demanded huskily, "When?"

"Late March, I think." She pulled his face down nearer hers and rained soft little kisses over his nose and mouth. "You are very potent, *señor*. Our baby will be born practically nine months to the day after our wedding."

"Do you mind?" he asked with a sensuous curve to his mouth.

She shook her head. "No. My parents had to wait years and years; I am glad we do not." She smiled impishly at him. "Besides, I want many, many babies."

"Oh, God!" he breathed thickly, "I'll do my best, tiger lily, I swear I will." He kissed her with a gentle hunger, and when she moved suggestively beneath him, the bath was instantly forgotten for a long time. . . .

423

They entered a new state in their life together, the delight of the coming baby momentarily pushing the dark clouds away. The second week of November, Brett had to leave for a meeting with his business agent in New Orleans, and a little forlorn at being left behind, Sabrina watched him as he moved about his room making certain that Ollie had overlooked nothing in the packing. Brett caught sight of her expression, and putting his arms about her, he asked, "Are you certain you don't want to come with me?"

She looked down at her expanding stomach and said ruefully, "You will not be gone more than a few days, and I think I would be more comfortable here." The pregnancy was proving to be an easy one but the week before she had been ill with chills and a fever, and she was still not fully recovered.

Reluctantly Brett bid her good-bye and left for New Orleans. He arrived to find the city full of news. News that both relieved and alarmed him. Had he been wrong about the map and Wilkinson, after all? Wilkinson, it appeared, had finally arrived at Natchitoches with his army in late September, and instead of commencing the war that everyone had expected, on November 5th, he had signed the Neutral Ground Treaty with the Spanish. The Spaniards were to retire to Nacogdoches; the Americans to Natchitoches, and the General had been quick to trumpet his triumph. He was a hero, having "complied with my orders in proclaiming the jurisdiction of the United States here." What he failed to mention was that the jurisdiction had not been established at all, the area in question having been made neutral ground. But Wilkinson had been satisfied, and he had taken himself off to Natchez, sending his army, under Colonel Cushing, to New Orleans. It was the presence of the army that alarmed Brett. Had New Orleans been Wilkinson's target all along?

That night as he lay awake in his bed in the town house in New Orleans, he wondered about Wilkinson's action. Obviously the General had averted a war with Spain, a war everyone had expected and many people had seemed to want. A war that would have given him the excuse to invade Spanish territory and seek the treasure Jason had revealed. Why had the General not done so?

The answer to that puzzling question arrived a few hours later in the form of Blood Drinker, Jason's Cherokee Indian companion. Brett woke at dawn to the chilling sensation that someone else was in the room with him, and when he would have reached for the small pistol that was never far from his side, a deep, melodious voice halted his movements.

"My brother, Jason, sent me to you," Blood Drinker said calmly as he found an oil lamp in the dark room and swiftly lit it.

The flickering light disclosed Blood Drinker's tall form as he moved nearer the bed where Brett had been sleeping. Blood Drinker was magnificent; tall, straight, and proud, his features undeniably handsome, with chiseled lips and high cheekbones and dark, fathomless eyes. His hair was blue-black, and he wore it parted in the middle, two long, thick braids lying on his chest.

There was a mystical air about the Indian, as if he knew things of other worlds that eluded ordinary men, as if he were capable of things that other men only dreamed of, and Brett suddenly understood Jason's confidence in Blood Drinker. Blood Drinker, he soon learned, was like no one he'd ever met. There was silence as Brett quickly shrugged into a robe and threw some water on his face. He motioned Blood Drinker to follow him into the other room, and when they were there he motioned his unexpected and slightly unnerving visitor to a seat. Blood Drinker shook his head and murmured, "I shall be here but a moment." And reaching inside the buckskin shirt he wore, he pulled out a crumpled piece of paper. "Jason thought you might like to actually hold it in your hands—he said it was yours to do with as you pleased."

Brett's hand trembled a little as he took the map from Blood Drinker. It actually existed, he thought disbelievingly with one part of his mind, his eyes roving curiously over the crude drawings and letterings. He looked at Blood Drinker. "How did you get it? When and where?"

Blood Drinker smiled faintly. "The General did indeed have it—he has carried it all this time in a thin packet about his waist. The only time it wasn't in his possession was when he bathed, and then he had it in his sight."

"But how did you get it?"

Blood Drinker shrugged. Almost apologetically he said, "It took me longer than I expected to discover where the map was, but once I had decided the General must keep it on him, it was easy enough to wait for a night when he had imbibed too freely and sneak into his tent and take it from him." A little gleam of amusement suddenly lit those opaque black eyes. "The General sleeps rather heavily," he murmured softly, as if that explained everything. Turning away, Blood Drinker began to walk back toward Brett's bedroom. "I will go now the way I came."

Reluctantly Brett followed him, watching as the Indian swung a leg over the balcony and prepared to make his way to the courtyard below. A grin tugged at the corners of Brett's mouth. "A bit unorthodox, wouldn't you say?"

"True, and Jason has often accused me of doing these things for effect—sometimes I think he is right." Blood Drinker looked back at Brett. "He will wish to see you when he arrives in the city on Wednesday. Will you remain that long?"

Brett nodded. "I can delay my return home for a few days longer." He stared intently at Blood Drinker and asked suddenly, "How long ago did you obtain this?"

Blood Drinker swung the rest of his body over the side, and just as he dropped from sight, he said, "Eight days ago."

Opened-mouthed, Brett stared at the place where Blood Drinker had been. Eight days ago would have been November 4th, the day before Wilkinson had struck the Neutral Ground Treaty. He laughed a breathless, pleased little laugh and stared at the scrap of paper in his hands. Had they altered history? Would a war with Spain have come about except for this one piece of paper? He didn't know, no one would ever know, but Brett liked to think that the disappearance of the map had completely changed Wilkinson's plans.

Seated on the edge of the bed, he stared at the map for a long time, and then slowly, deliberately, he reached over and brought the oil lamp closer. If all his suspicions were

426

correct, the map had already cost men their lives, it had nearly been the cause of a war, and all for greed. Not a greedy man himself, content with his own life, with deft, sure movements, Brett fashioned the map into a spindle and then, very calmly, fed it to the flames of the oil lamp. A moment later, there were only a few blackened particles floating through the air. Nolan's map was gone forever, and the Aztec treasure was safe until some other adventuring man discovered it.

Brett spent the next two days finishing up his business and also buying gifts for Sabrina. He wanted something special, something she would have always, and consequently he sought out a jeweler he knew in the city. Escobar and Sons had long been established in New Orleans. Their own work was superb, and they occasionally bought private collections, too. They would have the very best selection of anyone. Brett found several pieces that pleased him, and in an extravagant mood he bought them all.

His meeting with Jason on Friday was brief, but it confirmed their suspicions that the map must have been pivotal to Wilkinson's plans. Seated in the library of Brett's house, Jason said bluntly, "I've just come from a social call at Governor Claiborne's, and he had just received a letter from Wilkinson. A very interesting letter, I might add. It has the Governor rather concerned, for Wilkinson writes that Claiborne is surrounded by dangers and that the American government is seriously menaced. Wilkinson claims that there are spies everywhere and that within six days the President will be apprised of a plot that will implicate thousands." Jason grinned. "Much of it we can put down to Wilkinson's flare for the melodramatic, and of course he swore Claiborne to secrecy."

Brett cocked an eyebrow. "Yet the Governor told you?"

Jason's emerald-green eyes twinkled. "Don't forget, Claiborne knows that I am one of Jefferson's brilliant young men."

Brett laughed, but then his face grew serious, and he muttered, "It seems as if Wilkinson has made up his mind to betray Burr. What other plot could he be referring to?"

Shrugging his shoulders, Jason replied, "You're probably right, but we shall just have to wait and see. The next few weeks should be extremely diverting."

Eager to return home now, Brett left before dawn the next morning for Fox's Lair, and noon on the following day found him being greeted enthusiastically by his delighted wife. Her eyes sparkling with pleasure, Sabrina confessed breathlessly, "Oh, I have missed you! I did not think a week could be so long!"

Inordinately moved by this impetuous speech, Brett caught her more tightly to him. She must feel *something* for me to say such a thing, he thought bemusedly.

It was later that day, after dinner, when they were sitting in the salon, that he gave her the presents he had bought in New Orleans. The weather was growing cool and it had begun to rain, and consequently there was a merry fire burning on the hearth. Sabrina was seated on a green velvet sofa, and with childlike glee she opened the gifts he almost shyly presented to her. "I've never personally bought you anything before," he said with a deceptive casualness.

Sabrina was enchanted with the gorgeous necklace and earrings, the diamonds they were comprised of obviously expertly selected and just as expertly fashioned into jewelry worthy of royalty. "Oh, it is lovely," she cried with appreciation. There was a wide, happy smile on her lips as she opened the last package, but as she stared at the contents of the little box, her smile faded and she paled. Looking anxiously up at Brett, she demanded, "Where did you get this? Whom did you buy it from?"

Brett had been standing next to the fireplace, one arm resting negligently on the mantel, but at her expression and questions, he frowned and walked over next to her. "From a jeweler well-known in New Orleans. Why? Is something wrong?"

Sabrina looked again at the contents. It was a very lovely, very unusual brooch. Fine gold had been intricately fashioned to form a roaring lion; its eyes were tiny emerald chips, and its teeth were white, gleaming ivory. Sabrina had seen it before, had seen it often as a child. It was Señora Galaviz's brooch that had been stolen the night of the birthday fiesta over six years ago.

"Do you remember the bandits that were plaguing our area when you came to visit us? Remember that they robbed our guests as they left from my birthday fiesta?"

Brett nodded his head, his eyes fixed intently on hers. "Of course. I also remember that we killed them, although the things they had stolen were given up for lost."

Sabrina shook her head violently. "No, not anymore. This is one of the things that was stolen that night."

Brett's gaze narrowed. "Are you certain, Sabrina? Could this piece just be very similiar?"

For a moment doubt entered her mind. Could she be mistaken? It had been a long time, and perhaps her memory was playing her false. "I don't think so," she finally said. "It is too much of a coincidence for two such unusual pieces of jewelry to be made. It has to be the same one."

His frown deepening, Brett mused slowly, "Then either we didn't kill all the bandits . . . or someone else has found their cache and is selling it off."

Deliberately he picked up the brooch from the box and stared at it a long time. "I have to go back to New Orleans at the end of the month," he said thoughtfully. "I'll go to Escobar and Sons and talk with José Escobar. He'll tell me how it came into his possession."

They didn't discuss it further, but it lay heavily on both of their minds, and it was inevitable that they both would begin to speculate if there was any connection between this brooch and whoever had killed Alejandro. Was the robbery in which the brooch had been stolen totally unrelated to Alejandro's death almost five years later? It was a long time between events, but had one lone bandit remained from the original group? A lone bandit who had later met and murdered Alejandro?

Lying awake in Brett's arms, her head resting on his shoulder, Sabrina trembled with the need for vengeance. *Dios!* If only she could find her father's killer, even now, and take her own vengeance, perhaps it would ease some of the pain that still remained with her. The baby moved within her, and she smiled, a bittersweet smile. How delighted her father would have been! She was married to the man of his choice and would have been presenting him with his first grandchild. A small tear formed at the corner of her eye and trickled down to drop onto Brett's naked shoulder.

Feeling it, he turned to her with obvious concern. "Sweetheart!" he whispered softly. "What is it?"

Sending him a watery little smile, she muttered, "I was just thinking of Alejandro and how happy he would be about the child."

He drew her nearer, murmuring gentle words of comfort, and her heartache lessening, she drifted off to sleep. Not so Brett. He lay awake a long time, mulling over the lion-shaped brooch and what its appearance in New Orleans meant. Finally though, his speculations becoming rather wild, he, too, dropped off to sleep, wondering why he kept coming back to the fact that it had been Carlos who had shot the last bandit—at point-blank range, almost as if he hadn't wanted there to be any survivors. . . .

Oddly enough, Sabrina's thoughts, too, were of Carlos, but on an entirely different matter. During the time that Brett had been gone to New Orleans, she had dwelled a great deal on the events of that summer in Nacogdoches. She fully realized her own part in what had happened, and even now she writhed with shame when she thought of how easily she had accepted Carlos's words. How almost eager she had been to believe anything vile about Brett. Just thinking about it made her blush with despair. But there were still unanswered questions that nagged her, and mortified at the prospect of revealing to Brett how gullible she had been, how little faith she'd had in both her love for him and in him, she resolved to speak with Carlos. To demand the truth from him. Wise now to his lies, she was certain that if she met him face to face, she would be able to sort the truth from the morass of lies that surrounded what had happened. And she had two weapons that she hadn't possessed then—Brett may not have spoken aloud his love and he might never do so, but she knew with a fierce certainty that he cared something for her, that he cherished her and was very pleased at the prospect of becoming a father. She also had the strength to trust her own emotions, to trust her instincts, and instinct told her that Brett bore no resemblance to the man Constanza had described.

At first she considered going with Brett on his proposed trip to New Orleans at the end of November, but then she hesitated. It would be almost impossible to arrange a private meeting with her cousin in the city without Brett finding out about it. If Carlos was even still in New Orleans, she thought grimly. He could have left for Nacogdoches months ago. And feeling rather sneaky and underhanded, she finally decided that the easiest way to see Carlos without Brett finding out about it would be to have her cousin come to Fox's Lair while Brett was gone. It was risky, and the servants were bound to talk, but if she cautioned Carlos to come late at night . . . if she arranged some signal for him, so that he would only approach the house after the servants had gone to bed . . .

She didn't like it, but it was all she could think of. Meeting him privately somewhere else was out of the question —she wasn't *that* foolish! And though none of the servants slept in the house itself, their quarters were a little distance from the main house, and a piercing scream would bring them running. And then there was her knife. . . . Satisfied that she could hold her own if Carlos tried anything violent, Sabrina wrote her note.

Taking aside one of the servants, she gave him orders to deliver the note to Señor Carlos de la Vega. "You will have to go to the Correias' house on Condi Street first and see if my aunt is still there. She will know where he is staying. And if by chance she is not there, the Correias themselves will know whether he is still in the city and where he has gone." Hating herself, she said gaily, "And remember, not a word to my husband—it is to be a surprise!"

Guilt made the kiss she pressed on Brett's lips some ten days later especially fervent and yearning, and Brett looked at her with surprise. "I'm only going to be gone for four days, sweetheart," he teased. And gently fondling her swollen stomach, he added, "Rest and take care of our child. I wouldn't want anything to happen to either of you." His eyes darkened, and Sabrina was suddenly breathless as he muttered, "I think it would kill me if you weren't waiting for me when I returned."

Sabrina hugged those words to herself. Oh, he *must* care and care deeply for her.

CHAPTER THIRTY

◈ Carlos had been elated when Sabrina's note reached him. The intervening months since her wedding had not been happy ones for him. He had brooded a great deal of the time over the injustice of fate, unwilling to accept that once and for all Sabrina was out of his reach. He had drunk heavily, gambled and lost money foolishly—money he couldn't afford to lose—and he had fast gone through whatever had remained of his inheritance.

Francisca had left the city in September, taking a ship to Mexico City, where she would live with her sister, Ysabel. There was nowhere else for her to go, and not even Francisca would have dared return to the Rancho del Torres and boldly commandeer the house.

Francisca's departure had loosed whatever restraints Carlos had placed on himself, and as his money had vanished, he had begun to seek out low company, rubbing shoulders with smugglers, robbers, and the like. When Sabrina's note had arrived, he had been contemplating a not-very-bright future.

But all that was changed now. Sabrina wanted to see him clandestinely! Carlos was deliriously confident that she had realized at last that the gringo meant nothing to her. She must be seeking his help in escaping from her marriage. Eagerly he laid plans for their escape to Mexico City, and he could hardly contain his impatience for the day of his departure to rescue her. Sabrina's instructions had been quite clear, and on the morning of December 1st, he rode of out New Orleans toward Fox's Lair, avid for the meeting with his cousin the following night.

Brett had arrived in New Orleans late the previous evening, just five days after Wilkinson had appeared on the horizon blaring out that the city must prepare itself for an invasion by the rabble that Aaron Burr had gathered to attack the city. Wilkinson had demanded that Governor Claiborne declare martial law, and when the Governor had refused, he had gone about acting just as if it had been done. Civil liberties were suspended; he had ordered a curfew; he had accepted volunteers who were willing to repulse the rabid horde led by Burr, a horde that was expected any day. Every craft going up or down the Mississippi River was seized and searched. The city was panic-stricken and alarmed. All along the Mississippi Valley, people were fearful and apprehensive. What was going to happen next? When would Burr and his army appear?

Brett was astounded. The General, it appeared, was burning all his bridges behind him, and it was now obvious that Wilkinson was intent upon throwing Burr to the wolves and presenting himself in the light of conquering hero. He, Wilkinson, would save the city from Burr!

In view of the circumstances, Brett conducted his business as quickly as possible, not wishing to remain in this churning mass of fear and confusion one moment longer than necessary. Instead of taking two days as originally planned, he did everything that had to be done the next morning, and it was late in the afternoon when he paid a visit to the jeweler's, Escobar and Sons.

José Escobar greeted Brett genially when Brett was ushered into the little back room that served as the old man's office. Shrewd black eyes watched as Brett set down the box with the lion-shaped brooch in it. "Is there some defect?" José asked with concern.

Brett smiled lightly. "No, *señor*. It is perfect. It is just that I would like very much to know where you got it and when?"

José hesitated. He was known for his discretion, having handled many delicate transactions over the years. If it were learned that he had been indiscreet . . .

Indolently counting out several pieces of gold, Brett said casually, "You do realize that it is vital for me to learn this information . . . now?"

José eyed the gold. Señor Dangermond was a wealthy man, a man to be reckoned with, whereas . . . Cautiously he said, "It was one of several pieces I bought from a gen-

433

tleman about a month ago. Due to unfortunate circumstances, he was forced to sell his family's possessions."

"Who?" Brett demanded.

José sighed and looked at the small pile of gold again. Resignedly he said, "Señor Carlos de la Vega."

Brett wasn't the least surprised. He had almost been expecting it, and his face grim, he inquired harshly, "You said there were other pieces; may I see them?"

José shrugged and left the room, returning a moment later with a small velvet-lined tray. "Here they are," he said. "Some of them are quite exceptional."

Brett didn't even notice the other jewelry that lay glittering on the black velvet; his gaze was caught by one specific piece. Rage nearly blinding him, he reached for the lovely silver and turquoise bracelet. "This? He sold you *this?*" he got out thickly.

José nodded uneasily, not liking the sudden air of violence that radiated from his visitor. *"Sí,* he said that he got it—"

Brett's voice cut him off. "I *know* where he got it!" he snarled softly, and then controlling himself with a visible effort, he asked, "How much do you want for it?"

Escobar named a price. Brett threw the money down on the table and scooped up the brooch and the bracelet. A second later he slammed out of the little shop, murder in his heart. *Carlos had killed Alejandro!* The words were seared in acid across his brain, and he wondered if he could possibly control the fury that roiled through his veins.

All thought of leaving the city vanished, and there was only one idea in his mind. Find Carlos and kill him with his bare hands.

It was after midnight before Brett finally found where Carlos had been staying. From the Correias he had learned the name of the boarding house that Carlos had stayed in at first, and from there Brett had followed the trail that clearly revealed Carlos's disappearing finances. The last place was a squalid little inn in an unsavory part of the city. The slattern who called herself the landlady was quite open. "De la Vega? Yeah. He lived here—until this morning." Turning away, she muttered, "Said he was

434

going to visit that cousin of his that married a rich planter."

Brett caught hold of her shoulder, twisting her around to face him. "Are you certain?" he demanded urgently, unable to believe his ears.

Testily she replied, "Of course I'm sure! I was here last week when the note arrived from her, asking for him to come visit. He was quite pleased about it."

It didn't make sense! Why would Sabrina want to see Carlos? Coldly he tamped down the ugly thoughts that crept through his brain. With far more control than he was feeling, he asked tightly, "This morning? You said he lived here until this morning? Is that when he left to visit his cousin?"

"I just told you that!" the landlady answered grumpily, and jerking her arm from his grasp, she added, "Now if you don't mind?"

Brett left, his brain racing madly. Carlos had an eighteen hour start on him. . . . Why had Sabrina written to her cousin? Unless Carlos had just been lying to impress the landlady? Tiredly Brett rubbed his hand across his eyes. Well, there was nothing for it—he would have to leave immediately for Fox's Lair. He must see Sabrina and find out if she had written to Carlos . . . and why?

An hour later, in the dead of the night, Brett left the city. He was astride Firestorm, and as the big stallion's steady pace began to eat up the distance that separated them from home, Brett was unendingly battered by the conflicting emotions that flowed through him. His murderous rage against Carlos was momentarily submerged in his confusion about what he had learned from the landlady. He fought bitterly against letting doubt creep into his thoughts, but it was impossible. Why had Sabrina written to Carlos? Had all these months together been an illusion? Was she plotting behind his back? No! It could not be true! He would not accept it! There had to be some explanation! But what? And for God's sake, *why?*

The next evening, as she waited nervously for Lupe to finish fussing around and leave with Ollie for their own quarters several yards away, Sabrina was wondering the

435

same thing. Unexpectedly she was assailed with doubts about the wisdom of what she was doing. If Brett ever found out, how could she make him understand? Oh, dear God! Why did I ever write to Carlos? she wondered. Why didn't I leave things alone?

But it couldn't be undone now, and after Lupe and Ollie had bid her good night, she prepared for the meeting with Carlos. Getting out of bed, she fumbled for her green wool gown. Slipping it on over her nightdress in the dark room, she found her knife where she had placed it under her pillow earlier. It took another minute to find her shawl, and putting it around her shoulders, she slid the knife into the hidden little pocket she had fashioned at one corner of the shawl. There! The knife was in place and handy if she needed it.

Mindful of her step, she carefully made her way down the staircase and into the salon. The coals from the fire lit earlier glowed cheerfully on the hearth, and the sight of them warmed her. The knowledge that Ollie and the other servants were only a shout away gave her renewed confidence in what she was doing. Brett shouldn't be involved— this was between her and Carlos! It was *her* battle!

Her heart beating swiftly, she gave the signal she had written in her note—the oil lamp suddenly shining brightly then dimming. Then the same thing again.

Three minutes after she gave her signal, there was a furtive tap on the side door, and with a dry mouth, Sabrina walked over and opened the door. A pleased smile on his face, Carlos stepped inside. His smile vanished the instant his gaze fell upon her swollen stomach. "You're pregnant!" he said accusingly.

"Well, yes, I am," Sabrina replied defensively, "but I don't see what it has to do with you!"

It wasn't how either one of them had intended to greet the other, and trying for a lighter note, Sabrina said with forced politeness, "How was your journey? Did you have any trouble finding the house?"

Petulantly Carlos answered, "Your directions were adequate, but the inn you suggested I stay at last night was not particularly restful. And now I've had to spend the afternoon and evening lurking about like some thief!" Her pregnancy had both dumbfounded and enraged him. He might want Sabrina, but he wasn't about to be saddled with the gringo's bastard!

"Did anyone see you?" she asked sharply.

Carlos shrugged. "No. I *did* have a scare a few moments before your signal—I thought I heard a horseman coming down the road, but whoever it was must have gone on by."

Whoever it was *hadn't* gone by. The horseman had been Brett, and seeing the darkened house, he had stopped the sweat-flecked Firestorm, suddenly reluctant to face Sabrina with his suspicions. What if he were entirely wrong?

The signal that had shone out into the darkness a second later had given him his answer, and he had watched almost indifferently as a shadowy form had appeared from the underbrush near the house and had stealthily made its way to the side of the house. There was a curious numbness within him, and he was almost grateful for it—at least it held at bay the gut-wrenching pain he knew would follow later. There was no doubt in his mind now that Sabrina had written to Carlos or that the person he had just seen enter the house had been Carlos.

Brett was completely drained. He had been riding steadily for almost seventeen hours, driven by an increasingly urgent need to reach Fox's Lair. There were times he had been afraid that he was pushing Firestorm too hard, but the big stallion hadn't failed him. Unlike his wife, he thought with a bitter twist to his mouth.

He nearly turned away, going where he had no idea, but something stopped him. He couldn't. Everything he had ever wanted was wrapped up in one slim body, Sabrina's, and he had to see proof of all his dark demons with his own eyes. Silently he dismounted and wearily began to walk toward the front of the house. Just as silently, he opened the front door and walked into the foyer, Sabrina's voice carrying clearly to him.

The meeting between the two cousins was going badly. They had wasted several minutes with polite chatter, acting almost like strangers. But then Carlos was a stranger to Sabrina these days, and with surprise she noted the cruel curve to his mouth, the gleam of avarice in the black eyes as they passed around the room. Had he always been so? Or was she seeing him for the first time as he really was? She suspected the latter, and impatiently she listened to his idle conversation, wanting desperately to have this distasteful meeting behind her.

Carlos was sitting in a leather chair near the fireplace, Sabrina standing stiffly a few feet away in front of him. Speculatively Carlos eyed her, extremely curious about why she had written him and, in spite of her pregnancy, still not quite willing to relinquish his original plans. Aloud he merely said, "Did you know that Madre left for Mexico City in September? She's going to live with Tía Ysabel."

"Oh!" Sabrina replied blankly, and found herself muttering inanely, "She should like that. But tell me, why do you remain in New Orleans? Shouldn't you have returned to Nacogdoches?"

"Why?" he returned bitterly, his eyes on her face. "You're here . . . what is there for me in Nacogdoches? The only woman I shall ever love is here!"

Once those words would have made Sabrina feel sad and guilty, but not any longer, and her voice hard, she snapped, "Oh, stop it, Carlos! You don't love me—you never did! You just use your professed love of me as an excuse to hide behind when you're caught doing something reprehensible! You did the same thing after you almost raped me in the gazebo—would have raped me if Brett hadn't appeared!" Her features scornful, she added, "And if I would listen to you now, you would try to convince me that it was love of me that led you to tell Brett all manner of lies!" Eyes glittering with contempt, she demanded, "And what lies about him did you tell me?"

Enraged that she would turn against him this way, Carlos leaped furiously to his feet. "I don't know what you're talking about!" he blustered, a mad little spark gleaming in his eyes. This couldn't be happening to him! Not now, when he had been so certain, so confident.

"Yes, you do!" Sabrina flashed back. "That summer in Nacogdoches, you told Brett that I was after his fortune, didn't you?" She laughed angrily. "And me," she went on bitterly, "me, you told that he was after *my* fortune!"

Too stunned to think clearly, Carlos hunched a shoulder, and because it had always worked in the past, he whined, "But I did it all for you! Don't you understand, I was only trying to save you from him—because I love you so much and didn't want you to be hurt by him!"

Bile rose up in her throat. Did he really think that she was that much of a fool? That even now she would accept his patent lies? Almost defeatedly she said, "Don't tell me the same lie—I don't believe you anymore. I wrote you to come here because I have to know the truth and I'm too ashamed for my husband to learn how little I trusted him—how easily gulled I was by someone I thought I could trust implicitly." Her voice thick with suffering, she burst out, "I *trusted* you, Carlos! Believed in you! How could you betray me that way?"

Carlos wouldn't answer, his gaze fixed on her with a strange, unnerving intentness. This bitch had spurned him all these years, had married a gringo, was carrying the gringo's child, and she had the gall to berate him! How dare she!

Bluntly Sabrina demanded, "I want to know precisely what happened with the girl in New Orleans—the one *you* said he attacked with a knife. But most of all, I want the truth about Constanza." Steadily meeting his eyes, she finished, "I want to know if she really was pregnant with his child, if indeed he had refused to marry her because he wanted my fortune. And damn you! This time tell me the truth!"

Brett couldn't describe the powerful emotions he felt as he stood there in the foyer, stunned by the import of Sabrina's words. It is said that eavesdroppers hear no good of themselves, and he could definitely attest to the truth of that statement! But there was exultant joy mixed with all the ugliness as he realized fully how craftily Carlos had manipulated them both, had played upon their doubts. What fools we were, he thought impotently, as he listened to Sabrina's angry words. If only I had demanded an explanation from her then! If only I hadn't been so pig-headed-positive that it was *my* lack of fortune that had caused her to break the betrothal! He almost shouted aloud with sweet elation—there had been *nothing* separating them six years ago except their own mistrust. But never again, he vowed savagely, *never* again will I let *anything* come between us! And coolly he made his presence known.

"I, too, should like to hear the truth. It should prove most interesting," Brett said quietly from the doorway.

Her heart in her mouth, Sabrina spun around to stare at him in dismay. *Dios!* What was he doing here and what was he thinking?

Sabrina looked so adorably guilty, so horrified at the sight of him, that if the situation hadn't been so serious, Brett would have laughed. As it was, it was all he could do to stop himself from striding across the room, taking her into his arms, and kissing her violently. He had never loved her quite so much as he did in this moment, understanding the pride that would keep her from asking about the past, deeply moved that having been told the lies she had, she had married him anyway.

Brett was as weary as he appeared as he lounged in the doorway. His once-immaculate cravat was crumpled and half-untied, the bottle-green jacket was rumpled, and his breeches and boots bore signs of dirt from the roads. But moving a little away from the doorway, he lithely walked a few steps into the salon, repeating with commendable calm, *"Most* interesting, especially since my memory of that poor girl in New Orleans is that you cut her up, not me! And as for Constanza . . ." His voice trailed off, and he looked gravely at Sabrina, wishing he could deny the affair, damning himself for *all* the other women who had ever been in his life. Slowly, picking his words with care, he admitted, "I can't deny that for a short time after I first arrived in Nacogdoches, there was something between us. But I never got her with child, nor did I ever ask her to marry me—the question of marriage never arose. We shared a physical relationship and that was *all!*" Flatly he said, "I'm not going to apologize or make excuses for what I did *before* I began seriously courting you that summer —I'm entitled to my own past, and being a monk wasn't part of it!" Tautly he added, "As for your fortune, it never had a blasted thing to do with what I felt for you—I wanted to marry you because I loved you, and whatever wealth you possessed didn't matter a tinker's damn to me!"

It seemed as if they were the only two people in the

room, Carlos's presence momentarily forgotten as they stared ardently across the space that divided them. Sabrina swallowed with difficulty, not certain what to say. It was painful to hear him speak of Constanza, but so wonderful to know conclusively that she had been deliberately deceived that day. And he had said that he loved her! She made a helpless little gesture, so full of emotion that words failed her, and as the silence spun out, Brett said fiercely, "For God's sake, Sabrina! You might not have been the first woman in my life, but I swear to you that you are the only woman in it now—you will always be the only woman for me!"

Her voice still suspended by the dizzying jubilation his words gave her, Sabrina could only stare at him dumbly, fighting back a sudden foolish urge to weep with exhilaration. He *had* loved her!

Misunderstanding her silence, Brett looked at her with despair. Didn't she believe him? Couldn't she forgive him? His mouth twisting with pain, he asked in an anguished tone, "Don't you believe me?" Almost roughly he added, "I love you. I have always loved you—even when I fought against it and tried to use someone like Constanza to hide from it, it was there."

Her throat so tight with held-back tears of joy, half-laughing, half-crying, she got out, "Oh, Brett! Do you realize that this is the first time you've ever told me that you love me? That all these months I've been dying with love for you and so afraid that you didn't love me?"

With a snake's unblinking stare, Carlos's eyes moved from one joyous face to the other, and fury shook him. It had been bad enough that the gringo had married Sabrina, but that they would be happy together was not to be borne. Sneeringly Carlos murmured, "How touching! Dear cousin, do you really believe him? What makes you think that he isn't lying? He could be, you know."

His voice startled both of them, making them unpleasantly aware that they were not alone, and with pity in her gaze, Sabrina looked at Carlos. "Carlos, don't be a fool! Can't you see—I love him and he loves me. Your lies can't hurt us ever again." Almost pleading with him, she added, "Don't keep trying to destroy what we have found. If for no

441

other reason than the memories of our childhood, please be happy for us now."

Unable to believe that he had lost completely, unable to comprehend that she no longer trusted him, Carlos grabbed her hand and babbled wildly, "Listen to me, Sabrina, let me explain! You don't understand how it was, I can explain it to you!"

"I'm sure you can," Brett said harshly, and reaching inside his jacket, he suddenly threw on the carpet near Carlos's feet the brooch and Alejandro's bracelet. "Like how these came to be in your possession!"

The fading firelight danced over the two pieces of jewelry, the emerald chips winking in the lion's eyes, the bracelet a silver shimmer, the turquoise stones gleaming softly. Sabrina stared transfixed for several seconds at the bracelet, and then, not even aware of Carlos's hold on her wrist, she slowly knelt down and reverently picked up the bracelet.

There was a sudden, waiting silence, a tense silence, something deadly and dangerous stirring in the air. The enormity of what that bracelet meant sinking in with one painful thrust, Sabrina looked at Carlos with utter loathing and horror. "You?" she croaked. "You killed my father?"

Any half-mad, fading hope Carlos may have desperately clung to vanished, taking whatever remaining sanity he possessed with it. His eyes dilated; he glanced dementedly around the room. There was death here, he could smell it, and as his eyes met Brett's he saw it, too, glittering with cold promise in those jade-green depths. Deliberately Brett began to walk toward him, and losing his nerve, Carlos swiftly pulled out a small pistol from the leather belt around his waist. "Stay there!" he commanded in a curiously high-pitched voice. "Stay there or I'll kill her!" And he pointed the pistol at Sabrina's head.

Brett froze, his mind racing as he frantically sought and discarded a hundred plans to keep Sabrina safe from this madman. And seeing the madness in Carlos's eyes, he felt an icy fear creep along his spine. But more than that, he was suddenly, sickly aware that he had made a fatal mistake in his haste to enter the house—his own pistol was still resting safely in the holster on Firestorm's saddle.

Sabrina wasn't even conscious of her own danger. White-hot rage exploding through her body, without thinking she closed her fingers over Alejandro's bracelet, making a fist. Viciously she struck at Carlos's head.

Carlos was watching Brett so intently that he never even saw her fist when it came striking through the air, catching him violently across the face, the force of it knocking his arm with the pistol aside. He recovered in an instant, and even as Sabrina fumbled in the folds of the shawl for her knife, he brought the pistol down along the side of her temple, pushing her from him.

Brett was already in motion, fury and fear driving him forward like a bullet, but fast as he was, he was too late. Sabrina's body went flying, her head hitting the corner of a heavy table with a terrifying thud. She lay there motionless.

A stark, almost frenzied cry of pain came from Brett, and for the moment, Carlos was ignored. Kneeling by her side, with shaking fingers, Brett touched the bright curls, the faint trickle of blood that ran from her temple to her chin. She was breathing, but she was hurt—badly, he thought.

Like a great jungle cat, he slowly slewed around to look at Carlos. Rising with a deadly grace, Brett said in a lethal tone, "You're a dead man, Carlos."

Carlos laughed hysterically. "Threats, gringo? You are the dead man! Have you forgotten that I have the pistol, that I can kill you both whenever it suits me?" He giggled, the madness now out of control. His mouth twitching, he muttered, "I'd like to kill you, gringo!" Slyly his eyes slid to Sabrina's still form. "You and your whoring bitch of a wife!"

Realizing the dangerousness of the situation, Brett forced himself to stay calm, to think clearly. If only he could get that pistol away from Carlos. . . .

He took a cautious step forward, but Carlos said sharply, "No! Stay where you are!" Motioning the pistol backward, he added, "Get away from her!"

Brett hesitated, but seeing Carlos's fingers tighten on the trigger, he moved.

Sabrina's motionless body seemed to afford Carlos great satisfaction, and he growled, "She should have married me. I should have been the master of the Rancho del Torres!"

"Is that why you killed Alejandro?" Brett asked quietly, stalling for time yet desperate to get aid for Sabrina.

"*Sí!*" Carlos answered proudly. "He would not give me more money after my father died. And when I wanted to marry Sabrina, he proved stubborn. After you left, he could have forced her to accept me, but he wouldn't." His lip curled. "He was soft and foolish, and one day I finally decided that he would have to die if I was ever to gain the *rancho*."

Carlos's eyes went again to Sabrina's body, and Brett felt a thrill of pure fright. Frantic to divert his attention, Brett drawled infuriatingly, "You *are* a fool, Carlos! You're not man enough to run the *rancho*—you're too weak and stupid. You're not even man enough to meet me in a fair fight—you're a coward who has to hide behind a pistol."

Brett's taunting words had their effect. Everything was forgotten, and nearly choking on blind rage, Carlos uttered furiously, "We shall see, gringo, we shall see." He motioned toward the door that led to the foyer. "Let us walk outside and see if you crow so loudly after I prove to you that *you* are the fool."

Brett almost sagged with relief. If he could get Carlos outside, away from Sabrina, there was a chance he could goad him into making a mistake.

Forcing himself to walk casually, Brett made for the door, his body tense, ready to spring into attack if an opportunity offered itself. None did. The hair on his neck prickling, he was conscious of Carlos following directly behind him, of the pistol jabbed in the middle of his back. At the doorway, Carlos stopped long enough to pick up the oil lamp that Sabrina had lit earlier. He carried it with him as they walked out onto the portico.

Brett stopped and looked at him, but Carlos motioned him down the steps. Reluctantly Brett went down, an uneasiness growing within him. The two men stopped a few yards from the house.

There was an odd smile on Carlos's face, the flickering light from the lamp giving his features a diabolical cast. "Are you ready, gringo?" he breathed gleefully.

Not certain what he was getting at, Brett slowly nodded his head. At least Sabrina was out of his clutches.

"Then watch your wife die!" Carlos screamed, and madness giving him added strength, with a powerful movement he flung the oil lamp against the front door of the house.

The lamp shattered with a tinkling crash, the oil spilling across the portico, the fire igniting instantly, and Brett went crazy himself as he realized what Carlos had planned. Sabrina was to die and he was to be forced to watch it happen, and then Carlos would kill him, too. He could face his own death, but not hers, and with helpless horror he watched as the flames grew brighter, the fire spreading rapidly across the front of the house. The house was primarily wood, and the fire could ravage the entire structure in no time. It would be only a few minutes before the flames would reach Sabrina on the floor in the salon.

It suddenly didn't matter whether he lived or died, he couldn't helplessly stand by and watch his wife—his love and his unborn child—die in those flames, and with a snarl of rage, the jade-green eyes black with a deadly fury, oblivious of the pistol pointed directly at him, he lunged savagely for Carlos, his hands clawing for the pistol.

Carlos had been feverishly watching the fire, and Brett's crazed attack caught him totally by surprise. Frenziedly he struggled to escape Brett's vicious hold on his wrist. They fell to the ground, rolling over and over as they fought with a deadly determination to win this last vital battle between them.

The flames from the burning house danced over their twisting bodies, their breath coming in ugly, rasping sounds as they battled to gain control of the pistol. The pistol was between their bodies now, Carlos trying furiously to position it against Brett's body. But Brett was driven by an even greater fury than Carlos could imagine, and inexorably, he slowly, coldly, forced the pistol over Carlos's heart. Like steel talons, Brett's fingers closed over the trigger, and with a violent jerk the pistol went off, Carlos giving one great leap beneath Brett.

Brett didn't even wait to see what damage had been inflicted upon Carlos. He was already rolling away, rising to his feet and running toward the house, before the sound of the shot died away. His heart thudding rampantly in his breast, he stared with unmitigated terror at the sight before him. The entire front of the house was on fire, greedy yellow and orange flames already attacking the roof.

The smell of smoke had awakened the servants, and Brett was suddenly conscious of them moving about just out of range of the terrific heat that the fire generated. In the confusion, no one had noticed the two men struggling in the flickering shadows, but they had all heard the sound of the shot, and as Brett reached them, Ollie cried out, "What happened? Where's the missus?"

Brett had eyes for nothing but the house, and harshly he snapped, "Get me a blanket—wet it down with a bucket of water and *hurry!*"

Ollie's face with white with horror. "Guvnor, you ain't—"

"Get me that blanket, damn you!" Brett thundered.

A second later, the dripping blanket covering his body, Brett raced around the side of the house, and taking a deep breath, he plunged through the door where Carlos had entered such a short time before. A wall of heat blasted him, knocking him backward, but doggedly Brett struggled on, trying frantically to reach the place where he knew Sabrina had fallen. Thick smoke billowed through the breath-stealing air, obscuring his vision, but unerringly Brett found Sabrina. Bending down, oblivious to the falling, flaming debris, he cradled her close to him, fearful that she was already dead from the smoke and fire. Her soft faint breath touched his cheek, and with something between a sob and a shout, he lifted her up and stumbled back the way he had come, unaware of a huge, burning timber crashing down where Sabrina had lain only a second ago. His body screamed with exhaustion, and for one wild, despairing moment he didn't think he was going to get them out of the house. But then, with a final, instinctive lurch, Sabrina unconscious in his arms, he staggered out of the house, into the night, the cool air that rushed to meet them a balm and a benediction.

EPILOGUE

SWEET SPRING

Spring, 1807

Doubt thou the stars are fire;
  Doubt that the sun doth move;
Doubt truth to be a liar;
  But never doubt I love.

William Shakespeare
Hamlet

CHAPTER THIRTY-ONE

꿈 It was late May, and the weather was serene and unruffled, brilliant blue sky overhead and not a sign of a cloud in sight. The dappled rays of sunlight were warm on Sabrina's face as she gazed dreamily at the men moving about the rising structure that would one day be her new home. She was lying on a puffy yellow quilt some distance away from the construction, enjoying the intermittent shade provided by the spreading leaves of the towering oak tree behind her. Discarded slippers lay nearby, and with pleasure she wiggled her toes into the softness of the quilt, very glad to be alive and here once again at Fox's Lair, watching the new house rising from the ashes of the old.

The original house had burned completely to the ground that terrible December night, but Sabrina hadn't known of it for days. Hadn't know of Carlos's death, of Brett's frantic journey with her into New Orleans, of the anxious days that had followed as she had lain unconscious, unmoving; hadn't known of the anguish that had been undisguised in Brett's eyes. But three days later, she had regained consciousness, and though she had been weak and disorientated, she had gradually recovered.

All through the winter they had remained cozily immured in the house in New Orleans, planning the new home they would build, for the love that would be theirs. Love surrounded them, and during the long winter nights as they lay wrapped in each other's arms, they spoke freely of the past and of the things that only lovers do.

Wilkinson's "Reign of Terror," as the General's descent upon the city had been called, had ended ignobly when no sign of the rabble led by Aaron Burr had appeared on the horizon. And poor Burr, whatever his plans may have been, was arrested on February 19, 1807, on charges of treason. His trial was set for summer.

But those events meant little to Brett and Sabrina—there were too many other more wonderful things in their lives these days. And when their child was born in late March, Sabrina had known what real happiness was—her husband and her strong, healthy baby.

For a second her eyes strayed to where their child lay sleeping in a reed cradle at the edge of the quilt. Unable to help herself, she leaned over and peeked down at him. Alejandro Dangermond. What a handsome baby he was, she thought with a mother's pride, and wonderingly she stroked his soft cheek. Only two months old, he slept soundly, his extraordinarily long lashes like dark fans under his closed lids, his perfect little mouth moving gently as he breathed.

Sabrina sighed happily and leaned back against the tree. How fortunate she was! she thought gratefully, as her eyes moved unerringly to where Brett stood supervising the construction of the new Fox's Lair. He looked tall and very powerful as he stood there, hands on his hips, the white shirt revealing his wide shoulders and lean waist, the black breeches displaying the long length of his muscular legs. A faint breeze stirred the thick black hair, and impatiently he brushed aside a lock that fell forward onto his forehead.

The house was being built at an unusual speed, Brett determined that they would be living in at least a part of it by the end of summer. They were currently enjoying the hospitality of a gregarious planter who lived a few miles down the road, and of course there were always the house in New Orleans and the hacienda in Nacogdoches. For a while they had considered moving to the hacienda, but then they had discarded the idea—this was a new beginning, and neither wanted any reminders of the past.

There was one reminder, Sabrina mused sadly, that she would have treasured—her father's betrothal bracelet. Weeks after the fire, searching through the rubble of the destroyed house, Brett had found it, but the heat had twisted and melted it into a hardly recognizable mass. Sabrina had wept pitifully when he had placed it in her hand.

450

Through tear-drenched eyes, she had looked at him and murmured, "It was his most cherished possession." Gently Brett had enfolded her into his arms, comforting her as best he was able. He had taken the ruined bracelet away with him, not wanting her to look at it as it was and be reminded of that tragic night.

As if becoming aware of her gaze, Brett turned a little and glanced at her. She waved lightly, and he began to walk toward her. Reaching the quilt, he flung himself down on it, lying full length, his head resting in her lap.

With a soft smile, she looked down at him, loving him so much she thought she would burst with it. A little shadow crossed her face, though, as she wondered how they could ever have let suspicion and mistrust come between them.

Brett saw that expression, and concern in his eyes, he sat up and demanded, "What is it? Why do you look like that?"

"I was just thinking about how foolish we were—neither of us willing to trust in our love for the other," she answered simply.

He drew her into his arms. His eyes on hers, he said roughly, "Sabrina, I can't undo the past—oh, but sweet tiger lily, I *do* love you! I've loved you since you were a big-eyed enchantress, all of seven years old, and you've had my heart in your keeping ever since." Regretfully he confessed, "I just didn't want to admit it, and like a fool, I did everything in my power to deny it. But I think I've been well and truly punished for it—we've lost six years because of it." Pain in his voice, he muttered, "I've berated myself a thousand times, suffered a thousand deaths, every time I think of how stupidly we let our doubts and fears keep us apart all that time. However, I like to think that we have learned from it—that our love is stronger and more enduring because of it."

Sabrina felt hot tears prickle behind her lids, and she nodded dumbly, positive that if she tried to speak, she would burst into tears. Happy tears. Joyous tears. Their love *was* stronger, more powerful, because of what they had suffered.

Seeing the tears but recognizing them for what they were, he kissed her, and then he reached over to where his jacket lay on the quilt. The expression on his face somber, he handed Sabrina a slim, narrow package. At her look of surprise, he said with difficulty, "I had originally planned to give you this on our first anniversary, but I want you to have it now."

For a long time Sabrina stared down at the package in her hands, premonition telling her what it must be. With trembling fingers she slowly unwrapped it, savoring each moment, and then, when at last the contents were revealed, her heart shook within her breast.

Two slim, intricately fashioned bracelets of silver and turquoise lay on a bed of white satin. They were identical, except that one was obviously for a man, the other for a woman.

Her eyes shining like stars, she stared at him, and Brett said huskily, "I thought that these would be a symbol to both of us, a symbol of your parents' love for each other, and a symbol to remind us never to forget the past or what we have gained."

Gently Brett fastened one of the bracelets around her wrist, and solemnly she did the same to him. Her throat tight with all the love and rapture she felt, tears of happiness sliding unheeded down her cheeks, she looked down at their two wrists, the sunlight glinting on the silver and turquoise bracelets. Mistily her gaze traveled over Brett, her baby asleep nearby, and the framework of their new home. Her heart ached with a sweet joy, and suddenly, as if from a great distance, yet quite clearly, she heard her father's voice say warmly, "You see, *chica?* It is good, and it will be good . . . *forever!*"

BRAVE THE WILD WIND
by JOHANNA LINDSEY

Until a woman knows a man's desire, she can never know his love.

When she overheard him refuse to marry her, she swore to make him suffer any way she could. But Chase Summers wasn't a man to be trifled with. Even though beautiful Jessie Blair could hold her own against any man in the territory—and was running the ranch herself after land grabbers had murdered her father—Chase summers drove her to a fury of frustration.

In her innocence, she did not understand how very much he desired her. Her beauty haunted him, her arrogance enraged him, she defied and tormented him . . . until his passion spilled over into violence. Yet nothing could soften her stubborn heart, it seemed, but to tame a man's pride. And no woman tamed Chase Summers.

Yet when fortune called him halfway across the world, he realized how empty his world was without her. And the girl who had become a woman in his arms, knew at last in her heart where her destiny lay.

0 552 12628 4   £2.50

THE WANTON by ROSEMARY ROGERS

The things men did to her destroyed her innocence. The things she would do for the man she loved destroyed all her young notions of propriety. Trista Windham was drawn to Blaze Davenant with a passion that shamed her, with a yearning that left her powerless to hate him for spoiling her virtue.

In one unforgettable afternoon, in the sun-dappled heat of a secluded glen, her schoolgirl's fear turned to unafraid longing. And his demanding pride turned to the furious cruelty of lust. Though he betrayed her, and used her violently, his eyes spoke of desire that could never be satisfied.

From her Boston finishing school to the gracious twilight of the prewar South, from the golden land of California to the blood-soaked nightmare of the Civil War, Trista would be made to suffer the worst that men could do to her. Even the stepfather she had worshipped since childhood was driven to forcefully prossess her, and hurt her. But never would she let them take her dreams. Or the ruin the raging, sweet love that comes but once in a woman's life.

0 552 99179 1   £3.95

WHILE PASSION SLEEPS by Shirley Busbee

Beth Ridgeway was a violet-eyed platinum beauty—the kind of woman who made men burn with desire. Yet her husband didn't want her . . .

Rafael Santana was the handsome, arrogant son of a wealthy Texas family. As a child he had been kidnapped and raised by the Comanches. Even now, all his gentleman's breeding couldn't conceal the savage strength beneath his aristocratic bearing.

Beth thought he was cruel and insensitive, a man who used women only for his selfish pleasure and then tossed them away. Rafael thought she was a common wench—flirtatious and unfaithful—who took pride in breaking men's hearts.

Yet something had happened when their eyes first met at a dazzling New Orleans ball. Something their hearts could not deny, something neither the years nor the violent misunderstandings could diminish. Because,for the first time, both Beth and Rafael were awakening to the magnificent passions of love.

0 552 12362 5   £1.95

OTHER TITLES AVAILABLE
FROM CORGI/AVON

WHILE EVERY EFFORT IS MADE TO KEEP PRICES LOW, IT IS SOMETIMES NECESSARY TO INCREASE PRICES AT SHORT NOTICE. CORGI BOOKS RESERVE THE RIGHT TO SHOW NEW RETAIL PRICES ON COVERS WHICH MAY DIFFER FROM THOSE PREVIOUSLY ADVERTISED IN THE TEXT OR ELSEWHERE.

THE PRICES SHOWN BELOW WERE CORRECT AT THE TIME OF GOING TO PRESS (MAY '85).

All these books are available at your shop or newsagent, or can be ordered direct from the publisher. Just tick the titles you want and fill in the form below.

CORGI BOOKS, Cash Sales Department, P.O. Box 11, Falmouth, Cornwall.

Please send cheque or postal order, no currency.

Please allow cost of book(s) plus the following for postage and packing:

U.K. Customers—Allow 55p for the first book, 22p for the second book and 14p for each additional book ordered, to a maximum charge of £1.75.

B.F.P.O. and Eire—Allow 55p for the first book, 22p for the second book plus 14p per copy for the next seven books, thereafter 8p per book.

Overseas Customers—Allow £1.00 for the first book and 25p per copy for each additional book.

NAME (Block Letters)

ADDRESS .